BOOKS BY
Donald D Conley Sr.

Confined Visions/Poetry
Justice In Terror
Introduction To Justice
Fillmore Connection
West Coast Harlem
Imprints On My Soul
Earthly Inspirations
Life Without Hero's

WHAT'S DONE IN THE DARK

PART II

DONALD D. CONLEY, SR.

 www.trafford.com
North America & international
toll-free: 844-688-6899 (USA & Canada)
fax: 812 355 4082

ABOUT THE AUTHOR

Born July 20. 1950 in Chicago, Ill.
Children: Reba Conley Phillip Conley Danielle
Conley Brinston
Favorite Nephew: Carl Conley
Grand Children: Shawn Tasha Rocco

The year is 1988 Inside the Breakers of San Pedro Bay amid a thick blanket of Fog sits Terminal Island Federal Prisons South Yard, containing baseball field Track and weight lifting area which are all connected to a long one story building. The prisons Vocational & Wellness Center and the prison furniture factory, three razor wired sensory fences separating the prisoners from the water along with two manned gun towers at each end. Suddenly a bearded black man wearing kaki clothing is seen vaulting from the roof of the building on the very end, clearing the three fences and rocks below to land with the precision of an experienced High-Diver into the murky water.

A distance away from the prison in the water the man surfaces for air then returns under water and swims away from the prison undetected leaving the black pole he used to vault with floating in the water behind him out to sea.

CONTENTS

5 years later 1

The Home Invasion 7

Changing of the Guard 12

The Rendezvous 14

Loose Ends 17

The Trail 22

Old Habits 32

The Showdown 38

The Ploy 41

Sidewalk Café 46

The Resurrection 50

The Witness 57

The Total Experience 62

Hello Morning 64

77 th Precinct 68

The Legal Wheels 80

One Hand Washes The Other 83

Sundown 102

5 YEARS LATER

The story begins early one morning in Long Beach CA Ted Zackery is in the bathroom of his penthouse apartment washing his face. 45 years old six feet tall muscular build with shoulder length dark brown hair and a clean shaven ebony complexion. From the living room he hears the phone ringing and leaves to answer it.

The room is beautifully furnished and decorated with one of a kind hand- made furniture. The phone sat on a glass coffee table in front of a black sheep skin sofa.

"Hello?" Ted answers

"Good morning handsome" chimes the female voice from the other end of the receiver

"Rita? Is that you" he asks facetiously

"Now who else in their right mind would be up at this hour of the morning"

"What's the matter baby You calling to back out at the last minute"

1

"Of course not I just wanted to remind you that I left my belt in your car"

"That's right you did and that's where it still is" he stated.

Rita is standing by the phone mounted on the wall in her kitchen dressed in workout attire when she asks

"Do you think you can remember to bring it with you?"

He replies a bit sternly,

"Rita. The belt is in the car the car I will be driving so tell me how is it possible I could forget to bring it?"

"Oh! Excuse me mister particularity or whatever you call yourself being-" he cuts her off

"Here we go being touchy. Don't trip!" he suggests moving forward yet she injects

"Alright now I'm not the one"

"Come on babe it's too early for this but I'll see you in thirty minutes"

She takes the receiver from her ear looks at it saying

"He hung up on me" She replaces the receiver in its cradle and heads out the door

At the penthouse Ted reaches into the hall closet to bring out a black leather pouch and matching top to his warm up pants then a holstered snub nose 38. Revolver he straps to his right ankle then zips his pant leg down over it and heads out the door. He walks the short distance to the private elevator steps in and presses the garage button.

From behind the rising gate a late model Black Mercedes AMG pulls out of the garage with Ted behind the steering wheel listening to the CD of Nu Rah Ali, a local Los Angeles jazz vocalist singing her version of

Billie Holliday's Good Morning Heart Ache as he pilots the vehicle towards the Harbor Freeway.

The Mercedes pulls up and parks directly in front of the Crenshaw Fitness Palace. The sound of clanging weights can be heard as Ted exits the car from the driver's side walking cautiously to the sidewalk where he stops to take a careful look up and down both sides of the street then he enters the gym.

For such an early hour of the morning not many people were there. A few men and women all dressed in their workout attire busy with the free weights Treadmills pull down machines warming up with stretches and a small group of women taking an aerobics class.

Ted walks into the locker room where he changes into sweat clothes and secures the black leather pouch around his waist, hefting it a time or two checking its contents. Better to stay ready than having to get ready.

Walking on to the free weights lifting area where he approaches a man about his age in the process of spotting a barbell. Seated on the incline bench The woman is in good physical condition. Her name is Debbie. Ted addresses the man by his nickname

"Good morning mister mayor"

"Usually its Omar when you're not being cynical or when you want me to do you a favor so what is it this time?" he asks Ted suspiciously

'Aren't we touchy this morning You and Rita must have had the same dream she called me early this morning tripping too" Ted switches his attention to Debbie

"So what's up with him Debbie?"

"Don't pay him no mind Ted I believe my husband is going through the change at an early age"

"Well thank you for that brilliant bit of medical genius doctor". Omar speaks sarcastically

"Now are you finished" At that point Rita appears on the floor asking Ted

"Am I late?"

"No. As a matter of fact you're just in time to save me from these two". Omar has positioned himself on the incline bench now that Debbie is done and asks Ted,

"Can I get a spot here?"

"Yeah sure" Ted replies racing to the back or the bench "And Rita your belt is still in the back seat of the car out front"

'That's okay" she replies "I think I'll join in with the other ladies this morning How about you Debbie?"

"Lead the way girl let these men have their quality time to bond" giggling as she and Rita walk away. From bind the incline bench Ted speaks to Omar

"So what's happening with you man?" lifting the bar bel

"Ah its nothing" he replies while pressing the weight, "just feeling a little lame that's all"

"Lame?" Ted repeats

"Yeah you know regimented. My life is always the same nothing ever goes on or changes"

"Would you like to trade places?" Ted states more than asking Omar who replies

"I don't know I might like that. The life of a successful Business man and promising entrepreneur bachelor as well as Ladies man, so I don't know"

"Come on man drive the iron we don't have time for war stories, lets workout" Ted commands taking the role of motivator like he always does when they exercise together causing him to flash back on his past just at the age of twenty when he stood at a supermarket entrance firing a weapon outside until he hears

"Earth to Ted Earth to Ted!" Omar needing him to assist in setting the bar back in the rack He snaps back to reality

"I got it!" directing the bar with both hands back to the rack. They spend the next forty-five minutes concentrating on nothing but the exercise until it was time to go. Now at the front entrance with the two women trailing close behind

"Are we on for the same time Friday?" Ted asks Omar

"Oh yeah! Can't afford to miss one day Remember I'm going through that change thing" sneering back at his wife who is talking with Rita but clearly overhears his remark and replies

"That's all right Honey Snook-ums You still momma's sweet daddy" pinching him affectionately on his right cheek he expresses being slightly embarrassed

"The things I go through". Now outside on the sidewalk the two women embrace in parting while the two men give a high five

"That was a good one" Ted says in parting

"Alright you know it!" Omar exclaimed walking away with a bright smile leaving Ted and Rita standing close together on the sidewalk

"You know you hung up on me this morning" she informed him

"Did I?" he asked with surprise "I mean did you want something else?"

"No, but you didn't give me time enough to think

You hung up so fast I thought you had a woman you were trying to get back to"

"I know you didn't think that so don't even go there"

Knowing that she of all people knew him better than anyone and this ruse was simply her being a woman. She stands close to him lost in his eye. He has her car keys in his right hand as they stand beside her car parked behind his. He unlocks the door opening it for her passing her the key as she enters and is seated behind the wheel Ted leans down to hear what she is saying

"I'll call you later on tonight maybe we can get together or something". He smile's slyly, "Or something"

"Page me first" leaning his head inside to kiss her softly on her lips then dashes off to his car as the morning sun slowly takes shape in the sky.

THE HOME INVASION

An exclusive neighborhood near the Getty Center where a white panel truck sits containing one occupant inside A Black Man with a beard his hair pulled back into one long braid dressed in a midnight blue pin-stripe three piece suit. He is checking the clip to his 9mm as he is watching the house he is parked directly in front of.

The sun has risen awakening the chirping birds in the trees when a bald man exits from the house heading for the front lawn to retrieve the morning paper. Obviously still half asleep he is oblivious of the man with a beard with a gun at his head forcing him back inside his home.

He now has the bald man face down on the floor with his right knee in the middle of his back while he speaks calmly,

"Let's not make this a murder because you can always get some more money but you only got one life" As the victim is about to speak the bearded man strikes him viciously in the head with the butt of the gun causing him to fall to the floor unconscious. Pulling another pistol from the back of his jacket he starts up the winding stair case to inspect the house making sure no one else is there. There is a sound of running water. Slowly he approaches the bathroom door.

Steam from the hot water clouds the entire spacious bathroom as a middle age Latina Woman stands naked with her back to the door drying off with a large towel she then slips into a white bathrobe just as in seconds the bearded man is inside delivering a smashing blow to the back of her head rendering her unconscious.

Inside the foyer the bearded man has brought the unconscious body of the woman upstairs down to lay her beside the unconscious bald man.

The bearded man is slapping the unconscious bald man

"Wake up!...Wake up muthafucka...can you hear me!" The bald man is groggy

"Yeah..Yeah man I hea you" he moans pleadingly as the bearded man whispers

"Then make the choice. Life or death You know what I want so don't waste my time"

In another part of town considered only for those on their way to the top of their chosen careers, Rita is at work in her Real Estate business.

Standing in front of a one story Spanish style home with a FOR SALE sign posted out in the lawn She is talking with a tall dark complexion clean shaven man. David Coleman a police detective

"So what do you think?" he asks Rita

"Well, I'm sure your credit report is fine and once Escrow clears −" He interrupts "No! I mean what do You think about the house?"

"What do I think? I think you should buy it

I'm trying to make a living here" displaying one of those I am serious grins

David speaks slowly taking hold of her left hand

'What I'm asking is would it be a place where

You might like to spend some time and maybe visit once and a while?". The expression on her face is now one of total confusion as she withdraws her hand and clutches her briefcase in front of her as if it were a shield

"Mister Coleman-"

"David! Call me David" he insisted

"Okay David. I think it has a lot of promise and with the right touch I'm sure it would be a great place to live"

"Well do you know anything about that?"

"About what?" having no idea of what he is talking about

"Interior Decorating" he explains while she questions

"You mean you didn't notice that bit of information at the bottom of my business card? He reaches into his coat pocket to bring out her business card

"Ah! And so it is"

"Both sides of this business I enjoy a lot although I must admit that I'm somewhat partial to the Decorating side"

"I'll bet you're good at it too"

'Well there's only one way to find out" extending her right hand

"So is it a deal"

"Just show me where to sign" he affirms

In the living room of the Bald Man's home a number of uniformed police crowd around the motionless body of the dead Latina woman being carried out on a stretcher. The bald man is being attended to by a paramedic holding a compress to his head when Lt. David Coleman approaches the white officer standing near the injured man.

"What have we got here Phil?"

"How you doing lieutenant I'm sure you're familiar with mister Alvin Taylor here our victim otherwise known as The Sugar Daddy to all the Junkies".

"Piss on you white boy!" Alvin curses vehemently

"Now Sugar Daddy is that any way to speak to an officer of the law who is only trying to help you in your moment of need"

"You ain't funny white boy!" Alvin growls watching the lieutenant about to light a cigarette

"And don't lite that shit in here I got health problems!"

"What you do for a living causes health problems too" the officer chimes in causing Alvin to stand abruptly in anger snatching the bloody compress from his head as he yells

"Look you bastards! I pay my taxes and I broke

No laws. I am the victim here so why ain't you trying to catch the son of a bitch who did this!"

"Well for one you haven't really given us anything to go on other than he was black which isn't much even you have to admit"

"Why you faggot bastard!" Alvin spits as he lunges for the office but lieutenant Coleman steps in front

10

of him with a stiff right arm his palm pressing him forcefully in the chest

"Come on Alvin you don't want to do that and change your status from victim to criminal assault on a police officer". Switching his attention to the officer

"Phil I want you to go out and canvas the neighborhood To find out if any of the neighbors saw anything suspicious"

Without another word the officer goes as he is ordered leaving the victim with his superior officer.

"Come on now have a seat and tell me what happened" he calmly invites Alvin and he complie

CHANGING OF THE GUARD

A few hours away in Lake Elsinore Ted is sitting in the front passenger seat of a white Porsche 911talking with another man known as PD 50ish and slightly over weight

"Man I'm getting too old for this" PD says to Ted

"I'm seriously ready to pass the baton. When I do You know what that means, then the only thing left to talk about is how much paper I want" smoking a blunt.

"Well" Ted begins,

"You know your own mind and if you feel its time to back up I won't be the one to question that but before the old man died his only request was that I keep all his fronts alive"

"Yeah and I'm the main front but I want to get out while I can and that means you got to buy me out. I figure a million ought to let me rest real easy"

"Wheew! You want that paid to you like the lottery in payments over twenty years" with a chuckle

"That's real funny but you know you can make that back in three months. I just want to be so far away from all this until the Fed's think I done got off the planet".

Both men step out of the car and go stand by water's edge while PD sails flat stones across the surface of the rippling water

"Man that's a lot of paper but I got you no doubt" Ted states as the two standing at the edge skipping stones across the water until just before the sun is about to depart from the sky they slip off under the evening sky going in separate directions.

THE RENDEZVOUS

Inside the bathroom where Rita lives she is standing in front of the mirror tying her hair back wearing a bathrobe. Just as she is about to get into the tub the sound of the doorbell stops her. Securing the belt around her robe she heads out to the front door. Through the glass on the door she can see its Ted and quickly opens the door,

"I was just getting ready for my ba-..." without a word he takes her in his arms to kiss her passionately closing the front door with his foot.

Inside her bathroom Scented candles are lit all around the bubble filled tub. She invites him to join her She sits between his legs in the oversized basin as he plants loving kisses at the back of her neck and ears He caresses her breast with both hands arousing her to lean her head back allowing a duel of passion to engage in their heated desires with their tongues until the water had begun to get cold.

The bedroom lights are dim as Rita lay on her back in bed with Ted on top of her. Soft music filters through the room as he plants tender kisses all over her body.

He is holding her head in the palm of his hands making love to her, diligently and methodically as she reaches a convulsing climax just as the music crescendo's through the speakers there in her room leaving them both breathing heavily as though they had just run a marathon.

Together they lay in bed spent to satisfaction savoring the lingering sensations involuntarily surging through their bodies like small electrical currents.

Beneath the bed sheet they lay talking, he asks her

"You ever think about running away and starting your life all over in another place far off from here?"

"No" she answers slowly "Not really. Unless you're talking about running away somewhere with me now that would be romantic"

"I don't mean like that. I mean in order to straighten your life out-"

"Oh well, so much for the romance!" she injects with disappointment

"No wait hear me out" he implores as she repositions herself in bed away from him

"My life is just fine I was talking about us" she pouts while he makes light, mimicking an English accent

"Ah say my dear have I managed to rain on my lady's parade? Ah mean ah dent know my lady was into such things" grinning slyly while she has grown annoyed with his insensitive antics and gets out of bed reaching for her robe to cover her naked body then turns to face him saying,

"You just better be careful mister I might not be on the market too much longer"

"And that means what, you're serving me the news? He asks flatly

"No, not at all, it's just that today I was showing this house to a guy who I had to actually dodge an offer to move in with him on the condition he bought the house but I did get him to give me the redecorating contract"

"Hold it" Ted injects impatiently

"Why are you telling me all of this?"

"Because it was right then when I realized that I have been keeping life with other men away from me because of you"

"So you must like this guy since you're bringing him to my attention"

"No!" she hisses quickly taking a seat beside him on the bed

"I'm telling you because I will be spending quite a bit of time over there and I don't want you to get the wrong idea with him being a police detective and all"

"Police detective?" Ted blurts questioningly

"Yes, not that it makes any difference, or am I getting the sense that somebody is jealous ?"

"Don't be ridiculous !" he admonishes slightly blushing

"Why Theodore Matthew Zackery you are jealous" she says with a hint of glee

"If you believe that" he says "You believe the moon is Made out of green cheese"

"You mean it's not! "she questions with a facial expression of being serious.

LOOSE ENDS

Inside the third floor of a parking garage in downtown Los Angeles a sickly very old looking white man appears to be having a heart attack behind the wheel of his Cadillac Sedan De Ville and crashes into a parked white mini-van. The parking lot attendant immediately calls 911 and within minutes the entire area is filled with police cars ambulance and fire trucks with paramedics. A uniformed police officer is examining the white van that was struck only to discover that it was involved in a home invasion and murder earlier that day.

An unmarked patrol car pulls on to the crime scene and out steps David Coleman homicide police lieutenant. He walks over to the white minivan standing on the Driver's side with the door open while the finger print and lab technician's record and collect evidence. Looking down at the seat he goes in his pocket and takes out an ink pen to extract an empty half pint bottle of Bombay Sapphire gin handing it to the tech to store in a bag.

His cell phone rings

"Lieutenant Coleman"

The voice on the other end of the call is another officer

"Lieutenant it looks like we've got another two eleven like this morning except this time who's ever behind this has picked up another one eighty-seven"

"Who was the victim?"

"A male Hispanic shot in the head execution style"

"Any witnesses?"

"Yeah, an old lady from across the street said she saw a man go in and come out about half hour later with two briefcases. Said she got a real good look at him"

"That's good. Get her downtown so she can look at some mug shots-"

"One more thing, the dead man is Juan Hernandez, a.k.a. Don Juan Use to move a lot of heroin"

"Okay"

"Well sir, it looks like whoever did this was familiar with this guy they had a drink together judging by the glasses on the table"

"What were they drinking are there empty bottles?"

"Yes there's one half full"

"What kind is it?"

"Bombay Sapphire"

The following morning Rita is at her Real Estate Office on Century and Vermont seated at her desk in her office on the phone when David Coleman walks in

"I'm going to have to call you back" she speaks through the phone

"David! What a surprise I wasn't expecting you" She stands extending her hand

"I thought I'd surprise you"

"And that you did"

"Listen" he spoke in a soft and gentle tone "I was thinking that we might have lunch, then maybe a walk along the beach and later have dinner, you know, kind a make a day out of it"

"Oh lieut-...David I wish you would have called first because there's no way I can get away-"

"Am I going to have to place you under arrest or are you coming along peacefully"

"You wouldn't dare!"

"I don't think you'd like anyone to see you being escorted to a police car in handcuffs" looking directly into her eyes while she has a million thoughts running through her mind particularly closing the deal with selling him that property so she agreed to go with him

He takes her on Pine Street in Long Beach where outside dining in the downtown area is everywhere. There was a breeze that sent a waft of her perfume past him as she sat across from him at the table, arousing him without her knowing or having the slightest notion of anything intimate between them. Later on that afternoon they take a walk by the water off Ocean Boulevard discussing decorations for the home he is purchasing. Her focus was on the project so every time he would make an attempt to get on a more personal subject she would switch it right back to the remodeling project until the day had turned into evening and she asked to be taken home.

Standing outside at her front door David is standing in front of Rita nervously

"I don't know about you but I really enjoyed myself today" he testified

"Oh I had a wonderful time, it was great. Thank you!" she offers with a bright and beautiful smile

"No thank you!" he contends as he advances closer attempting to kiss her on the cheek. But when the kiss goes beyond friendly she pushes him away,

"Ahmm! Alright David, let's not ruin a perfect day"

Clearly apologetic he moves away and releases her from his embrace

"But I thought you enjoyed yourself with me today"

"I did" she speaks sternly,

"But that doesn't give you a green light for anything else!"

"Forgive me" he pleads from a distance

"I didn't mean to offend you it's just that I care about you and being with you today was really a-"

"I know!" interrupting him

"But let's not blow this out of proportion,okay?"

"Sure...and I hope you won't let this change your mind about our business arrangement"

"No it's alright now good night David" with door key in hand she unlocks the door steps inside leaving him alone out on the porch until he watches the lights come on from inside then he walks back to his car parked across the street.

Once inside his car he slams his fist violently on the dash board out of frustration. He sits for a moment in an effort to recompose himself when he observes a black Mercedes pull into her driveway. A tall man with shoulder length black hair exits and goes up to the front door. A moment later the door opens and he steps inside.

The police instincts kick in causing David to exit his car and walk cautiously back across the street in order to read the plate on the car. He returns to his squad car where he runs the plate number it comes back THEODORE MATHEW ZACKERY-LICENSE NUMBER NO WARRANTS NO VIOLATIONS

Coleman sits seething while watching the door the man name Theodore just walked in to.

THE TRAIL

The next morning David Coleman is in the computer room at the police station reading a print out and is visibly annoyed when a uniformed officer interrupts him

"Ah excuse me lieutenant, the captain is looking for you" but the lieutenant is so absorbed with the print out until he snaps

"Yes! What is it officer?"

"The captain sir he wants to see you"

"Yeah Thank you officer Close the door on your way out"

A short distance down the hall is the Captain's Office. The secretary allows him inside where the captain a large man of color sits behind a huge mahogany desk.

Captain Derrick Abrams, a large built balding Black man from Ohio sits amidst a pile of reports on his desk.. Coleman seats himself in a chair directly in front of the desk. The captain reads over a sheet of paper he holds in his hand,

"I've got a complaint here against you. It says you allowed one of your officers to verbally abuse a citizen during a robbery murder A one Alvin Taylor. Can you tell me about this and why does that name has a certain familiarity to it?"

"Alvin Taylor a heroin distributor we've been trying to nail for the last three years" The captain leans back slothfully

"Now I remember so tell me what went down"

"Somebody went in and cracked him over the head along with his girlfriend who later died from her injuries It's no way of knowing what was taken or stolen and you can bet ole Alvin is not about to make a police claim for any stolen heroin"

"Did Alvin get a good look at the guy?"

"Claims he never saw him before, said he was wearing some sort of disguise Dark glasses long hair a beard"

"What do you make of that?" the captain asks

"I don't quite know yet but something about the way he described the guy just sticks in my gut"

"So I take it he wasn't very forthcoming"

"Nope, he just kept yelling that he was going to Sue the department for slander but didn't ever say anything really solid about the guy who ran in on him. Hell, if it hadn't been for the gardener trying to get paid and seeing all that blood I doubt if ole Alvin would have said anything"

"So what do you make of all this; think it's just some dope fiend who got lucky?" the captain inquires

"I wouldn't go that far just yet"

"Well I'm sure you've got your people on the inside working the case as well"

"Most certainly, as we speak"

"In that case I won't keep you any longer but I expect you to keep me informed daily"

"Yes sir" the lieutenant replies with a salute and leaves the office.

In an unmarked police car Coleman is driving down Central in Compton He stops in front of a liquor store on Imperial and Central where a man resembling Captain Crunch on the cereal box is standing in the door way unstable in his balance after having recently injecting heroin.

When the grubby man notices the squad car he attempts to act normal aware that it is Coleman who use to be a Vice Cop and knows who all the local dope fiends are around the city having had to come in contact several times with Josh in the past In fact it was Coleman who turned Josh into a CI (confidential informant) when he was caught with a fully loaded automatic weapon in his car while still on federal parole. Coleman stops his car leans over to roll the window down on the passenger side but Josh gets in instead

"I hope you got something good to tell me otherwise you could a kept your stinking ass outside got my car smelling like shit!"

"Damn Man! You ain't got to be so raw, I'm trying To help you!"

"You mean help yourself cause I can still file that Gun case with the feds not to mention the money you get from all the cases you assisted law enforcement in convicting people who would love to see your good old snitching ass in there with them, so tell me what you got for me Josh"

Josh has his right hand extended rubbing his thumb and index finger together saying,

"Ain't you forgetting something?"

"I'm about to forget my patience and put my foot in your ass if you don't start talking! I'll decide if its worth anything or not"

"Oh All right Word on the street is some dude from out of nowhere is slinging some real good powder plus he got that dog food too"

"What do you mean some dude out of nowhere I need a name"

"Say man" Josh begins defensively "What I look like going around asking peoples for their real handles, they might think I'm a snitch"

"So then who are you, J Edgar Hoover reincarnated come back as a black dope fiend rat junkie. No you can do better than that" pressing the old dope fiend

"Well this ain't for sure but peoples say he hooked in with the police to be having it like that"

"Having what like that?" Coleman asks Josh who answers

"He be knowing when to move and he knows when the Players are holding. I ain't never done no business with the guy but I seen him a couple a times down on the front"

"What kind of car does he drive?"

"Always in rent cars"

"Is anybody ever with him?"

"Naw always by his self"

"What else can you tell me about him?"

"He jack that iron cause he swole"

"He lifts weights maybe he just got out of The joint"

"Maybe so, but it ain't likely cause this dude don't carry himself like that"

"What do you mean?"

"Ya see, a guy that's been Busted takes it easy when he first touches down Get to relearn the streets see who's doing what. But not this dude He been here a while" Coleman studies what the man has relayed to him when Josh repeats his compensation plea

"Check this man, I been straight with you so The least you can do is spare me a Sawbuck"

"Twenty dollars! No, it's worth a dime" going into his inside coat pocket taking a ten from his wallet and tossing it to Josh ordering'

"Now get your stinking ass out of here"

"Man you show talk to a brother bad" all the while Coleman is holding his nose attempting to avoid the offensive odor

"If you don't hurry up and get out of this car!" causing Josh to quickly exit the vehicle. With the windows down on the squad car Coleman issues Josh instructions

"Be some where I can find you tonight" and pulls away from the curb.

In the Crenshaw District inside a vacant restaurant Ted and Rita are walking through the empty building that Ted voiced an interest in which she was the agent conducting the sale. The area was popular for its shops and boutiques Even the nearby car wash was chosen as the site for the movie featuring Richard Pryor It was in a perfect location one of the most important factors in choosing Real Estate for a business

"This one isn't even on the market yet.

The owner ran into some legal problems forcing him to sell it, but when it was open business was good" she explains the history.

"Yeah I know I've been here a time or two" he affirmed

"Oh really!" she replied in curious humor

"You never brought me here, but I suppose you were having some kind of business deal going on". Recognizing her insecurity he soothingly places his right arm around her shoulder drawing her close to him

"Whenever I'm in the company of another woman You can rest assured that it can only be about business"

"Oh! So it was with another woman" she exclaims pretending to be upset with both hands on her waist lips pursed in a pout

"I cannot tell a lie" he mimics George Washington then says "Tell you what. How about the two of us getting out of here and head over to my place where we can spend some real quality time together" looking at her lovingly kissing her softly on her lips. Willing and eagerly she returns the kiss only pausing to ask

"But I thought you were in a hurry to locate some property?"

"I am" he replied

"Well I'm more in a hurry to do what you want to do"

Feeling slightly light headed from their passionate kiss she gleefully agrees as he takes her hand in his and they leave the empty building.

Inside the car with the sun shining high in the sky Rita is seated in the front passenger seat in a recline position looking out at the clear sky Luther playing on the radio as Ted pilots the sleek black vehicle towards Rodeo Drive.

He steers the car to an up- scale boutique, where he sits alone on a small sofa as Rita models different outfits for him each time shaking his no as to say he did not like it until the third time when she emerged wearing a satin strapless night gown causing him to eagerly nod his head in Yes along with a bright smile of approval.

At the cashier's Ted is in the process of paying for the number of boxes and garment bags. Rita standing beside him attempting to pay but he thrust several one hundred dollar bills to the woman behind the counter saying,

"It will take her forever to find anything in that purse" turning to Rita saying,

"We've got one more stop to make then we can get busy" displaying a mischievous grin. She watches him as he takes care of her purchases then together they walk off together back to the car

Later that evening he takes her out for dinner to the Queen Mary in Long Beach. Both dressed in formal attire seated at a table for two when in the middle of having dinner

"Alright do you want to tell me what this is all about?"

"What are you talking about?"

"You know what I'm talking about" she snaps back with a bit of sass

"It's not my birthday or Valentine's day and I don't know of any other special occasion we should be celebrating so why all the gifts and dinner?"

Ted sits back in his chair taking a sip from his glass of wine before he speaks looking directly into her eyes as though he is reading her thoughts.

"You know babe, it hasn't always been this good for me. I mean I've lived a hard life and sometimes I forget to take time out to enjoy some of the simple things like this just being with you and letting you know it"

She looks deep into his eyes searching as she tries to understand this sudden display of compassion and concern He continues,

"...if it's one thing I've learned the hard way is to appreciate the small things. The simple things like taking time to smell the roses watching the sunset"

"I had no idea you were so sensitive this way"

"Which is all my fault"

Rita is smiling warmly looking into his eyes

"No it isn't a fault. It's just the way you are and I accept that although I have to admit that there has been a time when I had just about given up on us" He takes his hand carefully away from hers to gently touch her cheek with his fingers

"No matter what life throws our way, don't ever give up on us" and kisses her softly

Rita stares longingly into his eyes then speaks

"May I ask what brought on this sudden sense for the need of reaffirmation?"

"You baby" he answers

"Me!" she feigns surprise

"They say love is proven through your actions and deeds. Lately I haven't been showing you much. I almost feel as though I owe you an apology for the way I seem to always have my mind else where. But I'm getting better"

From the table behind theirs a small party is going on. Champagne bottles pop with laughter erupting causing the couple to relocate outside to the front of the ship watching the fireworks and the full moon as it hovers over the ocean

"Okay I get a little carried away with my business but you know how it is sometimes being self employed" he defends.

"Sure I do but you still have to make time for the people you care about or else what's the sense in doing what you do"

"And you're absolutely correct I can't dispute that" yet knowing him as she does something in her gut tells her that something else is motivating his attention generosity affections

"Ted, do you want to tell me why you're being so agreeable tonight?"

"I told you" he answers without hesitation

"No there's more to it than just that"

"Well, I figured I better start paying attention to my love interest before I won't have any"

"So that's what this is about. David"

"On first name basis already?" Ted points out

"I thought we talked about this!"

"Obviously not extensive enough" he contends as she attempts to withdraw from their closeness by taking a step backwards, but he advances forward with her in an unspoken refusal allowing her to create the distance

"Ted this isn't about us it's about you trying to establish control over me"

"Control over my heart which is who you are"

"So you're saying you're not jealous?"

"Of course I'm jealous if it makes you feel any better hearing me say it so now you don't need to see this guy any more"

"I can't do that. Contracts were signed and I have my business on the line"

"It's just that everything good in my life was taken away from me when I was younger by the so called law, so I have a natural resentment against anyone representing it. I have had to sow a long and hard row in order to get where I am today. I know to pay attention to all of the signs"

She wraps her arms around his waist and is looking up into his eyes

"There is only one you and I'm not interested in any kind of substitute so you don't have to worry. I'll always be here for you. No matter what"

Another display of fireworks explode in the sky as he takes her in his arms and they exchange a long and passionate kiss...

OLD HABITS

The street lights make the deserted street visible from one end of the block to the other. A lone late model blue Cadillac is parked with the Bearded Man sitting behind the wheel. He picks up the mobile phone and speaks into it.

"I'm at the door right now. Hurry up let me in!" Stepping out of the car heading towards a darkened door way. It opens revealing the silhouette of a man. The closer the bearded man gets to the door the more visible the other man becomes

He is a light complexioned black man wearing a white shirt rolled up at the sleeves and surgical gloves. He steps past the man holding the door for him and without warning the sound of a silencer is heard and the man holding the door open slumps to the floor dead from a single gun –shot to the eye.

The murmurs of voices can be heard in the distance as the bearded man makes his way cautiously down the hallway towards the sliver of light beaming through the partially open door. He peers inside to see a large steel table with another man standing behind it dressed in hospital scrubs and mask. On the table is a triple beam weighing scale an electric blender along with mounds of white powder in separate piles. Totally absorbed in his task at hand completely unaware of the intruder lurking only a few feet away. He looks up straight into the barrel of the 38. The bullet striking him directly between the eyes as he slumps lifelessly to the floor The bearded man goes about collecting the drugs in a thick black plastic bag. From under the table he removes a mail bag filled with packs of hundred dollar bills, totally unaware of the young girl hiding under the table.

He places the mail bag inside the black plastic, looking around he finds a can of lighter fluid. There is an old dilapidated sofa with the foam now exposed from the torn cover. He saturates the sofa with the can of lighter fluid. Now empty he picks up the black plastic bag with one hand while tossing a lit book of matches with the other on to the sofa causing a SWOOSH! of flames behind him as he exits the burning building.

Inside Rita's apartment a trail of clothing leading all the way from the front door the front room and hallway up to the bedroom door where Ted is on top of Rita in bed lost in their passion. Her orgasm is evident as she convulses involuntarily. her whole body shivering and sensitive as if she had been exposed to a mild electric shock. Moments later as a result of the wine from dinner and after dinner on top of the outstanding orgasm she was fast asleep.

It was 11:40 p.m. when Ted looked at his Movado Wrist watch fully dressed and out of bed placing his car keys on top of the dresser where they are visible, then carefully he eases out of the door closing it as quietly as possible behind him.

Flames illuminate the night sky as three firetrucks along with a number of firemen shoot water from the numerous swollen water hoses into the flame engulfed building. A white fireman is standing with a partially clothed young girl. She is barefoot and holding a blanket around her shoulders when the unmarked police car pulls up.

A white uniformed officer steps out of the car and joins them. The scene is noisy and chaotic with high winds blowing causing them the need to shout when speaking in order to be heard with the news helicopter over- head reporting on the story.

"This kid says she was inside when the fire started. Says some guy came in and put a match to the place after he shot her two friends. The fire is too hot for anyone to enter yet and bring the bodies out"

"Is she hurt or anything" the officer asks the fireman

"No, just a little shook up. She says her name is Erica"

"Alright" the officer affirms,

"I'll take care of her from here" placing his hand on her shoulder leading her to his squad car where he opens the front passenger seat door for her then get goes around and gets in himself. Picking up the mic he radios ahead

"Car fifteen forty one to dispatch"

"Go ahead fifteen forty one" the female voice of the dispatch returns

"I'm here on Figueroa at the fire and I have a witness who says there are a couple of dead people inside. I need the Coroner down here and I'm bringing the witness in to talk with homicide"

"Ten four,fifteen forty one I'll patch you in to the Watch Commander"

While waiting for the call to transfer the officer speaks to the girl

"It's kind of late for you to be out here. How old are you?"

"Fourteen going on fifteen"

"What's your name child"

"My name is Erica an I'm not no chile!"

"Oh! That's right you are going on fifteen" shaking his head slowly in sadness as he looks at the girl

"Well tell me Erica, had you ever seen this man before?"

"What man?"

The man who you say came in and shot your two friends"

"Oh, yeah I seen him before"

"So you know who he is?"

"I don't know his name but I know he's a Mack Daddy He be down on the front all the time"

The officer pulls away from the curb escorting the witness down to headquarters to speak with a homicide investigator David Coleman.

Seated in a chair in front of his desk he speaks to Erica

"Now if you want we can wait for your parents to get here before I ask you any questions"

"No it's alright. My momma in jail and I my daddy could be anybody and anywhere"

"So you don't know who your father is"

"Nope sure don't and don't care" she concludes

"Oh-kay" he acknowledges "So what were you doing out so late and who were your two friends?"

"I don't know what they was doing cause I was in the back the whole time until I heard a funny noise and then I went to see what it was that's when I saw Chico on the floor with blood coming out of his right eye"

"Chico?" Asks the detective

"Yeah Chico and Essay from Compton"

"And you had no idea they were major drug dealers"

"Look, like I said. I don't know what they was doing I was just waiting in the back"

"Ok, now tell me about the shooter do you know how he got in?"

"I heard Essay talking to Chico saying tell him to come over and get what he wants"

"So Chico let him in"

"That was the only way" which meant they knew him but neither were alive to provide any information or leads to who the killer is.

"Is there anybody I can call to come pick you up?" he asks her

"Nah" she says simply

"Then I'll have one of my officers take you home. Where do you live?"

"With my Aunt on Vermont"

"Don't you think you ought to call her?" he asks the child

"She don't got no telephone and besides she don't Care what I do anyway"

The typical scenario of a child raised in a destructive environment, providing little or no hope at rising above the circumstances they have known their entire life. Placing his hand affectionately on her shoulder,

"Come on kid. I see that you get home myself"..

THE SHOWDOWN

Ted exits a late model Cadillac from the front passenger side. It pulls away as he walks to the front door of the Real Estate office. Inside the office Rita is seated behind her desk talking on the phone until she sets her eyes on Ted and speaks into the receiver

"I need to call you back" disengaging the call She is visibly agitated with him. He stands as the door with coat draped over his left arm

"And so! The prodigal lover returns"

"Why do I get the impression that you're upset with me?"

"Oh I shouldn't be!"

"I don't think so" he replies casually

"I had some business that couldn't wait. You were sleeping so peacefully I didn't want to wake you"

Rita gets up from her chair behind the desk to walk around to the front near him and sits on the corner. Her short skirt raises to reveal her shapely thigh

"And what was so im —No, strike that! I don't even want to know"

Ted is caressing her exposed left thigh smiling

"That's right babe. Let it go so we can move on to more productive things. You know honey you were incredible last night"

He stands massaging her shoulders when she replies

"Judging by the way you snuck out on me I have my doubts"

"Then maybe we ought to have an instant replay right here on your desk"

He leans in to kiss her when suddenly the office door opens and it's David Coleman walking inside

"Oh! Pardon me I didn't mean to interrupt" he utters in disappointing surprise as Rita jumps down from the desk attempting to straighten her clothes while Ted casually but smoothly looks straight into the eyes of the detective

"Ted this is David Coleman"

The two men advance towards one another Ted has his hand extended to shake

"That's Lieutenant David Coleman" emphasizing his rank

"I'm just Ted but how do you prefer to be addressed. Lieutenant Coleman or just David?"

"That depends on who I'm talking to. My friends call me David"

"I guess that leaves me at on hell of a disadvantage"

"Oh, how is that?"

"Because it's obvious you and I won't ever be friends" Ted releases his hand, then walks back to Rita and kisses her on her lips. Her eyes open wide in surprise as she smiles slyly.

"I'll be by later on tonight"

"Ah, page me first" She winks with a smile as so does he. Ted returns to the chair to pick up his coat when Coleman notices a bulge inside it but says nothing. Ted about to pass him on his way out says

"A pleasure to meet you Lieutenant"

"Like wise" and with that Ted leaves the office.

"Well, it looks like you two hit it off rather nicely" Rita states

"I ah…I don't think he likes me" David pointed out

"Now how can you say that he doesn't even know you other than you telling him you're a police officer"

He removes a pack of cigarettes from his inside shirt pocket as Rita clears her throat

"..ah hmm!"

"Oh!" he responds apologetically replacing the pack back in his pocket and he asks her

"What kind of business is your friend in?"

"He's a Developer, but I don't think you came here to talk about a man you just met"

"No I didn't. Besides I'm sure he and I will cross paths again one day" with a distant faraway look in his eyes.

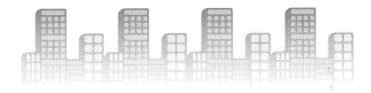

THE PLOY

Inside police headquarters David Coleman is in the office of Captain Abraham seated in a chair in front of the captain sitting behind his desk Clearly annoyed

"I never thought I'd see the day when law Enforcement would be asked to babysit a Drug Dealer"

"I understand how you feel captain but it's all we've got to work with. We know that Keno is the only major player in the drug business who hasn't been hit"

"What makes you think our man will hit him next?"

Coleman is drumming his pencil in the palm of his left hand,

"That's just it, with this guy we don't know what to think other than trying to think the way he does and get ahead of him"

"I don't know David. You're asking the Department to look the other way on one Killer with hopes that we can catch another"

David tosses his pencil on to the captain's desk pleading his case

"All I'm asking is for is a few days. We stake out Keno's gambling operation. Sure we've got enough on him to bust him right now, but with all those high price lawyers he's got, chances are like always he'll be back on the streets in no time"

"A bird in the hand is worth two in the bush, eh?" the Captain quotes

"I'm sure you didn't make it through the ranks By not taking chances" The captain smiles at Coleman's almost brash tenacity.

"Quite a bit can change in fifteen years David. Enforcing the law use to be cut and dry You do the crime you do the time. But with the way the criminal justice system is at this day and age, it's the crooks who are getting the last laugh instead of getting sent to jail"

Coleman continues his pleading,

We are in a war out there captain and we don't have the luxury of having too many good feelings so we can only go with what we know and hope we can make a difference"

The captain sits back in his chair in contemplation as the two men are silent for a moment. The Captain gets up from behind his desk to turn and stand in front the large picture window looking out over the city.

"It's been a many year since I worked a beat or was on a stake out. That was when not too many people had guns. It even felt like we were making a difference"

The Captain takes a deep breath almost sighing in sadness when he speaks to Coleman saying

"Do what you have to do lieutenant"

"You won't regret this Captain Sir" Coleman vows as he heads out of the office and back to his own.

He had just walked into his office when shortly afterwards with the door still open a uniformed white officer walks in holding a piece of paper in his hand.

"Lieutenant I've got the report from that fire last night. Two bodies were found both had a single bullet wound in the head. The fire investigators also dug through the rubble and found what was left of a triple beam weighing scale and an electric blender"

"They were cutting up dope" Coleman concluded

"Looks that way sir There was no need taking finger prints"

"Yeah I can imagine. Thanks officer Pierce" Coleman focusing on the name tag pinned on the officer's uniform

"You're welcome Sir" about to leave the office when the officer stops,

"Oh I almost forgot. Erica Thomas is here to see you. She was at the scene when the two men were murdered but was hiding"

"Okay. Send her in"

Before leaving the young officer awkwardly remembers to leave the report with the lieutenant and places it down in front of him on his desk then exits. Coleman is going over the report for himself A moment later the same officer is holding the door open for her as he announcer her

"Erica Thomas Sir".

Without looking up from examining the report he speaks,

"Come on in Erica and have a seat" then addresses the officer

"Close the door please officer"

He calmly puts down the paper to look directly in her eyes.

"According to this report you lied about your role in all this"

"No I didn't!" she defends

"Listen" Coleman starts off slowly

"If you want me to help you then you've got to be completely honest with me. You admit being there which makes you a part of a major offense. A double murder making you one of two things. A witness or you were part of it" Erica is visibly afraid

"No! I didn't have anything to do with that"

"Listen to me young lady. I believe you but that doesn't mean the District Attorney is going to which means you're looking at a very long time in prison"

Almost hysterical with fear she pleads "But I didn't have nothing to do with that I told the officer last night that I was there partying and this Mac Daddy who drives a blue Cadillac came in and killed-" Coleman interrupts her

"Hold it right there, you didn't say anything about Seeing any car last night"

"No I didn't, but I ran out and hid on the side of the building to see this Mack Daddy come out and get in a new blue Cadillac"

She looks as though she is about to bolt from the chair, "Take it easy now. Take it easy you're alright. I'm not going to let anything happen to you just take it easy.

Have you had anything to eat yet?"

"Just some potato chips" she answers with tears in her eyes

"I tell you what" Coleman starts

"I'll spring for lunch then we'll talk some more.

I want you to help me catch this guy. Okay?"

"Aw...alright"

Coleman picks up the telephone and presses out three numbers, then speaks into the receiver

"Yeah this is lieutenant Coleman, I need you to go down to the cafeteria and bring up a steak, vegetables salad and a carton of milk. Make sure the steak is well done"

He hangs up the phone only to pick it back up to dial out seven numbers while Erica is watching him carefully listening to what he says over the phone.

"Hi, I was hoping I'd catch you in. But listen,

I really need to talk to you if you can make time to squeeze me in today because, it is rather serious, something I'd rather not discuss over the phone" He listens

"Perfect. I'll see you then" hanging up the phone and smiles.

SIDEWALK CAFÉ

Lieutenant Coleman and Rita are seated at a small table at a restaurant on Crenshaw near 39th Two coffee cups sit on the table

"Thanks for meeting me on such short notice"

"Well you did say it was important" Rita replied

"It is. It's about your friend Ted"

Rita has her coffee cup in her hand about to take a sip. An expression of being slightly annoyed shows on her face

"Oh David please, let's not do this!-"

"Hold on not so fast!" he injects

"This isn't about anything to do with my personal feelings about the guy"

"Okay, then what is it, police business?"

"Exactly" he answers with authority.

She has a total look of surprise on her face as she sits looking at the police lieutenant curiously.

"I hope you aren't taking the meeting you two had the wrong way"

"Not at all even though it's obvious that he and I are vying for the same woman, but like I said this isn't about you" taking a sip of his coffee

"Then what is it about" she asks

"It's about Drugs and Murder"

Rita's eyes grow large as she is visibly startled

"What! So what's that got to do with Ted?"

"I'm not sure yet that's why I called you I thought purely for the sake of clearing him as a suspect you would help me"

"How can I help you?" still clearly concerned as she finishes her coffee only to signal to the waiter for another refill.

"First. by answering a few questions if you would?"

"Of course if I can"

"Okay, you told me that he was a Developer"

"Yes, I know that he's been involved with securing properties for people looking for a quick return"

"What do you mean Quick?"

"Property like Car Washes Laundry Mats and Motels"

"Does he work for a company?"

"As far as I know he's independent Most of his Clients are people who are directly connected with a coalition of investors of investors who are interested in giving something back to their communities"

Coleman listens intently as she speaks.

"But tell me why you think Ted might be Involved in these crimes?"

"Last night two more people were shot to death in what looks like a drug robbery but up until last night we haven't been able to get a solid lead on the person responsible"

"Until last night" she concludes out loud

"That's right" he answers

"We've got a witness who claims she actually got a good look at the guy"

Rita looks on in bewilderment as he continues,

"Our witness said this guy left in a blue Cadillac"

"But Ted drives a Mercedes" she defended

"I know that too because I saw him the other night at your house just as I was leaving but this morning when I stopped by your office I saw someone drop him off just as I was getting out of my car"

"I still don't see what that has to do with Ted"

The waiter returns to refill her coffee cup and asks if they plan to order anything else but is waved off when David tells her,

"He got out of a blue late model Cadillac but I didn't get a look at the driver"

She sits quietly studying what he said with an expression of total disbelief

"David, there are lots of Cadillac's in Los Angeles and Ted has a lot of associates who have cars like that so that still doesn't prove anything"

"You're absolutely correct but according to the description given by the witness, it's got Ted's name written all over it"

"That couldn't possibly be David because Ted was with me last night. All night"

"All night?" he echoes

"All night" she returns

"Then explain why someone had to drop him off This morning where was his car?

"It wasn't parked there all night if that's what you're getting at, only for a couple of hours or so until he came back and got it"

"Are you sure he didn't get up in the night an-"she interrupts

"He was with me all night David, we spent the entire evening together then checked into the Regency on Artesia Check it out"

The lieutenant looks at her with suspicious eyes,

"I hope you're not trying to cover for this guy Rita, because murder is a very serious offense"

She makes it obvious that she resents his insinuation

"Are you suggesting that I'm lying?" she asks the lieutenant

"No!" he answers quickly

"I'm not"

"Well have you considered talking to Ted"

"To be quite honest with you it hadn't crossed my mind until this morning when I saw him get out of that car. I've got the witness downtown looking at mug shots as we speak so I'm just following up on a hunch"

"Oh, so this isn't official?"

"Not yet" he answers stands up and leaves the office.

THE RESURRECTION

Inside police headquarters Erica is seated at desk with a white uniformed officer seated beside her. There are a number of notebooks filled with mugs shots she has already gone through along with empty paper plates sandwich wrappings and empty coke cans. There is mug shot of a Black Man with beard and close cropped black hair. The name under the chin is ROBERT MORRIS

Erica looks long at the photograph then proclaims,

"That's him right there!" pointing with her finger

The officer picks up the phone and presses out three numbers then speaks,

"Ah lieutenant, looks like she found our man"

"I'll be right there"

Moments later David Coleman enters the room and stands behind the chair Erica is sitting in

"Are you sure he's the one?" he asks

"Yeap!" she answers with certainty "Except his hair is longer"

The lieutenant pats the girl on her shoulder then picks up the photo speaking to her he says,

"Finish your food and I'll be back in a minute.
I want to check something out".

Walking through a maze of partitions he returns to his office where he takes a seat in front of his computer. He presses in some numbers the screen reads,

ROBERT   MORRIS---D.O.B.-7-20-50----
DECEASED-9-19-93---DATA COMPLETE---

Lieutenant Coleman looks at the readout for a moment then picks up the phone.

"Bring Erica to my office"

Moments later she is escorted into his office holding a partially eaten hamburger with the wrapping still around it and takes a seat in the empty chair in front of his desk.

"Looks like you picked out a dead man" giving her the photo again

"No, this is him! He is the one. I'm positive"

"Eric, that can't be see, the man is no longer living"

"I don't know about all that. All I know is what I saw. It's the eyes I remember most but that is him"

Lieutenant Coleman picks up the computer printout and reads it to her

"According to this report he died in 1993 apparently by drowning in the San Pedro Bay during an escape attempt from Terminal Island Federal Prison. His body washed up two days later"

"Oh well" she injects,

"Then he done rose from the dead because he is the one without a doubt"

Coleman sits back in his chair, arms folded right hand to his chin thinking

"I wonder …"

Across town Rita is seated behind her desk attempting to work but she is preoccupied with continuously looking at the phone in anticipation she is checking her Rolex women watch looking out the window and just as she is about to pick up the phone Ted walks in the door.

"Ah! At last it took you long enough

We have to talk"

"What's the matter Babe, you okay?"

"No I'm not" she admits

"Ted you've got to be straight with me. David thinks you're somehow involved with drugs and some people being murdered"

Ted remains expressionless and replies with,

"Sounds like the ole boy is really trying to put some locks on you which means he's got to get me out of the way first. Damn Baby, what you do to that man"

"This is no time for ill humor Ted. I'm in this mess too thanks to you"

"Me! Explain that one You're the one who looks like Camilla Harris and got his nose open so how is it my fault?"

"Have you been listening to a word I've said; the man Believes you are involved in drugs and murder"

"Yes I heard every word you've said, but what I don't understand is how you figure you fit in any of this"

"David asked me if I knew where you were at the time of the last…murder and I naturally told him you were with me"

"And I was so what's the problem?"

"So?" she echoes
"Ted you were not with me all night. Remember, I was asleep when you got up and left"

"But I told you I had some business to attend to"

She appears to be getting angry as she maintains her composure as she speaks to him

"How do you think this is going to make me look when the police find out that you weren't with me all night, they'll think I was covering for you"

"Covering for me for what? I don't know anything about these accusations"

"Why is it so hard for me to get a straight answer out of you?"

"I'm giving you straight answers. I don't know anything about any of this" He attempts to put his arms around her but she steps away

"Hey! Come on now. I mean I'm really touched by the way you're taking all of this out of fear for my safety but you're seriously making too much out it"

"Maybe I am" she admits "but even so I would think that if you really cared about me as much as you say you do, then you would be more than willing to ese my mind but instead you act like I'm working for the police"

'Well---- can't be too careful these days" he says joking attempting to embrace her. This time she does not resist too much

"Come on baby you just got to trust me on this. The guy is jealous is all it is. Besides isn't a warrant usually issued to a person in the case where enough evidence calls for an arrest?"

"I don't know" she sighs as he takes her in his arms "he just scared me with all of his questions and you don't seem to have one thought about it"

"I don't because it's nothing for me to care about and nothing for you to care about. This guy is just trying to throw his weight around like he's running something but don't take it serious" and they become lost in a passionate kiss, holding on to each other as though it were the very first time.

Later that night Ted is driving on the I Ten North heading towards the Ten freeway when he picks up the mobile phone on the console in its cradle quickly pressing out seven numbers. After a moment he speaks

"Listen we need to tie up our business and quick.

I've got a love sick cop sweating me over Rita and he might be trouble so I want to take care of this"

He listens a moment then speaks again

"No. From what I could tell he doesn't know anything but all the same I don't want to run the risk of getting caught up on a fluke, so I'm going to go close this deal then I'll get right back with you" replacing the receiver back in its cradle.

Inside his car Ted pulls off the freeway driving through the Crenshaw District on into Leimert Park. Just off Exposition he pulls over in front of a large home that has a late model Blue Cadillac parked in the driveway.

On the other side of town in a bar on 79th and Western one person sits at the bar with her head down.

She is the neighborhood drunk. In a corner alone sits Erica. The bar tender is nowhere to be seen at 4:00 p.m. when David Coleman walks in and takes a seat next to Erica at the table.

"Now we both know that you are not even close to being old enough to be in here" "sometimes this the only place I can go when I ain't got no money. The owner lets me stay in the room in the back for nothing"

"I find that hard to believe" he states as he looks around the run down club. "So, is this a relative"

"No see, most of the time I stay here by myself But sometimes he stay with me when his wife mad at him"

An obese apron wearing bald headed old white man walks up to the table introduces himself as Nick and asks if they planned to make an order

"What do you and you friend want here girl?

If you want to rent the room you better get a move on cause I ain't got all day!"

Erica attempts to warn Nick by waving her hand but he pays her no mind

"How much for the room?" Coleman asks "fifty bucks for the first hour. Twenty for each half hour after that"

"Is that with or without the girl?" Coleman asks Nick

"What are you nuts! Ain't nothing in life worth having Cheap. Pay me for the room and pay her for the Service"

The lieutenant goes in his coat pocket and pulls out his badge. Nick has an expression of utter fear as he stands urinating on himself

"Ahhhh Officer! Look I run a clean and honest business...and I don't want no trouble. Sure I rent out rooms but I don't got nothing to do with what goes on---"

Lieutenant Coleman holds up his right hand in signaling the man to be silent. Then he speaks to him calmly,

"If I wanted to I could shut you down haul your ass off to jail for the next thirty years in a federal prison for crimes against a minor"

"I didn't know!" Nick pleads "These little niggers come in here lying all the time with the fake ID" he stutters

"I pay my taxes. I got a wife a kid in clooege-"

In a calm tone of voice the detective speaks to the frightened pedophile

"Pay attention you piece of shit. As of this moment I own your sorry ass. Let there be no mistake about it. Now get out of my face!"

"Yes sir yes sir Thank you sir thank you " bowing all the way back out of the club running away meekly so frightened having wet himself.

Erica is hiding her face out of embarrassment

"He so stupid I didn't mean for you to hear that"

"It's alright" he conveys in a reassuring comforting tone of voice

"I know how it is down here. You got to do what you got to do to survive." Thinking to himself how the path for her life is already carved out unless she can somehow rise above her circumstances

THE WITNESS

It's early in the morning at the Crenshaw Fitness Palace, even the owner of the gym Larry was getting in his workout before the rush of exercise buffs made their way in before going to work. Ted is seated at the Preacher Bench with an EZ curl bar in his hands in the middle of his workout when he looks up to see David Coleman standing in front of him. He replaces the bar back in the rack

"The locker's are straight in the back" Ted directs the Detective

"My goodness!" Coleman speaks in surprised admiration

"I could tell that you were in good shape, but I had no idea you were put together like that!" while Ted shows he is not impressed with his spiel saying

"I don't like to hold conversations when I'm working out so if you came in here for that you came to the wrong place", wiping the falling sweat from his forehead with the back of his gloved right hand.

"Rita did mention that you work out here every morning so I got the idea to save time I would stop by"

"Like I said" Ted spoke sternly

"This ain't no conversation pit for me so you're going to have to catch me some other time during my normal business hours"

But the lieutenant will not be dismissed that easily and replies calmly,

"Well Ted, the way I figure it we can have this Conversation outside or we can go down town to my office. The choice is up to you"

Ted takes what he said as a challenge to step outside and battle out of the view of any witness's.

"Not a problem" he concludes with a slight grin and heads the short distance to the entrance stepping out on to the sidewalk to walk a few feet more on the street to stand next to his parked Mercedes at the curb He turns with Coleman directly behind him and says

"Let's make this quick lieutenant" as the sun slowly finds its way into the early morning sky Ted stands with both arms folded in front of his chest looking the detective directly in his eyes. Unaware of the occupant inside the black squad car parked across the street.

"Exactly what kind of business are you in Mister Zackery?"

"You'll have to excuse me but unless you have some sort of legal reason to ask me anything I am not obligated to answer anything, so what is this really about" "Truth is I'm conducting an investigation on a number of cases involving people being murdered and

I'm sure its just a coincidence but the suspect has an uncanny resemblance to you"

"Is that so" Ted quoted as he removed his cell phone from the pouch around his waist and pressed speed dial then spoke to the detective

"Excuse me for a moment while I contact my attorney"

"What for we're just talking nothing official no need to get nervous"

Ted leans in closer to Coleman speaking in a calm tone of voice,

"Listen lieutenant, if you want something soft to play with then I advise you to shit in your hand. Other than that if you want to talk to me make Sure you come correct"

"And that means?" the detective questions in reply

"Correct within the eyes of the law of course" with an icy stare

"I assure you" the lieutenant speaks,

"It's no need to get nervous. I just thought since we already met I would talk to you off the record"

"Yeah well," Ted invokes,

"This can be put on the record I do not associate with obvious adversity and I find you as exactly that" walking back inside the gym without saying another word.

Coleman walks back across the street to his squad car where Erica sits alone on the front passenger seat. He gets in'

"Well did you get a close enough look ;could you see his face clearly?"

"Yeah, but he look different in the day time. I always see him at night"

"But is he the one you witnessed put a bullet in your friend killing him?"

"I told you he don't look the same! Maybe he is maybe he not". Coleman sits back with a sigh of distress,
"There goes that one!"

Back inside the gym Ted is on the decline bench replacing the barbell in the rack when PD walks in
"Say man, I was sitting outside and I seen you with the police. I waited until he pulled off I could see too there was some broad in the car with him. Had me thinking she was trying to get a make on you".

"That's why that slithering low life wanted me to go outside ". Although annoyed by the idea of being set up for a clandestine line up still he smiles shaking his head. PD asks,

"Man you alright?" causing Ted to snap out of his thoughts

"Oh yeah I'm good. Listen, I'm just finishing up here then we can go and take care of this other business"

"Well I might as well do a set while I'm here" when they actually spend another thirty minutes working out then leave the gym together.

A telephone truck is parked outside a residence after normal working hours. Inside sit two undercover agents Richard Flannery is white Roberto Arteaga is Hispanic monitoring a particular residence. Both are young in their late 20's. Arteaga speaks with a heavy accent

"Say Main Chew ever been in a tie spot?"

""What do you mean?"

"Chew know, where chew have to make a choice"

"I don't quite understand what you're asking I make choices every day"

"I'm talking about with you and the other lady you got's on the side"

"I don't have a lady on the side. It's just me and Cindy, that's my wife and she's all I need"

"Ah come on!" he agitates with a Hispanic twist

"Don't give me that chit You mean to told me you don't like a strange piece of Ass"

"That's exactly what I'm telling you and if don't stop playing Russian roulette with you dick it's gonna fall off" causing Arteaga to laugh adding

""Yeah and when it do I hope it's in a nice round young blonds ass too!"

Outside the surveillance truck a late model dark blue Cadillac creeps down the street but slows down when it gets in front of one particular house.

From inside the van Flannery is watching out the front window with night vision binoculars and spots the blue Cadillac

"Wait a minute this might be our guy"

A police car appears cruising through the neighborhood and stops beside the car With window down he speaks to the driver. A few moments later the Cadillac pulls away Flannery is unable to make out the face of the driver but the beat officers having actually spoken with him was a plus

"Let's give it a few more hours, then I want to talk to the officers in that squad car"...

THE TOTAL EXPERIENCE

The sounds of Barbara Morison preforming a duet with Nu Rah Ali on the stage of the elegant supper club where men and women all fashionably dressed in their elegant attire and expensive jewelry enjoying the comfort and peace of mind in knowing that here is where a more elegant and safe setting made it easy to relax

Ted and PD sit at a front table with two drinks in front of them along with some papers they are going over,

"You can't lose with this. All you have to do is fix it where the money is automatically transferred into your account which means you can keep them Dames out of your business aside of all that pillow talk you be doing"

"Eh!" PD scuffs off the remark then asks

"Whatever, but is this a sure thing?"

"All you have to do is check it out the numbers don't lie" both men absorbed in the business in front of them not noticing Renaldo Ray the popular stand up night club comedian who walks up to their table,

"What you two pimps up to adding up all the Ho's ya'll done knocked today"

Speaking jovially to the night club regular Ted says,

"She—it Mister, you the real pimp when all you got to do is make a Dame grin and your money is a done deal. While me, I got to break a brick choke a stick and drown in a drip of water before I can get paid"

"Shit! After all that you deserve to get something" the trio erupts into laughter. Adding to the humor PD asks

"Say man, where that money you owe me?"

"That's why I'm up in here tonight trying to find a Dame who ain't shame to grin along with a budget to put me in," just as the Stage MC announces Renaldo Ray to the Stage, creating waves of applauds from the filled to capacity audience

A scantily dressed waitress appears at their table

"Would you gentlemen like another drink?"

"Please, two more Bombay Sapphire's" Ted directs holding a paper napkin around his empty glass wiping it clean of finger prints before he passes it to her...

As the sun slips away from the sky over the Hertz parking lot at LAX the bearded man is standing at the customer counter signing a form, then goes into his pocket to produce a thick wad of hundred dollar bills, peeling off a few handing them to the white male agent behind the counter.

Moments later a white Buick Road-Master pulls off the lot leaving a late model dark blue Cadillac in the Return section of the rental yard

HELLO MORNING

With suit coat draped over his right arm, collar open tie untied eyes red and clearly feeling no pain Ted is walking in the front door held open by Rita

"Well good morning mister party animal" she jeers as he continues to walk on into the kitchen where he goes directly to the refrigerator taking out a bottle of grapefruit juice then from the freezer he extracts a tray of ice separating the cubes while Rita sits down at the counter watching him He searches cabinet then asks,

"Didn't I leave a bottle of gin here a few days ago?"

"Top shelf behind the crystal" she instructs still half asleep with her right hand holding up her chin in an effort to stay awake. Along with the bottle of gin he brings down two glasses

"I hope you're not getting one for me!" she inquires

"Yeah Baby" he slurs,

"One time honey go against the grain and do something that just feels good" as he goes about mixing their drinks. She gets up from her seat to stand beside him

"Ted, *seriously I can't do this I've got two houses to show-*"

Without even looking up from what he is doing he says

"Reschedule it. No such thing as can't" Handing her the finished drink he pleads

"Come on Baby don't make me beg, just one Lil drink, Just one! Pweeze !" making it difficult for her to keep a straight face she reluctantly accepts the glass as Ted holds up his glass in proposing a toast,

"Live life with no regrets and in everything you do always do your best. Let the past stay right where it is so the future can show all the good it can give" They touch glasses and ted takes a gulp from his empting half his glass while she sips hers. He notices it and holds up his half empty glass showing her

"Baby, I'm not asking you to tie one on but I at least want you to feel it a little bit"

""I'm sorry but I'm just not use to this drinking early in the morning before putting anything on my stomach" she explains

"What!" he challenges

"you think I do this every day. I work too, ya' know!"

"I've heard that before" she mumbles but he hears her

"What's that suppose to mean?"

"Nothing" she conveys without hesitation

"Bullshit! I know you-" not finishing his sentence but takes a drink from his glass

"You know I what?" she asks he does not answer but continues to fix himself another drink

"Ted. Finish what you were about to say" she demands just as he has refilled his glass with gin takes a sip then sets it down on the counter

"I know you've been talking to your police lieutenant. He came down to the gym calling himself trying to press me"

"Press you about what?"

"About nothing so I told him where to get off".

She looks at him with pleading searching eyes

"What are you keeping from me?" she asks sincerely

"Nothing you don't already know since I told you a long time ago that I use to be in the fast life.

I was a hustler but I got away from all that yet my past still has the tendency to haunt me at times" Taking another drink from his glass staring out the kitchen window.

Two older detectives take over the night operations surveillance of the home where Keno lives. They don't think anything of it when they observe a black man going from door to door carrying a stack of what looks like newspapers A Jehovah witness going from one house to the next attempting to spread the word. So by the time the man reaches the home where Keno opens the door and allows the man in they have lost interest in him as Keno allows the man in and closes the door

On the other side of town in the bedroom Ted and Rita are totally naked together in bed. Luther Van Dross Keeping My Faith In You is playing softly through the speakers while together in syncopated passionate rhythm they make love. With her legs wrapped around his waist both arms clenching him to her she moans in delight and pleasure, arousing him to only want to please her more.

He kisses her neck then suckles her left breast as she locks her fingers into his hair. Her climax is evident. Explosive Her entire body trembles as she lay beneath him. He repositions himself beside her and attempts to caress her breast,

"No! No give me a minute" he places his right hand on her flat stomach to feel her still trembling when again she speaks

"No! don't do that Just give me a minute"

He smiles at her triumphantly laying back with hands behind his head he says,

"I would offer you a cigarette but I don't smoke"

Rita is still on her back with her eyes closed and hands are covering her breast so he can't tough them

"Very funny" was all she could muster to say.

77 TH PRECINCT

Lieutenant Coleman is sitting at his desk talking with an attractive black woman Undercover police officer Sheba Durden

"This will be the third buy you've made from Keno but this time I want you to buy half a key"

"Last time he propositioned me, said he'd give me anything I want if I let him go down on me, so is using sex as payment enough to indict?" she asks jokingly

"Sure we can. The only difficult part would be marking it into evidence" he snickers as she laughs

"I can see the prosecutor now turning red as a beet pointing to the people's exhibit A between my legs"

"Okay okay, let's get serious.-

She salutes him rises from her seat and leaves the office

The digital clock on the night stand read 10:15 A.M. when she opens her eyes turning to smile at the sight of Ted sound asleep from their all- night session of unharnessed sexual gratification over and over again. Suddenly it dawns on her that she has appointments She leaps from the bed heading for the shower leaving Ted still sound asleep.

11:45 shows on the clock as Rita stands in the door way fully dressed She looks over at Ted still asleep, smiles then quietly slips out of the room closing the door behind her.

On the other side of town police officers converge on the home where Keno lives, there he lay face down his head in a pool of blood next to a dead Rottweiler. Sheba Durden undercover and dressed provocatively along with the two officers from the stakeout are there in the house plus several other uniformed officers photographing the crime scene.

Lieutenant Coleman is clearly in a hostile frame of mind pacing the area talking to himself until,

"Will someone; anyone tell me how it is a suspect who is under constant surveillance is now on his way to the county morgue with a bullet hole in his head?"

Sheba Durden responds,

"The guy who did this is a Pro he knew Keno was being watched but that didn't stop him-"

"Oh you don't say!" the lieutenant cracks

"He waltzed right in here did his thing and he waltzed his ass right back out the same way under the diligent watchful eyes of your stakeout team" she points out

The two officers are huddled in a corner as Sheba steps to the lieutenant unintimidated by his rank

"And how did he manage to pull that off?" he asks

"Not mine to call so I'll let these two officers fill you in" waving to the officers to approach as she walks away.

The two male white officers walk up introducing themselves, the tallest of the duo speaks,

"I'm detective Fisher and this is detective Abbott"

"Okay, now which one of you gentlemen would like to explain to me how this happened"

"Ah Sir, you'll never believe the balls this guy had-"

"Try me" Coleman fires back

"Well Sir, we actually watched him go inside"

"You what!" Coleman shouts out in a rage

"Sir it's not unusual for these Jehovah witness people to be to be out here that time of the morning I mean he even came up to the window and asked if we had time for a message from the lord"

"Woah! You mean you actually got a look at the guy?"

"Yes Sir, just as sure as I'm looking at you now"

"Fantastic!" Coleman exclaimed as the other officer reports

'And sir it looks like his dog may have taken a bite of our perp"

"Let's not waste any more time but get back to the station where we can identify this bastard" Coleman directs the crew out of the house and back to headquarters

At her Real Estate office Rita is seated behind her desk when the phone rings

70

"Good morning Washington Realtor this is Rita speaking how can I help you?"

"Good morning pretty lady this is your friendly Neighborhood police lieutenant calling"

Rita sits stiffly in her chair waiting for him to speak but awkwardly she blurts out,

"Oh Ah Hello David I was intending to call you this morning about the house"

"Well, that's not why I'm calling. I'm trying to locate your friend Ted. You haven't seen or heard from him this morning have you?"

She pauses for moment before she answers

"Hello Rita are you still there?"

"Yes I'm still here but kind of in the middle of something-"

"But what about your friend?" he asks

"What friend?" she inquires

"Your friend Ted"

"What about Ted"

"I asked if you have seen him"

"Oh! Yes as a matter of fact I just left him a little while ago still in bed asleep at my house and I know he won't answer the phone"

Suddenly the lieutenant is silent absorbing what she just relayed to him along with his jealous obsession of Rita

He asks her,

"Is there any way you can reach him, other than having to go all the way back to your house or have you two worked out some kind of a code?"

Realizing his insinuation as if she is some criminal co-conspirator

"Listen David, I don't know anything about what's going on between you and Ted but I don't appreciate your insinuation!"

"Honestly I wasn't insinuating anything I just thought maybe you already had a standing agreement not to give out the other's phone number"

"Oh well, I can call him and he'll be able to hear my voice through the answering machine" she offers the lieutenant

"If you've got a three way there in your office then, why not call now?"

Again she hesitates to answer

"Are you still there?" his voice inquires through the phone as she has placed him on hold while she go through dissecting her options talking out loud to herself

"Oh God! I hope I'm doing the right thing" even though she trust her Man not to involve her in anything criminal, while on the other hand there was this mysterious side of Ted that had always peaked her curiosity.

She presses more numbers and the connection comes alive with the voice of lieutenant David Coleman already connected to the three way call. The connection clicks in

"Hi leave a message or page me I'm not in right now. Thanks. Beep! Hello Ted are you awake yet?"

Still in bed half asleep Ted picks up the phone

"Yes miss lady how may I assist you" still reeling from the effects of the gin and grapefruit juice the night before

"Ted I've got lieutenant Coleman on the other line" causing Ted to snap out of his intoxicated remnants and Coleman speaks

"I've been trying to track you down for hours" Coleman announces

"Yeah well you found me now what do you want"

"I need you to come down to my office this morning and for the record I might add, this is official"

"Not a problem lieutenant just as soon as I make contact with my attorney" Ted informs him

"Good. I'll look forward to seeing you in a couple of hours or so"

"Like I said" Ted corrects him

"As soon as I make contact with my attorney"

"Sure. Sure I'll be expecting you and thank you Rita" he clicks off the call and as Ted is about to speak she says,

"Hold on a second while I clear the line" after a moment she asks

"Are you still there?"

Ted is now sitting up on the side of the bed

"Yeah I'm still here"

"Is everything alright?" she asks

"As far as I know" he answers

"Then what does David want now?"

"Your guess is as good as mine but I'm taking Michael with me I'm going to call him now so I'll call you later. Don't worry. It's all good"

The connection clicks off.

At police headquarters David Coleman picks up the phone on his desk and speaks into the receiver,

"Get me the District Attorney on the phone" he waits a moment the line comes alive

"Good morning Artie. David Coleman, I was wondering If you had some time to sit in on an interrogation"

"What's the case about?" The DA inquires routinely

"Drugs murder and a character who is involved or knows something about it. I would just like your view from a different prospective"

"Sure, my schedule is pretty much clear, so when you set it up give me a call and I'll be right over"

"Good deal. Talk to you soon" and the line goes silent.

4:45 P.M. The interrogations room at police headquarters seated in a metal straight back chair his attorney Artie Weiss in another chair next to him sits Ted. David Coleman is seated on the other side of the desk along with the district attorney.

"I appreciate you coming in Ted so we can straighten out the confusion but what we have here is a long list of murder victims who were all in contact with you"

"So what. I know a lot of people who are dead now Everybody gets a turn we don't get out of life alive"

"Let me paint a better picture for you" the lieutenant speaks while thumbing through a stack of papers

"According to these reports, each one of these unfortunate individuals met with you hours prior to their deaths and that looks awfully suspicious if you ask me. These were your friends"

"No, I wouldn't use that term exactly. I had business dealings; legitimate business and nothing more"

"Oh I see and what may I ask was the nature of that business?"

"I locate property for them Income and Business properties"

"You mean you help them wash their drug money" The Attorney intervenes

"Lieutenant! My client has no knowledge what so ever about the sources or means by which his investors acquire their funds. He only assists them in the construction of their portfolio's"

"This isn't a court of law Counselor we're just having a conversation" the DA specifies but is not accepted by Weiss

"Never the less mister district attorney, the question is still suggestive and misleading something that could be used to imply that my client had an active role in some criminal plot which is totally ridiculous"

"Alright. Alright duly noted!" the DA concedes

"Okay skip that one "Coleman announces in moving on with the questioning

"Tell me, what hours of the day did you conduct your business with these men"

"Usually lunch or after the sun goes down"

Lt. Coleman gets up from his chair to pace a short distance to and fro behind his desk

"Have you ever had any late night meetings with any of your investors?"

"No"

"Have you ever had any late night meetings with any of the deceased?"

"It's possible"

"Either you have or you haven't Which is it?"

"Like I said It's possible but I don't have any specific recollections"

"Okay then, let's start with how you come to know these people in the first place?"

"I don't understand what you mean by These people"

"Drug Dealers" Coleman emphasizes

"Lieutenant!" Attorney Weiss reprimands

"Let me rephrase that" the lieutenant corrects himself

"Did these men seek you out or did you find them?"

"I'm going to answer both of your questions lieutenant,

I make it no secret that I was once involved with the Fast Life but I got wise and went straight. Never the Less"

Taking a sip from the bottle water

"In the course of my travels I've met all typesof people and I don't make it a habit of making any type of chronological characteristic of their personal business, my only concern is how much money they want to invest"

"You obviously make a good living at what you do"

"I'm comfortable with it"

Behind the one way mirror were the two stakeout officers and three elderly black women watching Ted being interrogated on the other side of the glass Coleman asks Ted

"So where were you between the hours of four and five?"

"I was in bed with my lady over her house having sex" displaying a deliberate display of pomposity with a wink

"You were there all night?"

"You asked me where I was this morning not where I was all night"

"Then what time did you get there?"

"I'm not sure. I'd had a few"

"You're saying because you had too much to drink is why you don't remember what time it was when you arrived where you slept"

"Oh we did a whole lot more than sleep if you know what I mean" emitting a needling grin knowing the lieutenant has a soft spot for Rita

"Well give me a ball park figure about what time you think it may have been"

"Maybe four or five"

"What type of alcohol do you drink?"

"Gin" Ted replies

"Any particular brand?"

"Bombay Sapphire"

"How often do you drink?"

Weiss interrupts the lieutenant,

"I don't see how that has anything to do with your investigation"

"You're right" the detective appears to be changing his approach

"That will be all for now but you don't have any. plans to go out of town any time soon do you?"

"Is that it?" The attorney asks the lieutenant

"Yes, your client is free to go I'd just like him to stay around in case I have any more questions" David speaks as he escorts Ted and his attorney to the door

"Thank you for your time and I apologize if I inconvenienced you in any way"

With Ted in the lead heading out of the room he and his attorney walk briskly out leaving Coleman alone with the DA who appears curious

"What is it David?"

"Get ready to have a warrant issued for our Mister Zackery" just as one of the white officers from behind the mirror walks in to report

"I'm sorry sir but nothing positive"

Outside police headquarters in the parking lot Ted walking to his car long side of his attorney says

"Thanks for that Artie. I've got something to check on but I'll give you a call later" walking off separately to their cars

Back at Parker Center Lieutenant David Coleman is in the office of the Medical Examiner His name is Frank a Kevorkian looking guy in his late fifties. On his desk is an open folder showing the name Robert Morris taken seven years before.

He questions the examiner about the report,

"So what you're saying is no positive ID was made, no DNA recovered from the body that washed up two days later after this guy escaped?"

"Not to my satisfaction" Frank answers

"You see, when a cadaver is submerged in ocean waters for that length of time the fish first feed on the soft tissue the eyes and eye lids the lips the nose and ears"

"Ahgg! Gross What about dental records?"

"Believe it or not, there weren't any. In all the time this guy put in he didn't see the Dentist one time"

"So how was he identified?"

"What was left of the remains had kaki pants and shirt

The same federal prisoners wear in Terminal Island"

Lieutenant Coleman sits in deep thought for a moment then offers,

"So let's say the body that washed up in Long Beach really was some other poor slob, but not ole Morris here. Then that means Robert Morris would be free to assume any identity he wanted to"

"That's right"

THE LEGAL WHEELS

Inside the Court House in Downtown Los Angeles on Spring Street Ted is going into the County Comptroller's office where he is greeted by the receptionist

"Good morning" she beams brightly

"I haven't seen you in a while How are you?"

"I'm good" he replies with a brief smile then asks

"Is the old Boy in?"

"No he didn't come in today and I don't think he will be in at all today but is it anything I can help you with?"

"Oh no I'll just check back later"

"Now you know you know you don't have to just need to see him in order to come back" He only flashes her a smile as he makes his way back out the door.

David Coleman is still talking with Frank the Medical Examiner in his office

"Tell me something Would it be at all possible for a man to swim in those waters to the shore from that distance?"

"Sure, anything's possible" he answers with a certain sense of excitement

"But even with the Breakers the waves get pretty rough out there especially with all those cargo vessels constantly in and out of the harbor. However! If he were a good swimmer he'd be able to make it under water"

"So you're saying it's possible"

"I'm saying this is strictly my own theory since no boats were seen in the area of the prison, the gun towers would have spotted one, but yes it is very possible". Causing the lieutenant to smile to himself with the thought of finding out that Ted Zackery really isn't who he says he is but in fact an escaped federal convict.

The Penthouse on the 12th floor of 501 Ocean Boulevard where Ted lives alone has a view off in the distance of Terminal island federal prison visible from the balcony Ted and PD are in the living room sitting in front of the glass coffee table each with a drink in hand talking

"I haven't figured it out yet" Ted says,

"but somebody is trying to set me up to take the wrap on all those High Rollers getting jacked and smoked"

PD takes a sip from his drink then speaks slowly,

"You got to always remember, whenever the kriss cross double cross and back stabbing jumps off check the closest thing to you. That's usually where the flaw is"

"Yeah I hear what you're saying but I don't carry mine like that. I'm not that open"

But PD is not in total agreement

"I don't know about that When you backed up out the Game a whole lot of Ho's was mad not to mention some jealous Negro's who was pissed at you for wising them Dames up to a better Game"

Ted sets his drink down on the coffee table then sits back in the sofa with a sigh of being tired

"Man! But that still don't add up for someone to go to all this just to have me knocked Besides don't nobody know for real what I do"

Maybe not directly from you but you know how those Negro's be running they mouth lying about lying to the police when they get pinched"

"I see what you mean" Ted concedes clearly in deep thought as PD continues,

"Not only that but negro's is naturally jealous. You got out the game but still rolling like the Blue Line while still a lot of them same clowns are still doing dirt bad, not to mention the Squares who ain't never had no game in the first place"

Silence envelopes the room as Ted rises from the sofa to go and stand out on the balcony looking off in the distance…

ONE HAND WASHES THE OTHER

At police headquarters David Coleman sits at his desk a sheet of paper in one hand telephone receiver in the other talking

"John it's David can you go ahead and issue that subpoena for Theodore Zackery I've got the lab reports back from the crime scenes and I need his to compare"

"I don't have problem with that but what else do you have to go on?"

"Truth is not much but that's only because I don't believe this guy is who he says he is"

"Wait! Run that by me again"

"I know it sounds weird but I've got a gut feeling about this one and if there is any problems from up stairs about it I will personally take the heat"

"You bet your sweet ass you will because this conversation is being recorded" causing a slight look of surprise to appear on the face of lieutenant Coleman

"Covering your own ass in the process right?"

"You got it pal!"
"Alright All- Right I can't fault you for that,
I mean look what happened with the OJ trial" the lieutenant recalls
"Yeah, tell me about it. Listen I'll see what I can do first thing in the morning. Is that good enough?"
"It's going to have to be. Talk to you later"
Lieutenant Coleman sits contemplating what to do next...

Ted is the driving down Imperial towards the Nickerson Gardens projects where from Central avenue all the way to Long Beach boulevard prostitutes and drug addicts parade up and down the streets either peddling their wares or looking for a Fix

He pulls in front of a liquor store on the corner of Wilmington and Imperial known as The Front where a person can buy anything from sex, drugs stolen merchandise even a life for the right price. Sitting in his car with the passenger side window down talking with a dope fiend standing outside the car The conversation is brief and he pulls away at 1:00 A.M

1:30 A.m. Ted is knocking on the front door, Rita is sound asleep until he knocks harder and rings the doorbell. Half asleep she comes to open the door for him
"I see I'm going to have to give you a key"

He walks in with an intense look on his face and goes to the sofa where he plops down Rita follows to sit directly at his right side resting her head on his chest and within moments she has drifted back off to sleep

Sometime during the hours of darkness Ted and Rita relocated to the bedroom where the morning sun light now begins to creep through the blinds She stirs out of bed heading for the kitchen to start to morning coffee then out the front door to retrieve the morning paper. In the driveway she notices a blue late model Cadillac startling her. David Coleman had asked her about Ted knowing anyone or owning a car like that Slowly she walks over to the blue Cadillac careful not to touch it as she looks inside after retrieving the newspaper then headed back into the house.

In the bedroom she walks over to the side where he lay asleep she puts the paper down then kneels on the floor with her head resting gently on his chest. He awakens to hear her whimpers and asks,

"What's the matter Baby?"

She attempts to hide her tears, wipes her eyes with the back of her hand then raises her head like a little child to look into his eyes.

"I'm sorry …I I'm just" she hesitates

"Hey! What is it What's this about?" he asks very much concerned as he sits up in the bed

"I'm alright" she lies

"I just need to be by myself for a while" her eyes avoiding his

He looks quizzically at first, then gets up and proceeds to get dressed to leave saying

"I understand- but before he can finish she blurts out

"Ted, David is investigating you For what I don't know All I know is it has something to do with that car parked in my driveway You can-"

He stops what he is doing to address her with,

"What on earth are you talking about?"

"Ted I know so you can stop pretending I know and David knows you've got to do something you've go-"

"Rita! Stop and tell me exactly what you're talking about! Seriously! I do not have the slightest idea of what's going on other than someone is trying to set me up". He then leads her out into the front room where they sit on the sofa holding on to each other he asks her

"Now start from the beginning".

In the neighborhood of Windsor Hills an unmarked police car sits in the driveway of the home Rita has sold to Lieutenant David Coleman. The entire house is void of furniture There are no lights only the glow from the rising sun through the curtain less windows Roaming aimlessly from one room to the other talking to himself

"This is where you belong Rita. Here with me The only thing stopping you is that imposter but he will be out of the picture soon " continuing his haunting of the empty home then suddenly he stops in his tracks

"You're right! We need to spend more time together Like the other day when we had so much fun. Yes!" He suddenly races out of the front door slamming it behind him jumps into the police car and burns rubber out of the driveway and out of the neighborhood.

In the living room Ted and Rita are sitting together on the sofa no longer crying but talking together when he concludes.

"And that's the truth! I know it looks bad, but if you ever believed in anything in your entire life I need you to give me that same consideration right now"

"Then how do you explain that car Ted?" she asked

"Just plain dumb luck" going to hos coat on the back of the sofa to take out the sales receipt from the rental then hands it to her

"Look at the date on it. I've only had it one night"

"But David told me he saw you get out of a car like that one yesterday morning when you came to the office"

"No Honey it wasn't that car I have an investor who has one just like it and I can prove it. Her name is Tameka Harris"

"A woman?" she inquires

"Yes, she and her husband have a spot on Florence and Western"

"Oh I don't know what to think It's all so confusing"

Forcefully he takes her in his arms,

"No it's not! You know me better than anyone alive so don't go getting flakey on me now just because some slick cop has the hot's for you–"

"But Ted he told me–"

"Forget what he told you! Listen to what I'm telling you! I am not the person he is looking for He is only trying to get at you by getting me out of the way"

She looks at him with trusting eyes as she locks her arms around his waist falling weakly into his embrace

"Oh Ted what are we going to do? Why can't you go to David and tell him what you told me?"

"It's not that simple to explain, but since you told me what your boyfriend is up to I better get rid of that car out there before your love- sick boy cop drops by" he laughs

"Don't joke like that He is not my boyfriend"

Walking to the front door Ted says to her

"All the same I'm taking this car back and get something else" Ted opens the front door and with gun in hand stands Lieutenant David Coleman Ted greets him,

"Well look Trick Willie is here"

"Hold it right there" Coleman commands

'Don't make any false moves just kindly step back inside" he directs as Ted complies and Rita attempts to intervene as he begins to pat Ted down

"David you're making a mistake-"

"I don't think so!" he barks at her

"Now stay back and let me do my job"

"Do like he says Babe" Ted advises her

"Where's the gun you had the other day?

I'll bet it's the same one you used on all those dealers you robbed and killed"

"What gun I don't carry a gun"

"You did the other day when I first met you at Rita's office"

"That's when you should of said something"

"It's called probable cause. I didn't have any but today that car outside changes everything"

Rita runs to the table to retrieve the rental agreement handing it to Coleman

"No David you're wrong It's not the same car" while keeping one eye on Ted he glances over the document

"For all I know this could be a fake just like

He is!"

"What?" she utters confused

"His real name is Robert Morris who escaped from Terminal Island federal prison almost six years ago and everybody thinks he ended up as fish food"

"Ted is that true?" she asks

"The ravings of a badge wearing lunatic with an over active dose of Super Stupid"

"Oh yeah, then explain those dog bites" the lieutenant announces

Speaking at the same time Ted and Rita speak,

"Dog bites? What dog bites"

"The ones you got from Keno's Rottweiler before You killed him." causing Rita to speak up

"I can tell you he hasn't got any dog bites on him and I've been all over his body"

Lieutenant Coleman clearly does not like her descriptive intervention and loses his composure

"Rita I told you to stay out of this You don't know what you're dealing with here so just get out of-" Ted kicks the gun from his hand then knocks the lieutenant to the floor unconscious with the same kick. Rita is in a total state of shock screaming hysterically

Ted picks up the gun to stand over the still body of the officer while Rita is watching him uncertain of what he is about to do. Ted looks towards her then steps over the unconscious law man handing her the officers gun and she asks fearfully,

"I don't want it! What do I do with it"

"Take it easy" he assures her,

"Give it back to him when he comes to but it wouldn't be a good idea for me to be here when he wakes up." He quickly takes her in his arms kissing her then bounds out of the house.

He jumps in the rented Cadillac and drives it a few miles away to park it in an industrial area abandoning it taking off on foot trotting down the street at a strong steady pace breathing through his nose.

Now down on The Front in Watts walking on the sidewalk when he notices a black man carrying a gas can Ted recognizes him as a Heroin user name Carlos

"Ted is that you?" he asks

"Hey Carlos" Ted replies and Carlos eagerly responds,

"Man am I glad to see you, but hey, why you walking?"

"That's a long story" he says casually looking over his shoulder

"Well check this brother man, my wheels done run outta gas up the street and I was on my way to my connection-" cutting him off

"Not a problem, in fact I'll fill up your tank get you fixed along with some extra if you can hang with me for a while"

"No shit?" he ponders

"No shit" Ted confirms

"My main man! That sounds like a plan to me."

Carlos drives an early model gray mercury Capri in need of paint but the engine in sound. Ted is driving while Carlos sits in the front passenger seat in a serious Nod from the effect of the heroin he so badly needed,

"Sa---y man...I really do appreciate that....

I...I been short real sho..." drifting off before he can complete his sentence

Ted glances as the man beside him being held in his set only by the seatbelt his head hung down in his chest

"Carlos." Ted calls out

"Yeah! Yeah I appreciate that man"

"It's all good, now tell me about this Dude who's been doing all the jacking"

"Man. I ain't gone lie. You know I always tell you the truth cause me and you go way back, but I was thinking it was you doing them dudes and so did a lot of other people"

"Why is that?"

"Cause the people who lived to talk about it all said It was you" going into another nod there in the front seat

"Carlos!" Ted repeats

"Carlos!"

"Yeah. Yeah man yeah!"

"What are you saying, talk to me!" in his drug induced stupor he says

"I ain't never seen him myself but this little broad got a make on him when Essay and Chico got smoked"

"What's the little girl's name?" But Carlos goes into another nod

"Carlos! What's the girl's name!"

"Oh! Ah Erica. That's it. She's a cute little hooker who works out of white boy Nick's spot"

"You mean white boy Nick on Figueroa?"

"Yeah he the one"

Lieutenant Coleman is now awake sitting up on the sofa. Rita is next to him with a cold towel holding it to his swollen face. Coleman is clearly upset but more so humiliated and embarrassed as he keeps pushing her hand away

"Hold still!" she commands

"I don't have time for this!" where she takes a firm hold of his arm forcing him to sit still

"Stop it David! I know you're angry but you have to believe me Ted is not the man you're looking for"

91

"I know his type better than you do now tell me Where did he go?"

"I don't know where he went or anything about what's going "

At that Coleman gets up from the sofa hastily heading for the front door

"That's fine. I'll catch him without your help then you'll see exactly how wrong you've been about this guy"

Nick's Bar located in a section of Los Angeles known for the place to go when looking for a Hoe, as Nick would rhyme in attempt to relate to his clientele which usually were the street corner hustlers who either spit balloons of heroin or choreographed some sort of elaborate scam to play some innocent sucker out of his hard earned weeks pay.

The sound of Bill Withers, The Same Love That Made Me Laugh rang out as Ted and Carlos walked through the door to see Nick behind the bar wiping a shot glass The juke box changes to Kim Waters version of Marvin Gaye's Got to Give it Up

"Am I seeing a ghost Ted! What bring you back to Hell" Extending his hand across the bar and the two exchange a sincere greeting

"So what's been up Nick?" Ted asks as he takes a seat on the empty bar stool

"Same ole shit. So what can I get you guys" Nick asks

""Bombay Sapphire make it two"

"Hey! Come on the clientele here not that classy but we got Tanqueray"

Ted looks over at Carlos who is in a deep nod asking

"Is that alright with you man? Carlos"

"Yeah man what happened?"

"You want a shot of Tanqueray with some grape-fruit juice?" as Nick is already in the process of putting the drinks together when Ted asks him

"Say Nick, is Erica around?"

"She ought to be in here any time now. It's getting close for the Regulars to be coming in" finishing with the drinks and brings them over in front of Ted and Carlos when Ted goes into his pocket to pay for them

"On the House" Nick insists

"Thanks man. I appreciate that" while Nick goes back attending to the glasses behind the bar as he continues to speak to Ted

"That's her table over there in the corner. She'll make a B line for it the moment she hits that door"

"In that case I'll just go sit over there and warm up atmosphere before she makes her appearance".

Nick nods his head as Ted stands up with drink in hand and walks over to the table in the corner Carlos is in deep nod and has not even touched his drink nor does her realize Ted has moved to another place.

No more than five minutes pass before this young girl walks in headed straight for the table in the corner, a young black man trails in after her he is clearly her pimp but he takes a seat in the booth next to Ted as she asks Ted

'Don't I know you?"

"Not yet Baby Sit down so we can kick the money" he invites

"I don't need to sit down for that It's fifty dollars up front" Ted goes in his left front pocket to pull out a roll of one hundred dollar bills

The young pimps eyes light up as Erica continues to bargain

"Then I'll make it worth the C Note" she offers and attempts to take the bill from his hand but he quickly pulls it away

"Hold on there! Not so fast is this your ah, man?"

"Naw he not my man" she answers defensively while Ted recognizes the play he stands up from the table replacing the money back in his pocket as he says to her

"Oh I see he just follows you around perpetrating a fraud" infuriating the young hustler who threatens

"Say old nigga don't let this Bitch cause you to get checked up in here"

"Listen Son" Ted speaks calmly

"Do yourself favor and take all of five seconds to get out of my face" looking directly into the eyes of his would be victim The younger man appears to be weighing his options but he decides to back down while Ted walks a short distance behind her in route to the back and the room when she points to Nick saying

"Pay him" as she continues walking back to the room

Nick looks up from what he's doing to wave him on past without paying anything not that he would have.

Inside the room is poorly lit and bare except for a bed on box springs but no frame that sits on the bare wood floor a wash basin on the side wall and a toilet Erica makes her way straight for the bed taking off her clothes asking

"So how you want it?"

"I want to talk to you that's all"

"Oh I get it you one of those kind who like to watch"

"No, I just need to ask you some questions" he replies flatly

"You know you do look familiar I done seen you somewhere before. You sure you ain't no Cop?"

"Not in this life" he replies going in his pocket to produce the thick wad of hundred dollar bills to peel off a few tossing them on the bed saying

"I need some answers and fast about a murder you witnessed" She sits down on the side of the mattress picking up the money when she asks

"Wait a minute! Was that you I saw, if it was then it's gonna cost you a whole lot more than this"

Ted speaks calm and slowly making certain not to frighten,

"Understand something young lady This money means absolutely nothing to me, but not for you"

She listens intently as he assumes a seat on the mattress beside her

"You see, the money is no problem for me because I can always get some more. But you depending on how you answer this could make a difference between the beginning or the end if you know what I mean"

"Okay" she concedes

"I didn't tell the police everything I didn't want no parts of this mess but the Dude that killed Chico told him he was collecting for the carrying charges whatever that meant cause Chico told him over the phone that wasn't part of the deal"

"Part of what deal?" he asks her

""I don't know but I heard Chico say on the phone when they paid for the building nobody said nothing about no carrying charge"

Ted is looking past her lost in thought as he blurts out loud

"That son of a bitch!", but manages to redirect his attention back to her

"Listen kid, everybody has to live their own life the way they see fit. You got your whole life ahead of you but at the rate you're going that could all be cut short depending on the choices you make" He peels off another few bills handing them to her as he advises,

"Do something for yourself with that, back up from this nonsense and come up with a plan for yourself. For your life"

"But I don't know what else to do" she says almost tearfully He places his arms gently around her shoulders when he answers

"You can do anything you want to do as long as you put your mind to it. Start using your imagination instead of your body to get over" then heads back out front to the bar.

Ted goes to the pay phone on the wall once the line connects the call he says

"I want you to wait until I call you back, then do like I told you"

He hangs up the receiver and walks over to Carlos who is in a deep nod so he turns his attention back to Nick,

"I want you to do something for me" passing Nick a "C" Note

"Tell him to hang here until I get back and if he Wants anything this ought to take care of it"

Nick accepts the money gleefully

"For sure he's in good hands" watching him as he is gone as suddenly as he appeared

Inside the Capri Ted is pulling off the 110 freeway towards the Westside headed for the Crenshaw District on into Leimert Park, turning off of Exposition on Duncan a neighborhood of beautifully kept expensive homes where he pulls in front of a home where a white Buick Road-master sits parked in the driveway.

As Ted is getting out of the car he reaches around to his back taking the snub nose 38. From the clip holster at the small of his back The street is clean and void of people walking around holding the revolver down by his side walking cautiously to the back door of the home

Cautiously he tries the knob The door is unlocked he eases into the kitchen to see a man sitting on the table with his back to him, bloody bandages on the floor sweat pouring off the man who is unaware that Ted is even behind him until he speaks,

"Did you really think you could pull this off Omar?"

Come on in man he says as though he was expected

Slowly he enters the room to see drug paraphernalia strewn across the table. Dingy water glasses, crusty bent table spoons with tiny balls of cotton in brown burnt crust. Omar asks Ted,

"You want a Speed Ball" clearly absorbed in his drugs as Ted looks over to another part of the kitchen to see what looks the body of a woman lying face down He rushes over to kneel down beside her checking her pulse. She is dead.

"Why?...Why the fuck you do this man!"

Breathing heavily, trembling as he continues preparing the drugs to use there on the table

"It was a accident. She was trying to take it stopping me from using it on myself but it went off"

Ted stands up and goes closer to the table where a Glock sits in front of Omar while Ted still has the 38.

He asks his friend,

"You want to tell me why you've been trying to set me up? I thought we were friends"

In the middle of plunging the needle in his arm Omar explains,

"It just happened. At first I didn't mean to make it look like you but it just happened The only way I knew to fit in was to look like you. I dress like you I got myself a hair piece to make my hair long like yours"

"But why did you kill all those people?"

"It just happened I didn't mean to make it look

Like you, but it just happened. After a while I just couldn't help myself I couldn't stop Besides they deserved it"

"Did Debbie deserve being killed too?"

Just as the blood registers in the syringe sticking in his arm Omar breaks the needle off in his arm crying in a fit of rage throwing himself to the floor sobbing uncontrollably

"What am I going to do Ted. You got to help me!"

"Help you! There is no amount of help on the Planet that can help you get out of this one and you will not make it in the penitentiary Omar"

The emotionally distraught man `attempts to recompose himself

"I know...I...I..I can't go to jail I can't You got to help me Ted" he pleads with visible finger nail scratches on his face from fighting with his wife Debbie before he killed her.

Ted goes to the telephone and dials as he sys to Omar,

"I can't help you now. Nobody can This is something you have to face all on your own the line connects and he speaks

"Do it now" then hangs up the phone redirecting his attention to Omar

"So now what What's the next move how are you going to fix this?"

While Omar has put together another syringe full of Cocaine and Heroin and is injecting it into his left arm before speaking. He removes the needle from his arm allowing it to fall to the floor

"Damn! That shit feels good All these years… all that time…damn…I…ah…..this" he rambles on.

Ted stands in front of Omar as he remains seated at the table,

"You try to be something you were not cut out to be and look what it got you I don't understand that, to throw everything away like that for the sake of what?"

"You're right one hundred percent, okay now tell me what to do!" he pleads to his friend but Ted replies calmly,

"I don't have to tell you what to do. You already know the only thing you can do, Omar"

Seated on the floor next to the body of his murdered wife he looks up at Ted with tears streaming down his face saying nothing while Ted turns and walks out the way he came in through the back door.

An army of uniformed police officers including Lieutenant Coleman are all over the home in West Los Angeles where two bodies were discovered, an apparent murder suicide the victims are the City Comptroller and his wife both found shot to death in the home David Coleman is on the phone talking to Rita

"I'm certain we've got enough evidence to prove the late Omar Bishop was the man responsible for those other matters but that still does not let your friend off the hook! We still like to talk to him

Has he gotten back in touch with you yet?"

"I haven't spoken with him yet David, but I think you owe me an apology"

"Not so fast!" he insists

"I still need to check him out to find out who he really is"

"Oh David I'm sure he will turn up soon I know him"

"I'm sure you do" the lieutenant replies as the phone goes dead in his ear Rita hangs up the phone and turns to Ted as he lay head in her lap on her sofa

"I get the impression that he is not a happy camper"

"Oh well" Ted yawns where he lay and she adds

"I just feel so bad for Debbie"

"I don't see why she's not suffering"

"You know what I mean I liked her and it's just sad the way she died"

"What would have been worse was if she had to go through living with the memory of what happened"

"I guess you're right, but what's going to happen to you now I mean weren't you selling property to these people with the help of Omar and the City Office?"

"Sure I did which was all perfectly legal and I cannot be held accountable for any of the actions he took"

"But what about David?" she asks in concern,

"I'm not worried about him because he can't force me to do anything My attorney makes certain of that"

"So you're saying the law will protect you?"

"That's what it's designed for isn't it?"

"But you're not really who he thinks you are
Are you?"

"Baby, I am who you think I am the same person who you not once had to question about anything so don't worry about it. I'll be fine".

SUNDOWN

The next day that afternoon in the 77th precinct parking lot Ted is walking away from the building accompanied by his attorney. They separate going to their separate cars. Rita is waiting in the front passenger seat in his Mercedes when he enters on the Driver's side

"You were in there forever!" she seem to sigh in relief upon seeing him Smiling brightly he first kisses her softly

"Yeah well, just like Luther Van Dross said,

It's All Over Now" quickly kissing her again causing her to purr

"Mmm let's go back to my place" she suggests

"I've got a better idea. Let's go on a boat ride" he counters

"Sure Honey, whatever you want to do"…

Tour boats frequent the waters of the San Pedro bay every day. Together at the bow of the boat holding on to the rail sailing through the shipping platforms that sit across from the Federal Prison. The boat passes at the back of the prison while the voice of the tour guide speaks

"..Directly in front of you is Terminal Island federal Prison that once housed Al Capone, and John DeLorean Was housed here during his drug trial along with other Notorious drug smugglers and Bank Robbers The gun Towers are manned twenty-four hours a day..."

Rita looks out at the prison as Ted standing beside her with no expression at all other than the harbor winds blowing in his face causing his eyes avoid it

"I wonder what it's like to be in prison?" she speaks not really asking a question

"Locked up for all those years" still he has no response. Finally,

"You're not even listening to me!" she pouts

"I'm sorry baby, what did you say?"

"What were you thinking about?"

"How cold that water must be" he answers

"The water?" she questions

"Never mind that Why don't you go in and get us a couple of drinks"

"I can take a hint" she reports then heads off inside to the bar

As soon as she has gone he goes to his pant legs to retrieve a holstered snub nose 38., Holding the weapon in the palm of his hand lost for a moment in time unaware that Rita is walking back from inside and can see him tossing something over the side of the boat. She comes to stand beside him again to inquire,

"Should I ask what that was you threw into the water or should I just leave it alone?"

"That depends" he responds without hesitation

"On What?"

"It depends on whether or not you're concerned for the future or for the past"

"I don't know how to answer that" she says with her arms now around his waist looking into his eyes

"Then the answer is, leave it alone"

They hold on to each other as the boat speeds out of the harbor when he asks

"So Baby, is that offer still good about going back to your place?"

She smiles warmly and replies

"Without question my love" becoming lost in a passionate kiss.

The End

LIGHTNING
Strikes

LIGHTNING
Strikes

Merriam and Her Merry Men 1

D A V I D   H U N T

LIGHTNING STRIKES
MERRIAM AND HER MERRY MEN 1

iUniverse books may be ordered through booksellers or by contacting:

iUniverse
1663 Liberty Drive
Bloomington, IN 47403
www.iuniverse.com
844-349-9409

ISBN: 978-1-6632-4143-6 (sc)
ISBN: 978-1-6632-4144-3 (e)

Library of Congress Control Number: 2022911592

Print information available on the last page.

iUniverse rev. date: 07/20/2022

THE TALES OF PROPHECY

My life has changed much since I began this journey. Being an Oracle of Prophecy has not been easy. My time at the temple of Athena was pleasant and placid. I spent my days deciphering the writings of the prophecy. The tablets handed down were timeworn and much faded in places. The language I learned as a child did not align perfectly with the translation. Some meanings have been lost over the eight millennia since my ancestor inscribed the tablets.

I must begin my story with the prophecy as I had translated it.

The usurper's fool opens the Box.
The Orb Flies once more, unleashing chaos upon the world.
The Oracle gathers the heroes' strong to send on the quest long.
Paladin bright champion of light.
Barbarian strong to right the wrong.
Archer true guards the right.
On the left the Rogue small to sense the trap and prevent mishap.
One for four flame of binding for warriors
The Cleric meek to heal the weak.
One from the past in the future last to guide and protect with lightning blast.

My task has passed through generations from mother to daughter. Nothing has been found other than the prophecy of ancient Sumeria. What horrible event could have destroyed such a shining civilization? I can tell from the translation that it was the orb. I may never know who created it or why.

I can tell you that my family left that land with almost nothing. The people of Sumeria scattered to the four winds settling in new lands. Like a pebble in a still pond, the people moved outward like a ripple. They merged and mixed with other people forming new civilizations.

Old gods vanished from history, and new gods began to arise. That is how my family became an Oracle of Athena.

There is little point in describing the process that brought my family from Sumeria to Athens. My ancestors suffered many struggles, but our line remains unbroken.

Prophecy tells me there is one who survives from that time. I cannot see him in my visions. I only get a hint that he will join us. He is the guide spoken of at the end of the prophecy.

I cannot say all that I know. The prophecy would collapse if I spoke too soon and someone acted out of place. That would bring untold disaster upon the world.

Right now, all my tools are in place. My paladin is on a mission to bring the king. Although he is not part of the prophecy, he does have a task to hold this country together. I only know that he must be present at the event.

There is not much time, so I must stay the course. I cannot let things get out of control.

Sophia Oracle of Athena
Memoirs of a fractured time.

C H A P T E R

Southend-on-Sea

"Sergeant Thomas," I said. "We seem to have made better time than we thought."

"Yes, Milord, but we can use the cushion later."

"A valid point, sergeant. We can use what we gain in time cushion later to rest."

"Hold the men here. I will go down to the docks and secure a ship. I see at least three of them in port."

Thoughts of my tasks ran through my head. Those thoughts led to Milady Sophia and the prophecy. I wondered if she was exerting some sort of control over me. I snorted and smiled to myself. She may not be a witch, but her beauty and compelling eyes make me want to obey her. That is all me wanting to follow her orders.

I walked along the docks looking at the ships there. One looked like it was about ready to sail. Walking up to the gangplank, I looked around. Seeing a sailor nearby, I asked. "Are you almost ready to sail, my good man?"

The man saluted. "Milord, we are just loading supplies."

"Good, I would like to speak with your captain if I may."

"Milord, I will get him now." He turned and ran up the gangplank.

A burly man in a blue hat and coat looked over the railing at me.

"I am Captain Lomas, and how may I help you, sir?"

"Do you have cargo, captain, and are you bound somewhere?"

"We are done unloading here and are bound for Ramsgate, hoping for cargo there."

"Well, now, captain, perhaps we can be of mutual benefit to each other."

"And how might that be, sir?"

"I am Sir Guy of Gisborne and need passage to Ramsgate for myself and two hundred men. We are also seeking passage back to King's Lynn."

"You are correct, sir. We can be of mutual benefit. Standard king's passage?"

"Yes, captain, plus bonuses for performance."

"I do like the sound of bonuses. I, however, require some coin upfront to lay in provisions for your men for such a long passage."

"Captain, I understand your position fully. Would two crowns be sufficient unto your purpose?" Digging into my purse, I pulled out two gold coins.

"Yes, sir, that will provide well for your men for this passage."

"When will you be ready to sail, captain?"

"We should be provisioned and ready to go on the morning tide one hour after sun up."

"Excellent, captain. We will camp for the night on shore and board at sunrise tomorrow."

"Very well, Milord, we shall be ready. Do you have horses or any other heavy equipment?"

"No, captain, just two hundred men on foot."

"Very well, in the morning, Milord."

As the first flush of dawn was beginning to lighten the sky, I led my men down the dock to the ship. The town was quiet at this early hour, with only a few people to mark our passing. There was more activity at the docks than in town. As sailors started work and gulls circled and screeched, looking for food.

The captain called down a greeting from the deck as his men began to lower the gangway.

"All is well, I trust?"

"Yes, Milord, my ship is provisioned for thirty days for two hundred fifty men. With my crew, that will allow for ten extra people."

"That should be more than sufficient, captain, and you know best on these matters."

"Yes, Milord, bring your men aboard, and we will show them their accommodations. They may not be the best, but it should serve well enough for them."

"My men are well-versed in the hardships of a long sea voyage."

As I looked down through the main hatch below deck, they had split the hold into two tiers.

The captain pointed. "Hooks on each side for one hundred hammocks on each tier. We also set up a seagoing cook area. Of course, if the weather gets rough, the cook fires will have to be put out."

"We are familiar with the procedure and will be on dry rations until the weather clears."

"Yes, I see you know what you are doing. Sir Guy, I will leave you to settle in while we put to sea."

"Sergeant Thomas, you heard the captain. By squads first ten on the upper deck last ten on the lower deck, carry on getting the men settled."

"Yes, Milord," said Sergeant Thomas.

The sergeant's voice faded as I made my way up to the stern rail out of the way.

Observing the men getting the ship underway, I noticed they seemed short of hands. I spoke up, making my way forward to the captain standing beside the tiller.

"Captain, you seem to have fewer men than needed for your ship."

"Aye, Sir Guy, a few men left on this last port call. It happens with these merchant ships. There is not much coin to be had sailing for a merchantman."

"About that, captain, I may be able to help. I have fifty men trained in sailing. You may use them to fill out your crew and give your men a rest."

"Thank you, Sir Guy, that would be most helpful."

"How long will the passage to Ramsgate be, captain?"

"The winds have been light but favorable lately, and I estimate three days."

"That would be just fine, captain. It is within my time constraint. I will head down below and join my men. I will send the sailors from my team to speak with your bosun. He can determine their skills and divide them amongst your watches."

"Thank you, Sir Guy."

Ramsgate

We entered the harbor at Ramsgate early in the morning. The port seemed busy, with only a couple of docks empty. A steady stream of men and wagons loading and unloading the ships docked along the wharf.

As we tied up at the dock, the men prepared to unload, and I approached the captain. As the captain had promised, winds were light and variable, leading to the trip taking one extra day.

"We should be back in three days at the latest."

"We will be here waiting for you, Milord."

"Excellent, Captain. We are off then."

The men followed me off the ship forming ranks as we moved down the dock.

As we cleared the busy dock area, we broke into a trot and found the road to Dover. The sun was touching the horizon as we reached the town and made camp.

I then made my way into town, looking for the captain of the fishing fleet. After some inquiries, I found him at the tavern having dinner. Getting two mugs of ale, I walked over to the man indicated by the bartender.

"Captain, I am Sir Guy of Gisborne, and I have a proposition."

"And what would that be, Milord?" The captain asked.

"First of all, Captain, how much would you make in one-day fishing?"

"Perhaps twenty silver but right now is not a very good time."

"How many men would your fishing boat carry?"

"A dozen perhaps if they squeeze in with my crew and me."

"Would all the boats in the fleet be about the same size?"

"Yes, Milord, we all run the same size boat because we all have the same catch."

"Do you meet with the French fleet from Normandy?"

"Yes, Milord, we work together to have at least a chance of the same catch."

"And how many boats in your fleets, if I may ask?"

"Twenty-five Milord and the French have thirty."

"That is excellent news, captain, and now for my proposal. I will pay you and every boat one crown for two days' work in both fleets. Do you think it would be acceptable to your men and the French?"

"Not only acceptable, Milord, a great boon to us."

"Good, my men and I can be at the strand at dawn. We will board your boats and then transfer to the French fleet. The following morning when you come out to fish, we move back to your boats and sail back with you."

"Acceptable, Milord. The French captain will be most agreeable as we have not had the best catches of late."

"Perfect, captain. I will see you in the morning."

Arriving at the strand first thing in the morning, we divided up among the fishing boats by squads. The sergeants each paid their captain the one crown fee. I did the same for the other five captains.

"The fee covers any chance you may have to carry men on our return trip. You get the same deal as I gave the rest." The other five captains expressed their profuse thanks.

Quickly boarding the boats, the fleet set off with the men helping row. The small boats made good time getting out to the fishing ground.

The meeting with the French fleet went well. All accepted the same deal, and the men transferred over. The French fleet took their time going back to their home port. This way, they would not arrive too early in the day, giving away the game. Thanking the French captain, I led my men up the strand and through the town. We made camp for the rest of the day in the woods just outside of town.

When dusk was beginning to fall, I sent out scouts.

"We will wait until after dark, Sergeant Thomas. Then we will move closer to the castle. I want to attack three hours before dawn."

"Aye, Milord, the watch will be lax by that time."

"Yes, we will also be aboard the fishing fleet and out to sea before anyone can find us."

We moved slowly up the road, and near midnight two of the scouts met us.

"Milord," the first scout said. "We have scouted the fortress. A cliff and curtain wall on the seaward side should be easy to scale. The fortress is not well defended due to a lack of manpower."

"Milady's vision was accurate. Sergeant Thomas, you will lead your men up the cliffs and over the curtain wall, quietly subdue the guards and then open the gate for the rest of us."

"Capture as many of these men as possible and lock them up. We are not at war, yet no point in killing any more than we have to."

We quietly moved on toward our objective. The sky was cloudy, which helped the men blend into the land. We met a scout waiting for us on the road about four hours before dawn.

"The fortress is just beyond the hill. A narrow rocky shore leads underneath the curtain wall. To the left, there is a path down the cliff. I am not a mountain man, but I could probably climb that cliff."

"Very well, Sergeant Thomas, good luck and godspeed."

Sergeant Thomas made a climbing motion and headed off towards the shoreline. The rest of the mountain men from the unit moved off behind him. Moving to the top of the hill, I watched the fortress. A short time later, there was movement around the walls. There was, however, no alarm given with the action. It must be the final changing of the guard before dawn. Very soon, the commotion settled down. About half an hour later, slowly, the gate creaked open. I began trotting towards the open gate.

When the rest of the men entered the fortress, squads covered each door. Moving over to the main doors, I pumped my fist three times, then dropped it to my side. At the signal, the men went through the doors, moving quickly. They subdued any guards they found, and ten minutes later, The fortress was secure.

I found King Lionel in the tower overlooking the sea. Taking a knee, I said. "Your Majesty, we are here to free you and bring you back to England."

"Sir Guy, we have been expecting you, although you seem to be earlier than expected."

"Your Majesty, the regent made a mistake and gave away your location."

"Oh yes, he is not the smartest. Thus we had hoped the court would have kept him in check."

"Any of your other men besides Jeffery around here, Your Majesty?"

"They were kept aboard the ship and moved somewhere else. We could only retain Jeffrey."

"Well, perhaps we can ransom them later, Your Majesty."

"We can only hope so. After this affair, King Philip may not be so willing to let our men go."

Sergeant Thomas entered the room. "Your Majesty, we are ready to move out."

King Lionel said, "very well, sergeant, lead on."

Moving quickly, we were soon back on the road to the village. We arrived back on the strand just as the first faint flush of dawn painted the sky. Boarding the fishing boats, we set out rowing quickly. We were soon far enough from land to escape notice. We met up with the English fishing fleet transferring over and thanking the French fisherman.

The king ordered a bonus of one crown for each captain.

The English fishing fleet returned us to Dover, receiving the same bonus.

Leaving Dover at mid-morning, there was a possibility we could make Ramsgate by nightfall. The king, however, was not in excellent shape. Instead, we decided mid-afternoon to stop for the night and rest.

"Apologies, Sir Guy. We are holding you up."

"No, Your Majesty. We have this planned and have plenty of time to make it to our destination."

"When does the event take place? Do you know?"

"Yes, Your Majesty, it will take place on the night of the fall equinox."

"That is only twenty-some days from now."

"Yes, Your Majesty, twenty-three days to be exact. We expect our journey to take fifteen days. However, the sea portion may take a little longer. We have a ship secured that will take us to King's Lynn, land, and go afoot. We will stop there for a few days while you rest and recover some."

"You have this well-planned out, Sir Guy."

"No, Your Majesty, Milady Sophia is the one who has this planned."

"That is the lovely young woman who has attached herself to Sir William?"

"Yes, Your Majesty, they may become an item soon."

The king laughed. "We suspect you are correct, Sir Guy. We will make sure Miladies reward is substantial for this task."

"I am sure she is not looking for any unique reward, Your Majesty."

"As king, that is our prerogative. We choose when we hand over awards."

"Of course, Your Majesty, no one doubts your willingness to reward good service."

"Well, now I daresay it is time we rested. Dawn will come early enough."

CHAPTER

The following day we set off, making good time to Ramsgate. We arrived just after midday at the dock and boarded the ship.

The captain met us at the head of the gangplank. Gaping astonished, he almost bumped his head on the deck, bowing low.

"Sir Guy, you did not say the king would be boarding my humble vessel. I will have my kit pulled out of my cabin and turned over to you immediately, Your Majesty."

"No, captain, that is your cabin. We shall stay below with the men."

"But Your Majesty, that is unheard of."

"That is true enough, good captain. When we are with our men, we share their discomfort and live as they do. We must follow protocol when a bevy of useless butterflies trails us."

"Very well, Your Majesty, please allow me to show you the way below."

"Captain, we are sure you have duties to attend. Perhaps we can dine together later. Sir Guy can show us the way and help us settle in."

"As you command Your Majesty, the tide is about to turn. We will cast off and get underway."

"Well, captain, we shall retire below now."

"This way, Your Majesty," I said. And I started walking to the main hatchway.

When the king and I got below, the squads were in place. Sergeant Thomas and his men set up a cot for the king.

I turned to the king. "Your Majesty, this may be safer for you. At least until you regain some of your strength."

"All right, Sir Guy, our bones are starting to feel the campaign trail. We think we will lay down and nap for a while. Wake us for dinner."

"I will, Your Majesty, rest well."

Leaving Ramsgate and sailing north, the winds were fickle. It added three days to the voyage. However, we made good use of the time. Exercise, good food, and sparing had the king back in shape or recovering well.

Docking in King's Lynn, we approached the captain, and King Lionel shook the captain's hand. I will reward you well, Captain Lomas. Where did you intend to winter?"

"Well, Your Majesty, we usually would winter in Ramsgate now. I am not so sure there will be room."

"Well, winter in London, I will be sure to look you up before the spring."

"As you command, Your Majesty."

"See, it was a fortuitous meeting."

"That it was, Sir Guy. That it was."

Disembarking, the men quickly formed ranks as we marched off the dock. We had made a set of our armor for the king and his squire, so they did not stand out.

"Now we have some leisure marching time. Perhaps you could tell us about this, Sir Guy." The king asked me, tapping the symbol embossed on his breastplate.

"Well, Your Majesty." I could feel my cheeks heating. "The men of my company adopted Milady Sophia as an honorary mascot. Hence this symbol that she wears upon a brooch. The men now call themselves Sophia's Own."

"The first thing she does is steal my top General? Now she has poached one of my companies?"

"Your Majesty, although they are still loyal to you, that is the case. The men worship her and would do anything for her."

"Ha, I will have to put Sophia, Sir William, and this company somewhere safe. Before we lose the rest of our kingdom."

"Oh, I do not think it will be that bad, Your Majesty."

"We shall see." The king laughed. "We shall see."

We began to double march at the edge of town. Sometime later, while trotting down a wooded road, We came on a camp. With a crash, twenty-five armored gauntlets slammed into breastplates as the men knelt before their king.

Looking at me, the king said. "I recognize some of these faces from the crusade. They carry the same symbol of Sophia as we do."

"Yes, Your Majesty, from my own company here to meet you. They have your charger and your bannerman ready to serve you once more."

"That is good, Sir Guy, but I have enjoyed my time marching with your men."

"Thank you, Your Majesty. We are most pleased to have you with us anytime."

Nottingham Castle

"Historian, I have a task for you. A box I wish you to research. It has no key, and I need to know how to open it."

"Do you have the box, Milord? I will need to examine it."

"Yes, come with me. I will show it to you."

I led the scholar down to the strongroom and opened the door. Around the room sat boxes and chests of treasure and other bric-a-brac. All were gleaming in gold and silver and bronze. A somewhat plain-looking box rested on a pedestal in the center of the room.

"There it is, scholar Pandora's Box."

There was nothing special about the box as the scholar walked around, examining it from all sides. There were ivory and mother of pearl inlays with an indent on the front decorating the box.

"May I touch it, Milord?"

"Whatever you need to do as long as it is not destructive."

Lifting the box to look at the bottom, the scholar noticed a small inscription. It appeared to be in some ancient language. The scholar

11

copied the inscription by grabbing a parchment quill and ink from his pouch.

The scholar then proceeded to draw a likeness of the box. He paid particular attention to the front, making as accurate a likeness as possible. The scholar filled the indent with sealing wax and a candle. Waiting for the wax to cool, he made some notes on his parchments.

I began to fidget. It was taking far too long. "How much more time will this take, scholar?"

"Oh, several weeks, Milord. I will need to go to Oxford to study in the archives there. There are a couple of tomes there that may help me translate the inscription. I also recall a scroll that speaks in detail about this box."

Having cooled enough, the scholar carefully pulled the wax from the indent, comparing the wax mold against his drawings and the impression on the box. He grunted with satisfaction removing a soft cloth from his pouch, wrapping the mold, and placing it in a hard pocket in his bag.

"How long will it take you to get to Oxford and back, scholar?"

"About three weeks, Milord, my donkey is not very fast."

"That will not do. You have thirteen days to accomplish this. At sundown fourteen days from now, I must be able to open this box."

"That will not be possible, Milord. It will take me almost seven days to get to Oxford."

"I will provide you, men, a carriage and horses. They will stop at garrisons along the way to change horses. You can be in Oxford in two days. Seven days after that, the carriage will make the return journey with you or just your head by your choice. But your research will be on that carriage. Do we understand each other?"

"Yes, Milord, by your command." The scholar said, quivering in fear.

"I will keep an eye on your family for you, so you have no worries to degrade your performance."

"Yes, Milord, I will leave at once."

"Very good we do have an understanding."

"Sergeant of the guard," I called.

"Yes, Milord," the sergeant said, coming through the door.

"You will arrange for a carriage and horses and four men to escort this scholar to Oxford forthwith. They may only stop to exchange horses until they arrive in Oxford. They will return here with the scholar and his research seven days after. Or if he has failed, his head will do."

"Yes, Milord, as you command."

"Come this way, scholar. There is a hard road ahead of you. We must get you in your carriage."

Once they had left, I picked up the box, examining the indent on the front. I had seen this before somewhere but could not recall where. Shrugging my shoulders, I carefully set the box back down. Exiting the strongroom, I locked the door, returning to deal with the day's business.

Forest Camp

I looked up from the task of fletching arrows as Little-Jon approached.

"Yes, Little-Jon, what is it?"

"Robyn, we are running short on critical supplies. Things we have to go to the market to get."

"Are these things we can get from Manchester or Lincoln?"

"Yes, but it will take twice as long."

"Very well, send four men and a wagon to pick up the supplies. We must avoid Nottingham for another week or so at least."

"You are concerned about keeping Merriam safe?"

"As you should be to you know she likes you."

"A big lummox like me only amuses her."

"No, my friend, she likes you for more than just your muscle."

"No, Robyn, she already has you and Will Scarlet vying for her attention."

"I sensed a great capacity in her for love. I believe she may surprise you."

"Speculation is not getting the supplies we need."

Turning away, Little-Jon went to gather the men and wagon to send for supplies.

Nottingham Road Junction

I looked up from my desk and said. "Milady, the companies should be starting to gather again. Are you sure of your timing? We can ill afford a miss here."

"Do not worry yourself, Sir William. I am as confident as anyone can be. I had another vision last night. Two companies plus the group with the king have started moving this way. You will be happy to know Lionel is much stronger now. Sir Guy was the right man to get him in shape."

"I suspect that could have gone two ways. Sir Guy and Sergeant Thomas either got him healthy or killed him before his time."

"Now, Milord, he would never harm his king. He will do all in his power to keep him safe." Sophia's tinkling laughter rang through the tent.

"Well, be that as it may, my heart fills with trepidation. I pray to the Lord to keep us safe from what we are about to receive."

"Where he can, he will help us when the time comes."

It was mid-afternoon the next day when my company turned into the main camp led by King Lionel. There was a flurry of movement as the men stood to salute the king. We stopped in front of the command tent.

Sir William exited the command tent and said. "Your Majesty, welcome home." Bowing and dropping to one knee.

Lady Sophia dropped into a deep curtsy.

The king nodded his head as he dismounted from his charger.

I turned in my saddle and said. "Sergeant Thomas dismiss the men."

"Milord," said Sergeant Thomas.

The king walked up to Sir William, saying. "Rise, my friend," and clasped his arm.

"Rise, Milady Sophia. It is good to see you again."

"Come, Your Majesty, please sit and rest."

"Thank you, Sir William. Some refreshments would be excellent. Then you can bring me up-to-date on the plans."

"I would be delighted, Your Majesty."

"Your Majesty," Sophia said. "Would you like to freshen up a bit first? We have had this sleeping pavilion set up for you over here. You can get out of your armor and wash."

"Thank you, Milady, that would be delightful."

The king went into the sleeping pavilion, and twenty minutes later, he came out washed, wearing clean hose and a royal tabard over a fresh and bright tunic.

Sir William guided the king over to the table and a comfortable chair.

I had also taken the opportunity to clean up a bit before refreshment.

The king looked up once he had sat down. "Please, my friends, there is no need to stand on ceremony right now."

Edwin brought over goblets of wine for us.

Then Jamie entered the tent, bearing a tray of meat, cheese, and bread.

"I am sorry, this is all that was available, Your Majesty. The cooks are just beginning to prepare dinner."

"It is just fine, Jamie. It will serve to take the edge off our hunger. While Sir Guy and I eat a little, please report Sir-William."

"Yes, Your Majesty." We are two days march from Nottingham Castle. Four of the six companies are in camp, with two arriving in the morning. The current plan is that we will move out the day after tomorrow.

We will march hard to cover more than half the distance on the first day.

The intention would be to march on the second day at a slower pace, timing our arrival with dusk. The order of march will be by company. The command group is in the center of the leading knights.

The second company will disperse around the market square, allowing the people to continue their festivities. The other four companies will surround the town, ready to defend or attack.

The first company is the critical element. They must reach the castle without interference. They will march straight into the courtyard pushing aside all opposition. If we move fast enough, it should not be a problem. We will be inside the gate before the guards can react.

"This is a sound plan, Sir William." The king said. "Your planning is to be commended."

"Your Majesty, this is not my plan but Sir Guy's. He has been training these men ever since the crusades began. These men are a well-honed blade ready to be wielded by your hand."

"How long would it take you to train up to twenty more companies of men like yours, Sir Guy?"

"A very long time, Your Majesty." The men I command are the top one percent in England. They were selected and trained by Sergeant Thomas and myself. These men have skills that no other men have. However, the rest of the battalion comprises some very good men. They have all the same basic skills and training as my men. I have given Sir William some documents outlining a method to train an army of similar skills. The problem, Your Majesty, is not finding the men but teaching them to command them. Performance by commanders during the crusade was dismal at best.

"Harsh words, Sir Guy, even if you are correct."

I paused a moment, unsure how to take the king's words. I then decided to take the plunge and use open heartfelt honesty.

Do not get me wrong, Your Majesty. There are enough men here to train and lead fifty companies. The other five companies in this command are the primary training cadre for your army. So it would be no hardship in training twenty.

The first problem would be the nobility, such as barons, dukes, and earles, taking command and wasting the units. Such as spreading them out on frivolous tasks without regard to their command structure.

The other problem would be speed versus competence. The current projection would be three years to have twenty well-trained companies. The five other companies in my command would split down the middle to form a two-hundred-fifty-man training group. That will give you the core of ten companies. It would take them about a year-and-a-half to train a like number of men. So each man would mentor another. We have found one on one training to be the most rapid.

After a year-and-a-half, each of those ten companies would be ready to twin again. The original two-hundred-fifty would be split with their mentees and then given one man each to mentor.

That, Your Majesty, would be a fast way, but it has drawbacks. Each time we split a company, they would be fragile for about three months. We would stagger each twinning by three months.

The plan that I have written down is for something on the order of a five-year training schedule.

Each of these companies is too top-heavy. If I do not break them up soon, the people will lose their edge.

"You say you need your king's help, Sir Guy."

"Yes, Your Majesty, I humbly beseech you to help my men."

"We will review these documents with Sir William and see what to do."

"Meanwhile, we endorse your plan for this event." The king said.

"Thank you, Your Majesty. In two days, we move," I said.

"Now, beyond war plans, what is that delightful aroma I detect?" The king asked us.

"If I may be so bold as to offer most likely dinner, Your Majesty.

CHAPTER

Nottingham Castle

My escort led me to the study for dinner. It was tasteful and well-appointed, from the desk under the windows to the seating area by the fire to the large dining table. The late duke decorated the room from what I had seen of the castle.

It did not help as the food tasted like ashes to me.

"Is the food not to your liking Milady Merriam?"

"The food is okay, Lord Sherriff. I am not hungry."

"How is your wine? It is one of the regent's favorite blends."

"It is okay. One wine is as good as another now."

"Very well, Milady, my question stands. Will you marry me in three days?"

"My answer remains the same. I would rather hang."

"Suit yourself, Milady. The dressmaker will be here in the morning. Guard, escort Milady back to her chambers."

"At once, Milord."

Camp 2

Will trotted into the Camp and headed straight for me.

"You are back early. Will, what is the matter?"

"We may have a problem, Robyn. The Sherriff sent a scholar to Oxford by fast carriage. This morning he returned all excited about something. I think he may have information to do with the event. Nothing else seems to be going on. However, they have tightened castle security."

"That may not be good." I waved over another man.

Looking back to Will, I said. "Write everything down, and Jack here can take it to Sir William."

"All right. Come on, Jack." Will moved over to a table with parchment and began writing a detailed message.

Friar Tuck rode into camp at that moment. But did not appear to be stopping.

I called. "Tuck, where are you going now?"

"Where the Lord and Annabelle will Robyn. She has determined that we must go to the junction."

"Well, if you are going that way, we can send our message to Sir William with you."

"Get one of your men to put a bucket of water and oats in front of her. She may pause for a few moments then."

"Jack, feed the donkey, so she stops. I have found another messenger, so you will not need to go now." I laughed.

Moments later, Will Scarlet finished writing out the message. Will then handed it over to Friar Tuck.

"There you go, Tuck. Hand this to Sir William as soon as you meet him."

"The Lord's blessing be upon you, my son. We will perform this task."

"At least with Annabelle's cooperation." Will laughed.

A few minutes later, her snack done, Annabelle set off again. Friar Tuck grumbled and complained about the pace.

Shaking my head, I turned back to Will. "Okay, Will you head back to the Inn. And we will meet you there in two days."

19

"So we are still sticking to Sir William's plan?"

"Yes, for now until I hear otherwise."

"Very well. I will see you in a couple of days." Will waved and trotted off.

Nottingham Junction

The group had just sat down to eat with all six company captains. When an unholy racket began at the gate, they could hear shouts and commands, the bray of a donkey, and the thump of a body hitting the ground hard. The guards seemed to be laughing at something.

Sir William stood with a smile and held up a finger. "I will be right back. If this is whom I think it is, there may be a message from Robyn."

I giggled. "I think another piece of the prophecy may have just fallen into place."

"You think so, Milady?" Sir Guy chuckled.

The king grinned. "May I be informed of the source of this commotion?"

"Yes, Your Majesty. That was the distinct sound of Friar Tuck hitting the ground."

"Yes, our cleric."

King Lionel laughed. "I have heard of this man. He seems to be the source of many jokes around the land."

"Yes, Your Majesty, also one of the most devout followers of God."

Sir William returned shortly after that with the inestimable Friar Tuck in tow. Smiling, Sir William said. "Your Majesty, this is Friar Tuck."

"Friar Tuck his Royal Highness King Lionel, Sir Guy of Gisborne Milady Sophia High Priestess Oracle of Athena. The rest of these fine knights are the captains of the companies surrounding us."

Groaning and holding his back, the Friar bowed saying. "Bless you, Your Majesty, and this repast before you. I have ridden long and hard to bring a message for Sir William. Would it be possible to share a small bite and sip in the furtherance of God's work?"

Jamie hurried over and set another place for the Friar.

"Please join us." The king chuckled. "You may pass on your news in comfort."

"God bless you, Your Majesty."

"Oh, and before I forget here, Sir William." The Friar passed a folded parchment.

Sir William quickly read the message and grunted. "So this is how he does it." Passing it to me.

"This explains the scholar in my vision. It also clarifies the scholar's bane in the prophecy."

I handed the message to Sir Guy, who read it and gave it to the king. He looked at me and said. "I still do not understand."

"The bane of every scholar is misinformation. That is why opening the box will have such disastrous consequences."

The king also read the message and said. "We must do something to prevent this at once."

"No, Your Majesty. It is no longer possible to change the course of this event. The prophecy began moving forward as soon as you recovered the box from its resting place."

"But surely if we stop this now, nothing will happen?"

"No, Your Majesty, this is the best we can hope to achieve. This event is the least terrible of all the possible futures I have seen."

"It would have been best if I had never taken this box."

"Your Majesty, this is the best course to avert the greatest disaster."

"Very well, Milady, we will defer to your judgment. Even though I may not like what will befall our world."

"Do not worry, Your Majesty. The heroes we set on this quest will help avert the worst damage."

"Oh, dear. I must go to the monastery and mobilize my brothers."

"No, my dear friar, your place is with Sir Guy, as one of the heroes I speak of."

Sir Guy looked at me, raising an eyebrow, and said. "The cleric meek meant to heal the weak?"

"Yes, my paladin, you have it in one."

"I am most undoubtedly meek. However, my healing skills leave much to be desired."

I felt a surge of power suffuse my body, causing my eyes to glow. The prophecy had taken over. **"The event will change you all. More than the sum of your parts, the power of the gathering begins to assert itself."** A light shone through the canvas, bathing Friar Tuck in a golden glow.

Gasping, Friar Tuck stood up, tipping his seat over. The light seemed to sink into his skin without harm.

Friar Tuck said. "I feel like someone is tickling me with a feather."

I slumped back in my seat with a sigh. "So it begins. Your God has infused you with his powers. You can now heal with word or touch. You will have the ability to remove poison or cast protections and charms."

"That is not possible, Milady. I have no witchcraft or magic."

"Sir Guy, take up your dagger and cut your arm."

He did as I asked, watching the blood run down and drip.

"Now, friar, point at the wound and speak the word heal."

The friar pointed at Sir Guy's wound and said. "Heal."

Suddenly the wound healed. The only evidence was the blood still on the arm.

Hissing Sir Guy said. "That hurt as much as cutting my arm did."

"Praise the Lord. A miracle."

"No good, friar. It is just a skill you now possess. Many people will find they have strange abilities soon. For most, they will not manifest until after the event happens. As for the pain of healing, Sir Guy, I suspect that is the result of reversing the damage from the wound."

Sir William spoke up. "You will need to proclaim this to prevent panic in the population, Your Majesty."

"Yes, I agree. The squires acting as scribes can make copies. I will draw one up tonight. As soon as we can."

"A wise decision, Your Majesty." Sir William replied.

"We are a king after all; therefore, we must be wise." The king said with a cheeky grin.

My laughter rang through the tent.

Sir Guy turned to Jamie, saying. "Prepare a cot in my sleeping pavilion. Friar, you can bunk with me until we leave for Nottingham."

"That would be delightful, Milord, but I should see Annabelle first and get my pack."

I glanced over, and Edwin nodded from near the door. "It would appear young Edwin has already brought your things in Friar Tuck. He took care of your donkey."

"Good young men are so hard to find these days. In that case, then I will gladly retire for the night."

"I will be in soon. Jamie can help you if you need anything." Jamie stood next to the door holding a candle.

Nottingham Castle

Once again, I sat on the throne of the audience chamber, and the scholar stood before me. I had most of the battle banners removed, leaving the walls bare. I was going to need to redecorate the hall soon.

"So scholar, a successful mission?"

"I believe so, Milord. All the evidence points to a ring that is the key. The shape of the ring matches the indent perfectly."

"Excellent," I said. "As I know, this rings location. Now I need to know the ritual to prepare the key."

"Simplicity in itself, Milord. You need but coat the ring in the blood of a virgin, and the box will open and release what your heart desires."

"I do not need to sacrifice this virgin?"

"No, Milord, you only need to make a small cut and smear the blood upon the ring."

Tossing a small pouch of coins to the floor in front of the scholar, I said. "Very well, here is your reward as agreed, thirty silver. Now be off. You are free to go."

"Thank you, Milord," said the scholar picking up the pouch of coins. He turned and left.

Alone again with my thoughts, they turned to my bride-to-be. *So maid Merriam holds the key to pandora's box. I wonder how she came upon this ring. Perhaps I will ask before I open the box."*

I know she will never willingly marry me. The whole wedding will be a sham. I have no doubt the night will be most enjoyable. Pandora's box will be well worth the effort. Once, the regent sits on the throne as my puppet. Then I will know true power. When England is secure, the rest of Europe will be ripe for the picking.

Nottingham Junction

At the faintest glimmer in the east, the camp began to stir. The command group had just finished getting ready for the ride. Men moved about taking down tents and packing equipment into wagons. The knights, of course, in armor Lady Sophia in a comfortable riding skirt. Friar Tuck was in his cassock.

"Milady, what has happened to me?" I could hear Friar Tuck asking. "My bald spot is growing hair, and I am losing weight wasting away."

Sophia giggled. "Your god, giving you the power to heal may have played a joke on you. Your newfound power is healing your body and making you fit."

I laughed. "Look at it this way. Annabelle should enjoy your new physique."

Everyone laughed at that statement.

A wagon rumbled up to the command tent. Several men rushed in to pack away everything and tear the tent down. The loading was complete within twenty minutes.

"I must say, Sir Guy, your men, are very efficient."

"Thank you, Your Majesty. The men will be pleased to hear your praise."

Sir William sighed. "We will be sleeping in bedrolls tonight."

"We are not looking forward to that. We are getting too old to sleep on the ground."

"You are not that old, Your Majesty. You are just not used to it."

We moved over to the column where our horses and Tuck's donkey were standing. By the time we got mounted, the packing was complete.

Mounting up, I looked at Captain Geoffrey. "Are we ready?"

"Yes, Milord."

Looking around to see the command group mounted, I nodded to Captain Geoffrey. "Very well, captain, we are ready to move out."

The captain moved to the head of the column and sent the scouts out.

The captain waited for the scouts to get far enough ahead. Raising his fist, he dropped it, ordering the column to march. The first squadron moved out at a fast walk. The rest moved by sections maintaining comfortable gaps.

"Why are we moving in such a fashion?" Asked the king.

"This way, we can change pace without bunching up."

After about two hundred paces of this, the command was double march. The column began to spread out as they moved into a trot.

The column maintained a grueling pace throughout the day. By late afternoon, they were no more than half a day's journey from Nottingham. The captain held up his fist, bringing the column to a halt. We moved to the roadside, dismounting and picketing our horses. Security and the horses taken care of, we settled down to rest.

Soon a wagon was seen moving up the road. Every few yards, the wagon stopped to hand out rations and water. Those units with horses got buckets of water and oats as well.

The king turned to me. "Sir Guy, why did the wagon stop at the column's head?"

"Your Majesty, as we pass the wagon, they hand us a water skin and travel rations in the morning."

We, in turn, leave the pails and our empty water skins by the road, and as the train passes, they collect everything and prepare it for the next night. If we were going a longer distance, it would repeat each night. Each company has two supply wagons that do this for that company. We have fifteen wagons in each company's train. Seven of them are devoted to food and water. We can march for fourteen days with the supplies we carry at this pace.

"I see. An interesting and novel approach to the problem of supply."

"Yes, Your Majesty."

We have found that we can gain approximately two hours per day. We acquire a surprise advantage when we appear four leagues from where the enemy expects.

"Sorry for dropping into lecture mode there, Your Majesty."

King Lionel laughed. "You have no idea how often Sir William has given me lectures on strategy. I call it good advice."

They curled up in their bedrolls when everyone had eaten and quickly fell asleep.

Nottingham Castle

The heavily laden wagon rolled slowly up the street to the castle gate. Guards stopped the wagon, preparing to inspect the load.

The guard sergeant demanded. "What is this wagon loaded with?"

"Oil candles and pitch." Said the wagoneer. "If you set this load on fire, you will have no drawbridge or gate and a dark, cold winter."

"Right." The guard yelled. "Move it over by the storerooms, and we can unload it after the celebration."

The wagoneer nodded, drove the wagon into the side court, and stopped near the wall.

The wagoneer looked under the tarp and said. "We are in position. I am heading for the Inn. Good luck, Robyn. I will hoist one to you tonight." There was no reply, none needed.

I looked up at the knock on my door. "Come," I called out.

"It is the dressmaker Milady and a maid to help you get ready."

"Very well, not that I can stop you."

"Yes, Milady, we have our orders under threat of punishment."

I sighed. "This is true. Everything that monster says is a threat of some kind."

"As you say, Milady. There is nothing we can do but get you ready."

The Forest

The column halted well back in the tree line outside of town. The men began pulling out the golden tabards with the lion rampant on the breast. The king's bannerman unsheathed the royal banner. His squire opened the purple velvet bag he was holding. Jeffery pulled the King of England's crowned helm out and handed it to King Lionel. Grunting, Lionel hung the helmet from the cantle of his saddle.

The king grinned at Sophia. "Milady helms like this have probably killed more kings than they have saved."

Sophia giggled. "Really, Your Majesty? It is pretty, so I guess it would make you a better target."

"Well, that, but no, Milady, the blasted thing is so heavy we tend to fall off our horses and break our necks."

Sophia broke out laughing. The rest of us chuckled around her.

"I have performed my task as the king for this mission. I have broken the icy claws of tension gripping us. I suppose the rest is up to you now, Sir Guy?"

"Oh no, Your Majesty, this part is on Captain Geoffrey. And the knights to lead us into the castle."

"As Milord commands." Said Captain Geoffrey.

I chuckled. "No, Captain, as Milady commands. We go on her word, not before."

"Then I will patiently await your command Milady."

"Soon, Sir Geoffrey, a few little things must happen before we can move. I think when I give the word, we will need to move fast."

CHAPTER

4

Dusk began to darken the courtyard. Will Scarlet poked his head from under the tarp. "All clear."

We quickly climbed down between the wagon and the wall. The five of us then ducked into the servants' entrance. Finding the staircase, we slipped up to the second floor. This area seemed to be old guest quarters. Moving down one hall to the corner, Will Scarlet held up two fingers, indicating two guards. Then pointed away, meaning they were facing the other direction. I slipped to the corner beside him and saw two alcoves midway down the hall. I pointed to myself, Will, and Jack, then to the alcove on the left. Then the other two and the alcove on the right. We commence slowly slipping down the hall and into the nooks. We paused to listen as a guard seemed to be talking.

The one on the right said. "Here, have a drink."

His partner replied. "Not while we are on duty. If the sergeant finds out, we will get flogged."

"Not likely between the study thing and the wedding. There will be no one coming this way tonight at all."

"True." Said the second guard. "We will be lucky if they remember us at all. Fine, pass me the bottle."

I pointed at Little-Jon, drawing a finger across my neck, and pointed at the guard on the right. Then I pointed to myself and the guard on the left. I then held up three fingers, dropping them one at a time. The last finger fell, and we moved silently down the hall. We grabbed our man by the head and twisted sharply, snapping their necks. Will Scarlet grabbed the bottle of wine before it could fall. Pulling the men back down the hall, we slipped into an empty room with the bodies.

"Jack, Allen, put on their uniforms. The guards may help us. Now we have information about what is going on to determine where we go next."

Will said. "I think the wedding will be in the audience chamber. But this other event seems to be secret."

"This is not something the Sherriff would be willing to share. The guard said they would be doing the ceremony in the study."

"If memory serves me. Back around the other hallway, the servant's corridor runs next to the study."

"Jack Allen, you remain here as guards. We will send Will back to get you if we need you for anything. Unless, of course, you hear a battle start, then come running."

"The uniforms fit well enough. We should be okay."

"Go," I said. We quickly retraced our steps, going past the servant's stairs. We soon reached the corridor. Looking into the service corridor, we could see a tapestry covering the far end.

I whispered. "We can get into position without being seen."

"We should go have a look."

Will's hand shot up three-quarters of the way along the hall, and we all froze.

Tilting his head slightly, he listened and then moved to the wall. Two paces past was a stone with a crest. He turned the crest slightly, and we could hear voices. Looking through the peepholes, he could see into the study.

Closing the peepholes again, Will came over to me. "We can watch everything from here. We will be able to see if Merriam is in danger. Do you want me to get Jack and Allen as well? The extra muscle would help."

"Yes, Will, we will wait here and watch you go and bring them."

Will darted off back the way we had come.

I moved up and opened the peephole to observe and listen.

Sophia sat placidly on her palfrey. Friar Tuck mumbled prayers beside her.

"How much longer, Milady?"

"Not long now, Milord, perhaps five or ten minutes. They are bringing her from the tower now. Once she is in the presence of the box, we can move."

"Why must we wait, Milady?" I asked.

"Once the key is in the presence of the box, the room will be locked in stasis. Nothing will be able to leave until the event happens. If we move too soon, everything we have wrought will sunder."

"That sounds very ominous, Milady." The king said.

"More than ominous, Your Majesty, devastating."

Will returned with Jack and Allen in tow as Robyn saw the door to the study open.

Accompanied by two guards and a maid, Merriam entered. She looked stunning in green brocade.

I did another headcount of four guards, a sergeant, and the captain.

I did not count the regent or the Sherriff as neither were known to be fighters. The presence of the scholar was not a concern. I signaled the others over to look at the disposition of people in the room. Closing the peephole, I turned to the others.

"When we go through those doors, the guards must go down fast. Will remain at the peephole and signal when the box opens. We will then rush the two guards at the door and burst through. Little-Jon, you must protect Merriam at any cost." He nodded, accepting. "We will keep the Sherriff alive for the king's justice as they should be marching into town at any moment."

Will open the peephole as we moved over to the tapestry and got set to attack.

The Sherriff spoke. "Milady Merriam, I am happy you could join us."

"Why have you summoned me, Sherriff? You should never see the bride before the ceremony. Even in a forest wedding, it is bad luck."

The Sherriff laughed. "I make my luck. Watch me open my wedding present to which you hold the key."

"You speak in riddles, Sherriff."

"Let me help clarify it for you. Give me your ring for a moment."

"Why would this help you?"

Taking the ring from Merriam, he held it by the band. Stepping in front of the maid, he said. "This may hurt just a little bit, my dear."

The guard grabbed one of her hands, cutting it with a dagger. The Sherriff then dipped the ring into the blood, ensuring it covered the whole of the stone.

"Now, Milady, observe the power unleashed by your betrothed." Placing the ring to the indent on the box, it popped open. At first, nothing happened, then a violet glow began to permeate the room.

Suddenly a fur-covered hand with long claws on each finger shot from the box. It grabbed the Sherriff by the throat, tearing it out in a spray of blood. A terrifying creature climbed out, throwing the body to the side.

The maid screamed and fainted. Merriam grabbed a dagger from the guard on her left and drove it up into his throat. She spun the other way, slashing the other guard's throat in a fountain of blood. Events began to transpire in blinking snapshots. First, a dark orb popped from the box. It moved around the room as if seeking something. A purple light began to shine in the center of the sphere. With an unholy scream, it flew into the night. Drips of purple light fell from the orb like raindrops. Each time one hit the ground, a monster sprang up.

Sophia shuddered and gasped. "Majesty, your presence is required."

The king squared his shoulders and yelled. "Move Out."

The men banged their breastplates with a roar, and the knights brought their horses into a steady trot. The foot soldiers closed the formation and began moving like a giant battering ram as the column crossed the empty open field at speed.

We entered the town at a quick trot, hoves and boots pounding the cadence.

The revelers in town screamed and jumped to the sides of the road. They saw the king's banner quieted and bowed low. The knights did not slow or waver as they thundered through town.

Sophia's laughter rang through the night, and she yelled to Sir William. "This is exhilarating."

The king just shook his head, and Sir William laughed.

We wheeled through the town square onto the road to the castle gates. Some guards tried to bar the way. They darted to the side when they saw the leading knights couch their lances. Captain Geoffery led his knights through the courtyard, up the stairs, and through the open keep doors into the entry hall.

The formation halted in the courtyard and turned outwards for security. Except for first and second squads, the rest of the foot soldiers deployed to secure the castle and arrest any guards they found along the way.

The command group entered the keep surrounded by the twenty men of the first and second squads.

Sophia gasped for breath and spoke. "Up there to the left big hall."

"Christ." Will gasped and raced past Robyn. "Go now. It is open." Running through the curtain into the hall, whipping out two daggers, and throwing left and right-handed. With blades buried in each guard's throat, they dropped like rocks. Will then raced to the door trying the handle. It was locked. Little-Jon lowered his shoulder, not slowing, hitting the center of the doors. They open with a splintering crack, knocking the guards inside to the floor.

Jack and Allen killed the men lying on the floor and stopped in their tracks. The reason for Merriam's scream crouched on the desk. A huge wolf-like ravenous beast was looking at Merriam. Little-Jon took a step forward, and the beast turned towards him.

"Careful, Little-Jon, it looks fast."

In the far corner of the room, a crackling portal formed. A shadowy shape stepped forth. The shadow raised a hand from which a lightning bolt shot out, blowing a smoking hole in the beast's chest and knocking it to the floor.

In the commotion, Will had taken care of the sergeant with a knife stroke. The captain stood guarding the regent, not moving.

Little-Jon quickly moved over to protect Merriam. Soldiers began to enter, and everyone tensed up for a moment. Then Will smirked. "Glad you could make it, Thomas."

At that moment, King Lionel stepped through the door. Noticing the tabards the men were wearing, Will Scarlet's face paled. Dropping to one knee and bowing his head, he said. "Your Majesty."

A voice shouted from the other side of the room.

"Awe fuck, the dumbass did it, didn't he. And you, Lionel Claymoore, are the one person in the universe who could fuckup my day."

Sophia stepped through the door, followed by Sir William and Sir guy.

She looked over at the shadowy man.

"The guide has come. The gathering is complete."

"Hello, little oracle." The man said as he stepped from the shadows into the light closing the box with a snap and tucking it under his arm. "I knew your ultimate grandmother and your many times great-granddaughter. You have all managed to look remarkably the same."

The man was dressed strangely in a tunic and trousers of shiny material. Under the jacket was a white shirt and bow tied at the neck. Over his shoulders, he wore a black cape with a white lining. On his feet, black boots shined to a mirror-like finish. A strange black device was like a chimney without a hole on his head. He had black hair to his shoulders and a neatly trimmed black beard shot through with tiny flecks of silver. He was tall but not broad-shouldered and fit, attested to by his rugged face and large strong-looking hands.

The king looked at the man and said. "You seem to have us at a disadvantage, sir. You seem to know our names, but we do not know yours. Or, for that matter, how you came here."

"Oh yeah, how rude of me." Removing his hat, he bowed at the waist and said. "My name is Merlin at this time. I will tell my tale over dinner and martini. Rather than remain standing in this slaughterhouse. The fewer ears that hear, the better."

Merriam then moved from Robyn's embrace. Stepping over the Sherriff's body, she picked up the ring from where it had fallen, wiped it clean of the blood, and put it back on. "Hello, grandfather."

"Hello, granddaughter, take good care of that ring as we will need it again. I gave that ring to your grandmother the day we wed."

"Yes." The king said. "I do believe this tale is going to require some ale."

With a rattle and bang, I dropped my helmet and shield. I had been so stunned up to this moment that I could not move. The vision before me was glorious. Pulling the chain and rings around my neck, I pulled the smaller one from its chain. Stepping forward, I dropped to one knee in front of Merriam. "Milady, I would offer you the moon and stars if you would do me the honor of becoming my wife."

Merriam sighed. "The final piece of my heart. There are conditions to my acceptance."

"Please, Milady, I would accept any conditions."

"Well, it is only one condition and has three parts."

"And what would these three parts be, Milady."

"Robyn of Loxley Wilfred Scarlet and Little-Jon. For they are the other three parts of my heart."

"I accept Milady, for I knew I would have to share." With that statement, I slipped the ring onto Merriam's finger.

Interlude

On another plane

I strolled with great dignity to the stone of judgment, where I settled on my haunches, wrapping my tail around me. Once I was in place, the narrow beam of light on me encompassed the entire hall. Evenly spaced outside were nine large platforms, each occupied by a different dragon species.

The stone I was on began to rotate until I faced a red dragon. Bowing my head slightly in acknowledgment, I waited.

"Stormavgaard, you have completed your training and faced your tribulations with honor and dignity. We have an assignment for you."

"You honor me, Elder."

"You have felt the disturbance in the Aether, have you not?"

"Yes, Elder, it is very disheartening."

"I understand, young one. We had hoped it would never return when the orb vanished last time. We had perhaps wished that this event would not take place."

"I concur, Elder. I have studied the materials from the previous event, and some information is missing. I am surprised we did not respond the last time."

"Yes, a different time with different elders. This time we are going to respond appropriately."

"Hence the reason for calling me here, Elder?"

"Yes, Stormavgaard. You are in line for mating, you are old enough, and we have a suitable candidate. Flashing a hologram before me of a white dragon of such exquisite beauty as to take my breath away."

"This is Shynne the Tender. As you can see, she is a healing dragon. She has seen your hologram and is very impressed with your credentials. She has also accepted the bonding. However, that will have to wait until you have built your eyrie on Earth."

"Earth Elder?"

"Yes, Stormavgaard. You will be our emissary and form a new clan with your mate, and you will have additional guardians from some other races."

"Our study tells us that England is the best place for you to go. While this is not the most central location, the event happened there. The tools of the prophecy have gathered there. We have noticed that these people are strong, just, and compassionate. We will give you a few minutes to consider."

I laid my head down on my foreclaws. It was a great deal to think about and decide. Scanning the data from Earth, I could see this was a fresh young world. Religion seems to hold a powerful place in their lives. That was okay. It is better to have them worshipping their gods rather than me. Having my eyrie and building my clan is a powerful draw for any dragon. The opportunities for wealth were also enticing. Also, if the elders are correct, the help I will get will be in the female form. They will build my necessary harem. The male dragons' propensity to procreate is powerful. It presents a problem as the female dragon has a five-year birthing cycle. It is not a problem in the bigger picture as we have lived for thousands of years. But when a male starts breeding, he requires many females.

"Elder, I will do this. My personal disposition is well suited for this task. Notwithstanding the idea I am helping a fresh new world, the enticements are the biggest draw."

"Are you fully prepared? Or do you need to collect anything?"

"No, Elder, I had just vacated my previous group lodging. I planned to seek a private place to build an eyrie, so I have everything."

"Very well, Stormavgaard, we begin gathering the power now. The place you are going to is Stonehenge, and it is some distance south of Nottingham. Good luck and fare you well."

I could feel the power building. I saw sparks begin to skip across my scales. I had to force myself not to draw the power. Suddenly a bubble formed around me, and with a lurch, I was elsewhen. With a thump, I landed on soft green grass. Taking a deep breath, I inhaled the wonderful scent of this world. Looking around, I quickly got my bearings, sampled the power levels tracked by my senses, and caught a faintly familiar scent of power. The Oracle and I now had a lock on her. Gathering my haunches, I launched myself into the air. With a couple of solid flaps of my wings, I moved over the ground at a leisurely clip.

CHAPTER

5

Merriam turned to assist the young maid stirring from her fainting spell. Helping the trembling girl to her feet, Merriam asked. "Is there a place where we can eat and relax in peace until someone cleans this room?"

The girl stuttered. "Y...yes, Milady, the duke's apartment is down the hall. Clean but unused since he went off to the crusade."

"Please show us the way," Merriam said gently.

Recovering her composure, the maid led us down the hall to the left of the grand staircase. She tried to open another double door, but someone had locked it.

"Oh, dear." She whispered. "I must search the Sherriff, as he has the key."

"No need to, young lady," I said. "Sergeant Thomas, search the Sherriff, find the chamberlain, and bring him here."

"Yes, Milord." Turning to one of the men, he said. "Find the chamberlain and bring him here at once."

"Sergeant." The man snapped a salute and ran off.

Another soldier trotted up to Captain Geoffrey and made a report.

The captain murmured some instructions. The man saluted and ran off.

Turning to the king, Captain Geoffery said. "Your Majesty, the castle has been secured. The guards have been locked up and are awaiting your disposition. The men are standing down to half-and-half watches for some dinner."

"Excellent, captain, most efficient."

Sergeant Thomas returned with a large key ring.

Handing her the keys, the maid opened the door.

Soon after, the man sent to find the chamberlain returned. "We found him in the dungeon, Your Majesty. He was not in good shape, and I left him in the care of our men to get cleaned and rest.

The maid squeaked. "Denby is the chamberlain's son and is learning to replace him."

I handed the keys to one of the men. "Give these to Denby and tell him to prepare some rooms for us."

The room beyond was dark, but a couple of men pulled candles from wall sconces. They went through the rooms lighting candles and the fire. The apartment was surprisingly clean for having been closed up for so long.

The king mentioned this, and the maid said. "We were let in here every week to clean, Your Majesty. This morning is the last time because the Sherriff planned on using this apartment tonight."

The maid was nervous but had regained her composure. So the king said. "Thank you, my dear. If you feel up to the task, go to the kitchens and arrange for some food."

The maid bobbed a curtsy and said. "At once, Your Majesty." She then hurried from the room.

The king moved over to the sitting area around the fire. Sinking into a comfortable chair with a sigh. "Come sit, and we will speak."

Roars and screams began coming from outside. "The devil?" Said, King Lionel.

"It is the first direct result of opening pandora's box."

Two Soldiers entered the room and saluted. "Your Majesty, Milords, we are being attacked from the woods. Monsters are trying to get into the town. We have managed to kill these monsters with arrows so far. But they are difficult to kill and fast."

"Silver is the best thing to use on werewolves. Barring that, cut their heads off, or they will regenerate. Decapitating them is the best way to deal with all monsters." Said Merlin.

"Has there been many so far?" I asked.

"Not many, Your Majesty, Milord. About ten scattered and not coordinated."

It will likely remain that way for a week or two, maybe a month. Then the werewolves will start to organize into packs. They will fight amongst themselves more than hunting humans, although they will not pass up a meal if it is easy to get.

"Very well, Captain Geoffery, Sergeant Thomas deal with the problem extra guards and roving patrols. How do you know so much about these things?" I asked as the men left.

I have had many lifetimes of training, research, and combat against monsters of all kinds. I have seen this before and will see it again.

"I must gather the brothers of my order, and we can force these demons back to the hell from whence they came. God will help us fight Satan. Where ever we should find him."

"These monsters do not come from hell, good Friar," Merlin said with a grave tone.

They are from other realms. Yes, even the demons have their realm. The orb contained in pandora's box is a gateway to these realms. Those drops of light you saw falling from the orb are micro portals and will randomly pull a monster through. On occasion, one will grow larger and draw an entire clan through. These clans can be anything from orcs to goblins and elves to dwarves. And pretty much anything in between. That is where the monsters are coming from and why we must find the orb and put it back in the box.

"The guide speaks truly of the task set before you."

"This is all well and good." Said the king. "I wish to know your story right now, Merlin."

"My story is a long one. I will attempt to condense it."

I am a wizard born and trained in Sumeria. Their most outstanding wizards were the ones who destroyed Sumer. Not intentionally but by creating the orb. They thought they would gain so much more power when what they did unleashed their destruction.

At last, when almost nothing remained, I found a way to contain the orb. Pandora's box was my sister's jewelry box, and we infused it with her essence.

She sacrificed herself in a battle with the orb that allows the box to contain it. I carried the box with me for thousands of years.

After much time wandering the world, I came upon a new civilization. The gods seemed strong, and I felt that perhaps I could pass on the burden and continue with my other work.

I turned the box over to a goddess with the key. She, unfortunately, was a trickster filling the box with old-world vices. She then gave the box to a young princess in the neighboring empire. When Pandora opened the box, she let out the seven sins. Realizing what she had done, she closed it quickly enough to keep the orb contained. But what she had released was enough to destroy her country. I arrived in time to save the box but not the young woman.

The myths and legends you hear of monsters like the minotaur or medusa are the monsters left over from the last time the orb was loose. It took me six thousand years to clean up the previous mess.

As for where I was when this happened? I was just under a thousand years in your future. Well, in a parallel future where this did not happen. I was leaving my home to attend an opera. Hence my tuxedo and top hat. I will have to see a tailor in the morning to get proper robes for adventuring.

Smiling, Merlin said. "Perhaps our journey will take us to China. I do so enjoy wearing silk as opposed to linen and brocade."

Sophia and Merriam giggled.

"Yes, these ladies understand." Both women blushed prettily.

"Very well. We must decide who these adventurers are going to be. Would a full company be too many or perhaps just a half?"

"Oh no, Your Majesty. The companions are in the prophecy. Chosen eons ago and gathered tonight."

"They have Milady Sophia?" Asked the king.

"Yes, Your Majesty, please allow me to recite the prophecy so you may understand."

The Usurper's fool opens the box
The orb flies once more unleashing chaos upon the world
The Oracle gathers the Heros strong to send on the Quest long
Paladin bright champion of light

Barbarian strong to right the wrong
Archer true guards the right
On the left the Rogue small to sense the trap and prevent mishap
One for four Flame of binding for Warriors
The Cleric meek to heal the weak
One from the past in future last to guide and protect with lightning blast

Merlin burst out laughing, tears streaming down his face.

Sophia quirked an eyebrow and asked. "There is something funny, Magician?"

Merlin gasped for breath waving his hand.

"A lot, really." he finally gasped out. "I told the first oracle it was too obscure and that you would fuck it up."

Merlin looked down at the floor, finally looking up with a deep sadness. So many centuries of knowledge lost. I am getting too old for this. Your translation Sophia is very close. You missed a couple of words, however. That one key line that confuses you was put there for a reason. It has more than one meaning. First, there is more than one meaning for the word binder and more than one for war. What that line should have read was.

"A firey leader bonded to the four warriors."

Sophia laughed. Merriam's eyes grew wide, and Sir William groaned.

The others sat with blank looks, although I was blushing furiously.

The king said with a bemused look on his face. "I do not understand. I get the usurper is my brother, and the fool would be the Sherriff. But the rest is just a meaningless riddle."

"Allow me to clarify, Your Majesty."

The heroes are from top to bottom. Sir Guy is the paladin. Then we have Little-Jon, the barbarian and Robyn of Loxley, the archer, and Will Scarlet, the rogue, small. The leader bonded to the four warriors is maid Merriam and the meek cleric Friar Tuck. Lastly, there is me, the guide. However, the lightning blast does seem a bit ostentatious, even for my taste.

"Well, you did shoot that monster with lightning. Protecting our Merriam." Little-Jon rumbled.

Merriam looked at her lap, blushing with a slight smile on her lips. While we warriors looked at her with some heat in our eyes.

Two servants entered the room and began setting places at the table. Two maids entered with trays of wine and ale, placing one at each seat. As they completed the plate settings, more servants entered carrying steaming trays of food. We all stood and followed the king over to the table. Before we could sit, Friar Tuck raised his hand in prayer. "Lord, we thank you for this bountiful feast. Continue with our care and forgiveness. Amen."

The king waved his hand at the table. "No need for ceremony. Sit and eat."

Everyone sat and dug in, filling their plates.

The majority of the servants left, leaving the maids to hover nearby.

"Sir Guy, do you have duties that require your attention?"

"No, Your Majesty, Captain Geoffrey is my second-in-command. He knows everything and will set the defenses."

"Good then, you will not miss anything said here."

The king looked at the two maids. "Young ladies, are you currently attached to anyone?"

The girls blushed and curtsied. "No, Your Majesty."

"Good." The king replied. "You were with Milady Merriam in the library. What is your name?"

"Alicia, Your Majesty." Replied the pretty blonde girl.

"And you?" The king asked, looking at the other girl. She had a tanned complexion with dark eyes and hair.

"Camila, Your Majesty."

"Wonderful. I promote you to Ladies in Waiting for Milady Merriam. You may also share duties with Milady Sophia. Unless you know other maids that may be suitable as well?"

Tears of joy streamed from the eyes of both girls. "Your Majesty." Both girls blubbered. Glancing at each other, Alicia spoke. "Mary, the mayor's daughter, and Rose, the merchant's daughter. We are eighteen, and they are seventeen. Although I think they both turn eighteen next month."

"Remain seated." Lionel rose and moved over to the desk. Taking parchment and quill, the king quickly wrote two notes. Affixing his seal to both, he called Jamie and Edwin over.

"Jamie, deliver this note to the merchant. Bring a squad of men to assist you as an escort and help carry the young lady's possessions." The king then counted out fifty gold splitting it into two piles. "You will give the merchant this letter and twenty-five gold as payment for his daughter's service as a dowry. Edwin, you will do the same for the mayor's daughter, Mary."

"Yes, Your Majesty." The boys replied. They then took the gold and letters and left.

Standing, the king moved back to the table.

"Sir Guy." The king said to me. "You will provide a dowry and letter to the parents of Merriam's Ladies in Waiting."

"Most certainly, Your Majesty, it would be my pleasure."

"Now run along, girls, and have the staff prepare rooms for your Lady and Milady Sophia. You may return when you have finished your task."

Both girls dropped curtsies and raced from the room.

Sir William chuckled. "They will not be much use for a couple of weeks. Many squires in this command approach the age to be tested for knighthood. They will be too busy mooning and spying."

We all laughed as Merriam replied. "I agree, Sir William. I think I saw stars in their eyes as they ran out."

A knight entered the room saluting, he said. "Your Majesty, we found the regent, and he went straight to the brothel with that captain."

"Oh, that is right." Merriam laughed. "Our best customer."

"Well, unless your girls make house calls to Inverness. Your business is going to take a hit. Is he sober?"

"No, Your Majesty, he can hardly stand."

"Very well, throw him in the dungeon. Put the captain with his men. I will deal with them in the morning."

"As you command, Your Majesty." The knight turned and left.

"Inverness, Your Majesty?" Sir William asked.

"Probably not there. The bloody Celts would likely set him free to make more mischief."

"You could send him to the world's end, Your Majesty, and he would still make mischief."

"Sir William. Thank you. You have given me a most delightful idea." Said the king.

The maids returned giggling and blushing. Behind them was Jeffrey, also blushing.

The king looked over at the maids. "Are the rooms ready for Miladies?"

"Yes, Your Majesty," said Alicia.

"Are we set, Jeffrey?"

"Your Majesty, I have selected a nice corner room."

"But Your Majesty. I thought you would take these quarters."

"No, these are the Duke's quarters once I have appointed the new one."

"You have someone in mind, Your Majesty?"

"All in good time, Sir William. We can meet in that office to break our fast in the morning."

We all stood and bowed or curtsied as the king left.

Soon after, Jamie and Edwin entered, escorting two pretty girls.

"Milords, Milady's, these are Rose and Mary," Edwin said, pointing to the two girls. Rose was a petite girl with sandy-colored hair, and Mary was a tall, brown-haired girl.

"Excellent. Rose and Mary, you will be Ladies in Waiting to Milady Sophia. Alicia, is there a room next to Sophia's where they may stay? We can figure out arrangements for accommodation in the morning."

"Yes, Milord, there is a room with an attached door next to both. Camila can show them where it is and get them settled. We can split them between us and show them what to do tonight. The Ladies' rooms are across from each other, so we will all be close together. We can all go together and show you your room, Milord."

"Thank you, girls. We will retire now, then."

The rest of us mumbled goodnight as they left.

"Jamie, have you found us a place to sleep?"

"Yes, Milord. If you will follow me."

I handed my helmet and shield to Jamie. "You can put these in our room for now. I will be inspecting the defenses before I retire. You can go to bed, and I will have a servant show me the way."

"Yes, Milord." Said Jamie, leading the others to their rooms.

I headed downstairs and spoke to a guard at the keep door for directions to the guardroom.

CHAPTER

Observing the activity as I crossed the courtyard, some men stood watch in pairs evenly spaced around the walls, and others patrolled in groups of five. Entering the guardroom, I found Captain Geoffrey and several men lounging around the table.

As they started to rise, I waved them back down. "You will have little time to relax over the next few days."

I would know how prophetic those words were soon enough.

"I will say in the morning when the king will be holding his levee. When I find out the king's plans, I will know more about whom to call. There will be a captains and sergeants meeting, to be sure, at some point."

"I am sure the king will not stay here long. Possibly, there will be movement orders in a few days."

"Yes, Milord. About time off for the men?"

"No more than fifty at a time, captain. We are here to protect these people, not cause more harm. And they better be on their best behavior."

"Yes, Milord, we can fit that into the duty rotation. Sergeant Thomas will break any heads that disobey."

I chuckled. "Only if Sergeant Thomas stays sober himself, captain."

The men around the table chuckled.

"Very well, if you have things under control here, I am off to bed."

"Yes, Milord and those attacks seem to have settled down. The monsters appear to have found us a tougher nut to crack than they thought."

"I expected no less, captain."

As I walked across the courtyard, something dropped to the ground with a screech. With the trained reflexes of a warrior, I drew my sword and lopped its head off in one motion. The captain and several men boiled out of the guardroom, and I called them to bring torches. Four men ran back inside and grabbed torches, bringing them over.

Shining the light on the creature, we saw a short snout like a cat with canines top and bottom. A leathery hide covered the beast. Spindly arms ending in claws and equally thin legs also with claws. The creature also had a long tail ending in a barbed tip. On its back were a pair of leathery wings. It stretched out the span of about six ft. It was about five ft tall from the head and looking at the body.

"Great captain, now we have a flying monster. Put a swordsman with each archer and no less than two men anywhere."

"Yes, Milord, I will take care of that immediately."

"And once again, Captain, goodnight."

"Good night Milord."

Suddenly there was more loud screeching as dozens of the creatures dropped from the sky. *Or not, I thought.*

The captain yelled "To Arms" as the alarm triangle began ringing.

The men with me quickly formed a hollow square, hacking and slashing at the creatures. They seemed to be very easy to kill. The creature's claws did not seem to penetrate the leather armor of the soldiers. However, any place unprotected by thick leather would receive a nasty gash from a claw.

Soon more troops came into the courtyard and began working from the edges inward.

The courtyard quickly became strewn with monster bodies and parts. It was not long before some of the creatures tried flying away. Archers around the yard shot them as they rose above the fighting. Within an hour of the butchery beginning, the attack was over.

"Captain, get work parties together. Use wagons and start taking these things out to the edge of town. The wind seems to be from the west. So take them to the east side of town and burn them. Any men that are injured send them over to the keep. I will have the servants attend to them and start preparing food."

"Yes, Milord, I will get on it right away," Captain Geoffrey replied.

Walking into the keep, I stopped a servant, asking them to get Friar Tuck.

I then asked another servant to help prepare a place to tend the wounded.

"Yes, Milord." He replied and ran off down the hall.

Another servant came from the back of the keep.

"Is there something I can do, Milord?"

"Yes, you can wake some cooks and have them prepare some bread and soup. My men have just fought a battle and are cleaning up the mess. When done, they will be hungry and could use some warm food."

"Yes, Milord at once." He then ran off.

There was huffing and mumbling as Friar Tuck stumbled down the stairs.

"What is it, Milord?"

"We have had an attack by flying creatures, and some of the men have wounds. They will be coming now, so do your best, Friar."

As wounded men entered the keep, I directed them toward the audience hall. Servants appeared from the back carrying bandages and water, and I also pointed them to the audience chamber.

Merlin came from a side room and said. "By the time I got down here, your men had engaged with the monsters too close for me to help. My magic can be somewhat indiscriminate, at least in melee. If things looked any worse, I would have stepped in any way, but your men are very good."

"Yes, thank you, Merlin. Do you know what those creatures are?"

They are a type of gremlin. The flying ones are more dangerous than those that do not have wings. They are a nuisance for groups of well-armed men rather than a danger. Once they are on the ground, they are clumsy and do not fight well.

The dawn was dark and dreary as heavy grey clouds scudded across the sky. I sat in the library reading reports that came in through the night. The number of incidents had declined to nothing in the early hours. It seemed the men had done well guarding the town against monsters for the most part.

There was a report of a winged beast larger than a warhorse, and it had a serpent's body, feathered wings, and the head of a lion. Fortunately, it was the only one seen. This one had killed five men before two knights at a full charge put lances in it.

The other was a man-like creature about ten ft tall wielding a club. The report said the thing had a hide-like tree bark and was tough to cut with a sword. Once again, the creature could not stand up to a charge with lances. Unfortunately, a horse was severely injured and put down on that charge.

Sir William and the king entered the study.

I stood bowing and greeted them.

The king said. "Are you first up?"

"That would imply I made it to bed, Your Majesty." I chuckled.

"What happened?"

"Quite a bit, Your Majesty."

I held up a stack of reports. To make it brief, we have been fending off attacks all night. Last night, it started with my inspection when we battled over a hundred flying gremlins. There have been twenty-two other attacks and two by giant monsters. One killed five men before succumbing. The other injured a horse badly enough that we had to put it down. The charges of mounted knights killed those two. Things finally settled down about two hours ago. The men have been on twenty-five percent alert in two-hour blocks all night.

"And the men?" Sir William asked. "How are they holding up?"

"Well, Milord, I spoke with Merlin last night. He thinks the incidents of attacks will drop as the monsters spread out."

"That is what I fear. If the monsters spread, they are going to find easier prey."

"Yes, Your Majesty, that is a real possibility. "But your people are tough, and they will survive."

Merlin entered the study, finding them bent over the desk, placing markers on a map.

"There are a couple of monsters here. We would like you to look at the reports on Merlin."

"Indeed, Your Majesty, always happy to lend my expertise." Looking at the report, Merlin said. "This first one is a manticore, and lances would be the best way to take them down. Manticores are immune to most magic."

"This other one, I am surprised. Wood Trolls are very reclusive and will hide, not fight. They are caretakers looking after forests, keeping them healthy."

"Pray, tell Merlin, do you have a book on these monsters?" The king asked, chuckling.

Merlin laughed. "I do, Your Majesty, twenty volumes. But they are all substantial about this thick." He said, holding his hands about a foot apart.

"Not likely to help us anytime soon."

"No. The volumes are not practical to carry around unless you have a bag of holding. I have one, but it was left behind. If I can find a half-day soon, I will call for it. It takes time and power to build the bridge for a calling."

"Very well, then." The king said. "We must gather our scholars to compile and record our guide."

The meeting broke up as the others started to enter the study. The group said good morning as servants began bringing food and drink. Once the immediate hunger was satisfied, they talked in the sitting area.

The king spoke first, outlining his agenda. We will have a commander's meeting before the levee. We need to coordinate units and dispositions. I am going to need to get back to Cambridge. The recall of troops from the crusade can begin then. I will be able to spread the men around the country in critical areas to protect the people.

Many appointments and promotions need to be proclaimed just in this area. Once that is taken care of in the levee. I want the mayor and the other town leaders there as well. Then we shall see what the rest of the day brings. But I want to be on my way to Cambridge no later than tomorrow.

I said. "Your Majesty, the second company, can escort you to Cambridge without difficulties. We can leave one company here to cover Nottingham. Then the rest can be spread out to cover key points in the country."

"Yes, Sir Guy, that will be in the commander's meeting. I will keep my plans to myself for now."

Very well, Your Majesty." Said, Sir William. "We shall arrange for the commander's meeting and subsequent levee to start mid-morning."

"Sir William, please remain. I value your advice. Sir Guy, you can make arrangements for the meeting and levee."

"Yes, Your Majesty." We both replied.

All stood and left the two men sitting alone.

In the hall, Merriam said. "I need to get my bow."

"I will come with you," said Robyn. "I need to send Jack and Allen to get the band."

"If you insist, my love. Jamie, go arrange an escort for Milady."

"Yes, Milord." He dashed off.

Sergeant Thomas appeared as if from the wall. "Sergeant Thomas orders."

"Yes, Milord," Sergeant Thomas came to attention.

First of all, send men to the companies. There will be a commander's meeting for captains and sergeants. Have the captains bring any men due for a promotion or special commendation. Second, send men to the town and invite the mayor and other business leaders to the levee to follow the meeting. I anticipate the session to last no more than an hour. So tell them two hours. "Have you got that, Sergeant Thomas?"

"Yes, Milord, runners to the commander's meeting in one hour levee to follow. Invitations to the town leaders for the levee in two hours." Sergeant Thomas saluted and marched out.

I then turned and entered the audience chamber. I looked around at tables set up for a celebration. Stopping a servant, I asked. "What is the meaning of this?"

"King's orders Milord to set this up for this morning."

"Very well, carry on."

Puzzled, I took a turn around the courtyard. Seeing Sergeant Boils, I asked him. "Did our patrols get away at dawn?"

"Yes, Milord, none less than ten men."

"Good, carry on."

A few minutes later, Jamie trotted up. "Milord, I have been ordered to bring you in to prepare for the meeting."

"Whatever do you mean, Jamie?"

"I have a bath drawn and clothing you are supposed to wear. King's orders."

"I do not know what he is up to, but we will find out soon enough."

"I hope so, Milord, because I am flummoxed."

"Get used to it, Jamie. Our king can be very devious sometimes."

"Yes, here we are. Let us get that armor off of you."

"Yes, Jamie, this may be a good idea. A warm bath may revive me."

"Yes, Milord, if you say so. Fresh clothes are on the bench, and I will brush out your boots and get you a fresh tabard."

I sighed as I settled into the warm water. Ducking under the water, I came up blowing and pushed my hair back. Then I grabbed a brush and soap and began scrubbing myself. Jamie had returned with my boots and tabard when I was drying off. Dressing in some black hose and tunic, I slipped my boots on and then put on the green tabard.

"You are sure this is what the king wanted me to wear?" I asked, looking at Jamie.

"No, Milord, Milady Merriam chose what each of you would wear."

"Each of us?"

"Yes, Milord the companions. The king directed Milady Merriam to choose your outfits for today's levee. You will see when we meet the others in the duke's sitting room. Now we must hurry, Milord."

"Then let us go," and we headed down the hall.

Entering the duke's sitting room, I stopped. Robyn, Will, and Little-Jon were dressed identically to me. Merlin had on hooded robes in the same colors. Friar Tuck had on robes similar to Merlin's in a warm brown. But what stopped me in my tracks was what Milady Merriam was wearing. She had on an emerald green brocade dress. It conformed perfectly from her breasts down to her hips and then dropped in multiple pleats to her ankles.

Walking over, I took her hand and kissed it, finally finding my voice. "Milady, you are stunning. I was rendered speechless at the sight of you."

"Pretty words Milord but I thank you nonetheless."

Merriam's maids standing beside her giggled, and the other men laughed.

I blushed slightly and said. "See, Milady, your radiance even blinded me to the sight of these others."

Merriam blushed even brighter and laughed. "You are such a charmer, Milord."

The rest of the men had moved up to surround her very closely. Realizing just how close we were, her breath hitched. I could feel our heat surrounding her.

We quickly stepped back at the sound of Sir William clearing his throat. Sophia entered with him giggling.

Sir William wore his usual blue hose tunic and tabard.

Sophia wore a dress in powder blue. Her maids accompanied her.

Sir William said. "You can cut the tension with a knife in here."

Sophia replied. "Yes, it is very delicious. Is it not Rose?"

Blushing bright, Rose giggled. "Yes, Milady."

Merlin laughed. "That was a close one there, Friar Tuck. You almost had to deliver the nuptials while they consummated the marriage."

"No," said Friar Tuck. "That would not have done at all. The Lord would have been most upset with me to leave it that long. There is, after all, the proper order for the marriage ceremony. We must have the nuptials. Then a time of feasting. Followed by drinking and dancing. Only then may the happy couple or group retire to consummate their vows."

The others laughed as we flushed and fidgeted.

"Enough fun, for now. It is time to be in the audience chamber."

We fell in behind Sir William and Sophia.

Entering the Audience Chamber, we made our way to the front. On the dais was a throne flanked by nine chairs. Sir William led us up the three steps, indicating the left side's five chairs. He then escorted Sophia to the second chair on the right side of the throne. He pointed to the other two seats for Merlin and Friar Tuck.

Soon after, we sat down. A much-recovered chamberlain pounded three times on the floor announcing. "Rise Milords and Miladies Sir Lionel Claymoore King of England."

The king walked at a stately pace into the chamber, followed by his squire carrying his scepter and his bannerman holding his banner aloft. Ten knights in full armor without shields or helmets flanked the king on each side.

Everyone in the room bowed as the king passed. As the king's foot hit the first step of the dais, the companions bowed as well. The ladies dropped into deep curtsies. The king stopped in front of the throne. Turning, he called out. "Rise, my friends." Then he sat down, and everyone followed suit.

The king spoke, Soldier's Knights Lords and Ladies. We wish to recognize you here. We thank you for your efforts to rescue us and protect our kingdom. We are most pleased with the efforts of all of you. But some of you have put in an outstanding effort. Sir William, please read out the list.

Sir William called several sergeants forward. Sergeant Thomas was among them. The king awarded them a purse of one hundred crowns and a small plot of land, making them landholders and gentry. The king made them captains of the realm, one step below knighthood.

The king knighted five squires. He then promoted four knights to captains, giving them a purse and land.

And finally, Sir William read. "Sir Guy of Gisborne, Robyn of Locksley, Will Scarlet, and Little-Jon. Kneel before your king." We moved to the lower step of the dais and knelt.

The king spoke. "For exceptional service to our realm. Sir Guy, I name you Guy Sherwood, Duke of Nottingham. Robyn of Locksley, I promote you to Baron of Derby. And finally, Will Scarlet, you are appointed the Sherriff of Nottingham. Little-Jon is now captain of the Sherwood Huntsman."

"Please rise and resume your seats. We will discuss details and your patents of nobility later."

"Now for a less pleasant task, gentleman. The military levee is complete, and the commander's meeting begins."

We need to dispatch men to protect the realm, and I believe we have enough men to the north for now.

The lands to the south are extensive and not well protected, which is the purpose of this meeting. We will be leaving for Cambridge tomorrow, and the second company will be my escort, and they will begin retraining the king's guard and protecting the area.

First Company will remain here as the core garrison for Nottingham. When I have recalled the troops from the crusade, We will send them here for training and then spread them around the south. For this reason, we will take the newly promoted captains as garrison commanders.

Each time we have five hundred fifty men available, we will send them here, and they will twin with one of the companies split and begin training.

Each company will only move out once it has trained enough to be effective. It will require excellent coordination as there will be near-constant troop movements.

We will maintain five companies around Nottingham. Three of which will form a core strike force. The companies that remain here will be under Sir William's direct orders, and he will have the discretion to send out smaller half-company units to trouble spots. At no time, and I repeat this. At no time will less than half a company be on the move. Every half-company captain will have a letter from Sir William, The Captain-General of England.

"Squires, you may now distribute the order packet."

Before you grumble, the first company to twin is the third company. The regent had two hundred fifty men here when we took over Nottingham. They are yours now. Captain Keating, use them as you please. When we get to Cambridge, We will send another three hundred of the guard to complete the twinning.

"Are there any questions then, gentleman?"

A murmur of no your Majesty's went through the group.

"Very well, dismissed." The king stood. Everyone bowed as the king walked out.

CHAPTER

We all gathered around, congratulating each other, slapping backs, and shaking hands. The biggest surprise was when Merriam threw her arms around me and kissed me.

She tried to break free and squeaked. "Sorry, Milord."

I laughed and kissed her again.

When I finally released her, her face burned furiously, and she was heavily panting. Robyn then pulled her into his arms for a kiss as well. He then passed her off to Will for a kiss. Finally, she shrieked when Little-Jon wrapped his arms around her and lifted her from the floor for a kiss.

The group broke apart as the chamberlain approached. "Milord Duke, do you need anything before the audience?"

"Your name, chamberlain?"

"I am called Digby, Your Grace. I have been in service to the Dukes of Nottingham since my father passed twenty-five years ago."

"I bow to your dedication and service. Are you recovered enough to resume your duties properly? Be honest, there is no penalty, and I only ask because you can have the time you need."

"I have my son to assist me, my Liege. He is not ready to take over, but he will be soon. Then perhaps I will retire and rest."

"Call over your son Digby and introduce him."

"Yes, my Liege," he waved over a younger man. "This is my son Denby."

I reached out and shook Denby's hand. "Do you feel ready to take up your father's mantle? I have another task in mind for him."

"My Liege, I am ready. My father will not hang up the mantle because he likes the job too much."

I laughed. "Then it is as I had suspected. What is the pay for chamberlain here?"

It was a silver per month before the Sherriff took over, and he felt room and board was enough wage."

"Well, that will change as of this moment. Your pay will increase to a half-crown per month, beginning the month of the previous duke's passing. You may work that out with my treasurer. Who happens to be your father, Digby. By the way, Digby, your wage is one crown from the same date as your son."

Both men stood mouths agape.

"Do you find this satisfactory?" I asked with a smile.

"We do not know what to say, my Liege," said Digby.

"I accept Milord would be good enough." I laughed.

"We accept my Liege." Both men said, bowing.

"Good. Hand over the staff and mantle of chamberlain to your son Digby. Then find the keys to the strongroom, as there must be a chain of office for you somewhere."

"Yes, my Liege, I know where they both are." Digby then passed the mantle and staff of chamberlain to his son.

"Excellent. Relax for the rest of the day, Digby. We will meet soon in the strongroom and review my expectations and wages for the staff."

"Yes, my Liege." He bowed and turned away, walking from the audience chamber with a spring in his step.

Denby said. "You have given my father new life, my Liege. He used funds for his retirement to pay the staff and me. He did not think I knew of this and must never know that I did."

"Well, then, Denby, you have placed me in a difficult position. To keep your secret safe, I must do nothing. However, seeing how happy he is, perhaps it is for the best."

"So, Denby, I take it the king's audience is to include a luncheon?"

"A feast of some sort, my Liege. The king would not fully disclose his mind, and I believe he tries to be coy. Perhaps he has some other surprise arranged."

"Ha." I laughed. "More like some mischief. We will retire to my quarters until things are ready and have some drinks and food sent up."

"At once, my Liege." And he hurried off.

Offering my arm to Merriam, Robyn offered his arm on the other side. She said. "I did not think Derby was a barony."

"No," Robyn said. "I guess I will have to find funds to pay for a manor house at the very least."

"If I am not mistaken, Robyn. Baronies come with a five hundred crown stipend per year."

Merriam gasped. "That is much gold."

I laughed. "Not really, my love. A portion of his taxes from the barony go to the king and me. From that money comes a house or castle and staff to pay, which you must first hire. Then recruit tenant farmers to work his land and soldiers to protect it. Plus, levee men for the king all before receiving any taxes. It would take three to five years before a barony could support itself."

"We can work that all out in the days to come. Will and Little-Jon have their work cut out for them."

"Yes, at my expense." I laughed.

"How is that?" Asked Will.

"It works out something like this." Said, Sir William.

Nottingham is the dukedom that includes Derby and four other surrounding baronies. These baronies pay taxes to the duke. The duke then pays a portion of those taxes to the king. From the taxes the duke collects, he must support the infrastructure of the dukedom. You, Will, are the Sherriff of Nottingham. The duke pays you two-hundred crowns a year. From that money, you must hire people to police the dukedom. It includes every village and town. These people would be an extension of your authority. Now, Will you also work with the huntsman led by Little-Jon. They take care of poachers and highwaymen. Their job is to capture them and bring them to you or the barons for justice.

"Yes, Robyn, you are one of my barons. So this means that for me to succeed, you must. If I am to be strong, I must make you strong. Now it just so happens I have five hundred men to use…well, they are Lady Sophia's men, but she lets me use them."

Sophia blushed and giggled, and Sir William laughed.

Merriam turned to me with an eyebrow raised. "Excuse me. You gave another woman five hundred men?"

"No, my love, she stole them from me, and Sophia bewitched them using some kind of oracle charm." I ducked my head.

The men roared with laughter.

Merriam pouted. "But I want an army too."

"I am offering you a fine castle, a large town with several smaller ones plus a giant forest. And do not forget a Sherriff and all his huntsman, and your army may end up bigger than Sophia's."

"Oh, in that case, it is okay." She flung her arms around my neck and kissed me.

Then she went over to Robyn and kissed him. As she pulled away, she said. "You can build the manor house for the summer."

"She then went over to Will kissing him. "And you can find us a hundred good policemen to protect our people."

And then she went to Little-Jon last, pulling him down for a kiss. "You can get me a hundred good huntsman to take care of the forest. Or maybe two hundred, as it is a big forest."

Merlin laughed. "You may not need so many, Merriam."

If you are cautious, Little-Jon, and leave the right kinds of gifts, you may gain the trust of wood trolls."

"Gifts for trolls, wizard?" Asked Little-Jon.

Honey oatcakes, fresh bread, vegetables, and that sort of thing are what wood trolls like, like fresh fruit, nuts, and berries.

Wood trolls roam a territory of about fifty miles. They will make little symbols to mark the boundaries, like small figures made from sticks tied with plaited grasses or stacked stones in patterns. One is a circle of eight rocks about three feet in diameter. Then they will place one stone on the Inside edge representing that spot outside their territory. You could leave a gift in the center of the circle, wait for a day and come back. If the gift is gone, he has accepted it. If it is still there, he has rejected you, so move away. Occasionally they will leave a gift in return. I can say that the only thing is never hunting in their territory.

"What a fascinating creature," Merriam said. "I would so love to meet one."

They are gentle creatures that would never harm anyone, even forest animals. That is what surprised me most about last night's attack. It reminds me Duke Sherwood. It would help if you put the word out to your men. Do not harm the forest trolls. Tell them to move out of the way if they come towards your men. It will be looking for something. It may be something harmful to your men. They have an instinct to protect all creatures. They may even be trying to heal one of your men. They are full of earth magic that includes a healing power. So if they smell sickness, they may just be trying to heal one of your men. They are trying to heal you if they hold out a glowing green hand.

"You will come in handy on this trip, Merlin." Said Will.

"I would suggest not antagonizing anyone that could turn you into a toad." Said Little-Jon.

"He would not do that. I am too essential to the mission. Who else is going to find the traps?"

"Gentleman, no bickering. God will show us the way."

"You are wrong, Friar Tuck. The gods are smart enough to hide behind the meat shields." Merlin laughed.

Servants entered with trays of drinks and pastries.

Merlin said. "What I would not give for a nice hot cup of coffee right now."

"What is coffee?" Asked Merriam.

Coffee is a delicious hot breakfast drink. We will have to wait until the discovery of the new world for that. Forget I said anything. I could spend all winter telling you of things you would never understand. Just take my odd references with a grain of salt and carry on.

After being informed of a delay, they sat and chatted amiably. The weather was a major topic. It was the first day of rain in some time, and it would be a month or two, at least, before we got any snow.

A servant came to the door and said. "Milords, the king wishes you to attend him in the study. He also requested that Miladies remain here with their maids in attendance."

I shrugged. "Very well, Milady, it is with the most profound sorrow, but we must part ways for a short time."

"We will be together soon enough."

Sophia giggled.

We filed out and headed for the study. Guards opened the doors as we approached.

We entered to find the king bent over the desk, looking at something.

We all bowed as Sir William said. "You called for us, Your Majesty?"

The king beckoned us to rise and come over. "No need for that frippery when we are together alone."

We have received five reports in the last hour, and they all came by fast horse. The first was from Derby. The town there was attacked. Fortunately, huntsmen stayed there and killed four of those werewolf monsters.

The following report came from Manchester. It predates the event and details an attack on a fishing village by persons unknown. The raiders killed the villagers but captured the young women. There are no survivors or witnesses.

The last three reports are all local. Last night, monsters attacked a hunting camp, logging camp, and quarry. In those cases, it was only a single monster. There were injuries as only the hunters had trained men.

"I am looking for suggestions here, gentleman, anything you can think of to help these people."

Sir William said. "I do not like it, but I am sure Sir Guy may have a solution."

"Yes, Your Majesty, I have a solution, however distasteful."

I would not say I like sending men out in penny packets, but that is against a coordinated enemy. It would be a temporary solution against ravenous monsters with no control or directions. Your Majesty, I will use the sixth company for this. Allow me to send for their captains and top sergeants.

"Very well, and then you can detail your plans."

Outside the door, I saw Jamie and Edwin. Calling them over, I said. "Jamie, run and get Sergeant Thomas and Captain Geoffrey immediately."

Jamie dashed off with a hasty. "Yes, Milord."

"Edwin, grab a horse and ride to six company. Bring back Captain Dorner, Captain Anders, and their sergeants."

"Yes, Milord." And Edwin dashed off.

I turned back to the room at large. "The first part can be explained in ten minutes, Your Majesty. Part two in half an hour or less."

"Very well, Duke Notting... That does not work very well as a name, does it?"

"No, Your Majesty." I grinned. "I am sure Milady would be less than pleased with it."

"Yes, I am sure she would not like it. Very well then Duke Sherwood it is. I hope that will be satisfactory."

"That is much nicer, Your Majesty. I am sure it will also garner fewer jokes from Baron Derby and the men."

The king chuckled. "Yes, I am sure you are right. Also, Robyn, as you are the last of your line and your lands no longer exist, we can call you Baron Loxley of Derby."

"Thank you, Your Majesty. I appreciate that. Will, I just thought, send a soldier to the... No, on second thought, you get Jack and Allen back here as quickly as possible."

"Right. On it, Robyn." And Will ran out.

The king raised his brow and chuckled.

"Your Majesty," Robyn said. "We have been friends for a long time, and the titles may take some work."

The king nodded. "I am sure they will. Jack and Allen are good men?"

"Majesty, they are my first choice for sergeants for the police and huntsmen. They are sharp and loyal to Merriam, as they have worked for her long term."

"Good, it looks like we will need loyal men around Nottingham while on this quest," I said, scratching my chin in thought.

"Yes, Milord Nottingham is the epicenter for everything."

"No, Sir William, not the epicenter, just the starting point. The orb is somewhere in France right now." Said Merlin.

"You can tell its location?" Asked the king.

"In the way that you can feel a pull like a fish nibbling at a line, I can sense a direction but not distance other than we are not close."

"So that is why you are the guide."

"Merriam and I are tasked with returning the orb to pandora's box. Your job is to get us there."

"I see, then we must be moving soon."

"There is no hurry. We cannot catch it, and the orb will meander until it finds a place to settle. Once it stops moving, then we can pounce. We must get going soon, but a week or two will not matter."

"Good, that gives me time to get things functioning here first."

"I have set in motion all the plans I can before I leave here." Said the king.

"Plans, Your Majesty?"

"In due time, Duke Sherwood."

CHAPTER

Captain Geoffrey and Sergeant Thomas entered the study and bowed. "You sent for us, Your Majesty?"

"Rise, men, we do not have time for that claptrap. Now for this plan of yours, Duke Sherwood."

"Yes, Your Majesty. Captain sergeant, look at this map. A quarry, a logging camp, and several small villages and farms are scattered around Nottingham castle."

"I presume they supply things the castle needs?" The captain said.

"Yes, there are a couple of hunting camps too, but we are not worried about them. The hunters, it would seem, can defend themselves, but we should check on them nonetheless. I need mixed teams of men consisting of knights, pikemen, and archers, and they can bring a wagon to carry supplies for five days. The archers can take enough extra arrows in the wagon to equal two quivers per day. That is many arrows, but I suspect they will need them if they run into trouble."

"I count fifteen places that need to be covered. I would suggest splitting this duty between the first, fourth, and fifth companies, as I have other plans for the sixth company, and I would like to keep the third intact for a reserve."

"Yes, Milord, I understand your plan entirely." Said Captain Geoffrey.

"Good, I will use the sixth company for further areas like Derby."

"Yes, Milord and the bulk of our men will act as a quick reaction force if more men are needed."

"Excellent, Captain, you may both carry on."

"Your Majesty Milord's." They bowed and left.

Will came back with Jack and Allen in tow. Both men started to bow, but the king told them not to bother.

"Come over here," said Robyn. "You are both now sergeants in the Sherwood Huntsmen. Get yourselves out to camp, and bring everyone back. You have a barracks here in town. Will is currently the Sherriff of Nottingham, and Little-Jon is the Captain of the Huntsmen. Report to them when you return; they will have other orders."

"Right, Robyn." The men said and ran out.

Robyn shook his head. "Yes, this will take much training, Your Majesty."

"Your people are remarkably calm and well-ordered, and I have not seen the slightest bit of panic in any of your men. I am glad I placed my faith in Sir William's recommendation."

Sixth companies captains and sergeants entered on the heels of a brief knock. They all bowed, and the king just shook his head and bid them rise.

"I waved them over. Captain Doerner, I am splitting your command in half."

"Captain Anders and Sergeant Scott will take half the company to Derby. Captain Anders, your task will be to guard the town and surrounding areas. My men send knights, pikemen, and archer teams to vulnerable areas. They take a wagon with five days worth of supplies and extra arrows for the archers. It is only a three-day mission, and they rotate back to town."

"I will have a problem with this, Milord, that will leave me very thin on the ground in Derby."

"Do you have a better solution Captain Anders?"

"Yes, Milord, half the men in roving squads. They will move each day to new locations to patrol and defend. Our men are getting accomplished fighting these monsters."

"Very well, captain, you have my blessing. We will see how your system works and adapt as needed."

Captain Doerner, your task is to investigate an attack on a fishing village south of Manchester. The population was slaughtered, and the village burned. I want your half company in that coastal village to see any clues. You know the type I think of, footprints and keel marks on the strand. You have the best tracker, so sweep southward to see if other villages are in danger or destroyed."

"Yes, Milord, we will move out within the hour."

"I will have part of the fifth company cover your quadrant. Oh, and take some extra wagons. There were no young women found among the bodies. So, you can expect the worst case, dismissed."

I turned back to the table and said. "That should take care of the defenses, Your Majesty."

"Sir William was right to place his faith in you, Duke Sherwood. Attend me, gentlemen. We have an audience to get through."

"The ladies, Your Majesty?"

"They will be along shortly. Before we begin the celebration, I have a few words to say."

"Yes, Your Majesty."

The King walked out, followed closely by his bannerman, squire, and the rest of us.

Descending the grand staircase, I caught the slight nod my chamberlain gave the king. Shaking my head, I followed along, playing the king's game.

As the king entered the audience hall, I thought the transformation was complete. There were benches, and people dressed in their finery at every seat. The servants decorated the hall with bunting, banners, and candles.

The people bowed as the king swept up the central aisle with Sir William. We were about to enter the door. The chamberlain shook his head slightly and twitched his fingers, indicating to wait. I quirked my brow at the chamberlain in a silent question.

The king ascended the dais to stand before the throne. Lionel lifted his hands before him, bid the people rise, and then began to speak.

"Good people of Nottingham, this is a day for multiple celebrations. We have returned from the crusades and begun to set right the wrongs committed by the regent and the previous Sherriff."

The king held his hands for quiet, and silence again fell as he spoke. "First, we would like to present." And he swung his arm toward the door.

His staff banged three times, the chamberlain announced. "Their honors, Wilfred Scarlet, Sheriff of Nottingham, and Captain Little-Jon of the Sherwood Huntsmen." They marched up the aisle waving as the people cheered to a spot indicated by Sir William. Then, the king held up his hands for quiet. "Next, it is our pleasure to introduce you to." He again pointed to the door.

Thumping the staff three more times, the chamberlain announced. "Sir Robyn Loxley Baron of Derby defender of the king." Robyn walked down the aisle smiling in embarrassment as he moved to a spot opposite Will and Little John.

Once again, the king held up his hands, waiting for silence to descend.

"Lastly, it is our pleasure to announce good people."

Once again, the staff of office banged three times, and the chamberlain announced. "Milord Guy Sherwood, Duke of Nottingham and Commander of the Northern Kingdom Army."

I marched down the aisle to the people's cheers and moved to the indicated space next to Robyn.

It took a few minutes longer for the kings waving to settle the crowd.

Then Lionel resumed speaking. Good people of Nottingham, these four men and the troops they command will restore order and protect you from harm. Since the last duke's passing, the regent and Sherriff have caused much mischief.

Our promise to you is that this will not happen again. We leave in the morning for Cambridge to restore order to the throne and kingdom. These men represent the beginning of a new order in this land. However, we must caution that the area outside town is unsafe unless you are in large armed groups. The men will escort farmers attending the weekly market from the castle and their farms. They will be protecting quarries and lumber camps.

Now that we have imparted the most important of the realm's news. With great pleasure, we turn to more pleasant matters. Servants filed in and lined up around the walls at a wave of the king's arms.

Friar Tuck entered dressed in a fine cassock holding an ornate bible, flanked by two squires carrying smoking miters of incense. The Friar and his escort stopped two steps below the king and one above the men and turned. Another man had followed the Friar carrying a small podium and setting it in front. The man took a knee in front and pulled an ornate box from his tabard. The Friar put the bible on the podium.

Raising his face and hands, Friar Tuck began. "Heavenly Father, bless your children at this gathering. Bless our king that he may stand firm, reigning over us for many years. Bless these four men that they may rule wisely and bear strong sons to continue their rule. Amen! In the name of the Father and Holy Spirit."

Your Majesty, Milords, and Gentlefolk. The king has entrusted me with strengthening the kingdom and, by extension, his Majesty. Today, we gather to celebrate much more than raising these men to power. What better way to celebrate than binding these men to their Lady?

The chamberlain pounded the staff three more times in a slow beat. His voice rang out. "Majesty Lords Ladies and Gentlefolk, I am pleased to introduce Milady Sophia, Oracle of Athena, maid of honor. Sophia began a stately slow walk down the aisle. The staff beat her first three steps in time, then the chamberlain announced.

"Milady Merriam betrothed of the Duke of Nottingham, Baron of Derby, Sherriff of Nottingham, and Captain of the Huntsman. Escorting Milady is her grandfather, the wizard Merlin."

Merriam walked through the doorway on her grandfather's arm. She was a vision of beauty in an off-shoulder snow-white brocade dress with lace ruffles. Her hair piled upon her head, with ringlets framing her face.

A gold belt cinched her narrow waist with a short pendant ending in a green jewel the same color as her sparkling eyes.

Merlin wore robes the same color as the gem. Smiling, he escorted Merriam to the center of the group of men, squeezed her hand then stepped back opposite Sophia as a witness. The four grooms stood stunned and wide-eyed. Friar Tuck looked up at the king as he chuckled with a big grin, clearing his throat.

Lord, we are gathered here today to celebrate a non-traditional wedding. This woman has taken it upon herself to love equally four men, and she only asks that they love each other and her the same.

I have been given vows written by the Oracle Sophia as she is also the High Priestess of the Temple of Athena. I can only agree to use them, as The Oracle is more familiar with this type of wedding. "Now to begin."

Dearly beloved, we are here to witness the bonding of five individuals into one soul, heart, and voice. Each of you has chosen to love, respect, and honor each other as one.

"Merriam, hold out your hands. Robyn and Sir Guy take her left hand. Will and Little-Jon take her right. Do you men pledge your lives, health, and wealth to care of Merriam. Without reservation in good times and bad to protect her and each other?"

We all replied. "I will."

"Merriam, do you take these men into your heart to love them equally without reservation through good times and bad sickness and health?"

Merriam replied. "I will."

"Do you all pledge to support and protect each other, your lands and people with unity of purpose that none may put asunder?"

We all answered. "I will."

The kneeling man opened the box and presented five rings to us.

"Each of you take one ring and repeat after me. With this ring, I pledge my bond in this joining forever more."

We each took a ring and repeated the vow while putting it on.

"Then in heart, soul, and mind, I pronounce you one in purpose and life."

"You may kiss the bride."

A stupendous roar of cheering shook the castle. We passed Merriam back and forth, kissing her until she could hardly breathe.

The king stepped down to the group Shaking the men's hands and hugging Merriam. The king returned to the throne and held up his hands for quiet. He then announced that the feasting and celebration would begin as soon as the servants returned. Thus began the formation of a long line of well-wishers.

As people sat at the tables and servants delivered food and drink, alarm bells rang.

"Hellfire and damnation, who invited the enemy today?" Cried Friar Tuck.

"Methinks we should have sent a proclamation for our day's activities so an enemy would not have interfered." The king laughed. He slapped the Friar on his back.

"Good people," I called out. "Please remain in the hall enjoying the food. My soldiers and I will take care of this problem."

The king, Sir William, and I headed to the entryway, followed by our other companions.

We met a knight coming through the entrance. His armor was scratched and battered, and he had a cut on one cheek.

Falling to one knee, he gasped out. "Your Majesty, an army of monsters approaches."

"Where were you, and how far out?" I asked.

"Milord, I was with the team heading south to protect the lumber camp."

We were about to turn off the road when we encountered monsters. There were five creatures man like about this tall. He held his hand over his head with a mix of armor, weapons, and bucklers. They shot arrows but were weak and did not penetrate our armor. They did not last but a few minutes against the Infantry. What gave us the problem was a huge dog-like creature one rode.

"Damn," said Merlin. "Wargs orcs breed them as fighting mounts, and they are tough to kill with their sharp teeth and claws. The men had greenish skin and tusks growing from the bottom jaw?"

"Yes, Milord, as you describe them." After dispatching their scouts, we followed their trail and ran into a large body of these creatures advancing. We got into another tussle with their advance guard, and there were too many for us to disengage. The sergeant told me to ride hard and warn you.

"They will be in a position to attack by nightfall, or they could wait for the morning."

Merlin said. They are intelligent but not very smart. They form village clans of one to five hundred fighters. Standard practice is rape and pillage in a small area until they run out of loot. Then they will set up a farming community, hunting and gathering to build strength. One will get the idea that he is a warlord and combine several communities on the warpath. Do you have an idea of how many there are?

"A few thousand Milord, they hit us too quickly to get an accurate count."

"Right," Merlin said. "It is your turn, Lord Duke. They will not turn away, have poor tactics, and tend to fight straight ahead. The woods could be a problem if there are many of them."

"Sixth company is out of it as they went by the north road," I said. "They are coming from the south and have more than a mile of open field to cross before they hit the town."

"Jamie, ask Captain Geoffrey to pass the word of an all commanders meeting in the study in twenty minutes."

"We should have enough time to set up an excellent reception for our unexpected guests."

"I like the way you think." Said the king.

"Come, let us get out the town map." Said, Sir William.

As we went up the stairs, Merriam asked. "Grandfather, what would you say is the range on their bows?"

"A hundred paces max sixty accurately, I would guess."

"Interesting," Merriam said. "Guy, my love, is it not customary for armies to stop just out of bow range to consider their options?"

I flashed Merriam an evil grin. "They stop at what they perceive is the maximum bow range."

"So dearest, if I was to drop an arrow at their feet when they reach two hundred paces, would they stop then?"

"Yes, my love, I believe they would."

Robyn gave a tight grin. "The average longbowman can hit a man with enough force to puncture armor at three hundred paces. On the other hand, my men can hit a soft target at four hundred paces. Our little lovely here practices on apples starting at four hundred paces and can range out to five hundred."

"Hold up." The king said. "That is not possible. Most can not even shoot an arrow that far, and I would bet for a woman half that distance at most."

"Oh," chirped Merriam. "A bet?"

"Hide your purse away, Your Majesty, because I have seen her do it dozens of times. Merriam has an extraordinary bow, which I cannot pull, and she is stronger than any other man in this room."

Then Robyn saw Merriam's pout and started laughing. "No, my love, you are not allowed to rob the king."

"Well darn, in any case, my men and I pick off any leaders and the wargs. We may be able to make this battle easier."

"Most people move when they see arrows flying."

Standing on her tippy toes, she kissed me on the cheek.

"Did you see that coming?" She asked with a cheeky grin.

"No, but I predicted it."

"That is the beauty of them attacking this evening as the sky darkens. It will be harder to see, and the orcs will be so far away that they will not hear the twang of the bow until the arrow has struck. How difficult do you think it would be to give orders with a mouthful of an arrow."

I gave her a vicious grin. "Very, I should think. How about you, Your Majesty, could you give orders like that?"

The king laughed. "All you need to do is position your troops to the best advantage."

CHAPTER

9

We had made our way to the study by this time, where I found the needed map.

Your Majesty, I have just the formation for this situation if you look here on the map. We will use the infantry of three, four, and five companies on this line with the archers behind them.

The first company will garrison the castle and provide a fallback point, and they will also supply fifty-man flying squads to counter-attack breaches. The second company will use teams to fill breaches in the main defense line and provide fallback points for the primary defense if they are overwhelmed.

As the men get into position, we will withdraw the townspeople to the castle.

The only dangerous part will be if the enemy has overwhelming numbers. If the line does not hold, we may lose archers as they try and retreat. We will use the knights to crash the flanks.

If these monsters are, as you say, Merlin, they will loot houses as they go. That will slow them down even more, but I do not anticipate that eventuality. We will plan for it as always; we plan for defeat, but the focus will be on victory.

The king said. "A toast then to victory, may it be cheap."

We drank the toast as the captains and sergeants filed in the door.

I spent half an hour explaining the plan to the men. A captain or sergeant put forward ideas, and we also discussed them. We implemented the change if they had merit and improved the overall strategy.

One idea got a resounding endorsement from everyone. The young sergeant ducked his head in embarrassment. "No, sergeant," I said. "This a brilliant idea."

The king spoke up. "Excellent idea, sergeant one I would like to use against the charge of French knights. I will be sure to keep it in mind."

"Very well, gentlemen. Armor up and prepare the defense."

The king remained seated while the men bowed and left.

The king waved Sir William back to his seat as we left to get ready.

"You have chosen your protege well, William."

"Thank you, Your Majesty. He is a brilliant young man. I will enjoy my retirement knowing he is in my place."

"Bah, you have a few good years left yet, my friend."

"I think we will sit behind the center barricade in town and watch the battle. If needed, we will be close enough to intervene and far enough away to allow this young man free rein."

"Yes, Your Majesty, a wonderful idea. You will like Guy's ability and acute sense of timing. Knowing when to pull some trick, he and that devilishly clever Sergeant Thomas have cooked up."

"Yes, I have noticed that about Sergeant Thomas. Why is he not a captain himself?"

"Apparently, according to Sir Guy, they found him about to be hung. He was tutoring for some lord in Reading, and he was caught as he had just finished a lesson training the lord's twin daughters in carnal delights."

"Twins, you say?" I laughed. "God, I wish that had been me."

"Yes, apparently, they were seventeen and quite pretty. The lord was extremely upset when he found he no longer had maidens to offer as he had been arranging very advantageous marriages for them."

"Putting the shoe on the other foot. If it were my daughter's, the sergeant would not have made it out of bed."

"Your Majesty, I do not suppose he would have. The lord in question, however, was old and somewhat feeble."

"Well, my old friend, I will have to inquire about these twins. Could they still be available? Perhaps I shall elevate the good sergeant to the peerage and marry him to them."

"You are a very evil old man, Your Majesty, very evil." Laughed Sir William thinking how that would shock the stoic sergeant.

"I know, right. Suppose we should get armored up ourselves."

"Yes, Your Majesty, I will send Jeffrey in on my way out."

The companions met in the entry hall except for Sophia.

"Where is Milady Sophia?" I inquired.

"She is not one for battle." Sir William said. "She is helping set up a hospital in one of the barracks. She also mentioned organizing the town folk to carry the wounded back from the front. They will not leave the town confines, but any man that makes it back to the barricades will be loaded up on carts and brought to the hospital."

"That is an excellent idea." The king said. "It will build the sense of camaraderie between the troops and the town folk, and knowing they have participated somehow will give them a sense of accomplishment."

"That was Sophia's thought, Your Majesty." Said, Sir William.

"Well, we should mount up, make our way down to the front, and see how the defenses are shaping up." The king said.

They all mounted, and the bannerman unfurled the king's banner.

I laughed. "You know, Your Majesty, that banner will be like waving a red flag in front of a bull."

The king looked over with a tight grin. "That was the idea, Duke Sherwood. If they focus on me, they will not be looking at the flanks."

"I see, Your Majesty, if you are the prettiest maiden at the ball, everyone will want to dance with you alone," Merriam said.

Everyone roared with laughter, and the tension seemed to melt away from the troops in the area.

"Well done, Milady, you gave the men relief from pre-battle jitters."

Moving up to the barricade, the king said. "It is hard to believe we just came down this road yesterday."

"I thought that myself, Your Majesty," I said. "A lot has happened in just one day."

Merriam said. "Yes. And some gentlemen and I have unfinished business to attend to."

The men all laughed, and we managed to look sheepish.

"Is that platform for me?" Merriam asked, pointing to the highest platform behind the defense line.

Looking side to side, I said. "As there were only enough made for your Huntsmen. Yes, I do believe that one is yours."

"Oh, thank you, my love, it is taller and bigger than all the rest. I love it."

"Good, then I will join you up there, Merriam." Said Merlin. There is a slight chance they will have a shaman with some magic ability. Typically it is not very effective, but some have dabbled.

"Good, then you can protect Merriam from them." Said Robyn.

"My pleasure," Merlin replied. "I will have an opportunity to create some mischief."

"Be careful, both of you," I said. "If the line looks to be collapsing, get back to the castle."

"We can tie our horses right to the platform."

Little-Jon said. "I will be near the middle. If things start to go badly, I will fall back on their platform."

"Oh, Jon, do be careful. The fighting in the center will be the fiercest." Moving her horse next to his, she gave him a big kiss.

She went around and gave her other men a deep kiss as well.

Merriam and Merlin rode over to the platform, dismounting and tying their horses to a brace. They quickly climbed to the top. Looking at the front rail of the platform, Merriam saw dozens of arrows placed for easy access.

"Oh, ho." She said, giggling. "I should join the army. They know how to provide for their archers."

Merlin laughed. "Look down there beside you between the platforms. That is how the army treats archers."

The archers stood a pace or two apart with a wicker basket of arrows in front of each man.

"Well, that is a sound system too. There is a better chance of you fumbling your grab for an arrow still reasonably fast."

"After all, the standard is forty arrows in ten minutes. I usually shoot sixty more than that accuracy goes down too much."

"I am impressed with you, granddaughter. You use that monstrosity all the time?"

"This monstrosity, as you call it, is named Flama."

"As in inflamed?" Merlin asked.

"No, grandfather, as in passion. My passion for archery."

"Then why not call it passion?"

Merriam giggled. "My grandmother called me little flama when I was very young. When I asked her what it meant, she said I was passionate about everything."

Merlin chuckled. "From what I have seen, you are still that passionate little girl. Perhaps I will call you Flama from now on."

"I would like that, grandfather. The way you say it makes me warm inside."

"Anytime now, they will appear at the woodline."

"This is good. The rain is letting up, and the wind is dying down." I reached into an inner pocket and pulled a fresh string for my bow. I quickly restrung the bow. Rolling up the old line, I shoved it in another pouch. Then pulling out a small yellow block, waxed the new string.

I selected an arrow from my quiver and checked the message tube.

"Why that arrow?" inquired Merlin.

"It is a message arrow. The fletching will vibrate with a whistling noise as the arrow flies, making it easier to find and retrieve a message."

"Oh, what a grand idea. Our enemy focuses on the arrow and sees where it lands."

"Yes. By the way, do orcs understand English, the written part?"

"No, for the most part, orcs do not read English or even speak it. But I can both write and speak Orcish."

"That would be perfect. Here is charcoal and parchment. Please translate this." I said, pulling a note from the message tube.

Taking the message, Merlin read it and doubled over laughing. "Their leader will go berserk when he sees it."

Quickly Merlin translated the note to Orcish and slipped it into the message tube.

"Whatever are you two doing?"

Merlin yelled down. "Sending a brief message to our guests."

"Oh? And pray tell what does it say?"

"Your Majesty's message reads. The best part of you ran down your mother's leg. Respectfully Lionel Claymoore, King of England."

Every man who heard the message roared with laughter. The laughter spread to the ranks and into town as word of the letter was passed.

"Goodness Milady your message is giving heart to our men. That will get their blood boiling, and they will attack without thought to our defenses."

"That was my intention, Your Majesty. Distracted minds do not fight well or think clearly."

"I should abduct you, Milady, making you a princess back in court. Then I could use you to balance the dried-up cronies on my council."

"I think my husband's get to use me first, Your Majesty. Otherwise, you may spark a rebellion." I laughed.

"A wise king knows when to bow to the desires of his subjects."

"Wise indeed, Your Majesty." Quipped Sir William.

There came a series of howls and the sounds of stamping feet and jingling metal.

"Not very good at sneaking up." Observed Sergeant Thomas dryly.

"No." Said Merlin from the tower. "Orcs are not known for their subtlety."

"Well, that is my cue to move my post."

"Be well, Your Majesty." Said the Duke.

"And you, companions, as well. We do, after all, need you for a time." Said the king as he rode off.

Little-Jon said. "Come, Sergeant. Let us move to the front of the line. I do not wish to miss wetting my blade." He pulled a massive battle-ax off his back, giving it a few test swings.

Sergeant Thomas barked a laugh as they moved up.

The Duke said. "Are you going to take that other platform, my dear baron?"

"Yes, My Liege, I believe I will. I can do much damage myself at long-range." Robyn chuckled as he walked away. "Take care, my brother-husband."

"And you." The duke laughed.

I laughed in delight. "Brother-husband, I like that you will have to use it all the time."

"Yes, it has a certain comfortable ring. Will you stay here near our wife in case of a breakthrough. You can guard her in retreat. In a case like that, I may be too busy to watch over our wife closely."

"Most certainly, my brother-husband, my duty is to protect our love."

"Oh, well, said Will," I called from the platform.

Merlin laughed, then pointed as the first of the enemy broke from the tree line.

Orcs on wargs rode into the field about a hundred paces and stopped. Looking at the defenses, they waited.

I knew from that side how it looked, a shallow trench and dirt berm with a line of men standing on it. A shield wall of pikemen, and they may have seen a few more men behind through gaps in the formation.

The appearance of weakness should entice them to attack on a broad front.

More orcs began moving out of the trees filling the area and moving forward.

Young Jamie scrambled up to the platform between Merriam and Merlin. He pulled an abacus from his tabard and counted. Soon they stopped coming from the woods and just stood in an unruly mob.

"Just over thirty-one hundred, My Liege." He called in a crackling warble. He turned bright red in front of Merriam.

Merlin laughed and clapped him on the shoulder and said. "No worries, lad, your voice is starting to change, and it will settle into a deeper, more manly tone."

"Oh, dear." Laughed Merriam brightly. "The young ladies will be in trouble."

Jamie blushed even brighter and stammered. "Y...Yes, Milord and Lady." He then scrambled down from the platform.

Merlin then called down from the platform. "Duke, we are fortunate. Only about two hundred wargs in the army, and they will stay with the enemy through most of the charge. Only in the last fifty yards will they drive ahead in an attempt to leap over the front ranks."

"Excellent," I said. "I was hoping the wargs might try that from your description of these giant dogs, and I have prepared a surprise for them."

"Oh, how delightful." Sang Merriam. "I love surprises."

I laughed. "Not for you, my love but our guests."

"But if it is unpleasant for them, it must be nice for me."

"Put that way then, light-of-my-love. It will be a delightful surprise for you." I laughed.

"You say such nice things, husband making it hard to decide."

"Decide what?" I asked.

"Who will be last." She laughed.

Merlin laughed. "You are such a tease, Flama."

"I know, right." Her eyes sparkled.

Then there was a voice from the back of the orcs, and the enemy stomped forward two steps. Then the sing-song voice was heard again, and the orcs ran ahead ten steps and roared as one.

"No, worries," called Merlin. "They are psyching themselves up to attack. They think that Merriam, in her finery, is our Queen. This demonstration of intimidation will continue until they reach bow range. It may cause them to concentrate on the center."

"So they play into my hand," I said with a vicious grin. "Was that big fellow on the warg in the center their king?"

"Most likely grandson."

"Oh, that caught him, off-guard grandfather." Merriam giggled as I spluttered.

"Yes, I did." Merlin chuckled.

"Looks like they are getting close to the marker," said Merriam.

"There is a marker out there?" Asked Merlin with a raised brow.

"Yes, the small bush with the broken branch," Merriam pointed.

"Oh, yes, I would have never noticed that."

"That was the idea. The orcs will not notice it either, and they will make another pause just about ten paces from the marker."

Raising her bow, she got ready to pull. She pulled the bow about halfway and released it in one smooth motion. The orcs stopped and roared.

Everyone could hear the whistle fading as the arrow traveled the distance. At the top of the arc, it curved down point first into the ground twenty paces to the right of the bush.

The orcs yelled and laughed. A few arrows were fired from their side, reaching half the distance to the defensive line. Men on the line pounded their shields and laughed back.

An orc scurried out, grabbing the arrow. Bringing it back to the line and fumbling for a moment, it opened the message tube. The orc returned the message to the leader, handing it to him.

Merriam selected another arrow, checking it for straightness and tight fletchings.

The orc king began screaming in outrage. Drawing a huge curved sword, he hacked down the messenger.

"Well, that is about right," said Merlin. "Kill the messenger instead of the one who sent it."

"Now, my love?" Robyn called from his platform.

"Yes, now," Merriam called back.

CHAPTER

10

Merriam drew her bow back to her cheek, aimed, and released.

As her bow thrummed from the shot, twenty-five other bows fired as one.

Her aim was true, taking the orc king's left eye and knocking him from the saddle. He was dead before he hit the ground. Twenty-five other arrows struck, and twenty-five more leaders died. The wargs they rode went wild, attacking others, and orcs had to kill them.

With a roar, the orcs charged, and as one four hundred archers fired with a powerful thrum. The front rank of the orcs melted away at the onslaught, but they kept coming in a mindless rage.

In a perfect seamless cadence, the archers kept firing. They began aiming for the rear ranks carving them up. Each round of arrows brought their aim closer. The orcs kept coming in front, thinking they ran under the arrows. By the time they got too close for ranged fire from the archers on the ground, more than half were dead behind them.

The archers on the platforms continued firing as they could see over the ranks of men in front of them.

The hundred or so remaining wargs gained speed for their leap in front of the army. As they gathered their haunches to jump, they began stepping on the caltrops scattered in front of the defenses. Many wargs fell howling in pain, rolled over their riders, and further wounded themselves.

At a shouted order, men in front of the archers pulled on ropes. Large spears lifted from the ground and angled towards the leaping wargs. The spears impaled the wargs that managed to leap and became easy prey for the men in the rear.

The orcs had also reached the caltrops and began to go down. Many more made it past having to kill the wargs laying in front of them as they lashed out in pain at their masters.

The following line of defense was the shallow trench before the berm. A layer of burlap covered the real trap. The orcs found sharpened stakes in the bottom when they ran into the ditch. These took care of another row of attackers.

Finally, they reached the berm to find a tightly locked shield wall and men well-versed in using the pike. These are primarily a stabbing weapon thin enough to pierce openings in helmets and armor pieces. A spear of about four feet with a narrow blade and cross guard prevented enemies from running up the spear shaft.

In the center was Little-Jon standing head and shoulders above the soldiers. The blade of his battle-ax flashed in the waning light covered in gore. The orcs began to back away from him in fear.

I allowed this to continue for a few minutes calling up to Merlin.

"How many would you say are left?"

Merlin yelled back down over the din of battle. "I would say less than a third, Milord. Short of a thousand, the trench is starting to fill in."

"Thank you, Merlin. Jamie, the signal."

Jamie took the special arrow wrapped on the head soaked in oil. He handed the arrow to an archer. Once, he had knocked the arrow and drawn it. Jamie struck flint and steel to spark a light as the arrow began to catch. The archer aimed it at the sky and fired. The arrow glowed green and grew bright as it arced over the field.

The knights began to ride out. Cantering leisurely, the knights spread across the field by squadron behind the enemy. Turning in, they formed squadron wedges and began to pick up the pace. They were lining their formations up and moving as one. The knights lowered their lances and charged from a hundred paces at full gallop.

Some orcs turned at the sound and began screaming, but it was too late. Seconds later, the knights hit with a tremendous crash. They took two or even three orcs on their lances before dropping them. Then unsheathing their swords, they resumed the slaughter. The men on the berm stepped back, dropping their shields and pikes, and drew their swords. It allowed space for the billmen to attack, adding even more chaos to the enemy's ranks. After another ten minutes, the slaughter was over.

The men cheered their great victory, organized work parties, and cleaned up the bodies. Runners began reaching me from the flanks. Teams of men moved toward the castle as the reports came in. I smiled wider and wider as the king rode up, and I could contain myself no longer.

"Your Majesty, this is an incredible victory you have won today. Not one lost man. A hundred or so wounded are on their way to the hospital."

The king replied. "No, Duke Sherwood of Nottingham. It is your victory alone. Outnumbered, you have achieved something never seen before. Since William the Conqueror at the Battle of Hastings, such a victory has not been won."

Woodsmen went out to collect wood for fires. Other men loaded the bodies of orcs into wagons, and they piled them near the woods for burning. The men worked hard to clear the trench area immediately in front of the defenses. I then ordered half the men to rotate out for food. The chamberlain was to have the hall ready to feed many men.

The wind was light but steady from the west, making the battlefield the ideal place to burn the bodies. Soon great fires began to be lit as men began rotating for a hot meal. The first company, which was not engaged in the battle, sent out patrols on foot in the area, and these were only three-hour patrols.

When the second group of men returned to the castle for the food, we joined them. We all had good hot food and a couple of tankards of ale. We headed for the study after the last men returned to cleanup work.

We all sat around the fire as squires poured wine for everyone.

"A toast to the Duke of Sherwood. A fine victory, and may he have many more."

Everyone agreed and drank the toast.

I replied. "To the king without whose guidance, none of this would have been possible."

Everyone cheered at that, and we drank again.

The king said. "Now that that is out of the way, to business. There is much that needs doing. William, my friend, you will remain here to run things while the duke is gone. Who knows what other surprises are in store for us. I cannot be everywhere, so I must trust others. For the time being, those others will be your captains, Duke Sherwood.

Thank you for that trust, Your Majesty. As you have seen, my men are competent. Captain Jeffrey and Captain Goodson each have a signet like this one. I pointed to the ring on my right hand. Any reports we send will have this mark on the seal. Captain Jeffrey has one for you as well. We will only respond to orders with this mark unless you have handwritten them in front of one of our men. We have our system of couriers we will use for our orders. Any reports for you will be hand-delivered to Captain Jeffrey. He will give them to you in person to avoid the chance of alteration.

"That will be perfect, Duke Sherwood. No system is proof against tampering, and we can only do our best to make it so."

"I will be staying here, Your Majesty," said Sir William.

"And you will keep an eye on this area while the companions are on their mission. Too many things could go wrong to leave Captain Geoffrey in charge.

"I agree, Your Majesty," I said. "The Captain, with the Sergeant's assistance, is a capable military man. But I have not had time to break him in for domestic use."

Merriam giggled. "To be housebroken, the captain needs a suitable lady."

"Yes, I will see what develops here," Sir William said.

"Will Milady Sophia be staying here with you, Sir William?" I asked.

"Yes, she will. Her tasks are not complete, and there is something else she must do."

"That is good news because I understand there are three or four older Maids who would make good ladies-in-waiting."

Sir William said. "Excellent. She will have several companions to take under her wing."

"Merlin, can we expect more of these attacks?" Asked the King.

"I doubt it, Your Majesty. The attack today, I think, was an accident. At most, I suspect nuisance raids now. These orcs were more likely on the warpath and marched through a portal. There may be something from goblins as well, but less likely."

"Goblins?" I asked.

"Yes, they are smaller than orcs but more cunning. On the other hand, they are also more cowardly and easier to kill."

"Can we expect other races that will not wish to fight us? Because it would be nice if we could get some help as well."

"Oh, yes, Your Majesty, that is possible. You could see dwarves, elves, shifters, or even halflings."

There is even the possibility of dungeons popping up, and they could be a boon or a curse depending on the monsters that spawn.

"Dungeons?" The king asked with raised brows.

"Yes, Your Majesty, they can take many forms. Most are caves and have many levels, but their loot can be very lucrative."

"Lucrative? Loot?" Merriam perked right up.

Robyn chuckled. "Now, those are powerful magical words for Merriam."

Everyone else laughed.

"Well, we will just have to be on alert. We will respond to each crisis. However, we need to. I now have an early morning and a long day ahead, and I shall retire. Good night everyone."

We all stood and bowed to the king.

"Now, grandfather," Merriam said. "What about these dungeons? And how do we go about plundering them?"

Merlin laughed. "If any of them should appear, you would need to form a party."

"A party?"

"Yes. A group of like-minded individuals fights through the dungeon's monsters. A party generally consists of melee fighters and ranged fighters with bows or magic. A healer keeps the party healthy and rouge or ranger to detect traps and scout.

"So you are saying that we are an adventuring party?" I asked.

"This is precisely what I am saying."

"In general, though, it is best to form guilds."

"Guilds?" I asked.

Guilds serve two primary purposes. First of all, they organize and regulate adventuring parties. Secondly, they regulate the prices of loot and equipment. They will also set up quest boards. So merchants and others can post quests for specific items. These could be ingredients for potions, crafting materials, or killing a particularly nasty monster. They also keep track of adventurers' levels. Right now, our party would be at mid-level 'D.' By the time we finish this quest. We may reach level 'A' or higher. The levels go from 'F' at the low-end to 'A' at the top with an 'S' and 'SS' level. Monsters work in the same range. The Gremlins you fought would be an 'F'-class monster, whereas the orcs are 'D.' The wood troll and the manticore would be a high-'C' or low-'B.' I would place your army in the upper 'D' as far as skill and ability. It remains to be seen if we can check our levels. But we will learn that as time goes on. I will retire to my room for now and write some of this down. That way, the king can have a copy to take with him. It will at least give him some idea of what is popping up.

We all said goodnight to Merlin, followed by Friar Tuck, checking the injured.

"Well," said Sir William. "As Milady Sophia spends the night with the injured, I think I will head to bed myself."

Merriam giggled. "I will take my maids and get ready for bed myself. Jamie has set up a room for you to bathe in, and he will have laid out clean clothes for you. I will see you in about an hour or so."

"We will be there soon," we mumbled.

Merriam swept out of the room with her blushing maids behind her.

I groaned and said. "Milady might be the death of us before morning." The others grumbled out their assent.

Jamie then stuck his head in the door. "Milord's, I am here to show you your baths. You will have nice hot water, and I have also taken the liberty to set out a tankard of ale for each of you."

"Lead the way, Jamie. Hot water and cold ale sound perfect right about now."

The others quickly stood. We followed Jamie down a side corridor.

We stepped into a room and found four large tubs of steaming water with ale soap and washcloths nearby. And a bench with clothes and towels folded on them.

Stripping off our armor, Jamie said. "I will have your armor ready for you by morning, Milords."

"We can handle it from here. You may retire for the night."

"Yes, Milord's, good night."

We climbed into our tubs, groaning in delight. Picking up my tankard, I drank.

"That hits the spot." The others took drinks, agreeing.

"Now, Will this adventurers Guild. The Huntsman would be perfect for setting it up."

"That is a perfect idea, Guy. My crew would be ideal for that task. Most of the people in my group are basecamp-type people. The huntsmen's barracks would be an excellent base to build the guildhall by adding a forge, farriers, training yards, and armorer. Will and Jon will look into that tomorrow and get back to us. Jack Allen and Clarice are good administrators, and they used to keep our base camp running smooth and well-supplied."

"That would be excellent, Robyn. We could let Merriam be the guild leader and go adventuring in our spare time once this quest to destroy the orb is over.

We will see what we can set up in the next two weeks."

"Good," said Will. "There are other matters we need to deal with tonight."

"What would those be?" I inquired.

Grinning, Will said. "Maid Merriam for one. "And how we are going to work this brother husband thing."

"How do you mean?" Little-Jon asked.

I said. "First of all, there will be no titles among us, and we are Guy Robyn Will and Jon, the husbands of maid Merriam."

"Not after tonight." Robyn chuckled.

Jon Rumble a laugh. "I suppose at least one of us will get lucky."

"That was the point of my question."

"I think we will not have a say in that." Said Robyn. "That will be Merriam's choice, and we must respect it. The only way for this marriage to work is if we accept her rule of law."

I said. "I am sure there will be some give and take, and we will have arguments and disagreements. That goes without saying in a marriage between two people, never mind five. Whoever is leading has control at the moment. And I guess in the bedroom. It will be Merriam."

Jon said in his low rumble. "Will is trying to get at who gets her maidenhead, and the answer is Merriam will choose."

"It is, after all, not for us to decide."

Will said. "This is true, my brothers. I have had maidens, and the first time is the least pleasurable, no matter the passion. Even for the man, they can be so tight as to be uncomfortable."

"I have had a little experience with bought women," I said. "I found them to be less than satisfying."

"I know what you mean," said Robyn. "They are more focused on the coin than on your actions."

Jon rumbled. "Yes, unfortunately, that is very true. I would use my hand or seek a man for pleasure."

Will said. "A little goose grease can ease the passage, and men know what they like and reciprocate in kind."

"During my recovery, the attendants and I would exchange such services from time to time."

"Well, Jack or Allen and I have shared blankets occasionally." Said Jon.

"It is the way of the world. Priests say it is a sin, and yet they commit it themselves. My first time was as a choir boy." I said.

"This is true." Said Robyn.

"Not meaning to change the subject." I said, taking a drink. "But this is delicious ale and has a sweet fruity flavor."

Robyn laughed. "Oh yes, that is the brewers doing. He chops apples into the barrels before putting them up, and it is the finest ale for five hundred miles in any direction."

I said. "I do not think we will put the brewer to the torture as long as we can enjoy the fruits of his labor. And he has an heir to pass the skill on to."

The others laughed.

"I must leave this tub before falling asleep."

So saying, we all began washing up and climbing from our tubs to dry. Quickly stepping over to the benches, we began dressing.

Walking into the room, a servant said. "Good Milord's, you are out of the tubs. You may sit here, and I will shave you and fix your hair.

The servant then proceeded to groom their hair and shave them. Carefully he trimmed Jon's beard. Throwing our tunics on, we then headed for the duke's quarters.

CHAPTER

11

We came to our door, and I knocked softly.

One of the maids called just a moment, please.

It was a few moments until Alicia and Camila slipped out of the door closing it behind them, Alicia said. "Milady awaits within. Please enjoy your evening."

Blushing brightly, they both rushed off giggling.

Will said. "Those maids have such a vivid imagination."

The rest of us chuckled.

Robyn opened the door, and we filed in Will closing it behind us.

And we stood in line, frozen at the vision before us.

Merriam reclined on a chaise. Her glorious auburn hair brushed out, framing her face. Her left side rested against the raised end of the chaise, her typically emerald eyes a darker shade of jade.

A diaphanous gown of see-through white material covered her from neck to ankle. The shift blurred but did not hide the curves of her figure.

The light from the fire and the few candles cast highlights and shadows along her body, enhancing her lush figure. She grinned, eyes gleaming at the effect she had on our hose.

"Please join me, my loves, for tea before bed. There are a few things we need to discuss."

We moved to sit awkwardly in the seats artfully arranged to give us the best views of her reclining forum.

Clearing my voice twice, I stuttered. "Why, what do we need to discuss?"

"A few things, my love. You recall Sir William mentioning that he knew me a long time?"

"Yes."

Well, I first met Sir William as a young squire nearing his test for knighthood. That was some twenty years ago. You see, dear husbands, I am older than you may think, and there is a reason for that, which I will get into soon. Does any of this bother you, my loves?

A mix of mumbled no's head-shaking and shrugs answered her.

Good, she said. I am what is called a druid. We are not entirely human, but we are not immortal, and we live as long as we need to and remain healthy. Merlin has mentioned several times that he is thousands of years old.

Well, I am his granddaughter. My mother was his daughter, and I have lived for over three hundred years.

When Merlin found my grandmother and fell in love, he knew what would happen. My grandmother was mortal, and he could do nothing about it. My mother was born, and Merlin trained her and stayed until my grandmother passed. Once Merlin felt my mother's training was complete, he gave her this ring and left, pointing to the ring on her right hand. That was many years before I was born.

My mother then moved to another village. She met a blacksmith and married him a year later, and I was born. Knowing my father would not live as long as her, she stayed with him until the end.

We then moved on to another village some distance away. We became midwives, not staying in one place for more than a few years.

About fifty years ago, there was a disturbance in the earth. We both felt it, and my mother knew it was time for us to part ways. It was time for her tasks to begin. I have not seen or heard from her in all this time. But before we parted, she handed me this ring and told me I would feel the box move. I knew my time was coming when the king touched pandora's box. The part I did not realize was the prophecy. But I could also feel you four my husband's in my heart. I also know that my mother is still out there. I do not know where she is, but I can feel her.

"My love, how can you know these things?" I asked. "Are you some sort of seer like Sophia?"

"No, it is hard to explain what it is. It is like that feeling you get when someone is watching you. Like you know something is there, just not quite where."

"Okay," said Robyn. "I can understand that and relate to it."

The others nodded in agreement.

"You have power." Said Will. "Is it like Merlin you can shoot lightning bolts?"

Merriam laughed. "No, silly man, but I can do this." She flicked her finger at Will, and a small flame shot out and lit the candle beside him.

Will jerked and nearly upset his chair, gasping.

We all laughed, and Merriam said. "I do not have much control over it yet, but grandfather can teach me."

Jon said. "I hope so. That is a valuable skill to have."

"Yes, it would be." Said Robyn. "She can light Will's britches on fire if he misbehaves."

They all laughed, and I said. "Maybe, but Merriam could also light our campfires."

"Really?" She said. "Is that all the uses you can think of for me?"

Merriam then sat up, leaning forward to place her cup on the table. The move pushed her breasts against the thin material, and her nipples peaked as she saw our looks of lust.

"Time for bed," Merriam said in a husky voice as she stood up. Grinning, she reached up, pushing her hair back from her shoulders, which forced her breasts against the gown even tighter, and it also pulled the material back to display her lower stomach and triangle of hair on her mound.

Groaning, we stumbled to our feet. "Good Lord, woman, you test a man's restraint,"

"Something else you should know, my loves. While a virgin, I lost my maidenhead years ago riding horses. Also, I may not have that much experience; but I have run a brothel for fifteen years now."

Robyn and I ripped our tunics off with those words, casting them aside, exposing our erections, pushing out our hose.

As one, we wrapped an arm around Merriam's waist and palmed one of her breasts to a peak.

Merriam gasped as she felt the firm pressure of hands on her. She was looking at Will and Jon as they stripped utterly.

Robyn ran a hand up Merriam's back slowly. She shuddered as he found the first bow holding her gown closed and pulled it undone. Merriam shook inside as he moved his hand to the back of her neck, undoing the second bow. She groaned at the heat loss as we stepped away, pulling the gown from her shoulders and letting it fall to pool around her feet. Jon stepped forward, wrapping his arms around her waist. Each hand gently cupped her bottom and lifted her to wrap her legs around his waist.

She nuzzled her face into the base of his thick neck.

Jon turned, walking over to the giant bed. Will moved to the other side, and I joined him on this side as we turned the covers down.

Jon stepped onto the bed, laying Merriam in the center. He then began kissing her forehead, nose, cheeks, and lips down to the hollow at the base of her throat. Then continued down her breastbone to both sides to quickly lick and suck on her nipples. Then moving back to the center, he worked down her stomach.

Merriam was moaning and squirming the entire time. She briefly giggled and twitched as he tongued her belly button. He began working his way down toward her core. Gently caressing her inner thighs as he kissed and licked at her hips, he started kissing and licking her inner thighs. Merriam began to squirm, flushing with heat.

She gasped. "More, please."

Will kissed her, pushing his tongue out to dance with hers. She cried out, muffled by Will's mouth as Robyn and I began to lick and suckle at her breasts.

Merriam reached out to try and touch us. Her hands found my and Robyn's erections. Wrapping her hands around them, she began to stroke.

Then Jon pushed her thighs further apart, licking her wet heat from the bottom to top, flicking her clit at the end. Merriam screamed and bucked in orgasm from all the stimulation, and we groaned at the scent of her sweet release.

Circling her tight bud with his tongue, Jon began to push a finger into her vagina, gently sending shivers through her body. He drove the finger in slowly. As her vagina relaxed, Jon started rolling the finger around, loosening her up. Then he pulled back and began using two fingers. As she got used to that feeling, he began to scissor them, stretching her out even more.

By this time, she was again approaching climax. As John pulled back, he said, "she is ready. Who will be first?"

Will stopped kissing and caressing. "Who do you want first, my love?"

Merriam said. "All of you at once."

Will laugh gently. "You do not have enough openings, love."

"Then I will alternate in my mouth. Get on your back, Jon, and I will ride you. You can take my back passage, Will there is some of that lovely oil we use at the brothel in the bedside drawer."

Will crawled over to get it while Jon lay on his back. Robyn and I helped Merriam mount Jon. She grabbed his enormous shaft and positioned it at her opening. Taking his head in, Merriam groaned and slid down a little more. Jon grumbled and bit his lip, trying not to come from how tight she was. Merriam moved up and down a few times, grunting, getting the feel of being filled.

"Hold her steady, Jon, and I will lube her up." Jon wrapped his hands around her hips, supporting her. Will began to rub his oiled finger around her anus. Pouring more oil down her crevice, he began to push his middle finger against her ring. As Will pressed in, he told her to bear down. As she did, his finger popped in, and she grunted.

"I can stop moving if that hurts," Will said.

"It just burns a little and makes me feel full."

I have used this oil before." Said Will. "There is a bit of a numbing effect that should work as I add oil."

He then dribbled more oil on his finger and in her anus, working in and out. "That's it, love, it is getting easier, and I will put in a second finger."

She said. "That is starting to feel so good."

Will introduced the second finger, pumping in and out in a twisting, scissoring motion to loosen her hole. Within a few moments, she responded by thrusting back and moaning.

"You are ready now, my love." Palming some oil, Will spread it onto his shaft, making it slick. Inching forward, Will pressed the head to her opening. Inch by inch, pressing deeper until he was fully seated. Slowly sliding into her anus Will growled.

Merriam shook and shuddered the whole time. She hung her head, panting as we waited patiently. Soon Merriam began to wiggle and squeeze her anal and vaginal passages. Gasping, she looked up, eyes wide.

"Full."

"Move."

"Please."

Her mantra of one-word sentences caused us to smile. Slowly Will drew out. As he started to slide back in, Jon withdrew back and forth, alternating they began to speed up. Merriam grabbed Robyn and my shafts in both hands, pulling us up to reach them with her mouth as Will and Jon filled her passages with an alternating rhythm. She was licking and sucking Robyn and me. She would take one in her mouth for a few strokes, then the other. Using her lips to follow her hands up and down our cocks. She soon built up a good amount of saliva, so her hand slid easily.

We five quickly began to reach our peaks. As Will and Jon began to lose the rhythm and shake, she could feel all four cocks start to swell. She quickly pulled the heads of Robyn and me into her mouth, stretching it almost uncomfortably. She started stroking us hard. Jon reached down and pressed hard on her clit, feeling his imminent climax.

Merriam screamed, and we all climaxed together. She tried her best, but the two cocks spurting in her mouth were too much to handle. As sperm dribbled over her chin and neck, Merriam pulled back too soon, so a couple of shots from us landed across her breasts. She giggled at the mess and moaned as Will withdrew slowly from her anus. Will trotted to the washstand, grabbed a cloth, wetted it, and quickly cleaned himself.

Discarding his cloth, he grabbed four more and wet them. He handed one to each of us. We quickly wiped Merriam's breasts, neck, and face clean. Then we helped Merriam lay forward on Jon as Will gently wiped between her thighs and butt cheeks, cleaning her. Jon took advantage of having her lying on his chest and kissed her thoroughly while Will cleaned her.

We rolled her to the side, and Jon cleaned himself up, walked over, and dropped the cloths by the stand.

Robyn and I moved Merriam to the center of the bed and lay beside her, kissing her. Will leaned over Robyn and kissed all three of us as Merriam giggled. Jon came over and kissed us all, and she laughed outright.

Then she said. "That was the most wonderful stimulating, and exhausting thing I have ever done. Thank you for making me feel good and so loved."

"We are here to do nothing less than make you feel that way every day for the rest of our lives," Robyn replied.

"How do you feel about twenty children?" I asked.

I slowly became aware of the heat made by two walls of muscle. An arm was around me, and a calloused hand cupped my breast. Then I was aware that firm biceps supported my neck. This last caused me to wiggle as heat bloomed between my legs. That made me aware of something hard poking between my nether cheeks. And there was another hard poking in my lower belly. I felt two hands clasping my leg and hip as more awareness returned.

The erection in the back lined up as I squirmed, and I moaned softly. Suddenly a breath brushed my ear, a voice whispering, "lubricant love?"

I reached behind me, grasping the shaft at my back entrance, and Will poured oil over my hand and the cock. I spread oil over the entire length and put some into my opening. I pressed back, sliding the cock into my ass, sliding the other member down my belly, and bumping my clit. Moaning, I grabbed that shaft pressing it to my wet opening.

The snores of Robyn and Guy turned into groans as I squirmed on the tips of the shafts. My breath hitched, and I moaned louder as the two waking men pushed into me deeper.

I made my way to the washstand over behind the door. I nodded and winked at Jon as he sat up against the headboard. I got three washcloths ready for the cleanup. I turned towards the bed to watch the action, which had gotten much heavier. A knock came from the door beside me.

It opened before I could react, and Alicia and Camila walked in.

"Good morning Mi...eek." They both blushed bright red getting an eye full of the action. The men had Merriam's leg raised as both thrust hard into her lower openings.

Spinning around, they came face-to-face with me naked and fully erect, holding washcloths. They both squeaked and fled the room, slamming the door.

Jon and I, who had sat up by this time watching and stroking his erection, laughed. The other three wrapped up in their lust and moaning, never even noticed.

I got back to the bed as the three cried out in orgasm. The two men caressed Merriam for a moment to catch their breath and hearts to slow down. Rolling way, taking a cloth each, they cleaned themselves and got up.

I got on the bed, lifting Merriam's leg as she had not moved from her side. I cleaned between her legs and the cheeks of her sweet behind. She smiled and moaned, wiggling a bit as I cleaned her up.

Smiling and following me as I left the bed to return the cloth to the dirty hamper, she sat on the bed's end. When I turned to walk back, Merriam giggled at the sight of my shaft bobbing and weaving while I walked. Grinning widely, I asked. "See something you like, my love?"

"I most assuredly do, my husband. It is staring right at me." She then dropped to her knees in front of me. She licked me from bottom to tip, grasping my shaft at the base. Merriam took my rod into her mouth, rising on her knees for better balance, and this presented her delectable rear in a position Jon could not resist.

Stepping behind her, he dropped to his knees, pushing into her dripping vagina. Merriam moaning around my shaft almost caused me to lose my load. I carded my fingers into her hair to hold her head still so I would not finish too soon. Once Jon entered her fully, he nodded to me. I moved back so the tip of my cock was in her mouth. I then placed her hands on my thighs. I pulled her mouth down my shaft as Jon pushed her off his. When her nose touched my pubes, Jon pulled her back onto his shaft and off mine.

She hummed as she caught the idea pushing forward onto me and then back onto Jon. Backward and forward, she soon found the rhythm. She began to speed up, slamming back and forth as fast as possible. Suddenly she pounded back on Jon, and clenching her climax erupted. That set Jon off as he sprayed into her womb. Screaming around my shaft in her mouth, she pushed forward on my length, setting me off. I exploded into the back of her throat, and she began swallowing as quickly as she could, licking me until my softening shaft was clean.

Robyn stepped before her, wiping her face with a clean cloth. Guy handed Jon a cloth to clean himself and bent over to wipe between Merriam's legs. He took care to be gentle around her still quivering, sensitive opening.

Merriam moaned at the level of after-care she was receiving. Robyn and Guy helped her sit on the bed while Jon and I put on our clothes and slipped our boots on. With all four of us dressed. Guy said. "We will send in your maids and meet you in the library for breakfast."

I snickered, and Jon rumbled with laughter. "If they have stopped running and are not too embarrassed to come back after what they saw earlier."

Merriam asked. "Whatever do you mean?"

"Well." I snickered. "The girls walked in as you were on the bed, leg in the air with those two buried balls deep. Jon was sitting watching, stroking his staff, and I got washcloths. So as they turned away, they also got a perfect look at me. Then they both bolted from the room."

Robyn and Guy looked sheepish as Merriam threw her hands over her face blushing bright red.

Jon and I laughed and again headed for the door.

I pulled the door open, and Alicia's hand in the air was about to knock. She screeched and covered her eyes. Then I noticed Camila behind her, also covering her eyes.

Quivering, Alicia asked. "Is it safe?"

"Yes, my dear." Said the Duke. "Milady awaits your assistance."

We headed for the study, flagging down a servant to order breakfast.

We met the king, Sir William, and Sophia at the door to the study. We all made our greetings and went inside to await breakfast.

CHAPTER

12

Where is Milady Merriam?" The king inquired?

"She will be along shortly, Your Majesty. Her maids are getting her ready."

Sophia giggled. "Rose mentioned the girls running back to the room and saying they saw something."

Robyn and I blushed as Will laughed.

Will said. "Yes, they walked in as the three engaged in amorous activities.

The others laughed as the king said. "It must have been a sight to behold."

"Yes." Said Will. "It was from my point of view. I was standing behind the door, almost beside them, when they walked in."

"Oh, the poor dears." Laughed Sophia, tears running down her face.

"I would bet they were terrified." Laughed Sir William rubbing his chin.

Jon chuckled. "I am sure they will have some memories to keep them warm on cold winter nights."

Soon after, Merriam arrived, and on her heels were Merlin and Friar Tuck.

A couple of servants bearing trays with platters of food and drink came almost right behind them.

"Merriam, how were your maids this morning?" Asked Sophia.

Merriam blushed, giggling. "Somewhat flustered Sophia, doing their best to take it in stride. I will have a long talk with them later."

Everybody chuckled at that.

"You are still leaving, Your Majesty?" I inquired with some concern in my voice.

"I am afraid I must." The king said. "I need to recall the levees, so you have troops to train. I can only do that from Cambridge."

Times have changed. England needs a standing army of well-trained men with competent leaders. Despite what they think, a patent of nobility is no measure of one's skill or intelligence.

"Which reminds me. I want that sergeant that came up with that brilliant idea with the spears yesterday."

"Your Majesty," I said. "He is the second sergeant in the company you are taking, so you already have him. Do not break him, as he is an outstanding soldier."

"Oh, I do not intend to harm him." Said, King Lionel. "However, the nobility may not agree, and they may wish to take his life."

"There should be no problem in that case. Sergeant Stone should be able to reduce the expense of paying many useless popinjays." I laughed.

"Well said, Duke Sherwood." The king laughed. Everyone joined in the humor.

"I do not deny that it may sound humorous, but he is a brilliant tactical fighter."

"Good. I may need the sergeant's services."

"As I say, Your Majesty give him your thoughts and turn him loose. You will be thrilled with the results."

"Well." Said the king. "I have enjoyed my time here, and the conversation, the food, and the combat have been most stimulating. But I believe I can not leave the court in Cambridge waiting in good conscience."

"Yes, that is probably true," said Sir William.

"Come on, my old friend, and we will share some last few thoughts as you walk me to my horse."

The king walked out with Sir William, their heads close together, speaking quietly.

Robyn asked me why Sir William stayed here rather than helping the king build his army.

"Because Robyn Nottingham is where we are building the army. The companies we are sending out will train here as they twin."

We folded the regent's men into the third company. When the second company gets to Cambridge, they will send three hundred here to complete the third's twining

Each time the king sends us five hundred fifty men, we will twin another company. They will then begin training as one unit for three months and split and train as separate companies for another three months.

Do not say anything yet, but I have a plan within this plan to help Sir William.

We will not be here for the start, but supplies are coming from all over England to Nottingham. We will send the first two companies to Derby. You, Robyn, will be the commander of that battalion. As we recruit each company in this first battalion, it will move out to my baronies. But that is something we need not concern ourselves with right now.

I already think we will change unit structures, and the current company sizes are too bulky for peacetime purposes. I will have to work that out later.

"In any case, we will see about getting a start on building your castle and the manor house."

"That would be good. It would be nice to have a home to go to when I eventually make it to Derby."

Stepping into the courtyard, we saw second company formed up and ready to move out.

At the top of the stairs, the king took Merriam's hand, brushed a kiss over her knuckles, smiled, and said. "You have been a most gracious and exquisite hostess Milady. Your display of prowess with the bow is legendary."

"Thank you, Your Majesty," Merriam said, blushing and curtsying deeply. "You have been a wonderful and entertaining guest. Please do come again anytime we are home, of course."

The king chuckled and shook everyone else's hand. He stopped at Sir William. "Try and stick with the plan this time, old friend. I do not think my heart could take any more deviations."

Sir William chuckled. "I will do my best, Your Majesty."

Reaching Sophia last, he took her hand, bowing and brushing his lips over her knuckles. "I hope your visions will show us the way clear soon." Then leaning in, he whispered something in her ear.

Sophia giggled and said. "Soon, Your Majesty, very soon."

Sir William cocked his eyebrow. "And what are you up to now, Your Majesty?"

"All in good time, old friend, all in good time." The king turned, marching down the stairs, and mounted his charger. Waving, he turned and headed for the gate.

A squadron of knights wearing the king's tabard rode in front to lead the column through the gate. The rest of the company, in close marching formation, followed behind.

Once the tailing squadron of knights passed through the gate, the companions turned and headed back inside.

Sir-William said. "Let us head back to the study, and we can talk there."

We all moved up to the study and gathered around the long table with maps.

Sir William asked. "How do we determine what you will need for this mission?"

"Do we know where we are going?" Asked Robyn.

Merlin said, "only in the broadest sense of the word."

The orb Is moving, although I still understand the direction. There is no way for me to determine the distance. We will need to be a lot closer for me to get a sense of how far we may be. We will need gold to purchase supplies, as there is no way we will be able to carry everything we need. Horses at the very least because this will be a very long trip."

"How long do you think it might be, grandfather?" Asked Merriam.

"Do not plan on being home for a year or more. We will likely be back in the holy land before this is over, and potentially we could go even further."

"That does not sound too promising," I said. "You sure this thing will not settle down sooner?"

"Anything is possible," Merlin said. It will be working its way towards an energy source. While it has much power, it will need to feed off the earth's energy to keep the portals open. It went to Stonehenge first but did not stay there long. Then it moved over to Normandy, where the ancient stones are there. After that, it moved north before heading south again. It was too far for me to tell if it was moving east or not. Now all I can say is that way.

We will need food for the road, possibly tents to set up a camp. Likely a couple of pack animals to carry that equipment. We should also take sufficient gold to buy more food and stay in town's inns. What it comes down to is what we need to carry. That will be our clothes and weapons, which could be a problem. Arrows for your bows will be few and far between.

"Robyn and I can make our arrows as needed," Merriam said. "We need to carry spare arrowheads and fletchings, is all."

"Is there anything special you will need, Will?"

"No, I am good. With my knives and my short swords, I also use the bow. That will help with ranged weapons and also being a rogue. I am better at hunting than most. That will help with food on the road."

"We should be all right for moving. The less we have to carry, the better. Gold is more valuable than tons of supplies at this point. Then two extra quivers of arrows should be sufficient for each of you. Monsters will be more problems than people, and towns and villages will be safer than wilderness areas."

"What about you, Jon anything you need?"

"A good whetstone, my ax, and shield are all I need."

"The same for me," I said. "I will not take my heavy armor but my leathers. The heavier armor is a liability for most of these monster attacks."

"I disagree." Said Merlin. "You will be our tank drawing the fighters and monsters we encounter. You may want to carry a couple of lances if we run across some bigger monsters."

"Yes, that is probably a good idea. With spare tips, I can make more anytime. But what is a tank?"

"A heavy front-line fighter able to take and deal damage. Jon will also fill that role at your side."

"Well, I can use the lance." Said Robyn. "Perhaps we should carry two, just for safety sake. I should not need my ranged weapon without warning, which will work out okay. My sword is perfect for melee in case we get ambushed."

"Yes, most of our problems will be during travel." Said Merlin.

Sir William said. "So the next question is when you want to leave?"

I thought for a moment, rubbing my nose, and said. "A week or two, at most. That will give me time to set up things here at the castle. I would not, after all, wish to leave you with all the work Sir William."

"I suppose it will give you a chance to know your people, Sir Guy."

"I am afraid, Robyn, we will not have much chance to set up your barony."

"It is just as well, Guy. I would not want to walk away leaving a job half-finished, and besides, Derby has been operating well enough without a baron until now."

Sir William chuckled. "True enough, I suppose. I will see what I can do to get things organized for you. I will have some men sent out to survey the lands around Derby, and they can perhaps select a few locations for the castle. I assume you will want the manor house in town or nearby?"

Actually, no, Sir William, on the eastern side of town, north of the road, a large rocky hill may be a good location for the castle. To the southwest of the town is a scrub forest with a sizeable stream and lake. Forresters can cut the trees for firewood to clear the land. It would be a good location for the manor house and fields for horses and cattle. There is a bit of higher ground on the north side of the lake to build the house. The land is relatively rocky, so I suspect why the trees do not grow there so well.

"I suggest we split up and go do our things. We can then reconvene at lunch to make further plans."

"Merriam, you should go meet with the staff of the castle. Get to know them and see what they need."

"That is a beautiful idea, my love. Sophia and I can also look into the winter stores; we will know what else is needed."

"A good plan, my love. I will also be meeting with the treasurer Digby and the town Elders."

"Will, you and Jon should check up on your barracks and people. They must have everything they need to survive the winter and function while we are gone."

"Yes," Will said. "Jack and Allen should be back now. We may be the rest of the day or longer, so do not wait up for us."

I chuckled. "You are not children and do not have a curfew."

Will and Jon laughed as they went out the door. I stood kissing Merriam on the cheek. "Until later, my dear."

CHAPTER

Merlin followed me into the hall and said. "I will accompany you as I may have some ideas or insights that help."

"Thank you, Merlin. I will welcome your company."

As we walked toward the treasury, the ladies and their maids followed behind in a cluster, whispering and giggling as they headed for the back of the castle.

I grumbled as we headed downstairs. "That sounded rather ominous."

Merlin laughed. "I have visions of lacey curtains and doilies all over."

"God's, I hope not." I groaned. "Nottingham is a castle built for war, not a bordello."

Entering the strongroom, we could hear the clink of someone counting coins. I spotted Digby behind a table full of stacks of gold coins.

Digby quickly stood and bowed.

"Rise, Digby." I chuckled. "There is no need for that when we are alone."

"Yes, Milord." He said quietly.

"So, how goes the treasury count?" I asked.

Well, Milord, I was double-checking the counts and recounting a few bags of coins for accuracy. I have found that you have five hundred thousand crowns in gold and silver coins. Another hundred bars of gold are in that corner, pointing to the back left. Then pointing to the right, he said. We have two hundred bars of silver, which would come to an additional two hundred thousand crowns. The next room has numerous gold and silver serving sets in crates. I have also found two casks of all different types of jewels. It will take some time to put a value on. It may take weeks to sort and catalog them.

I held up my hand, bringing Digby to a stop. "So what you are saying is the Sherriff has been pillaging the land for some time?"

"It would appear to be the case, Your Grace. I have ledgers of taxes, extortions, and thefts performed by this man."

"Very well, Digby, I want a list of all taxes paid by our people and what that rate was. I want to know how much they should have paid in the next column. In the final column, list the difference that we owe them. I am sure some are dead or gone, and we will never find them, but we should pay their families if they had any. Then we shall see what we have left."

"This will take some time, Milord, and I will likely have to hire some helpers."

Merlin hummed. "If I may make a suggestion, Milord. You have a few idle squires hanging about that could use this experience."

"That would be most helpful, Your Grace."

"That is a capital idea, Merlin. Digby, give Merlin a purse of two hundred crowns, as he will need to purchase personal items for our quest."

"Oh, and before I forget, have a purse put together for Milady. Two hundred crowns should do, as I am sure she will want to do some shopping."

"Thank you, Sir Guy. It is challenging to buy things I need if I do not have the currency. I appreciate that." Said Merlin.

I chuckled. "You are family, and you have been most helpful. But one should have some coin to spend."

"Now about this other stuff, jewelry trinkets, whatever. Is there any way to identify where they came from or to whom they belong?"

"I will bring in the town jeweler, Your Grace. Some of the items may have makers marks on them, and we may trace where they belong. As for the loose gems, I think the Sherriff may have been taking apart jewelry and melting down the gold and silver for bars."

"In that case, I may go through and pick some out later. Then I can talk to the jeweler about making some trinkets for Milady."

"I will speak with the jeweler, Your Grace when I see him. Perhaps he will have some ideas for Milady."

"That is an excellent idea, Digby. I will let you handle that."

"I have another idea for you as well."

"What is that?"

"Gems have great value, but they are not a very functional currency. You have gold and silver bars for settings and large quantities of gems with no settings."

"Ah, I see putting those two together with a jeweler, and we would both gain a great deal of profit."

"Exactly," Merlin said. "Digby and the jeweler could work out commissions for each piece and sell them for your profit."

"I will speak with the jeweler in a couple of days. Digby, you can set that meeting up for us. I do not think there is any hurry as we have abundant coins to work with now."

"Yes, Your Grace, as you say, you have enough coin now. For the time being, I will just have the jeweler sort the gems, and he can put an estimated value on each type."

"Yes, that will work nicely," I said. "I will speak with you again later, Digby."

"Yes, Your Grace, good day to you for now."

Heading back up to the entryway, Merlin and I stepped into the courtyard just as a messenger rode in on a lathered horse.

Seeing me, the messenger lept off his horse before me and saluted.

"Milord a message packet from Derby."

"Thank you, where is your escort?"

"They are coming along behind me, Milord. A couple of the men are injured and moving at a slower pace. We had just gotten to the treeline when I rode ahead."

"Very well, go get some food and ask Captain Geoffrey and Sergeant Thomas to attend me in the study."

"All right, Merlin, let us head back upstairs and see what new disaster awaits."

"Yes, this could be interesting," Merlin replied.

Entering the study, Merlin and I went to the map table. Robyn and Sir William looked up from the desk.

"Something wrong there?"

"Maybe," I replied, using a knife to open the packet.

I then began reading the dispatches.

Grunting, I began looking at the map tracing my finger over the route to Derby. I said, pointing. "That is where the company we sent to Derby ran into an ambush. Here, where the road forks northwest is the route to Manchester, and the west road goes to Derby. Some monsters have set up a fort and charge people tolls to move through the area."

"What kind of monster?" Asked Merlin with an amused glint in his eyes.

They are between four and five feet tall and just as broad with a long beard. The report says they are incredibly belligerent.

Merlin laughed. "Dwarves are miners. They deal in weapons, armor, and other metal-crafted items. They think it is their territory, and everyone must either pay a toll to pass or trade with them."

"Then that explains this next part."

Captain Anders reported he spoke with the leader of the dwarves and reached an amicable agreement. The dwarfs will recognize the king and rank structure of the land if they get the right to form a mining guild.

Merlin chuckled. "Yes, they are rough but fair and the finest metalsmiths in any realm."

"I will need to ride up there and discuss agreements with their leader."

"Oh, hell." Merlin blurted out.

With dwarves out there, chances are you may find elves. They average about six feet tall, male and female, with long pointed ears. They will appear to you when they are ready. Elves are consummate scouts and wood-crafters, and you will never spot them or find a trace of them unless they let you.

"Damn, I best warn Will and Little-Jon."

"Yes, they must warn their men to be careful."

Sir William spoke up. "I had best get writing some dispatches for the king then."

"The question becomes what other creatures may we run into in the next while?"

"Anything from gnomes to dragons, I would think." Said Merlin.

"Oh, joy." Said, Sir William. "Dragons, you say?"

Dragons are not as evil as you might think. They are thoughtful and intelligent and hoard shiny things like gold and gems. But for the most part, they trade in information. Cultivating good relations with dragons is the best idea as they are almost impossible to kill.

"What about Gnomes?" I asked.

Gnomes are not bad for merchants. They are uncanny at getting the best deals. They also make great servants and innkeepers. They are very diligent and clean people. If you hire one, you get the whole family, consisting of up to twenty gnomes.

A knock at the door heralded Captain Geoffrey and Sergeant Thomas entering. "You asked to see us, Milords?"

"Yes," I said. "We will need a team to run dispatches to the king as soon as Sir William writes them. I will also need a platoon ready to ride with me within the hour. Make it Sergeant Boils and another squad with a squad of knights. We will need equipment and rations for a week. I do not anticipate being that long, but you never know. What else might we need, Merlin?"

"Does the dispatch say how big the clan is?"

"Yes, three hundred Dwarves and half as many wives and children."

"Okay, ten barrels of ale, vegetables, flour salt, and some cattle and sheep."

Right, that changes things, Captain. We will need a hundred men for the escort with the supplies. Robyn and I will be leading twenty knights and archers the balance in pikemen in their night fighting gear. We will be leaving in the morning as it will take some time to gather these supplies. Send some men out to purchase the cattle and sheep. Make sure they have at least one ram and one bull. I will speak with the chamberlain about the other items.

"Yes, Milord." The captain and sergeant saluted and left.

"Merlin, you should stay here and help Sir William with his dispatches and the descriptions for the people the king may encounter."

"Great, I can do that."

"I will be back shortly."

Leaving the study, I headed downstairs toward the back of the castle. I turned in the direction of the kitchen and saw the chamberlain coming from a side passage.

"Denby, just the man I am looking for."

"Yes, my liege, how may I help?"

"I need to put together some supplies for a mission. I hope we can purchase what we do not have on hand from the town."

"What is it you need, my Lord."

"I need staples for about five hundred people for one month, maybe two if we can do it. So we are talking flour, salt, vegetables, spices, perhaps some bolts of cloth and things like that."

"Yes, my liege, we can supply most of what you need to start a small village out of the castle supplies. I can add a few casks of salt, beef and pork, beans, and dried fruit and oats to make gruel. We also have some heavy wool for winter clothes and blankets."

"Perfect, you may start loading those supplies into wagons. The expedition will be leaving in the morning."

Denby bowed and said. "At once, my liege."

Denby called for people as he headed for the storeroom.

Meriam came up from the kitchens at that moment. "What is all the commotion about, my love?"

"We have some new tenants in our dukedom."

"Oh, my, who are they?" She asked as she leaned in and gave me a peck on the cheek.

I replied. "Dwarves are a guild of miners and smiths, and they seem to wish to fit in with our kingdom."

"Marvelous, we must help them. I will go pack, so we are ready to leave as soon as possible."

"Hold up, my love. I plan to leave in the morning. I will lead the expedition as I need to make trade agreements with them."

Meriam covered my lips. "Hush, my love, you will need me along as I have much experience with trade. But I also wish to meet these people; they will be mine."

"Very well, my love, you may come along. Denby is working on getting the supplies together, and my men are purchasing sheep and cattle."

"Good, I shall go start packing. Come, Alicia and Camila, we must hurry."

I shook my head as the ladies rushed off to pack and headed for the study.

Entering, I found Robyn, Will, and Jon looking at the map. Merlin and Sir William were over at the desk writing dispatches.

Will looked up as I entered. "What is this about dwarves?"

"The troops I sent to Derby ran into a group of dwarves camped on the Manchester crossroad. They are miners and wish to open trade and join the dukedom. We are leading an expedition to negotiate and bring supplies to them."

Will chuckled. "If Merriam hears of this, she will take over the whole mission."

I laughed. "Merriam already accosted me when speaking to Denby about the supplies."

"So I presume she is coming?" Asked Robyn.

"Yes, I could not stop her."

"We will need to provide guards for her." Rumbled Little-Jon shaking his head.

"I will have a hundred men with me as an escort."

"We should bring Allen and a few men," said Will.

"Let us not get carried away here, as we must leave some people here if something happens."

"I will be here." Said, Sir William. "It will be an excellent short-term test for when you leave on your mission."

"I will leave some orders with Jack and the rest of our people. Then I can go pack," said Will.

"You know we will only be gone three or four days."

"You can believe that if you want, but I will not."

Sophia swept into the room with Rose and Mary on her heels. "Bring lots of arrows. You will need them to complete the mission."

I groaned. "How? Never mind, you have had a vision."

"Yes, of a battle to protect these people. It will secure your agreement, and it will also add more benefits than you may expect. Bring the cleric. They will need his services."

"That sounds somewhat ominous," said Will.

"Not too bad." Said Sophia. "I only see a few injured men. But I do see many sick children."

"Right, I guess we better get packed."

"I will let the Friar know."

"Thank you, Merlin."

The men left the room, leaving Sir William and Sophia alone.

"Is this another test?"

"Somewhat," said Sophia. "It is more of a side quest to prepare them for the journey, and it will give them a chance to work together. The warriors will learn how well she can lead, and Merriam will also find a new skill."

"Should we tell them?"

"No, it is something they must discover for themselves."

"Well, I have these dispatches done for the king." Sir William said as he pressed his seal into the wax.

"Edwin," Sir William called.

"Yes, Milord." He said, coming from the side room.

"Take this message packet and hand it to the riders waiting outside. Tell them these are for the king posthaste."

"Yes, Milord." Edwin took the package and ran from the room.

CHAPTER

14

Dawn had begun with a pewter glow as I awoke to a knock on my door.

"Good morning, Milady." Said Alicia as she opened the curtains.

"It will be a fine warm day." Camila followed up.

"Where are my husbands at this ungodly hour?"

"They see to breakfast Milady, among other things."

"Here are some clothes they suggest you wear. Although I do not think they are fitting for a lady of your station."

Stepping out from the privy, I saw the clothes laid out for me.

"Yes, well, I will be riding all day, and there is a possibility of a fight, and I will need to be ready in that case."

Pulling the blouse over my head and slipping into the breaches, I tucked the shirt in. I noticed the thighs had hard patches sewn into them. I then pulled on the boots and laced them up. The heavy leather would protect my lower legs and feet. Next, I picked up a heavy leather vest. As I put it on, I noticed it was reinforced like the men's leather armor.

"I am going to be like a turtle in this thing."

Alicia giggled. "I had heard they wanted to put you in plate and chainmail."

Merriam giggled. "This will be hard enough to move in. I do like the bracers with arm guards built into them. And what is this? Special gloves for archery? These will be just perfect."

"As you say, Milady. You should get some breakfast before the men eat it all."

Stepping to a cupboard, I opened the door and pulled out my swords, slipping the harness over my shoulders, hooking the clasp between my breasts. I then pulled out my bow case and quiver of arrows and headed for the study.

Striding down the hall, I smiled as the guard's eyes bulged at my sight. They fumbled to open the doors quickly.

Thanking the guards, I walked into the room. I was a vision of deadly grace.

Sophia giggled as the men's conversation stumbled to a stop.

"Well, the armorer certainly got the measurements right for you." Said Sophia.

"The fit is perfect, and they are comfortable."

Robyn growled. "We are in trouble."

My face lit with a dazzling smile as I came over and kissed each of my husbands.

Sitting down, I proceeded to fill a plate. "Everything looks delicious this morning."

Sir William chuckled. "The last good meal before the road always tastes best."

Breakfast passed quickly with nothing but inconsequential chatter. Once we finished, we headed down to the courtyard.

Guy turned to Sir William. "Keep an eye on things here while I am gone. I do not expect any problems, but you never know."

"I am sure we will be fine here with most of four companies of troops in the area. Are you sure you do not want to take more men?"

"Not with me, no, we will not be moving that fast. Please send the third company along behind us. Wait half a day, then send them. They should catch up just about the time we arrive."

"Then it will be as you ask." Sir William replied.

Clasping forearms with Sir William, I turned and mounted my horse. I headed for the gate with the companions and the rest of the formation following. We met with the men herding the animals at the edge of town. Slowing to the pace of the animals, we moved on.

We had fended off three separate attacks by packs of wolves without loss by midday. I said. "This is becoming very annoying. We should not be getting these attacks."

Merlin replied. "It is most unusual. Something is driving them into us, and some larger force has been pushing them away from their claimed territory."

I called out. "I want five scouts ranging out to the north and west of us. Will, we will use your woodsman for this task."

"I will go as well." Said Merriam. "I have more speed and better stealth."

"How can we possibly protect you, my love. You need to stay with the formation."

Merriam laughed gayly. "I have been running alone in these woods longer than you have been alive. Trust me, I know what I am doing."

I gave a long-suffering sigh. "Very well, Milady, try to stay close to Will."

Robyn said. "I will take a few more men and range to the south. It may be they are trying to distract us."

"Good idea, Robyn," I said. "That is a genuine possibility. Meanwhile, we will take a short break to let you get ahead and then press on."

After a short break, the column resumed the march. Soon one of the scouts from the north trotted out of the woods in front of us.

I held up my hand for a stop.

The scout said. "Milord, we have a problem. There is a large group of what Milady calls goblins to the north. We cannot get an exact number as they are widely scattered, and there are at least a couple hundred. Milady sent me to let you know she is bending to the south to see how far they stretch."

Merlin said. "Goblins are not very good fighters and are generally poorly armed and disorganized. However, the numbers suggest they have a large village nearby or are trying to build one. They tend to be thieves and raiders and prefer fighting from ambush rather than storming an enemy."

"Thank you, Merlin," I said. "Sergeant Thomas, I want half the archers behind the knights and the rest down the column. Keep an eye on the trees overhead. Move out."

Minutes later, scouts appeared from both the north and south side of the road. Once again, halting the column, I prepared to receive the report.

The scout from the south reported first. "There are very few goblins to the south Milord, and they are in small parties likely hunting. However, a group of about twenty are preparing an ambush up the road from here."

The scout from the north then reported.

"Indeed, Milord, the same thing can be seen from the north. Although the bulk of the goblins is advancing toward the dwarven encampment."

"What are they using to block the road?" I asked.

The scout replied. "They have set up a gate consisting of a pole across the road. It is only the thickness of a lance, and one of the chargers could ride through it without even slowing."

All right, then you men call in your scout teams. We will crash the gate and rush through to the dwarven camp. At the same time, we wait for the scouts to return. Sergeant Thomas, please form your men around the herd animals to push them along. Four archers in each wagon, the rest spread along the column for cover. Captain, use your squires as mounted guards for the column, and they can assist with protecting the animals.

You, captain, will not be able to move slow enough, so I want you to charge through any barricades on the road. You can clear the rest of the way for us, and you may inform the dwarves of the impending attack and help prepare the defenses. It is not that far, so we should be close behind. Here come the scouts. Everyone be ready in ten minutes.

"How did it look out there?" I asked as Merriam ran up.

Merriam chuckled. "I could wipe them out myself if I had the arrows. They have no discipline or formation. They are like an unruly mob of children running in and out of the trees. The direction does tend towards the dwarven camp. Beyond the gate, they have erected between here and the dwarven base. Goblins do not pay much attention to what is behind them."

Merlin chuckled. "Typical, goblins have no real sense of danger. They are very primitive and tend to follow whichever one is loudest or strongest."

I said. "Right, then we will drive through before the goblins get organized. Captain, you may begin your charge."

The ambush proved no deterrent for the knights. The following forces of companions and archers finished off the remaining goblins.

The column moved down the road at a steady trot. Archers took out the goblins we faced along the way. Thirty minutes later, the column broke from the tree line to see a beehive of activity at the dwarven camp. The knights had formed their horses, one squadron on each side of the open gate.

Beside the captain was a man with a beard down to his waist. He was perhaps five ft tall and just as broad. He had an intricately decorated breastplate over a chain mail shirt that fell nearly to his knees. On his head was an open-face helmet with a pair of horns on top. He had a massive battleax slung over one shoulder.

I pulled to the side with the companions and directed the column through the gate. I dismounted and approached the captain and dwarf.

"I see you had no trouble getting here. Introduce your new friend if you please." I raised an eyebrow at the tankards in their hands.

"Yes, Milord, this is Clan Chief Dworkin. He leads these people and cares for them."

"Dworkin, this is Sir Guy Sherwood, Duke of Nottingham and defender of the realm." The dwarf bowed low enough that his beard touched the ground.

"Dworkin," I said, holding out my hand. "You do not need to bow to me."

"Nae, you are great lord. Dworkin needs show respect. You help will take knee before you. We pledge our might and skill to you. Drink are we, then fight goblin. Bond of drink blood and war. Excuse common talk is rusty, not use much."

"Very well," I said. "We will drink, and we will talk about your needs. But, first, my wife Merriam and brother-husbands baron Robyn,

Will Scarlet, and Little-Jon. Merlin the magician and Friar Tuck, our cleric, are with us."

"Pleased to meet you all. Come to board for ale and meat." The clan chief led them through the gate to a longhouse with a table full of food and tankards of ale.

"Now, this is my kind of hospitality." Said Friar Tuck.

Will snickered. "Food and ale are always your kinds of hospitality."

"Your cleric has the right of it." Said Dworkin. "He will need some strength as we have many sick among our clan. Drink, eat, and you can see them soon."

"Why do you have so many sick?" Asked Tuck.

A sad tale. We hit sour gas in our mine, and many miners got sick, and some died in the mine. The gas spread, and we had to abandon our town. We were marching to elves to find healers, and poof, here we are.

Friar Tuck said. "This can not wait. I must see them now."

Dworkin pointed to a dwarf. "Follow him he will show you the way."

The rest of us companions sat at the table and began eating and drinking. Turning back to Dworkin, I asked. "What else can we do for you?"

"Help with food is good. We are craftsmen, not farmers, so we trade for things we need. We get the food, and, in exchange, you get better armor and weapons. We can also make pretty baubles to please your woman."

"Baubles? As in jewelry?" Asked Merriam.

Robyn laughed. "Possibly the only thing that would take her mind off food."

"First, a demonstration. I need a set of your armor that is spare."

I turned to Sergeant Thomas. "A set of spare knight's armor and infantry armor."

"Yes, Milord." Sergeant Thomas hurried out. A few minutes later, he returned with the spare armor.

Dworkin took the armor and hung them on a stand. "Sergeant Thomas, strike each piece with your sword." The Sergeant caused some damage and much less to the breastplate than the leather.

"As I thought," said Dworkin. "Good enough for your weapons but not what we make."

Dworkin stepped to a side table and grabbed a short sword. Passing it to Sergeant Thomas. "Now try with this."

"I would not want to damage this blade, as it is well made but too delicate for battle."

Dworkin laughed. "That is one of our cheaper ones, very common. They are made by apprentices by the dozen, and you will not harm the blade."

Thomas grunted and swung at the leather armor, slicing cleanly through it. He then swung at the heavy breastplate with the same result. Both halves fell to the floor with a clang. He then inspected the blade.

Sergeant Thomas looked up in wonder, as there was no mark on the blade. He then looked to Dworkin. "How fast can you make these like my falchions?"

"With the raw material one hundred a day. They could be black like yours. But first, we must continue the demonstration." Pointing to another table, Dworkin asked. "Milady, if you would be so good as to hang that armor for me."

"Certainly." Said Merriam picking the armor up. She heaved overbalanced and fell on her backside. Dworkin grinned, and all the companions fell over laughing.

Merriam exclaimed. "I have night shifts that weigh more than this, and it is so light that it will never protect anyone. She then hung the armor on the stand.

"For this demonstration, Milady, please use your bow."

Merriam said. "If you insist and there is no one behind the wall." She then walked to the other end of the longhouse and drew an arrow.

Dworkin turned to the others. "Stand over there." Once the others had moved far away, Dworkin asked Merriam to go ahead.

Drawing fully, she aimed and loosed the arrow. The arrow hit the breast with a loud crack and shattered into pieces flying to the sides.

Eyes wide and mouth agape, she walked over to the armor. Placing her finger right where she hit the armor, she rubbed at it.

Turning back to the Companions, Merriam said. "There is no mark on this and not even a scratch." Turning to Dworkin, she said. "I want now."

"In a moment, you can be measured and fitted. But first, grab that armor and toss it onto those rocks."

She took the armor off the stand and threw it on the rocks. The armor made almost no sound when it landed.

I looked at Dworkin. "And this can also be made black? How fast can you make them?"

"We can have a set made for your companions and the sergeant. And a heavy armor set for the captain before the goblins become a problem. But first, Milady put on this hood. Each of the rest of you should try it on as well. When you put it on, the ridge goes in the back to be able to see."

Merriam picked up the hood and inspected it. She saw there was no opening in the front. "How do I see?"

"Just put it on, and you will see."

Merriam flipped it over her head and gasped. "It is incredible. I can see so clearly even in this dark hut." Pulling it off, she handed it to me. "Try it is fantastic."

We, including the captain and sergeant, tried on the hood gasping in amazement at how well we could see and breathe.

Merlin waved his hand over the hood. "A fascinating enchantment vision, breathing, and hearing. Your people do excellent work."

Yes, Mythril accepts magic and enchantments very well, and it even requires magic to work it. I am not sure if we can teach our method to your people. We will need to see if your craftsman can learn; if not, we will need to provide craftsmen for your army.

Leading the companions from the longhouse, Dworkin pointed to a building. You can go in there, Milady, and get fitted as that is the woman's crafting hall. If you men follow me, I will take you to the men's hall. We can work on new ones if I may also have your weapons for a few minutes. Not your bow Milady. That one is god-crafted, and we could not match its power."

Merriam raised her eyebrow. "You know how some god made this bow?"

"No, Milady." Said Dworkin. "We can see the magic, and it is potent. You will no longer need to carry arrows when you unlock your magic."

"Excuse me?" Merriam asked. "What exactly do you mean by unlocking my magic? I can do this." She made a small fireball in their hand, dropping it to the ground and leaving a burn mark in the dirt.

Excellent, great lady, that is the first step. You must draw the magic to your left hand and link it to the bow. Then bring the fire into your right hand and pull the bow. You will create an arrow of pure fire that will be strong enough to bring down a greater dragon.

Merriam gasped. "I will have to think about this. Grandfather, perhaps you can help teach me?"

"I most certainly will, my Flama." Said Merlin.

Everyone turned over their weapons to a couple of dwarfs standing there. We then entered a hut nearby. A short time later, we all came out and reclaimed our weapons.

Back at the longhouse, Merriam said. "It was like being fitted for a new dress, and they even measured between my legs like they were making underwear. They had me posing, drawing my bow, and using other weapons like I was fighting."

Dworkin chuckled. "It is vital to get the fit right. You would not wish to have something pinch or dig in at the wrong moment while fighting."

"That is very true." Will chuckled. "Having armor pinch you between the legs at the wrong moment can be very distracting."

Merriam laughed. "I would not want any critical man bit damaged by accident."

"Heavens no," said Robyn, wincing.

CHAPTER

15

After a couple of hours of chatting about trade and other things, an armored clansman entered the longhouse.

Coming over, he spoke quietly in his language to Dworkin.

Dworkin grunted and replied. The dwarf turned and left the hut.

Dworkin then turned to us and said. "There are two things of note. First, your armor is ready, and you can try them on in a moment. Next, the goblins appear to be gathering in the woods, and we suspect they will wait till dark."

Merlin said. "That is quite possible. Goblins are raiders who will wait for the dark, seeking an advantage."

"Quite true." Replied Dworkin.

"In that case, we have time to try our new armor. We can then look at the defenses. There are still two hours before dark." I said.

Dworkin rose and led the group from the longhouse.

Merriam headed to the woman's craft hall with a skip in her step.

We husbands chuckled as we headed for the other hall.

We laughed at the squeals of delight coming from the other hut. We quickly dressed in our new armor and stepped outside to wait for Merriam. We examined each other's armor, noting the crests embossed on our breasts.

Thomas was carrying his normal bandoliers in his hand. His armor had sheaths included, and he kept running his hands over the grips.

I quirked, my eyebrow smiling. "Is something missing, Sergeant Thomas? You keep touching every grip like one is missing."

"No, Milord, that is the point. Each one is in the correct place. It is even better because, on occasion, my bandoliers would slip. The men will be most pleased with this armor."

"Yes, by the look of Captain Geoffrey, the knights will be most happy to."

"More importantly, Milord, the horses will be most happy." Chuckled the captain jumping a few times. "A knight in complete armor mounted will weigh half what they do now."

"I noticed you move better than in your old armor," I said.

Sergeant Thomas chuckled. "Our old leathers were heavier than we are wearing now. I feel almost naked for how comfortable they are."

Dworkin laughed. "This is nothing yet, Milord. Captain sergeant, speak the words I taught you."

Both men spoke loudly. "For the King."

On the breast and back of both men, a large square turned to gold. The lion rampant blazed forth on the patch in red like a fire burning.

"Now that is some fun magic." Said Merlin.

"Wait for Milady, and then you will see some fun magic." Laughed Dworkin seeing our questioning looks.

The door to the other craft hut opened, and a dwarf woman stepped out. She spoke in a low deep tone.

"I am pleased to present the lady Merriam Duchess of Sherwood."

Merriam stepped through the doorway, and the men all gaped at her. The armour she wore was even more perfectly form-fitting than theirs.

The men removed their helmets and dropped to one knee.

I found my voice first. "Milady, you are stunning to behold."

Merriam giggled. "You have seen nothing yet, my love." She spoke loudly, "Flama," and her armor burst into flame.

Our eyes bulged from our heads as we looked on.

I groaned and said. "The enemy will either run screaming or charge with a vengeance. How by all that is holy do we protect her looking like that?"

Merlin laughed hard. "At the right moment, if Flama lights up like that and starts shooting flaming arrows, she will break any army."

Merriam then spoke aloud, "dark." Her armor went back to black and appeared to drink the light.

Robyn laughed. "She can wear that all the time. With her bow and that armor, nothing can harm her."

Dworkin grunted. "Never say nothing. Some legendary weapons can damage this armor. Be wary of glowing weapons, for they are magical in nature."

"Speaking of magic, grandfather, why did you and Friar Tuck not change?"

Giving a belly laugh, Tuck said. "Our robes may appear the same, but the lining is the same armor as your britches. The hoods are the same as your helmet with the face shield."

I stepped up and held my hand out for Merriam to take.

"Let us walk around the defenses now."

Sergeant Thomas spoke up. The defensive walls are weak on the north side, Milord. Most of the rest of the walls are sturdy and easy to defend. I recommend one squad for each of the other walls. We can then put four squads on the north wall. And have three squads as reenforcement in the square. Then we can divide the archers between the squads equally.

"Captain Geoffrey, how does this sound to you?" I asked.

"It is the way we planned it, Milord. We recommend keeping knights as a mounted reserve in the square."

By this time, we had reached the north wall. Looking it over, I saw it was the weakest.

"I approve your recommendations, gentlemen, with one caveat. Captain, I want your knights at the west gate. Due to enemy numbers, you can sweep in from the flank if we become hard-pressed on the north."

"Yes, Milord, an excellent compromise."

"Gentleman, take up your defensive positions. And have the men on the east wall keep an eye out for Captain Keating, as I suspect he should be along shortly."

Both men saluted and moved off.

I tugged Merriam's hand. "Come, my love, we will climb the wall and have a look."

"Good idea, love. We can see how well these headcovers work."

"Yes, I did want to test these as well."

Climbing up first, Merriam looked over her shoulder and smirked at the men's staring. She gave her hips an extra shimmy as she stepped onto the walk.

Laughing, she said. "You can see much better from up here." We shook our heads and quickly climbed up beside her.

Will said. "You are a terrible distraction, my love." He patted her on the backside as he stepped around her.

"Good," she replied. "At least I know your eyes are not wandering."

Will laughed. "If my eyes wander, it is only to increase my appetite for the sumptuous meal at home."

We laughed as Merriam blushed.

Turning, we put on our head covers and looked into the woods.

"This is amazing," said Merriam. "I can see where the goblins gather under the trees."

"Yes," I said. "This is incredible. How can dwarfs make these to see even in the dark shadows under the trees?"

"It is a fascinating part of the vision spell. Notice the green cast to the light under the trees. That is part of the spell that uses starlight." Merlin said.

Dworkin replied. "They also work well in mines with no light. Because the colors are tinted, it takes some training to pick out the different ores."

"That is interesting, but I make it about three hundred goblins gathered."

Robyn scanned the area and said. "I see another hundred over there on the left as well."

Will said. "I also see another group gathering on the right."

Little-Jon replied. "A hundred so far, but more are coming in."

"About five hundred at the minimum," I said. "That should make it entertaining once the third company arrives. Dworkin, how many of these hoods do you have?"

Dworkin said. "We should have enough for all the men and some to spare. We need these for mining, so they are one of the first things we make."

"Perfect," I said. "Give one to each of my men. They are the best night fighters we have, and their armor should be good enough against the goblin's weapons."

Dworkin replied. "They have inferior weapons and armor. They do not fight well in groups or at all."

"I have spotted a good place to fire my bow from," Merriam said. She was pointing at a large building.

"The best, my love, the north part has a flat place on top. Our longbows should have no trouble reaching the woods from there. It would appear there is enough room for all the archers."

"I will join your men on the wall," said Merlin. "There is a chance I can get a couple of good spells in."

"Very well, Merlin. We will be happy to have you on the wall."

Sergeant Thomas climbed up to join the group. "Milord, the troops, are set, and hoods, issued to each man. They will stand down below walls until the goblin attack."

"Good," I said. "We do not want to appear too strong for the goblins and scare them off."

"Suck them in, then slaughter them." Dworkin chuckled. "Good plan. Great lord, did you mention another company coming? Are there as many men as you have here?"

"No, my friend, there are five hundred in that company." I smiled. "I plan to have them take over guarding Derby. Then I will have the half company there come here to protect you, and you can concentrate on mining and crafting."

Dworkin snorted. "We do not need protection. We carry our weapons to the mines."

I laughed. "I understand that. My job is to protect the people on my land. I do not do this because I do not think you are capable. I do this because it is my bond with the people. Tell me how long it would take to arm and armor two hundred fifty men? They would be similar in makeup to the half-company that came through two days ago. And how much would it cost my king?"

Dworkin hummed and hawed and began counting on his fingers. He then called to a dwarf standing nearby. The dwarf walked over and handed him an abacus. He flipped the beads back and forth with speed. A minute later, he looked up.

We can start smelting in a week if I put all my lads and lassies to work in the mines. We would need another week to build our reserve. Then I could call the craftsman back to work. We can make twenty-five sets of armor and weapons each day, and for your regular men, ten gold for your heavy knights and horses twenty gold each."

I grunted, pulling a bag from my belt. "Here is a hundred gold to cover us, Dworkin."

"This is for myself and my companions. Each man coming here will have the gold to pay for his armor."

Dworkin barked a laugh. "Keep your gold duke your companions armor, and yours was free, and this will cover the sergeant and captain, and we have made a good deal this day." Dworkin then counted off thirty gold and handed the rest back.

"I feel I have somehow cheated you. We pay up to ten times that amount for armor. We are building an army that needs this equipment and will be twenty thousand strong. It will take a couple of years, but you will have steady work. Do your people work in stone as well?"

Dworkin's eyes grew wide at the numbers. "Yes, we have some of the finest castle builders and stonecutters in any realm."

"Your people are talented crafters, and we will have much work for you over the years. We have many devices that you can likely make much better."

Dworkin waved over two dwarfs pulling a cart. "Here, Little-Jon, for you." Dworkin reached into the cart, pulling out a sizeable double-headed battleax. The blade glowed blue with an engraved scene on both sides, and the shaft was also intricately carved.

Little-Jon took the ax and stared reverently at the engraving. "It is almost too beautiful to use as a weapon."

Dworkin laughed. "It was forged for the heat of the fiercest battle and will cleave hundreds of foes, and not even Mythril will stand up to it. Go ahead and try it on that training post."

"Okay," Little-Jon said as he stepped over to the post. Swinging his arms around, he took a couple of practice swipes.

"Are you sure I will not damage this ax? It seems very light."

Dworkin laughed. "It is more than strong enough to strike the post."

Little-Jon took a mighty swing. The blade cut through the post like it was straw. He overbalanced and spun around, almost falling.

Everyone was laughing and clapping.

Little-Jon said. "That was incredible. I hardly felt the strike." Taking his old battle-ax from his holster, he tossed it in the cart, and the wood groaned from the weight.

Will laughed. "It was hard enough to hide that big ox. Now he will glow in the dark, but he will make a matched set for our wife in the sparkly battles."

We all laughed hard at that.

"Use the word dark." Dworkin laughed. "To light up again, shout for glory, and the duke."

Little-Jon held the ax out and spoke the word. He began swinging the blade around as it turned black and almost vanished.

"Now speak the word backstab."

Little-Jon held the ax in front of him, speaking the word. With a thunk, a two-foot spike appeared between the blades.

"Oh, my. That will surprise someone." Said Merriam.

"Withdraw is the word to retract the spike." Said Dworkin.

"Do you see how my ax sits? Now for the last trick." Dworkin reached up, gripping the shaft, and said. "Release." His ax came free, and he swung it around. Then Dworkin brought it back up into the same place and said. "Stick. Yours will do the same. It will never come loose, and only you can call it to battle."

Merriam looking in the cart said. "This bundle must be for our good Sergeant Thomas, as there are many stabby things in it."

Sergeant Thomas chuckled and stepped over to open the bundle. A feral grin spread across his face, and he began replacing the knives on his armor and tossing the old ones to the front of the cart. At last, Thomas pulled a pair of falchions from the bundle. He walked to a practice post and swung the short swords around, limbering up his arms. Getting to the post, he started the first steps in the dance of a blade master. Soon a blizzard of wood chips flew through the air as Sergeant Thomas moved. Suddenly stopping, he stood straight up, walking back toward Dworkin, and lifted his hands, sheathing both blades. Clasping forearms with Dworkin, he said. "Thank you."

Both Robyn and I pulled a hand-and-a-half bastard sword from the cart, putting them through several forms two-handed and single, and sheathed them.

Robyn said. "These will take some getting used to. They are so much lighter than our old swords."

"Yes," I said. "We will need to work on our form. The blade had me off balance quite a bit."

Will pulled another bundle from the cart, containing a saber the same as he used and several throwing knives. There was also a bow similar to Merriam's but black. Seeing a pocket on the grip, he pulled out a string. "This is not gut," Will commented.

Dworkin said. "No, it is Mythril treated to be flexible, and it will not stretch when wet. Also, it will not grow brittle when cold, so there will be no issue with breaking. You can use the bow even in the heaviest rains. You will find it much better than your longbow."

Suiting action to Dworkin's words, Will quickly strung the bow.

"The pull feels the same as my bow."

"You will find the pull set the same. But because of the recurve, it will have more power. Clear the lane." Yelled Dworkin.

Several people moved to give Will a clear shot at the target on the wall.

Will knocked an arrow, drew, and fired in one motion. The arrow went high, exploding against the wall. Will huffed in discontent, knocking and aiming another arrow. He fired this time, hitting the bullseye. But the arrow went through the target and again exploded against the wall.

Turning to Dworkin, Will said. "Yes, not as much backlash as my other bow. But it is going to be hard on arrows."

Dworkin replied. "Yes, that is a feature we had not expected with a bow made this way. You were the first to test it as we are not tall enough."

"I am happy enough with the results." Said Will. "Dworkin, I thank you and your craftsmen."

Robyn pulled another bow from the cart, stringing it. He also fired two arrows with nearly identical results.

Robyn said. "I also thank you, Dworkin. You and your craftsmen have my undying gratitude."

"You are most welcome, Baron Robyn. And here, Milady, is a new string for your bow.

"Okay, we have less than an hour until sundown. Get the men some food and water they can eat where they stand." I said.

CHAPTER

16

Darkness settled over the land as the men stood below the wall. I stood on the wall, looking toward the forest.

"They are starting to stir. It should not be long now before the goblins attack. Archers onto that platform and standby. Sergeant Thomas, get your men on the wall and keep them low."

Everyone quickly moved into position. Dworkin and about twenty dwarves formed up at the gate. Little-Jon, Sergeant Thomas, and a squad added to their numbers.

I looked down at one of the runners. "Pass the word, archers; hold your fire until Milady commands."

Looking over the wall, Goblins began screaming as they charged from the woods.

"Not very stealthy, are they," I said to Merlin.

"Not really. Goblins see very well in the dark and think no one else can."

The goblins were about halfway across the field when they cleared the woods.

Looking back below the wall, I said. "Fire the signal, arrow Will."

Will drew the arrow he had knocked on his bow. Touching the tip to a torch, he aimed nearly straight up and loosed the arrow.

As it reached its peak, the arrow burst into intense red light.

Looking over the wall, Merriam saw the goblins come to a halt. A goblin jumped and gestured toward the wall, and she drew and fired an arrow. The goblin leader died before the signal arrow's light faded to black.

All the other archers opened fire at that moment. The steady thump of released bowstrings was a counterpoint to the screams of dying goblins. I could hear a thumping noise faintly from the woods.

I looked from the wall and hollered. "Will tell Captain Geoffrey to exit the west gate, hit the flank, and bring the reserve squads to this gate."

"Sergeant Thomas, be prepared to attack. Dworkin, I am adding some extra men to your force for the attack."

Dworkin called a command, and thirty more Dwarves ran towards him.

Sergeant Thomas looked at Dworkin. "Your men are heavily armored, so you take the center. Little-Jon, you will take half my men left, and I will take the rest to the right."

Dworkin laughed and looked at Little-Jon. "You may wish to shine for this, so call for the duke and victory."

Merlin looked over the wall at the approaching horde. "Well, they seem to be in my range now."

Raising his hands, he called a word of power, and a bolt of lightning split the darkness hitting the front ranks. The lightning began to fork and jump between goblins. Merlin then called out two more words, and again more lightning bolts arced out, cooking another thirty or forty goblins. Each one hit fell to the ground, smoking.

"I can see what you mean by your power being indiscriminate."

"Yes, the more metal one carries, the greater the effect. One pair of bolts would have taken out a hundred knights in armor."

Merriam cried out. "Flama." And her armor lit up in full glory. She then drew her empty bow and released it, and a lurid flaming light shot from her bow struck a goblin, and it exploded, incinerating everything in a twenty-foot diameter circle.

"Yes." Merlin cried. "She has done it."

"Done what?"

"She has linked her power to the bow. She must hold her fire soon as your men get too close."

"Merriam's power is almost as indiscriminate as yours."

"Yes, that is the problem with magic. Great for an area of effect but not much good for single opponents. Unless you are one on one and wish to obliterate your enemy."

"Well, by all means, fry a few more before they get too close." I laughed.

"With pleasure." Merlin laughed.

The thumping from the woods stopped, and three hundred pikemen stepped out. Behind them, another one hundred archers began firing into the goblins. As the goblins turned to the new threat, a rumble came from the east, and one hundred knights in gleaming armor rode from the east road. They lowered lances and charged as they entered the field, forming a wedge. At that moment, Captain Geoffrey and his twenty knights thundered around the west wall with near-perfect timing.

The gate opened, and Dworkin and his dwarves ran from the entrance with various cries. The dwarven warrior's armor and weapons lit up with attributes. Little-Jon cried out. "For Sherwood Glory and Victory," his armor lit up in my colors. His battleax began to glow.

Sergeant Thomas called out. "Sophia and Victory." And his armor lit up with Sophia's color and her crest. His falchions began glowing with a blue light.

As they crashed into the goblin ranks, panic spread. The goblins ran every which way trying to escape. They even attacked each other, trying to get away. There was, however, no place for them to run. The slaughter was total.

The troops began the gruesome task of hauling the bodies into piles to burn. The companions gathered at the gate with Dworkin to await third companies, captains and sergeants. When they arrived, I made the introductions.

"Dworkin, Captain Keating, Captain Nordson, Sergeant Wilson, and Sergeant Gaines. Gentleman Dworkin clan chief of these dwarves."

"Happy to meet you, men," Dworkin replied. He stepped forward, clasping arms with each. "And now a drink to victory."

"Captain Keating, no more than one tankard for the men on guard duty. Place five archers and one squad on each wall to stand guard with the dwarves."

Captain Keating said. "Sergeant Wilson, see to the guards."

"Aye, Sir."

"Captain Keating, your men may make a cold camp inside the walls. There is more than enough room."

"Yes, Milord. Sergeant Gaines pass the word cold camp inside the walls."

"Yes, Sir."

Looking back at Captain Keating, I said. "Captian Nordson will move out with his half company in the morning to replace Captain Anders, who will move here. He will have an instruction pack on what you will do there. You can carry on with that operation until you are relieved."

"I have already sent my stonemasons with your men, and they will layout your castle and start building."

"You do not need these men to help with your mining operation?"

"No, Milord, they are not miners; their skills are stone carving and laying. They have some skill at smelting and would let us know if they find anything. For now, we can get what we need in five places in this area."

"Very well, we will carry on as we are."

"Captian Keating will stay here until Captian Ander's half company arrives. When Captain Dorner returns from his mission, he will join them. I expect them back within two weeks so that the sixth company will be equipped first. That puts the kernel of a plan in my head I will need to develop with Sir William."

"Yes, Milord, we will begin mining in the morning. It will take two days to get the first mine set up. It is a vast deposit of Mythril which we will need for your armor. While setting that mine up, we can arm and armor some of your other men. We do not have enough raw material to do all your men but perhaps a third."

Sitting at the table with a tankard of ale, I thought. Scratching at the stubble on my chin.

Merriam leaned over and said. "A small sample group to send to the king with dispatches about this discovery?"

Setting my tankard down, I cupped Merriam's cheeks in my hands and kissed her hard.

"What a brilliant idea, my love. Captain Geoffrey detail Sir Penrose and his squad, plus two squads of pikemen with their archers. They will be armed and armored by the dwarfs, and we can then send them to the king with my detailed report on the new armament plan."

Dworkin grunted. "Tell the king to come here and meet us. Tell him I will equip him with magnificent armor. His only cost will be an agreement to set up the guilds, and I will draw up a proposal outlining how our guilds work to send with your dispatches."

"That would be a good idea as we have many jokes about the standards of workmanship for our equipment." Said Sergeant Thomas grinning.

"Yes, we have seen this when talking to your men. I propose making things standard for crafting skills, making prices standard, which is good for the economy."

Merriam began laughing hysterically and, when she composed herself enough, spoke. "King Lionel will have a fit when he sees that report. His last words to Sir William were, do not mess with the plan."

"Gods." I groaned. "I need to sleep on this before attempting the report."

"I agree." Said Robyn. "We can resume with fresh minds in the morning."

Dworkin said. "There is a cabin next to mine, and it is large enough to accommodate you all in comfort."

"Thank you, Dworkin," I said. "A good night's sleep would be best for all of us. But first, here is the gold for eleven knights, twenty Infantry, and ten archers. What would you recommend for the squires? They are still growing boys."

"Thank you, Milord. We will put this gold to good use. As for young boys, I would recommend training armor, and it can be adjusted to fit and not compromise the protection. They come in several sizes, and as the boys grow out of one set, they can exchange them for a larger set passing the old armor down."

The following day dawned clear and cool, and the chill in the air spoke of the lateness of the season.

Merlin took a deep breath as he exited the hut. "We must move soon, or the winter storms will catch us."

We will head back to Nottingham tomorrow and take a couple of days to prepare ourselves to move on with our quest."

We all moved toward the longhouse for breakfast. Stepping through the doors, we met a wave of heavenly smells from the kitchen area.

"Oh, my goodness." Said Merriam. "The smells are incredible."

We all chuckled at a rumble from the area of Little-Jon's stomach.

We joined Dworkin at the head of one of the tables. We no sooner sat down, and servers brought platters of food, water, and wine.

Dworkin grunted and said. "Eat."

Without further comment, we began filling our plates with food. Soon we were all stuffed and pushing our plates away, and servents rushed over and cleared the dishes.

I turned to Dworkin and said. "I need writing materials to compose my dispatch to the king."

Dworkin waved over a dwarf. "Please get the duke a desk set and bring extra paper and pens."

"What is this paper you speak of?" Asked Merriam. "For that matter, what is a pen? We have quills and parchment."

Dworkin laughed. "We used to have such rudimentary writing materials. Then we invented a better way to communicate with writing."

Merlin grunted. "It would appear you are about to advance three hundred years in a moment."

The dwarf returned, placing a box on the table before Dworkin. The box had an angled top except for the back three-inch wide strip at the top that was flat except for a couple of grooves carved in it in a shallow indentation and a cork near one corner.

Dworkin flipped a latch and opened the lid. Taking out several sheets, he set them on the table. Dworkin then reached in and pulled out three shiny cylinders with rounded ends. Passing out a sheet of paper to each companion, he said. "This is paper. We have a process that uses wood chips and scraps, which is too tedious to describe. We can then cut the finished sheets to any size."

Picking up one of the cylinders and pulling the short end off, they saw it was hollow. "This is just a cap that protects the nib." Dworkin then pulled the cork from the flat top of the box. He dipped the exposed tip into the ink and pulled a recessed lever on the cylinder, pushing it back down flat again. When you lift the lever that pushes the ink out and pulls it in when you push it down, you can empty the pen when you finish writing.

Then Dworkin began to explain. The critical thing to remember is that you must lift the pen just like a quill when you stop.

Placing a piece of paper on the sloped desktop, Dworkin handed me a pen and slid the desk in front of me. After taking the other two pens out for the others to try.

I said. "This would be a boon to scholars. One would typically have to dip a quill after each word, and I can write a whole page with this pen and not even have to press like a quill."

"This thing is marvelous. I want one." Said Merriam.

The others expressed a similar interest.

Dworkin laughed with delight. We have a couple of different types. This one on the table also has a stand, so you do not need a table. We also have a lighter version that hangs around a scribe's neck so they can move while writing. We also have one attached to the arm for clerks. Pens cost one gold, and the desk, as you see it with ink and paper, five gold. Paper refills and ink are one gold. The ink will last for five hundred sheets of paper hence why the ink and paper come as a set.

"What do you think, husband?" Merriam asked. "One for the king and his scribe, then one for us?"

"One for Digby, and he can share with Denby."

Merriam said. "That will do for now but expect more orders, Dworkin. We should throw in two refills for the king... I just thought that one for Sir William and one for Sophia makes twelve. Ah, make it thirty refills."

Robyn laughed and pulled out a purse. "Here is a hundred gold, and make it as many refills as the gold will cover, Dworkin."

I began writing, grumbling as the ink blotted when I paused. I was about to crumple the sheet of paper when Merriam stopped me.

"You are having troubles, my love. Why do you not just continue practicing on that sheet until you get the hang of it? Then you can start the king's missives on a fresh sheet."

"That is a good idea, my love. Although I fear I will waste much paper before finishing."

Merriam giggled. "It will take some getting used to writing with these pens."

"We will leave you to your writing, my love. We will go out and do a little bit of scouting and hunting. We will be back before dinner, possibly with dinner."

"Have a lovely trek through the woods, my love." I returned to concentrating on my writing.

Merriam giggled as she and the others left the hall.

A few hours later, I stretched and groaned. Looking at the shadows, I had been writing for about three hours, quickly getting the hang of the pen. The pile of crumpled sheets was not too horrible.

Carefully folding and sealing each message, I placed them in two packets. Walking out of the hall to look for Dworkin, I saw Sir Penrose in his new armor.

"How do you like your new armor, Sir Penrose?"

Turning, Sir Penrose said. "It is incredible, Milord. So light and comfortable. I am surprised it protects so well."

"Yes, it is fantastic. I am going to entrust you with a special mission. You and the men selected for special armor will be heading straight to Cambridge. You will make a brief stop in Nottingham to deliver a packet to Sir William. Then you will head for Cambridge. Do not stop or delay until you hand the king his packet. You will also have two other items to deliver to him. Come, I will show you how to use them so you can show the king and his scribe."

"Yes, Milord." Sir Penrose followed me back into the longhouse. I spent the next half hour showing Sir Penrose how to use the desks, pens, and paper, and I concluded by saying. "There will be extra paper ink and pens in the chest you will deliver, and there will be an additional message from clan chief Dworkin."

"Yes, Milord."

"How long before the rest of your men are ready?"

"About two hours from now, Milord. The dwarves did say about the noon meal. But getting the king's messenger symbol to work takes a bit longer. Three tabards seem to be the limit for the armor, and it takes longer to add new ones."

"It must be some sort of limitation to the magic."

"Yes, Milord, it would appear so."

"Very well then, you and your men can leave at first light with us. Stay with the king while he reads his messages; he may have questions. Depending on how the messages are received, you may have the king for company on the way back. In any event, do not delay, as you need to be back as soon as possible."

"As you command, Milord." Sir Penrose said, saluting.

CHAPTER

17

It was mid-afternoon when I leaned back in my chair. Scrubbing my hands over my face, I said. "That takes care of my armament plan for the army, Dworkin. You have already armored forty-five men from the first company so that they will deliver that much less gold. In contrast, other companies will need all their men equipped."

Dworkin grunted from his place at the table. "I have completed my proposition for the king. Here is a guide on how guilds work, and the second part is a proposal about setting up guild training halls around the kingdom. There is a copy for you to share with Sir William."

"Excellent," I said. "Much more than I had hoped for, Dworkin."

"Some of these things are standard or trade-specific. Most guilds operate similarly, using the same rules and trade practices. It is what keeps prices from getting out of hand."

"Well, for myself and my dukedom, I accept your proposal. I am certain the king will jump at this, and the people will be more than happy with this system."

"I need to get up and stretch my legs."

"I guess I should take a walk around town myself. I need to check on my men's progress and preparations for leaving. I shall see you for dinner. Dworkin."

"Yes, Milord, I have a few things to look into myself."

We both walked out the door and headed our separate ways. I observed men training with dwarves in combat maneuvers, and other men seemed to be talking with craftsmen.

Captain Geoffrey and Sergeant Thomas were meeting with Captain Keating and Sergeant Wilson. I walked over to join them, and all four men gave crisp salutes.

"Yes, Milord?" Captian Geoffrey inquired.

"How are things going, gentleman? All preparations are in hand?"

"Certainly, Milord, all the men have been kitted for the trip to the king. We will be ready to move out in the morning as well."

"Excellent," I said. "And what else is going on here, Sergeant Thomas?"

"The men are doing a little cross-training, Milord. Some are learning dwarven tactics or are teaching our tactics. Those men there are learning care and cleaning armor, and they are also learning how to make some new things."

"Very good," I said. "As long as we are ready to move out in the morning."

"Yes, Milord, there will be no problem with that."

"Good, then I shall continue my stroll."

"Yes, Milord." The four men replied, saluting.

Soon, I approached the north gate where the battle had occurred the night before. Coming close and hearing a commotion, I hurried my steps to see what was going on.

One of the dwarves on the wall called down commands, and the gates began to open. Moments later, Merriam rode through the gate with the other hunting companions close behind. The cart behind them seemed to have several animals in the back.

"Loves," I called to them. "Your hunt was successful, I see."

"Yes, my love." Said Merriam. "We got four large bucks on our hunt and bagged a scouting party of orcs and wargs, but we left them for the carrion birds."

I chuckled. "It is probably just as well. I do not imagine orcs taste very good."

"No kidding, their smell is off-putting." Merriam giggled.

"And where were these orcs headed?"

"They were to the east of us and seemed to be heading toward Lincoln," Robyn said.

The garrison there should be strong enough to handle a few orcs. But I should have Captain Keating send a squad to warn them."

"I recommend sending them on the north road, as that is the first bunch we have seen to the east."

"That is true," I said. "I wonder if the orcs are after the goblins, and we just happened to be between them."

"That is a genuine possibility." Said Merriam.

"I think I will chat with Merlin before forming an opinion."

"Yes, Merlin may have some insight into this problem." Said Robyn. "Little-Jon, you and Will take the cart to the cooking hall."

"We can take care of that and meet you later at the main hall for dinner."

Robyn waved as they headed off.

The rest of us headed for the crafting house where Merlin most likely was.

Merlin was less difficult to find than expected.

There was a resounding boom, and several dwarfs ran out of a building in a cloud of smoke. Merlin was in the middle, and they all stood talking and gesturing with their arms as the smoke dissipated.

Merriam giggled as we walked up. "What in heavens name are you trying to do, grandfather?"

Merlin turned around, looking sheepish even with his face covered in soot.

"The plan was to make gunpowder for a mining explosive. We were just slightly off the saltpeter sulfur and fertilizer mix."

There was another loud woosh, and flames shot from the door and windows. Then with a sad groan, the building slowly collapsed in on itself. With a gesture and a word of power, a cloud formed over the remains and began raining, quickly putting out the fire.

"It sounds and looks very dangerous," I said.

"Not at all," said Merlin. "In the hands of an artist, mining can be made very easy with dynamite."

"I have a question for you, Merlin."

"What is that, Milord?"

"Merriam said she took out a couple of orc scouts on wargs while they were hunting. They were scouting towards Lincoln to the east, and was it possible they were looking for the goblins?"

"Absolutely," said Merlin. "Orcs and goblins have no love for each other. Sir William may have to take the time to eliminate this problem while we are gone."

"That will be good training for our troops. Having an enemy to attack is much better than just practicing." I said.

"Yes," said Robyn. "Dry training can only do so much."

"We need to get back to Nottingham," I said. "There is too much to do before we can leave."

"No, my love," said Merriam. "Sir William can handle that while we get on the road. This weather will not last much longer, and I would rather not be on a boat when the storms hit."

"You are right, my love. We must get going soon, and we will relax for tonight, leaving in the morning."

The following morning, a commotion came from the west gate as we formed.

We mounted our horses and rode in that direction to see what was happening. We arrived at the gate just in time for the messenger.

He rode up to me and stopped reaching into his messenger bag. He passed over a letter.

I opened the letter and quickly skimmed its contents. I then told my companions. "This is good news, as Captain Anders will be here by noon."

Just then, Captain Keating rode up. I said. "Your replacements will be here by noon."

"Good," said Captain Keating. "Captain Nordson, made good time then."

"Once Captain Anders arrives, you may pass on his orders and head to Derby."

"Yes, Milord." The captain replied.

"Let us move out," I said.

We returned to the column and waved them forward. As soon as the last man cleared the gate, we broke into double time.

Mid-morning found us about halfway to Nottingham. A large creature sprang from the underbrush in front of us. We halted. The creature looked like a cat but much larger at fifteen feet long, nose to tail, all white with black stripes in bands to break up the white.

"Merlin?" I called as he rode up. "What is that?"

"That, Milord is a magnificent example of a Siberian tiger, probably a shifter."

The cat was licking a forepaw this whole time from which sharp claws protruded. Cocking its head to one side like it was trying to decide something, the air around it began wavering. In seconds, a woman of impressive stature stood before us. She was more than six ft tall. She had white hair with one black stripe over her right eye running down to the tip around her waist. She wore a leather bustier and a skirt to mid-thigh. The armor left her shoulders, arms, and abdomen bare. She had on boots laced to the knees. The hilts of two swords protruded over her shoulders, and she had several knives sheathed on her.

Holding her hands up to the sides to show they were empty, she spoke. "I am Tarija of the Snow Elk Adventurer Guild. Are you the Lord of this land, and do you speak common?"

"I am Duke Sherwood of Nottingham. I care for this land in the name of King Lionel Claymoore of England."

"Damn all the gods of ill luck. I delved into the grim caverns with six companions when undead wolves beset us. I jumped back from an attack and found myself lying in this forest. I was looking for a familiar landmark when I caught a most delightful scent."

"What scent would that be?"

"Him." She said with a feral grin. She pointed to Sergeant Thomas. "He smells like my soulmate, and I must now test his worth in a spar."

I looked over to see Sergeant Thomas staring in wonder. "Do you wish to spar with this woman, Sergeant?"

"God, yes, and so much more! You are magnificent, Tarija. My name is Ulysses Thaddeus Thomas."

Merriam snickered. "Ulysses Thaddeus?"

Sergeant Thomas flashed her a grin. "My mother, may God rest her soul loved the Iliad."

Sergeant Thomas stepped forward, rolling his shoulders and cracking his neck. He drew his swords as Tarija drew hers, dropping into a fighting stance. Without a word, they exploded into action. They slashed, blocked, spun, and kicked in a flurry of movement. She moved with feline grace and he with economic power, neither giving ground except to make a new strike or block.

Suddenly they came together, swords locked overhead in a strength test, almost touching noses. Pupils dilated, a grin spread on her lips, and she kissed Thomas then stepped back, sheathing her swords in one motion. Sergeant Thomas stood stunned for a moment when he shook himself and sheathed his swords.

"Ulysses Thaddeus Thomas." Tarija said. "You will make an excellent father to my kits."

Kneeling before Tarija, Sergeant Thomas took her hands in his, kissing both palms, and replied. "I will strive daily to increase my worth and make you happy."

Merriam sniffled and wiped her eyes. "That was so beautiful. Now we should take a break for lunch and get to know Tarija."

"That is an excellent idea, my love," I said. Glancing over at Sergeant Thomas, I saw him mesmerized by Tarija. Chuckling, I shook my head. "Captain Geoffrey, have the men break for lunch."

"Yes, Milord, it would appear the good Sergeant is a bit gobsmacked."

We all laughed at that as we dismounted.

We walked over to join Tarija and Sergeant Thomas.

We were just in time to hear her say.

"I recognize this style of armor. Where did you get it from, Ulysses?"

"Go a half-day back up this road, and there is a village of dwarves run by a man named Dworkin."

Tarija said. "Dworkin is a fine craftsman; his clan makes some of the best equipment any adventuring guild can buy."

"You know Dworkin?" I asked.

"Oh, yes, his people made my weapons."

"What about your armor?" Merriam asked.

"No, this was made by an elven enchantress. I did a quest for the Elven Queen, and this was my reward. It has legendary full-body protection against all weapons and most spells."

147

"Wow!" Exclaimed Merlin. "That must have been some quest."

"Yes, it was long and arduous. We lost four members of our party. I was on this delve to test a new party, plus, I was close to leveling to 'C' rank."

"We have wondered about this leveling system," said Merriam. "How can you tell what level you are? Or what level your equipment is? Or what someone else's level is? Or..." And Merlin clapped his hand over her mouth.

"Let the poor girl answer." And everyone laughed.

Merriam just blushed and stomped her foot. "Fine."

Tarija laughed. "So, the leveling system has not appeared here yet?"

"No," Merlin said. "Or at least we have had no indication of it."

"Wow," Tarija said. It is hard to explain, but a window appears if I look at my hand and think about my status. It shows my name, clan, guild affiliation, and class. Then it details my experience and how many points to the next level. I currently need two hundred experience to reach level 'C' warrior."

I can draw a status chart when we get where we are going. While I was still in cat form, I was scanning your party. Some of you, including Ulysses, wear exceptional dwarven Mythril armor. In contrast, most of your men are wearing good common leather armor.

Moreover, some weapons are exceptional and do high levels of damage. Your bow Milady is God-wrought, and at such a high level, all I see are question marks for damage. The only other thing I can tell about your bow is that it is soul bonded to you, which means you are the only one who can draw that bow.

"So," I asked. "Have you seen any monsters in your travels today?"

"No, not in this area, only what I consider prey animals."

Will said. "I have a bad feeling about this. It has been way too quiet today."

"Yes," I said. "Since the event, we have been under almost constant attack, and why this peace suddenly?"

"That is easy to explain." Said Tarija. "Anyone with magic should be able to feel the power approaching from the south."

"That is what that abnormal pressure is in my head?" Asked Merriam. "It feels like it moves around depending on where I look."

"Turn your head until that feeling of pressure is between your eyes."
Merriam did as Tarija asked and was soon facing just west of south.
Merriam said. "That is where the pressure comes from."

"Every magical creature and monster can feel that pressure as well.
Monsters are simply terrified of it and running away."

*I could not believe my good fortune. Tarija was magnificent in every way,
and her eyes were a smoldering amber with slitted pupils like a cat. Tarija partly
hid her great strength under her soft golden tan, but I could see the flow of her
muscles as she gestured. And her smell was like fresh falling snow in a pine
forest, so crisp and clean. I have had many women in my time, which was why
I became a soldier. To be brought before this glorious goddess, those twin beauties
were worth the price.* I shook my head, rejoining the world.

"Right then," I said. "We need to get mounted up and moving, as
I want to be inside Nottingham's walls when whatever this is arrives."

It was mid-afternoon when we arrived back at Nottingham castle.
Stopping in front of the doors to the keep, I turned in my saddle.

"Captain Geoffrey dismiss the men and then collect Sergeant
Mackey and meet us in the study. Sir Penrose, take the balance of the
day and work on your kit. Make yourself ready to leave first thing
tomorrow possibly."

"Sergeant Thomas, you and Tarija will accompany us." We
dismounted and headed into the keep. There was a brief cacophony
of noise as orders echoed around the courtyard and men made replies.

As we approached the doors, they opened, and Denby stepped out.

"Milords and Miladies, welcome home. Your mission was successful?"

"Yes, Denby, thank you. My mission was eminently successful."

"Should I arrange for baths and refreshment in your quarters,
Milord?"

"No, we must speak with Sir William first. Send some refreshment
to the study for now."

"Yes, Milord, I will arrange that right now." He said, turning away.

As we climbed the stairs, Will began to laugh.

"What has you in such high humor, brother-husband?" Robyn asked.

"I just had a marvelous idea. When the guards throw the doors open, Merriam, our love, should light herself up as she steps in."

The companions laughed. "Yes," cried Merriam. "That will be perfect."

I said. "That may give Sir William a stroke, but a great idea, as it should lead nicely into our report."

Robyn and I formed up on either side and just behind Merriam. The remainder of the group fell in behind us.

As we approached the doors to the study, I signaled for the guards to open them.

As Merriam's foot hit the threshold, she cried, "Flama," and her armor lit with fire.

Sir William shot to his feet, gasping for breath.

Sophia clapped with delight crying out. "So pretty."

We called out. "For the Duke." And my ductal shield blazed forth on our chests.

Sergeant Thomas called. "Sophia's own." And her crest was emblazoned on his chest.

Gasping in wide-eyed wonder, Sophia said. "Oh, my, that is glorious."

Sir William managed to gasp out. "What the bloody hell?"

We all called out, "Dark," And our armor returned to black. I said. "We have much to report, Milord."

"Yes, it would seem so, Duke Sherwood."

Servants entered carrying refreshments for the group.

I said. "That will be all for now."

The group gathered around the table and got food and drinks as they preferred. As we all settled in our seats, Sir William said.

"You should probably be starting this report from when you left."

"Yes, Milord," I said. When we were out of sight, we were attacked and harassed by wolves. Shortly after noon, we spied a large force of goblins, and they appeared to be moving towards the dwarf village. It may have been their movement driving the wolves into our column. We came upon a flimsy barricade the goblins were using for an ambush. Sending the knights forward, they smashed through the barrier, clearing the way for us. We hurried to the village, where the dwarves received us with open arms. Their clan chief Dworkin shared a tankard of ale with Captain Geoffrey as we arrived.

Dworkin immediately pledged allegiance to the king. They were happy to receive the gift of food and livestock.

After we sat down to eat, I began negotiations. Dworkin's only demand was the need for them to set up proper guilds.

"Guilds?" Asked Sir William.

Yes, Milord, mining, smithing, woodworking, masonry, that sort of thing. They have pledged to me as their Duke to follow my rule. Of course, I accepted all of this, pending the king's approval.

Dworkin felt that was not enough and decided on a couple of demonstrations first. We will now perform for you because you will not believe us if we tell you.

There was a knock at the door, and Captain Geoffrey and Sergeant Mackey entered.

"Oh, yes," I said. "There will be some changes to my command."

"Sergeant Thomas, attention to orders."

Sergeant Thomas stood to attention, saluting.

"Sergeant Thomas, you are promoted to Command Master Sergeant for the Northern Army. You will report to Sir William in my absence, and your current function has been extended to include the entire Northern Army.

"Sergeant Mackey, attention to orders."

Sergeant Mackey snapped to attention, saluting.

"Sergeant Mackey, you have been promoted to First Sergeant of First Company."

"That is all for orders." I stepped forward, shaking Thomas's hand while the rest of the companions gathered around to congratulate him. I then turned to Sergeant Mackey taking his hand and slapping him on the shoulder.

"You and Captain Geoffrey head down and set up that demonstration in the courtyard for me. We will be down in a few minutes, and you can celebrate your promotions later."

"Yes, Milord." Said Sergeant Mackey.

Turning to Captain Geoffrey, I said. "I knew he would be your first choice as a replacement for Sergeant Thomas."

"Yes, Milord, thank you very much."

"Now, before I forget," I said. "This is Tarija. She is a tiger shifter, and we met her on the road back here from the dwarf village. She has chosen Sergeant Thomas as her mate, and they will both move into the castle."

"Perhaps Milady Sophia, your maids could find them a suitable apartment near yours."

"Thank you, Milord." Said Tarija. "I could have found rooms at the inn."

"No, I will not have you separated. The things you know will be most valuable to everyone. At the same time, we will be able to help you adjust to this world."

"That is true, thank you, Milord," Tarija said.

"Now, Sir William, let us move down to the courtyard where they have the demonstration setup."

"Very well." Said Sir William as we all stood.

CHAPTER

18

Arriving in the courtyard, we found a stand holding three armor sets.

"Milord, take your sword and strike all three armor sets."

"You know what damage this sword will do, Duke Sherwood?"

"Yes, Milord, that is the point."

Sir William struck the leather armor first, leaving a relatively large gash. The knights' breastplate was dented and had a smaller gash. Rolling his shoulders, he stepped in front of the dwarf-made armor. Taking an overhand swing, he cried out as his sword bounced off the armor, not leaving a mark.

"My God." Sir William said. "I nearly broke my wrists. How is this possible? My sword has never failed me before."

"Yes, Milord, that was our reaction to the demonstration. Here try my sword on the old armor, as the dwarves also made it. Do not touch the blade with your hands." I handed him the sword by the sheath.

Sir William drew the sword, and I smiled at his surprise at how light it was. Turning back to the old armor, he said. "Are you sure this blade is strong enough? It looks pretty flimsy for such a big weapon."

"It will be fine, Milord. Take the same swing as you did before."

Sir William did as I asked and yelped in surprise as the blade sheared through the armor and the post supporting it.

Sophia giggled as Sir William staggered to the side, losing his balance. Sir William swung at the other armor set with much the same result. Sheathing the sword, he handed it back to me.

"Who has these weapons and armor?"

"All of us and Sir Penrose with his knights and a thirty-man team. The only exception was my love's bow, which is God-wrought, and dwarves cannot make something that powerful."

Sir William's eyes widen at that.

"However, we have bows nearly as powerful and indestructible. Come over here for the next demonstration. It will be safer."

Moving about twenty-five paces from the armor, Merriam giggled. "It is my turn now."

Removing her bow from the case, she quickly strung it with her new Mythril string.

"Milord, observe the new armor for this event."

"Very well." Sir William replied.

Selecting an arrow, Merriam drew and fired in one motion. Everyone watched as the arrow shattered on impact. Sir William gasped, walking up to the armor and inspecting it closely.

He turned to say in wonder. "There is no mark. I want a set of this armor."

We all laughed, knowing how he felt.

Tarija said. "Why did you use a common arrow, Milady?"

Merriam laughed. "This castle is my home, and I wanted to leave it standing. We are demonstrating the armor, not the bow."

Eyes widening, Tarija said. "That much power?"

"I do not know yet, as I have not had a chance to test my bow."

"We will find such a place soon, my love."

"Now," I said. "You and every man in our army will have a set of this armor. The process has already begun, and the only reason so few of us have it now is the lack of raw material. They are in the process of opening mines for the ore they need."

As we headed back up to the study, Little-Jon stopped by the cart and grabbed the chest from the back, bringing it with him. He sat it by the end of the table, and once we were all seated, I resumed my report.

Reaching into my pouch, I handed Sir William a sheaf of paper. "This first part is my dispatch to the King, and I detailed the agreement with Dworkin and a plan for arming our troops, including the cost."

Sir William was looking at the paper and not paying attention.

I finally laughed. "Okay, maybe that invention first. Then we will get back to the report." Standing, I opened the chest, taking out two bundles of poles.

Coming back over, I handed one to Merriam and then began unfolding it, setting the frame on the floor by the desk, and Merriam did the same in front of Sophia. Then we went back to the chest to get a writing desk, bringing them back to set on the stand. We then pulled out a paper and pen from the desk.

I then began explaining. "This is a portable writing desk, and it comes with five hundred sheets of paper, three pens, and an inkwell here at the top."

I held up the pen, uncapped it, and filled it while explaining the procedure. Merriam was following along, showing Sophia. Taking a bit of cloth, I wiped the pen's tip clean and explained how to write with the pen.

When you get the hang of lifting the pen, each time you stop, it becomes easier. You can write a hundred pages before you have to refill the pen. It takes practice to get the flow without leaving blotches on the paper.

"By all the Gods." Said Sophia. "This is fantastic, and the demonstration has been impressive far beyond the rest."

Merriam said. "Sophia scholars worldwide will be clamoring for these, not to mention nobles and merchants."

"Did you perhaps pauper the kingdom for these things?" Asked Sir William.

I chuckled. "No, Milord. The desk with pens, paper, and ink cost five gold. Replacement pens or a refill of paper and ink cost one gold."

Sergeant Thomas's armor and weapons as a set were ten gold. A set of knight's armor, including for the horse, costs twenty gold.

"Good Lord." Said, Sir William. "My armor cost five times that."

I chuckled. "It weighs ten times what this armor does."

"Why did you not just bring me this armor set?"

"Therein lies the rub Milord. The dwarves need to measure you very carefully to get the fit right, and I had to go through a complete set of sword forms to get the measurements perfect. It takes about a quarter of a day. Then you can go relax, and about mid-afternoon, the dwarves will have your armor made."

"What?" Sir William exclaimed. "How can that be possible? It took two months for my armor, and it still pinches."

I smiled. "I know. I wondered why we did not have these dwarves before."

Sophia giggled. "Because the Sherriff had not opened the box. Therefore the orb could not drop a clan of dwarves in your lap."

"This is very true," I said. In any case, things will go a lot faster once the dwarves set up their guilds. For now, there are only five hundred of them, and they can train anyone if they are capable of learning the magic. The biggest problem with Mythril armor is that it takes magic to work. Each time they have enough people, they will split off to form guildhalls in towns and cities. For now, we are limited to one clan. Capable as they are, they can only outfit twenty-five men daily and, by that standard, outfit one company every month. Dworkin says it will take two weeks to stockpile the raw material needed.

There came a knock at the door, and Denby stepped in. "Milord, dinner will be served in one hour. If you and your companions wish to bathe, tubs are ready in your quarters."

"Excellent, Denby," I said. "Could you have a room set up for Sergeant Thomas and Tarija near Sir William's room?"

"I have arranged a nice room, Milord. I also have a maid arranged for lady Tarija."

"Thank you, Denby, that will be all."

"We can resume this over dinner, Sir William."

"Yes, I will write a cover letter for these dispatches to the King."

"Those documents are for you. Milord, Sir Penrose has my dispatches with him. You can include your letter in his pouch."

"They leave first thing in the morning for Cambridge."

"Why not just use the king's messengers for these dispatches?"

"Sir Penrose and his men are the other forty-three entirely armed and armored by the dwarfs. They will also be bringing two desk sets for the king and his scribe. Among other gifts from Dworkin. They also have the scriptorium tabard built into their armor."

Servants began filing in to set the table for dinner. We broke off the conversation to take our baths and freshen up.

We spent an enjoyable evening dining with Sir William and Sophia. We completed our story of the past two days and what we had accomplished.

Sophia nodded as Merriam related the tale of Tarija and her mating ritual with Sergeant Thomas.

Sophia asked Tarija. "Do you not get married?"

Tarija replied. "No, Milady, a soul-bond mating is far more potent than any willing wedding ritual."

Sophia said. "Friar Tuck will be most disappointed."

Merriam giggled. "Tuck will have many more opportunities to marry people."

The only part of the evening that worried me was how quiet things had become.

By the time we got to bed, we were so tired that we had just gone to sleep.

I climbed out of bed. The steely light of dawn was beginning to sharpen the horizon. Being careful not to disturb the others, I pulled on my armor and gathered my weapons. I waited until I was in the hallway to put my boots on. Moving quickly down the stairway, I stepped out into the courtyard. Sir Penrose and his men were preparing to leave. I went over.

Coming to attention, Sir Penrose snapped a salute and said. "Milord."

"Sir Penrose. Are you ready to depart?"

"Yes, Milord, we are just finishing loading the wagon and saddling our horses."

"Excellent, Sir Penrose. Godspeed and a safe journey."

"Thank you, Milord. With the wagon, we should make very good time."

"I am sure you will. As I said, do not push yourself so hard that you get ambushed. Some of these monsters are pretty difficult to kill."

"Yes, Milord, I was part of killing that Manticore. An experience I care not to repeat."

I chuckled. "You have done better than me then. I killed a few gremlins. In any case, be safe now, carry on."

"Yes, Milord, we shall be back soon with or without the king."

Walking away with a wave, I headed for the guardhouse. I found Sergeant Stone staffing the desk.

Leaping to his feet, Sergeant Stone snapped a crisp salute. "Milord. I did not expect to see you this early."

I smiled. "You know me better than that, Sergeant Stone. I am always up with the dawn."

"Yes, Milord, but now you have a good reason not to be." He smiled.

I laughed. "But it is hard to change the lifetime of habit."

"Aye, Milord, I wager that is very true."

"What have you heard from the patrols overnight?"

"Every patrol reports nothing, and we have not had an encounter in two nights."

"That has me worried things are too quiet for my liking."

"Aye, Milord, it is like that itch you get between your shoulder blades. That sense of impending doom."

"Yes, Sergeant, you have it exactly. I will go out and continue my rounds."

Leaving the guardhouse, I turned, climbing the stairs to the wall. I continued up into the gate tower. I waved at the men to carry on before they jumped to attention. "I just want to look around, and things have been tranquil."

"Yes, Milord." One of the men said. "It has been very quiet these last couple of nights."

"Milord." One of the men pointed slightly to the southwest just above the treeline. Faintly I could hear a whoop, whoop noise coming from the west. As the sound grew, a herd of deer burst from the forest. Out of the darkness, something huge was flying toward the castle.

"Sound the alarm now," I said. The men jumped and began ringing the bell.

The huge something folded, its wings back, and stooped like a hawk. It landed on the herd with a resounding thump that shook the castle.

Rushing down the stairs from the wall, I grabbed the first man I could.

"You run to get my wife, husbands, and Lord Merlin down here in full armor." Running into the stables, I called out. "Saddle horses for my companion's Captain Geoffrey and Sargeant Thomas." I stepped back into the courtyard and saw men forming or racing to man the walls.

I saw my companions running up as hands began bringing mine and the other horses from the stables.

Merriam was leading but not by very much.

"Mount up," I said. "We are going to be in for an exciting morning."

"What was that noise and shaking?" Merriam asked.

"That, my love, was the sound of a greater dragon stooping on a herd of deer behind the castle."

"A Greater Dragon?" She screeched.

"What can you tell me, Merlin?"

"Approach slowly with confidence and be very polite. Keep your weapons down, grandson. They will do you no good. Merriam, if this goes badly, your bow may be the only thing that can kill it, not with a natural arrow but a magic bolt. You will see a lighter patch of scales at the base of the neck. That is where the heart is. Do not miss it."

"Grandfather, have you ever known me to miss a target," Merriam said with a huff.

We rode through the gate and raced to the edge of town, where we slowed to a walk. Merlin said, circling out onto the field so we could approach from the front. "Hold up."

"The dragon is feeding. We will wait until it is finished. He has seen us, but if we do not approach, he will leave us alone for now."

We waited quietly until the dragon finished the third deer it had caught. With its meal ended, it lay down and folded its wings and tail curled around its side.

With a deep rumble like an earthquake, the dragon spoke. "You may approach humans, and we will speak of many truths."

The companions and I rode forward slowly, stopping ten paces away.

"Lord Dragon," I spoke up. "I am Sir Guy Sherwood, Duke of Nottingham and this castle's caretaker. Our wife, Duchess Merriam, Merlin the Wizard, The Oracal of Athena, Lady Sophia, and Sir William are with me, and Captian Geoffery and Master Sergeant Thomas of the king's army. These are my brother-husband's Robyn of Loxley Baron of Derby, Will Scarlet Sheriff of Nottingham, and Little-Jon Captain of the Huntsman.

"Good, I have found the companions gathered. My name is too long for you to remember, so you may call me Stormavgaard. I have some wisdom to share now that I have broken my fast. I will transform into my other forum so we may retire to more comfortable surroundings to speak."

The air seemed to waver around the dragon as he shimmered. When the air cleared, a man as large as Little-Jon stood before us wearing a loincloth.

"Oh, my, he is a big one even in this form." Giggled Merriam.

"No, you cannot have him, my love. Our bed is already full." Said Will, chuckling.

"Little-Jon, your clothes should fit him."

"Yes, dear, I thought of that as I came out here. I also had Sir William bring an extra horse."

"Milady?" I asked.

"Yes, dear one, he is part of this."

Dismounting, Sir William led the extra horse over to Stormavgaard. He held the horse while handing over the clothing.

"It is just loose breeches and a tunic for the time being. We can have tailors brought in later to outfit you."

"Thank you, Milord." Said Stormavgaard. That will not be needed as I have plenty of clothing in my bag of holding. What I am wearing now just happens to be suitable clothing for where I was. Some women with larger breasts will wear something up top to support them. But for the most part, this is all we wear. Quickly dressing in the clothes Sir William brought, he took the horse's reins. Mounting, he showed horse skill as soon as Sir William was back in the saddle. We all rode back to the castle.

Dismounting at the doors to the keep, I turned to the troops in the courtyard. "Sergeant Mackey, we could put a bit more polish on that response time. You may dismiss the men for breakfast."

"Right, you lot you heard Milord. You can feed your faces, and then we will come back and do some more drills. Dismissed." Barked Sergeant Mackey.

CHAPTER

19

"Please, Stormavgaard, this way," I said, moving toward the doors.

As we entered, I saw Denby and waved him over. "I will need to speak with you further but have breakfast sent to the study for now."

Turning to the others, I said. "Sir William, if you would be so good as to lead our guest to the study, I will be there in a moment."

"Certainly, Duke Sherwood. Stormavgaard this way if you please." He then led them up the stairs.

A few moments later, Denby rejoined me.

"Denby, how much more room do we have in this castle?"

Your Grace, your wing is full, but we still have the south wing on that floor. That wing contains a set of royal apartments. Then on the third floor, we have the apartments the regent was using with several other apartments for minor nobility or diplomats. Then we have the west wing above the study for a significant Noble and large entourage of thirty or more.

Lastly, we have the south wing on the third floor, just a series of large comfortable rooms, but they have been closed for many years.

"Very well, Denby, here is what I want you to do. Hire some extra servants, maids, and footmen primarily. Clean and open all the rooms, as the way things are going we may need them very soon. Keep the royal apartments available for the king. And when I have talked to Stormavgaard, I will decide where we will put him."

"Yes, My Liege." Denby hurried off, and I headed for the study.

I entered the study just as the others were eating and joined them at the table as Sir William began the meeting.

Sir William asked Stormavgaard. "How long will you be staying here?"

"This is now my world as much as yours. Of course, I will find a suitable place to build my eyrie with your king's permission. I recognize dwarven wrought armor and weapons. Does this mean you have a clan nearby?"

"Yes, Milord," I said. "A clan led by the dwarf Dworkin arrived not far from here. We have met them, and they have pledged allegiance to the king, and their only request was to set up guilds."

"Excellent," Stormavgaard said. "If they have masons, I will engage them to build my eyrie."

"Yes, they have masons, and they have been sent to Derby to build the Baron Loxley's castle.

"Oh," said Stormavgaard. "Is this castle to be built in a high place?"

"Yes," said Robyn. "The location is a five-hundred-foot hill with a sheer drop on one side."

Stormavgaard said. "I would look at this location. If you are willing, may we share this castle?"

Robyn chuckled. "The purpose of this castle is to house the troops to protect the area. I will have them also build a manor house for the summer. Because we are all married, we will spend most of our time here in Nottingham."

"Did the dwarves arrive in good shape?" asked Stormavgaard.

"There was a sickness affecting them from a previous mine. The dwarfs moved to a new location when they stepped through the portal. Our cleric Friar Tuck healed the sick, and they are doing fine now."

"Good, often, clans or groups get broken up by these portals. Part of my purpose is to create portals to rejoin the clans."

Sir William said. "You can open portals to send these monsters back?"

"No, Milord, my portals are only one way like the orb. The only difference is my portals are more stable to facilitate the transfer of groups."

Merlin said. "I wish we had you here when my fellows created the orb. At least then, we may have had some help, and I might even have been able to save my country and my sister."

"Yes, our greatest regret was not sending a dragon the first time. We thought the problem had been solved when the orb stopped opening portals."

"With my sister's help and sacrifice, I managed to trap the orb in this box," Merlin said. He held out pandora's box for him to examine.

"Yes, I see the soul essence magic in this box is very powerful. I also guess your purpose is to return the orb to this box."

"The prophecy demands we succeed in this task. Thus the reason for us companions."

"Our scholars recorded the prophecy as written some eight thousand years ago. It was before my time as I am only a thousand years old."

"I see." Said Merriam. "Like we druids, you live just as long as you need to."

"Yes, something like that, although I do not know of any personally. In any case, to get back on the subject. Once you find this orb and contain it again, I will ensure its destruction."

"Unlike most beings drawn in by the orb, I have had time to prepare myself."

Servants entered to clear away the dishes. On their heels, Sir Penrose entered.

"Milord," said Sir Penrose. "Unless you state otherwise, I have delayed my departure until this situation resolves itself. I thought you may have additional dispatches for the king."

"Thank you, Sir Penrose, that is quick thinking. We must wait until the morning, as we will have further dispatches."

"Duke Sherwood, may I ask a question of you, Sir?"

"Certainly, Sir Penrose, ask anything you like."

"Well, Milord, I overheard you mention to Baron Loxley that the companies were too bulky."

"Yes, I have thought about it for a while now, and I have just not had time to sit down and plan anything."

"Well, Milord, I have been thinking about this myself. I have an idea based on increasing the size of our companies, calling it a battalion, and dividing the battalion into smaller companies and then platoons. It would give you multiple configurations for any situation. The team I am leading now equals a platoon."

"Okay, stop right there for just a moment. My love, would you be so good as to lend Sir Penrose your desk?"

"Certainly, my love, I do not need it today that I can think of."

"Good, Sir Penrose, you have the rest of the day to write up a proposal for this configuration. I will want three copies for myself, Sir William, and the king."

"Yes, Milord, I will get to it right away."

"Good, my love, if you would take Sir Penrose and give him your desk."

"Yes, my love. This way Sir Penrose." Merriam said, leading him from the room.

Merlin said. "That sounded very close to how armies are configured in the time I was from."

"The concept did sound intriguing." Said, Sir William.

Stormavgaard said. "I chose wisely in placing myself with your people. You are quick to see a good idea and adopt it."

I chuckled. "I have been watching that young man for some time now, and I knew he was capable of something like this. I planted the seed and want to see what grows from it."

Sophia gushed. "Well said, dear one. I love to see people expand their horizons."

"Yes, Milady Sophia." Said Stormavgaard. "Now on to the other interesting subjects."

"Lady Tarija of the Snow Elk guild. You got drawn into this world, and I have not seen you since your rank 'D' quest."

"Yes, Milord Dragon, I jumped back to avoid an undead wolf when I found myself here. And contrary to all cat expectations, I landed on my ass."

We all got a hearty laugh at that.

"I suspected as much and checked the archives. Your companions made it safely back but had great concern for you, and I have sent an update through our archives telling them you are safe."

"Thank you, Milord. I have found my soulmate and have no desire to return even if I could." She said, wrapping her arms around Sergeant Thomas.

Stormavgaard chuckled. "You adventurers are all the same. I want to point out that the guild and your companions expressed interest in coming here."

"There have been no indications of dungeons in this realm, and at least none are close, or I would have smelled them. Please send them a message saying we will wait and see if dungeons and the leveling system appear."

"That would be a good idea, Lady Tarija. I have been thinking of building an adventurers guild myself. Perhaps, for now, you could oversee our effort. Then should dungeons appear, you could have the basics for your guild to merge on ours."

"That is an excellent idea, Milord Duke. It will take some time for a dungeon to mature enough for me."

I went to the desk, grabbed a piece of paper, and scribbled a note. Coming back over, I handed it to Tarija. "See my treasurer Digby, and he will pay you."

Tarija looked at the note, and her eyes grew round. "One hundred gold, Milord? Whom do I have to assassinate?"

I laughed. "The king made your mate a Captain of the Realm, and he was gifted land and a one hundred crown stipend, and I could not pay you less in good conscience. It reminds me Sergeant Thomas look around Nottingham. Let me know if you see a piece of land that strikes your fancy."

"Yes, Milord, I will do that very thing."

"Take your time. There is no hurry."

Stormavgaard said. "While we are on the subject of land Baron Robyn. Perhaps you could show me the castle site on a map."

"I would be delighted, Stormavgaard." Robyn moved over to the sideboard. "Let me see. Oh yes, here it is." Grabbing a map, he returned to the table, rolling it out.

"Here we are, Nottingham, and here is where Dworkin has set up his town. Then another half-day march on the west road from that fork is Derby. Just where the road enters the village on the northside is a large hill where the castle will be built."

"Good, I will fly up there this morning and take a look. I can be back before dinner, no problem."

"You should hold off for a couple of days, Stormavgaard. We can send a messenger to warn the troops and prevent accidents."

"That would be no problem." Said Stormavgard. "I could take Robyn and Milady with me."

The ride would be quite safe, as I can carry passengers like diplomats and royals from kingdom to kingdom. We provide this service at a cost to royalty. We dragons are mind-linked from birth. It is one of the many ways we build our horde when we are young. As well as being advisors and sounding boards for scholars our trade is information. We all know what each dragon knows, not mind reading as we cannot talk mind-to-mind. We have the information like a library in our minds, a place full of books to research data. We can even pass notes back and forth between us.

Merlin cried out. "So that is what it is."

You have something like the world wide web in your minds. All the information you have ever learned is linked to one source. The humans of my time built a net to present electronic data spread worldwide, and anyone could access it anytime. Dear dragon, you will be obsolete in about nine hundred years.

"However, due to your longevity, if you build a clan and build the web yourself, you would be rich beyond compare."

"As I am the only dragon on this planet," said Stormavgaard. "I must procreate and build a clan. The first step is to build my castle or expand a castle with suitable accommodation. Once the castle is complete, I will build my nest, lining it with my horde. Then it will be time to call my first mate to me. I need to see this castle as it must be substantial to accommodate a dragon eyrie. Are you ready to leave, Sir Robyn, Milady Merriam?"

"What about flying monsters?" I asked.

Stormavgaard laughed. "Have you seen any monsters around in the last couple of days?"

"Oddly enough, no," I said.

That is because I am the apex predator in this world. All the monsters within two hundred miles of my presence runaway."

"Well, that explains it, my love. You have my permission to go. Enjoy your flight and have fun."

Squealing with delight, Merriam jumped up and ran from the room.

Robyn held his hand up, smiling. "Any second now."

Merriam bolted back through the door, grabbing Robyn. "Come on, Stormavgaard, let us go, hurry."

Everyone at the table laughed.

"Do not forget your weapons even if you are riding the most fearsome creature in the world."

"We should watch them leave to have some idea how this works," I said.

"I agree." Said, Sir William.

When the group got to the field outside of town, Stormavgaard turned to us. "It would be better if the dwarven masons came here after building our castle. This way, they can add a landing tower to the back of your castle. Building platforms at every castle will take some time, but it will make things easier."

"So, how does this work?" Asked Merriam.

"I will move over here, and once I transform, I will lie down, and you may step on my right claw, and I will raise you. Ten spines on my neck and shoulders are flattened on the front side, and you sit between them and use them as a backrest. The spine in front of you will have handholds."

"I usually wear a riding harness. But it will not be needed for this short flight."

"Derby usually is a two-day ride from here with wagons. As the crow flies, we would be talking thirty miles by road forty."

Stormavgaard laughed. "My size is very deceiving. I can cover forty miles in about ten minutes unburdened. Having passengers and no harness, it will take about thirty minutes."

Stormavgaard walked over about thirty ft away, turned to the side, and transformed. His huge sixty-foot bulk lay down. He turned his right front claw over, making a cupped platform. We could all see the flattened spines from the base of his neck to his wing root.

Stepping onto his claw, Stormavgaard raised Robyn and Merriam. They stepped off and sat between two spines with Merriam in front. They reached for handholds and took a firm grip. Turning his head, Stormavgaard asked. "Ready?"

At their nods, he said. "Now hang on tight as the take-off can be a bit of a jolt."

Stormavgaard gathered his haunches, opened his wings, and leaped into the air.

The group on the ground heard Robyn's yell, almost drowned out by Merriam's screech of joy. They could still hear her laughing as they crossed the treeline.

Sir William said. "I am not sure I want to try that anytime soon."

Sophia laughed. "It would be quite the experience by its look."

"Only if you like heights, Milady." One of the men behind them grumbled.

I glanced over my shoulder and saw Sergeant Boils' mining squad, who was the escort.

"Yes, Sergeant, I will keep that in mind if I send troops by a dragon."

"Thank you, Milord. That would be most appreciated." Said the Sergeant.

Chuckling, Sir William said. "Best get back to the keep, I have work, and I am sure everyone else has tasks to perform."

"Yes, I have a schedule to write. One that will allow the units to cycle through the dwarven village for arms and armor."

"That is an excellent idea." Said, Sir William. "I will assist you once my letter is written. I suspect the king will be coming this way once he reads this report."

"Good Lord," I said. "That means his bevy of butterflies will descend upon us soon."

Will laughed. "I will have the dungeons cleared out and prepared."

I actually thought about that for a moment, then shook my head. "No, just clear out the extra barracks and the top floor of the south wing."

CHAPTER

20

Laughing and yelling, Merriam pointed to the north and ahead of them. "Look there," she called. "You can see the dwarven village from here; the view is incredible. I can see for miles."

"The view is fantastic. We could have saved ourselves much trouble on the crusade if we had a dragon."

Stormavgaard looked back. "We would not have given you that kind of an advantage. We do not fight or make war except in self-defense, and our purpose is to negotiate and find a better nonviolent way to do things."

"Stormavgaard," said Merriam. "I am afraid you have found yourself in the wrong world for peace. Our existence has been nothing but a battle for survival."

"Then it would appear I have my work cut out for me." Said Stormavgaard.

I was doing paperwork when the commotion began. Grabbing my sword, I ran out to see dwarves running helter-skelter. "Kristoff, what is going on?" I called.

"We must prepare the lord dragon comes this way, and we must stop construction until he makes his wishes known."

"A dragon? You say. Sergeant Wilson call the men to arms and prepare the defenses We may have a battle before this day is over."

"Oh, no good, Captain, you would not defeat this dragon. Your men should be ready to greet him as is befitting a great lord. We must keep this space on top of the hill clear for his landing". Another dwarf pointed east. "And it looks like he has riders."

Looking up, I squinted. "Yes, I believe you are right, and it does look like riders. My god, he is enormous. We would have never stood a chance in a battle."

"That is correct, Captain, about the only weapon that may take down a great dragon, would be the Lady Merriam's bow.

The dragon stooped and flared his wings as he landed with a thump.

Miladies voice screamed. "That was great. Do it again."

The dragon gave a rumbling chuckle. "I thought you might like that, Milady."

Baron Robyn laughed. "We need to take off again. I think I left my stomach up there somewhere."

"Yes, that was so much fun." Cried Merriam waving her arms.

Raising his claw to let the couple down, when they got clear, he transformed.

Mariam said. "I thought you would be dressed in a loincloth again."

"No, Milady, what I wear transforms with me. By then, they had walked over to us, waiting for them. What I wore before was customary for the warm, humid place I was in."

I snapped a salute. "Milords and Milady. May I present Master Mason Kristoff?"

Merriam said, "Captain Keating and Kristoff. May I present my husband, Robyn Loxley, Baron of Derby. This Is Milord Stormavgaard."

Stormavgaard said. "We have come to inspect the building site for this castle, as the Baron has graciously allowed me to share it with him."

"So, you require an eyrie?" Said Kristoff.

"Yes, said Stormavgaard, "one large enough to host troops to guard the area when I am away."

"Excellent. "said Kristoff. "We should step over to my tent. I have plans for several magnificent creations you may choose from, Milord. Perkins, have the men gather up the markers. There will be changes."

Robyn turned to Captain Keating. "You may dismiss your men to their duties, captain. Your men performed very well forming up. I appreciate your diligence.

"Thank you, Milord. Perhaps you would join me for lunch when you are done looking at plans."

"We would be delighted, captain," said Merriam.

"Excellent. We will see you later then, Milady and Milords." The captain turned away, giving orders to dismiss the men.

Following Kristoff, we walked into a tent where he moved to a table, rolling up some plans. Putting them into one of the tubes in a rack and then pulling out a thick roll of drawings. Setting them on the table, Kristoff said. "Flatten." The bundle of drawings rolled flat.

Robyn laughed. "I hope we can teach our maps that magic. That would come in handy on a campaign."

Stormavgaard laughed. "It is a handy enchantment for scrolls and maps."

Kristoff grunted. It also helps to keep the paper from tearing. Now, these are all view drawings of castles I have designed. This first one was the one I was building. As you can see, it was a simple keep meant to house five hundred men, a baron, his family, and staff. The next few are similar, increasing to five thousand men. He pulled each back showing ever more impressive castles, letting them hang over the table's edge. Now we come to the first of the eyries, and I gasped.

"That is gorgeous. Well, the castles were all gorgeous. But this one with the tower is impressive."

"Thank you," said Kristoff. This one will house five hundred men, two dragons, and one hundred staff."

Stormavgaard said. "This will be much too small. It is likely to be my home base. I will need room for an entire clan."

Kristoff said. "Yes, Milord Dragon, I merely showed the lady a starter castle. Please look through the drawings and see what you like. We can make adjustments to all of them to suit any purpose."

I began flipping through the drawings. "These are all so glorious," I said. "How can we possibly choose between them?"

Robyn grunted. "We only need one, my love."

"For now." She quipped. "I think Nottingham is going to need a makeover. After all, if Stormavgaard is to be part of the family, we will need to accommodate him at our home castle."

Robyn shook his head. "Yes, my love, we will see what the duke says."

I continued flipping through the drawings. When I suddenly stopped crying out. "This one."

"An excellent choice, Milady. This one offers accommodation for three thousand troops and a thousand staff, and you would be able to host five hundred guests. As you can see, the eyrie rises behind a hundred feet. It will accommodate a clan of twenty dragons and a harem of thirty for you, Milord. An aquifer below the hill would provide more than enough water for twice that number."

"I do like the shape of this castle." Said Stormavgaard. "I would like the larger eyrie on this design." He said, pointing to another drawing.

"Humm." Said Kristoff. "We could do that by building this mountain eyrie out of the cliff at the back of the hill. This eyrie could accommodate up to sixty dragons. Once your young are ready to mate, I assume they would move away to find their own eyrie."

"We saw that sheer face as we were landing."

Robyn said. "I admit they are beautiful, but how would they stand up to an attack?"

Stormavgaard chuckled. "Crafters will infuse the walls with magic, and there is not an engine made that could damage them. It would take some potent magics to breach these walls as if I would let anyone get close enough to try. Kristoff, I see there is room for expansion in this design."

"See, love, we could have the most beautiful castle complete with our watch, dragon."

The men all laughed, shaking their heads.

"Yes, Milady, you may have three or four dragons in a hundred years."

"How long do you take to grow?" I asked.

Stormavgaard said. "We are very slow to grow. It takes fifty years, and we can molt ten times to reach thirty ft or about half my size. After fifty years, our growth slows, and it takes up to two hundred more years to reach full size. By then, a Drake has had the training to begin diplomatic work."

Robyn said. "I guess that comes with being so big and long-lived."

Stormavgaard said. "Elves take up to fifty years to mature and live up to two thousand years."

"An eyrie for sixty dragons would be most suitable for my needs. Now, Kristoff, is this fully equipped for the cost? I want the most formidable defenses you can make."

I believe the plan for troop dispositions is only to have a thousand men here. Perhaps we could shift the staff quarters and increase guest accommodation by a thousand, giving us room to house more people in case of a siege.

Yes, we could do that with no problem. The staff and troops are mainly housed in the walls. With maximum effort, Milords and Lady for this design would take about four months to build. It would take another two months to finish the interior to make it livable. The craftsman would simultaneously add the finishing touches. The armorers and wood crafters will have their separate schedules for you. I would think that with overlaps, eight months will complete this castle. One hundred thousand gold should cover it unless there are further changes."

Robyn and I gasped at the price and build time.

Stormavgaard laughed. "That is not very much at all." Reaching into his tunic, "here are five bars of Mythril and five bars of platinum."

I gasped in wide-eyed wonder. "How much are those bars worth?"

Kristoff chuckled, "a bar of Mythril is worth fifteen thousand gold, and platinum is running at five thousand gold. These are much easier to transport when making large payments. These should cover it nicely, Milord. I thank you very much."

"Excellent," said Stormavgaard. "Now, Baron Robyn, your castle portion will be small. I would think it fair you kick in ten thousand gold."

Robyn cringed a bit at the cost. "As I do not carry that much on me, would it be okay if I sent the gold directly to Dworkin?"

Stormavgaard laughed. "No, Robyn, I have paid the total price. Give the ten thousand to me, and we will be square."

"Once we get back, we can just pay you out of the treasury at Nottingham."

"That will be good enough." Said Stormavgaard. "I think it might be time for some lunch. Master Mason, we shall let you get to work."

"Thank you, Milord Dragon. I have always dreamed of getting this opportunity."

Stepping out, the group moved over to Captain Keating's tent

Stormavgaard said. "This is a rich land with little population and many resources."

"I know." Said Robyn. "The village of Derby there is barely getting started. Once the castle is built and the mines have opened, there will be an influx of people. That reminds me, captain, you had best-put word out the dragon is friendly and will not harm people."

"Yes, Milord, they may take some convincing, but we can do that."

"This has been a great visit," I said. "We must spend time here when we return from our quest."

"I agree, my love. By then, the dwarves will have the manor done as well."

"You are building a manor house? Why not just live at the castle?"

"We will have quarters in the castle, but the plan is to use the manor as a summer house. We were going to spend our winters in Nottingham."

"That is fine. Your troops and I can enjoy the hot and cold running water to ourselves."

Captian Keating chuckled. "I am requesting this castle as my posting."

"Pardon me?" I said with a raised eyebrow. "Running water inside? No servants tracking through the house with pails for a bath?"

"Well, no, Milady, plumbing runs to each suite of rooms. They will put a bathroom with tubs, toilet, sink, and shower."

"When Kristoff completes this castle, Sir William will have to move here for a short time. I want Nottingham rebuilt with all these features. We will keep this from the king because I want to hold a grand ball unveiling this castle."

"You are an evil woman, my love. Do you have any idea how many nobles will die from jealousy? And I can hear the screams from the king now."

"Yes, dear, that is the plan."

The men all laughed.

Stormavgaard chuckled. "As much fun as this is, we should be getting back."

"Yes," said Robyn. "There is still much to be done before leaving. Thank you for your hospitality, captain, and I will pass on word of the excellent job you are doing."

"Milady and Milords, have a safe trip home." Captain Keating said.

I giggled. "There is nothing safer than on the back of a dragon."

"This is true." Said Robyn.

Making our way to the top of the hill, Stormavgaard quickly transformed. We settled in place, and Stormavgaard launched himself into the air. The ride home was just as quick, and we soon landed in the field behind the castle.

As we dismounted and Stormavgaard transformed, a carriage approached Jamie and Edwin driving.

"Milords Milady, we thought this would be more convenient." Said, Edwin.

"A capital idea." Said Robyn. "We thought we would have to walk back."

"No, Milord, as soon as guards saw you approaching, they told us to come to get you."

"Well, let us talk to Guy about robbing the treasury, my love."

"According to our vows, it is my treasury too." I giggled.

Stormavgaard laughed. "She has you there, Baron."

"Yes, well, get in so we can get this over with, cheeky woman."

Settling into the carriage, the boys drove us back to the castle, dropping us in front of the keep.

Sir William and I had our heads together at the desk, working on the schedule for arming the troops. I looked up when the doors opened, and Merriam entered with Robyn and Stormavgaard.

I stood and stepped over to Merriam, kissing her. "You are back so soon, my love. Robyn, Stormavgaard, how was your trip?"

"Very expensive, brother husband." Laughed Robyn shaking my hand.

"You would not believe how well it went, my love." Said Merriam. "You may give Stormavgaard ten thousand gold for our portion of the castle."

"Ten thousand?" I asked. "That does not seem very much for a castle to accommodate a dragon."

Merriam pulled the sheet of paper from her pouch. Unfolding it on the desk, she said. "This is what you are buying. It has hot and cold running water inside. But keep that a secret from the king for now, as I want to surprise him."

"This is incredibly beautiful," I said. "How many years will it take to build?"

Stormavgaard laughed. "We are talking about dwarves and their magic. It would take about six months to make it livable and eight months to complete."

Sir William whistled. "Hot and cold running water inside?"

Merriam laughed. "Yes, like open a valve and water pours into your tub."

At that moment, Sophia walked through the door. "Into whose tub?"

"The ones in my new castle." Said Merriam.

"And now we see the proper mindset of a married woman." Merlin laughed.

"And what would that be?" Stormavgaard inquired with a puzzled look on his face.

What is yours is mine, and what is mine is mine." Merlin laughed.

Everyone laughed while Merriam stamped her foot.

I rose to step around the desk and kiss the pout off Merriam's lips. I said. "Why not go rest until dinner, my love? Meanwhile, Stormavgaard and I will go to the treasury and settle accounts."

"Good idea," Merriam said. "Come, Robyn, we can go and take a nap."

Robyn raised his eyebrow. "A nap?"

"Well, maybe a short one after." She said, pulling Robyn from the room.

Sir William said. "I will have Jamie and Edwin make copies of this document for the company captains while you give away all your gold."

I laughed and said. "Come on, Stormavgaard, let us go rob the treasury."

In the treasure room, I called out. "Hello Digby, how are the counts going?"

"Very good, Milord. We have put a value on some of those gems and pieces of jewelry, but the more extravagant ones are harder to place a value on."

"So bottom line, net worth?"

"Approximately three million gold Milord if we were to liquidate all assets. That includes things like artwork, business holdings, but not these pieces of jewelry over here that I cannot place a value on."

Stormavgaard wandered over, looking at the pieces pointed out by Digby.

"What of these pieces over here?" Stormavgaard asked.

"They were special commissions and had no jeweler mark on them, and therefore we cannot find an owner or place a value on them."

"I am afraid we may just have to break them up and melt down the gold." Said Digby.

"No." Said Stormavgaard. "I have a better idea." He then walked over to Digby's desk. Reaching into his bag of holding, Stormavgaard began pulling metal bars out. Setting six of them on the desk, he said. "These are Mythril, and each bar is worth fifteen thousand gold. I will take this necklace for these six bars." He said, walking over and picking up one of them. "This piece alone is worth a hundred thousand. It is for a queen, which evens our score on the castle, and you get something extra for something I want."

"Sounds very reasonable, does it not, Digby?" I asked.

"Yes, Milord, very generous if we had taken that piece apart, it would only be worth about twenty thousand."

The value in these pieces is not the gold and gems but the artwork. I can tell you now these three are worth eighty thousand and those two hundred thousand and that Crown there two hundred fifty thousand.

So there, your treasury went up seven hundred ninety thousand or as near as makes no difference.

"Gods do not tell Merriam how much is in here. She will want the biggest, most spectacular castle in the world."

"Oh, heavens no, Milord. I have informed Milady we have sufficient funds for five years of operations, or about two hundred fifty thousand."

"That reminds me," I said. "Stormavgaard, if you would be so good as to keep Digby company for a moment, I will be right back. I need to get something."

Running upstairs to the study, I grabbed another desk set. On my way back down, I called Denby to follow. Coming back into the treasury, I set the desk on the table.

"This is for you both to share," I said. I then spent the next half hour showing the men how to use the desk.

"Milord, this will be a boon for doing my ledgers."

"Yes." Said Denby. "It will save so much time doing castle accounts."

"That was my plan all along. You are most welcome and need not say anymore."

"Yes, Milord." They said in unison.

"Stormavgaard, do you see anything else you might like to buy?"

"I may be interested in a few things, but it will have to wait until my eyrie is built. Once I see my eyrie, I will know what might be suitable." Stormavgaard chuckled.

I laughed. "Dinner will be ready soon, so we should get back upstairs."

"Yes, Milord." Said Denby, "Dinner should be ready in half an hour."

"Thank you, Denby. I will see you later, Digby. I will have another set of books for you to look after."

"Yes, Milord, that will be no problem."

We quickly returned to the study to find our two squires working diligently.

"How are things going, Sir William?" I asked.

"Very well, the boys are just finishing up the last copies."

"Excellent, dinner will be ready very soon," I said.

CHAPTER

21

Entering our chambers, Robyn began removing his armor. Alicia came from the bathing room with Camila on her heels as he was about to pull down his bottoms.

Alicia asked. "Milady, how was your trip? It was exciting to see you fly, and was it as much fun as it looked?" She then squeaked when she saw Robyn standing in nothing but breeches.

Camila had stopped in the doorway, eyes wide, staring at Robyn.

I laughed. "It is okay, girls. Milord and I will care for ourselves. You may go find something else to do and come wake us at dinner."

"Yes, Milady," Alicia said, and both girls rushed from the room, giggling.

Robyn laughed. "We are going to give those girls a complex. They keep seeing us in the most compromising positions."

I giggled. "Those girls will have plenty of ideas for when they get married."

"So true." Robyn laughed as he finished stripping.

We entered the bathing room to find a large tub and two buckets full of water. We used one bucket to soap each other down and the other to rinse. We settled into the tub with me laying back against Robyn's chest with sighs of contentment.

I asked. "Can you imagine how this will be when we have running water in our bathing chambers?"

"In some ways, my love. But I wonder what that shower thing was they were talking about."

I moaned as he kissed the back of my neck. Then I sighed as he began fondling my breasts. Nibbling up my neck to my ear, one hand slid down and explored my nethers. Robyn then pinched my nipple and flicked my clit at the same time. I moaned and squirmed as he inserted one and then a second finger into my vagina. I began panting as Robyn pumped his fingers inside me and the heel of his hand pressed on my clit. His other hand was moving back and forth, pinching at my nipples. Suddenly I spasmed as I tipped over the edge into orgasm. Robyn slowed his movements as I came down, shuddering a few times.

I then spun around, straddling Robyn's groin. Grabbing his iron-hard shaft, I slid down over the top of it.

Robyn's head fell back, groaning. "You are tight like a vise, my love."

"You fill me, and it feels good," I replied.

Robyn grabbed both my breasts and began suckling on the nipples.

Moaning, I slowly began sliding up and down his shaft.

Sliding his hands down, he grabbed my hips and began speeding my motion up. I grunted and gasped as he slammed into me faster and faster.

Soon my vagina began fluttering with another impending climax. Robyn slammed into me again as I screamed my release, and I felt his load spray against my womb.

Shaking and panting, I lay against Robyn, nuzzling his neck.

"That was so wonderful, my love. Thank you."

"The feeling is mutual." Said Robyn. "Let us dry off and climb into bed."

"I think I could use a nap now."

Robyn chuckled and helped me from the tub.

"Oh dear, we have made a mess."

Robyn laughed as he dried me off. "Yes, the servants may be mad at us this time."

Drying himself off, we climbed into bed and cuddled for a nap.

I finished making a copy of the cost for reequipping the army. It was the one that was going to Digby so he could maintain the ledger.

Sir William finished reviewing the copies of the schedule the squires had made.

"Excellent work, both of you." Said, Sir William. "Edwin, ride out and invite the fourth and fifth company captains to dine with us."

I told Jamie. "You will take this document to Digby in the treasury. As it is the cost breakdown for the rearmament, he can construct his ledgers from that. Then go invite captains Geoffrey and Jenson to our dinner."

"Yes, Milord." Both boys exclaimed. Taking the document, I handed Jamie, and they ran from the room.

Grumbling Merlin came through the door. "Someone is going to get run over by those two someday."

"They are keen to please." I chuckled.

"It is a good attitude if it does not kill anyone."

Sir William laughed. "The injuries would only be minor, and Friar Tuck could care for them no problem."

"True enough." Laughed Merlin shaking his head. "I would still not wish to be on the receiving end of a collision."

They all laughed as Merlin poured some ale from the jug on the desk. "So, what are the plans now?"

Sir William said, "You have a trip to prepare for, and I will keep operations running smoothly. The staff is more than capable of running the castle, leaving me to direct people where they need to be."

I laughed. "And to write reports to appease the king."

"Yes, there is that as well." Grumbled Sir William. "I will also likely have the king and a bevy of court butterflies descending on me in about a week."

"You are correct. We will have to be out of here before then, or we may never get away."

"You would abandon me in this time of darkness, you coward." Sir William smiled.

We all began laughing at that statement.

"Milords, I passed on the messages and gave Sir Penrose the rest of the dispatches. He said he would leave first thing in the morning." Jamie came back into the room and reported.

"Excellent, Jamie, you may sit and rest."

"Thank you, Milord." As he sat near the door nursing a cup of ale.

Soon after, Edwin appeared at the door. "I delivered your invitations, Milords, but something unusual happened when I got to the fifth company, so I hurried back. The Sherriff came out of the woods from the west, leading a group of about fifty strange tall people who were slender but almost as tall as Milord Dragon."

"Elves, I would suspect." Said Merlin. "Looks like you will have some more tenants, Duke Guy."

I looked over to Jamie. "Tell Denby we will have dinner in the grand dining hall. It would appear we are going to have more guests than expected."

"Yes, Milord." Jamie darted from the room.

"Get a drink and sit down, Edwin. We may require you again."

"Thank you, Milord." Said Edwin as he sat next to where Jamie had been.

"What else could happen to delayed dinner?" Asked Sir William.

As if on cue, the alarm bell began ringing.

"You just had to ask." Laughed Merlin mumbling about some god named Murphy.

We lept to our feet, grabbed our weapons, and headed for the door.

Bells startled me awake jolting Merriam off my chest. "The alarm," I said. "Armor up."

"By all the hells, I had such a nice dream." Complained Merriam.

With my breeches half-up, Alicia and Camila darted into the room.

"Milord Milady,"… she squeaked, seeing me with my pants half up.

"You will have to get over this," I said. "Help Milady into her armor. There is no time for blushing and being shy."

"Yes, Milord." They both rushed over to help Merriam. With the girl's help, Merriam was ready the same time I was. Grabbing our weapons, we headed for the top of the stairs.

Joining the groups coming from all directions, we headed down the stairs to the front doors. We ran across the courtyard up the stairs to the wall over the gatehouse.

I snapped at the first man. "Report."

"Milord, fifteen flying things are coming from the north. When they got near the edge of the treeline, they started flying around to the west. There they are." And a soldier pointed.

Stormavgaard spun around and looked at the flag above the keep. "They come to talk, not fight."

"How can you tell?" I asked.

The wind is out of the north. They would have come in from that direction if they wanted to fight. That way, the wind would help with their speed. They are circling to come in from downwind and putting the wind in their face slowing them down and making it easier to land.

Looking over the wall, I called down. "Sergeant Mackey, send a runner to fourth company and ask captain Paulson to escort our visitors to the keep."

"Yes, Milord." Said Sergeant Mackey pointing at a man. "You heard the Duke move out."

"Yes, Sergeant." And the man trotted off.

Merriam had put her hood on to observe the incoming flyers. "They are so beautiful and graceful. My goodness."

"What is that, my love?" I asked.

"Our guests are some of the most beautiful women I have ever seen."

Whipping my hood on, I took a second look. "My God, you are right. They also have strange arms and armor, each carrying a short spear and round shield. I can not make out more detail from here, but their armor does not seem to cover them entirely."

"Yes, love, it is very peculiar, but I recall seeing or reading about them. For the life of me, I can not remember where."

Merlin was also looking through his hood. "God's, this could get insane. If I am not mistaken, those are valkyries. It is a good thing they come to talk. Even with our armor and weapons, I do not think we have enough men to defeat them in battle."

"They may be good warriors." Said Captain Geoffrey. "But there are only fifteen of them, and their armor appears very skimpy."

Merlin laughed grimly. "These are Odin's shieldmaidens. Their primary task is to bring heroes who have died in battle to Valhalla. The only one who might harm them is Merriam with her bow. Those are Godforged throwing spears and have the same power and accuracy as Merriam's magic arrows. The only difference is that when those spears strike a target or deflect, they instantly return to the thrower's hand.

Sergeant Thomas grunted. "I would like to try sparring with them."

"You may well get your chance, sergeant." Said Merlin. "Because here they come."

While speaking, the valkyries landed in the middle of the field in a perfect v formation. Without a moment's hesitation, they began trotting forward. Meeting captain Paulson, they spoke for a minute. Exchanging some words, they formed up with captain Paulson and broke into a ground-eating trot. By the time they arrived, we were down in front of the doors to the keep.

The group slowed as they crossed the gate and marched up to us.

Captain Paulson saluted and said. "This is Yrswen Black Strider, leader of the valkyrie company."

I stepped forward, bowing to the woman, "I am Sir Guy Sherwood, Duke of Nottingham, Commander of the Northern Armies for the King of England. May I present Sir William, Commander of all the armies of England?"

Transferring her spear to her shield hand, she brought her fist sharply to her breasts. I am Yrswen Black Strider, and this is my valkyrie squadron. I would speak with the Dragonlord, for it is him we seek.

I said. "This is Stormavgaard, the Dragonlord."

Stormavgaard stepped forward. "I am the one you seek. What is your message?"

"First, would you please transform great one? It is with your dragon form that we must speak."

"Very well." Said Stormavgaard turning to me. "Be so good as to clear the courtyard, as it should be large enough."

"Sergeant Mackey guards to the walls and the remainder of the men to their barracks."

185

"Yes, Milord." Said Sergeant Mackey. "You men clear the courtyard unless you want to be stepped on by a dragon. If you are not on guard, duty on the walls, get into your barracks. Move."

"Captain Paulson, dismiss your men back to your company. You should remain here for dinner." I said.

"Yes, Milord." Said Captain Paulson. "Sergeant Corwin, return with the men to the company and resume your duties."

"Aye, Sir." Sergeant Corwin replied. "Double time march."

Captain Paulson and I joined our companions. We turned to watch the proceedings.

The valkyries turned to face the courtyard as Stormavgaard transformed and lay down with his head resting on his crossed foreclaws.

"Lord Dragon, Freya chose us to be your spear and shield. As she spoke, they all began to remove their armor.

"Only an honorable death allows us to return to Valhalla to sing with our sisters. Our task is to protect and serve as long as you live." Once she had stripped, she stepped forward and pressed the top of her left breast against Stormavgaard's claw. She opened a small bleeding wound. Speaking again, she said. "I bond myself to be your shield and spear with my blood. I so pledge."

The tip of Stormavgaard's tongue flicked out to lick the blood from her breast, leaving a strange mark. He then spoke in reply.

"With the taste of your blood. I mark you as mine and accept you as shield mate."

She bowed, returned to her gear, tears of joy streaming down her face, and began dressing again.

Each maiden stepped forward after another to make the same pledge. Stormavgaard accepted each, and they returned to dress, tears of joy streaming down their faces.

The last pair stepped forward together and spoke as one. "We are Rohildr and Rehildr, the twins." They then proceeded to perform the same ritual in a united voice. Both turned from him to get dressed again, and Stormavgaard spoke.

"I, Stormavgaard, accept your bonds and pledge myself to provide for and guard you with my life."

Transforming back to his human form, Stormavgaard walked up to me.

"Come, my friend, we have much to celebrate. Your servants must pour ale and wine and put meat on the board we feast."

"That was so beautiful." Blubbered Merriam wiping tears from her eyes.

Sophia said. "Another part of the prophecy becomes clear." As she also dried her eyes.

"Oh, yes." Said Merlin. "The dragon shall take fifteen spears to his death. I thought I would have to rescue you, my friend."

Stormavgaard laughed. "As I now have a blood bond with all fifteen, you will not need to rescue me. They will all be part of my harem and my guardians."

Robyn choked out. "Your harem?"

Yes, my harem, they are mates and guards. When my first wife arrives, she will command them, and at all times, there will be at least two of them in my presence. In this world, they are valkyries; in others, they could be any other flying creature. My father's fifteen guards are eagle shifters. When my mate arrives, another fifteen will join us to form the harem guard.

As Will walked up, he said. "Stormavgaard will not be much good for a couple of days. What with all the consummating that will be going on."

Stormavgaard laughed. "You have no idea of my stamina."

Stormavgaard then turned to the two following Will and began speaking in a musical language. The two bowed and replied in the same musical language.

With a hearty belly laugh, Stormavgaard said. "Please, friends, speak in the human language so they may know our hearts."

Bobbing their heads, they replied. "Yes, Lord Dragon."

"This is Sir Guy Sherwood, Duke of Nottingham, master of this land and wood."

Continuing, Stormavgaard introduced the entire group to the Elves.

Turning to us, Stormavgaard said. "This is Tholci of the Wood Elves and Alvos, the Academic of the Light Elves."

Going to each and clasping forearms, I said. "Please, friends, bring your people into the great hall, and we will feast and talk."

"Thank you for your kind invitation," Alvos said. He called and waved to the other elves to bring them over.

The group then entered the great hall, where we found tables in a hollow square. The previous Sherriff had removed the decorations, and the staff had not yet replaced the typical banners and tapestries.

"Please," I called. "Sit anywhere, mix and mingle. It is not a time for formalities but for getting to know one another."

Then I went over suiting actions to words and sat near the end of one leg, between an elf and valkyrie.

"Hello," I said to both of them. "I am Duke Guy Sherwood, and welcome to my home, castle Nottingham."

The elf replied, "I am Erhile the agile. One of the queen's guards."

The valkyrie then said. "I am Eydra spear hand shield maiden and guardian."

"It is lovely to meet you," I said.

"Please excuse me a moment as host. I must give the first toast." Standing, I raised my goblet and waited for the crowd to quiet.

I then said. "Companions, guests, new friends, and future allies. Although we celebrate Stormavgaard's bonding with the valkyries, we also celebrate meeting new people, the elves. To new friends, I saluted and drank."

Everyone called out. "To new friends." And everyone else drank.

CHAPTER

22

Sitting back down, servants began bringing platters of food to the tables, more jugs of ale and wine. It was a general hubbub of people speaking and eating. I glanced around Eydra and caught Stormavgaards eye.

"My friend?" I asked him. "What were you laughing so hard about when you first spoke with the elves?"

Stormavgaard chuckled. "Alvos was in a quandary. Perchance is your king unmarried?"

"No." Said Sir William. "He has never found the time. Why?"

"The elves have asked me to assist them by bringing the rest of their clan from the other world. They know this works as I can not send them back, so I must create a portal for the rest."

"Well, there is enough room in the dukedom for more people. I would like to know their skills, so I have some idea where to place them."

Tholci spoke up. "We are the best woodsman and hunters you will ever see if we let you, and wood elves are also the best carvers and carpenters. "Genlyn, pick a piece of wood and show Milady your talent."

A young-looking elf girl went to the fire and handpicked a log about a foot long. She reached into her belt pouch, pulled out a tool, and began carving.

Alvos said. "While she is working on that, I will explain some of our other talents. We, the light elves, have many academic and magic skills and run a school for magic."

Sorac, there is an alchemist who not only makes potions and other alchemical items but teaches alchemy to those with talent. We also have many healers and herbalists that can make creams and poultices, drawing out poison and healing. We also have magic crafters who make things like holding bags, self-cleaning clothes, and valuable items."

"Oh, I like the idea of self-cleaning clothes." Said Merriam.

I chuckled. "Okay, I agree your people are accepted."

I saw a virtual blizzard of wood chips near my wife. Oddly enough, the chips flew through the air, and they all seemed to settle back into one container. *Now that is an interesting bit of magic, I thought.*

"Okay, Stormavgaard, back to your tale leading to my king."

"Oh, no, my friend, this is on Alvos now."

"Okay, then Alvos, please connect the dots."

"Queen Evadhi, The Guardian, leads my clan. She carries the seed of our home tree. For her to quicken the seed, she must, in turn, have the king of the land quicken her."

Sir William had just taken a large mouthful of wine which he proceeded to spray all over the table while choking.

Robyn laughed hysterically as he pounded Sir William's back.

Gales of musical laughter rang from the other end of the table.

I laughed as well.

Merriam said. "Payback will be such a sweet dish."

Merlin laughed. "Yes, granddaughter, you already have a plan in that devious little mind."

"Oh, grandfather, this will be much more than fun. Alvos, I hope your queen is a happy whimsical sort because she will need to play the part well."

"Yes." Alvos laughed. Our queen loves acting in plays, which is one of her most endearing qualities."

"Good. Stormavgaard, how long to get the elves here?" Asked Merriam.

Stromavgaard chuckled. "In the morning, Milady, that will be soon enough."

"We shall all ride out to meet our queen, and the boys can have the carriage gleaming for her by morning."

I laughed. "Slow down, my love. Let us give them time to get some sleep first."

"Yes, I guess we can do that." Said Merriam. I chuckled at Edwin and Jamie's sighs of relief.

"Alvos, is there anything else we need to know?"

"Yes." Said Alvos. "We light elves also number fifty warriors. Half male and half female to protect the king and queen, and they will also be the king and queen's harems. You look shocked, Milord."

"Well, except for our circumstance, typically relationships are monogamous."

The elves laughed. "We are more free-spirited."

Part of that comes from controlling our biology to some extent. It takes mutual consent, and a fifty-year commitment before elves can procreate. If one partner has the tiniest bit of doubt, nothing will happen. The fifty-year commitment is because it takes that long for an elf to mature. A couple is committed to raising and training their young together, and it is unusual for a couple to raise more than one child together.

"Well," I said. "If that is the case and these guards are half as good as Stormavgaard's valkyries, the king should be well guarded. That could free up second company to move elsewhere to twin."

Yrswen spoke. "Perhaps a skill test to see if their abilities match up. Rangilde Brandy Head front and center. A valkyrie with amber-colored hair lept from her seat, landing in the center of the floor. My companion Erhile stood, placing one hand on the table, and cartwheeled to the center of the floor.

Facing the valkyrie, Erhile pulled a pair of Sabres from behind her head, and Rangilde pulled a couple of falchions from her back.

Merriam said in wonder. "Where did the weapons come from?"

Merlin laughed. "From a bag of holding granddaughter. They can carry many things."

"I want one for my trip." Said Merriam.

"We will all need them." Said Merlin. "I think I know where we will get them from."

Alvos spoke up. "Yes, I can craft them with no problem. Guild price is ten gold apiece."

"Alvos, see me in the morning," I said.

Yrswen spoke up. "The purpose of this contest is to test skill, not injure. Ready? Fight."

There was a clash of swords in the center of the floor. At first, it seemed to the companions they were in a deadlock, and the sound of blades striking seemed to speak otherwise. As the contest continued, I noticed they were not standing completely still. And then I began to see flickers of movement between the two. Occasionally one or the other would lean back a hair. At other times it would be a slight shoulder movement. Neither seemed to be getting the better of the other. My brain could not process the speed of the combatant's arms.

After five minutes of the seeming stalemate, they lept back a few steps from each other. They reached up, and their weapons vanished behind their heads again. Stepping forward, they embraced each other and kissed. Turning back to the leaders, they bowed.

Rangilde Brandy Head spoke first. "Erhile, The Agile is skilled in combat, and the elves will be more than adequate for protecting the king and queen."

Erhile then spoke, "the skills of this mighty warrior Rangilde and the valkyries will be more than adequate to guard our Dragonlord."

"This is good. Then we may speak of other matters." Said Yrswen.

The combatants walked over, holding hands, and sat beside me.

Sir William raised his eyebrows and looked at Stormavgaard. "Now, what is that about?"

Stormavgaard chuckled. "They are sharing the bond of the blade."

They will spend the night together trying to recruit one another. Once their passion is spent, they will realize it, and no harm will be done. It is funny because though they may become lovers, the elf is blood-bound to the queen, and the valkyrie is blood-bound to me. We need to make suitable quarters ready for the elf queen.

The west wing of the third floor is for your group Stormavgaard. The south wing of the second floor has the Royal Apartments for the queen and her guards.

Seeing some guests slumping in their seats, I waved Denby over.

"Denby, have quarters been arranged for our guests?"

"I have already taken the liberty of using the top floor of the north wing for these guests. The top floor of the west wing is ready for Milord Stormavgaard and the valkyries."

"What about the quarters for the queen?" I asked.

"I will have them scrubbed out first thing tomorrow. I hope the elves have means for looking after their queen as we do not have enough trained servants for a royal guest."

Alvos leaned in. "Do not worry about the queen. Her guards will look after her as is our custom."

"Thank you, Milord." Said Denby. "That removes the pressure off my staff."

Alvos laughed. "For the last hundred and fifty years, after our queen matured, she has lived in a simple two-room cottage as we all do. So this extravagance and luxury might be a bit uncomfortable for her."

"Oh, yes, we shall do our best to make the queen's time here as carefree and comfortable as possible."

"Thank you, Duke Sherwood. We appreciate your effort. Our people may be very talented, but we prefer to live simple lives."

Standing, I rang the bell. Once I had everyone's attention, I said. "Captains, we have some matters to discuss. Please attend me at the side table."

I excused myself from my companions and headed to the table by the wall.

Sitting down, I waited for the men to sit as well. "This is not a formal briefing, so relax, gentleman."

The men nodded in reply.

"You have had a chance to look over your orders and the schedule?"

The captains all nodded.

Rather than have the men carry their gold to pay for their armor, the quartermasters will come to the castle and draw the total amount for your company. When your turn comes, you will drop off the gold for your company at the dwarven village. Then you may proceed to Derby for your stay there. You will relieve the company stationed there to get fitted for their armor. You have seen you have thirty days at each location. It is because winter is coming on, and the weather may affect your movements. It is crucial, gentleman. You may delay your departure from any location if there is a storm. I do not wish to lose any men because you got caught in a blizzard on the road. You are here to fight the enemy, not a random storm. Am I clear, gentleman?

They replied in the affirmative.

Now you have all heard about Sergeant Thomas's promotion to master sergeant?" They all nodded, smiling. A couple even said here, here, or it was about time.

I chuckled. "Yes, I am aware Master Sergeant Thomas's promotion was long overdue."

He will be working with Sir William to oversee training and troop movements. Do not be surprised if he shows up to guide your training or to chew you a new one for less than stellar performance.

"That is all I have for you, gentlemen. Enjoy the rest of your evening. We get back to work tomorrow."

We all rose and rejoined the party.

Seeing several people had left the party presumably for bed, I rejoined my companions as they seemed to have clustered together. Sitting next to Robyn, I watched how the conversation had gone. In front of Merriam was an exquisite carving of her in a gown.

Merriam asked Stormavgaard. "So, could I fit a person in this storage space?"

Stormavgaard laughed. "Milady, things that are alive do not survive the storage space. So you will be unable to tuck your maid in there to carry along."

Merriam pouted and wrinkled her nose. "Well, it was a thought."

The men laughed, and Robyn said. "Do not worry, my love. We will look after you very well."

I said. "Yes, we will wash your back when you bathe and brush your hair at night."

Will snickered. "I will rub that sweet-smelling lotion all over you that keeps your skin soft."

We all laughed as Merriam blushed.

Merriam replied, "however, womanly needs cannot be met by a man like the simple act of conversation. In any case, I am off to bed. Try not to stay up all night drinking."

"Goodnight." We all replied as she rose, kissing each husband.

Will then spoke. "Jon and I have some wood elves to tuck in and other work to take care of, so we will see you in the morning."

Stormavgaard spoke up. "Do not worry, gentlemen. Your wife will not be starved for female companionship."

I have looked over your prophecy, reading it from front to back and from both sides. There is mention of the dragon's eyes remaining close. As far as I can parse this out, I will be sending two of my valkyries with you. Because of the blood bond, we all know where each other is at all times. We can reduce or even turn this off if we need to, but it usually is on. I can see what they are doing through their eyes, and no, I have not been following Rangilde. However, I think the two blushing beauties behind me have been.

The twins giggled and got even redder, if that was possible.

Two more will fly in every two or three weeks to replace them, and when you have read and formulated a reply to any dispatches we send you, the other two will fly back here. This way, we are all kept up to date.

"That is a most excellent plan." Said, Sir William. "The king will be most pleased with regular updates as well."

"I am sure he will be happy to keep track of us," I said.

"Oh, I think the king will be too busy to worry about you." A giggling Sophia said.

Yes, he will storm through those doors and be struck dumb by what he sees on the throne, and there will be no more extraordinary ethereal beauty than that of the guardian. And now we should all be off to bed, as it will be another busy day tomorrow.

We made our way upstairs quietly, entering our chambers. Merriam was curled up in the center of the bed, fast asleep.

I whispered, grinning. "Merriam has had a long day. Let her sleep."

Robyn nodded his agreement. We stripped off our clothes and washed up for bed.

We carefully climbed in on either side of her and kissed her gently. She sighed in her sleep and resumed her gentle snoring. We laid back, and I fell asleep almost immediately.

A knock on the door heralded the arrival of Alicia and Camila to wake us up.

Alicia sang out in a bright, bubbly voice. "Good morning, Milords and Milady, It is a sunny, beautiful day." She giggled and caught the pillow flying toward her.

Merriam grumbled. "It is much too early to be that cheerful."

I laughed. "It is not all that bad. My love, you are the brightest thing in this room."

Merriam sighed. "That is so sweet." As she kissed Robyn and me, she asked. "Now, what should I wear today?"

I said. "If you are leaving the castle, armor. If you are staying here, whatever you want."

Robyn snickered. "Or nothing at all."

The maids both giggled and blushed.

"Milord." Said Camila. "That would be scandalous."

"Well, I would think if we meet the queen of the elves, I will wear one of my best gowns. I should not need armor or weapons with all you men, especially with a dragon in our midst." She giggled.

"This is true." Robyn laughed. "With fifteen valkyries, I think it should be safe enough."

Alicia giggled, walking over to the armoire and opening the doors.

"Well, we will be wearing our armor," I said, slipping out of bed.

Alicia squeaked and blushed as she turned back to the armoire. "Well, what do you think, Milady green satin or perhaps blue brocade?"

Getting out of bed, Merriam sashayed over to the armoire as both of us groaned.

I hurriedly grabbed the rest of my armor. "Merriam did that deliberately just to tease us."

Robyn grunted in agreement as he grabbed the rest of his gear.

Merriam laughed, and the maids giggled as we left the bedroom.

We finished dressing in the sitting room. I then stuck my head back through the bedroom door and said. "We will see about breakfast. Meet you in the dining hall."

"God's, I hate becoming aroused in armor." Said Robyn.

"I entirely agree," throwing on the rest of my gear.

Stepping into the hall, we ran into Denby.

"Your breakfast is being laid in the great hall, Milords."

"I take it you are informing everyone, Denby?"

"Yes, Milord, I am passing the word around now."

"Well, then, Denby, carry on."

"Yes, Milord, thank you."

Walking onto the landing above the stairs, we met Stormavgaard.

"Good morning Milord Dragon," I said. "Did you have a good night?"

Stormavgaard chuckled. "Yes, it was most pleasurable. We did not get much sleep, but it was fun."

The Valkyries all blushed a deep shade of pink.

Robyn laughed. "Well, there should be plenty of food for breakfast. That will help restore everyone."

Stormavgaard asked. "And where is Milady Merriam?"

I chuckled. "Unlike us warriors, she has wardrobe choices to make. Meeting a queen is a huge deal for a woman like her."

Yrswen asked. "Milady is not a warrior?"

Robyn chuckled. "She is an excellent swordswoman and extraordinary archer, but Merriam does not think of herself as a warrior. Her grandfather Merlin will teach her much while we are traveling. So while she is very adept at using her weapons, she considers herself a druid first."

"I see." Said Yrswen.

"You will find out soon enough when she pulls her bow from its case things tend to get..."

"Annihilated." Robyn finished.

"That is the word I was looking for, Robyn," I said. "Merriam tends to annihilate her targets, and while she does not always wear armor. She never goes without her bow."

"I look forward to discovering more about this bow," Runeror said.

Merriam's voice came from behind us as we entered the dining hall. "I would love to show you whenever we could compare notes on our bow's strengths."

Robyn laughed. "Not inside the castle, my love. We do not need any holes in the walls.

"Why not inside the castle will be torn down eventually," she said.

"Yes, my love," I said. "But we need this one until the other castle is built."

"Fine," she said. "I will wait till we get into the forest."

Everyone laughed at that.

CHAPTER

"Come sit anywhere and eat," I said.

"Anyone of any station is allowed at my table, and only for formal occasions are any rules imposed."

"Which reminds me, Denby, please have a formal dinner arranged to welcome the queen tonight."

"Yes, Milord." Said Denby. "We have already started preparations for this evening."

"Excellent. Get with the elves and see if any unique customs need to be observed."

"Already done, Milord."

Merriam rolled her eyes. "Meddling in household affairs does not become you, my love. That is my job."

I blushed as everyone at the table laughed.

I just shook my head. "Stormavgaard, how will this whole portal thing work? And how many men should I bring as an escort?"

Stormavgaard thought for a moment. Flicking his fingers like he was turning pages to read a document. I suggest fifty armsmen, twenty-five knights, and no archers with the elves around. I will need a clearing for the portal where the elves first came through. If your men stay back two hundred paces, they should be safe.

Alvos spoke up. "The clearing we came through is about a quarter-mile around. Oak trees surround it, and this trail runs through it."

"That should be perfect then." Said Stormavgaard. "I assumed you were in your village when the portal opened?"

Yes, it was a bizarre coincidence. We had gathered in the town square to embark on an expedition. We had heard about a dwarf clan in need of assistance.

I laughed. "I suppose that dwarf clan was Dworkin's?

Stormavgaard chuckled. "The prophecy does work in mysterious ways."

The portals we dragons open have a blue rim around them. When I open it, I will throw a unique capsule through it. These capsules are the only thing that can travel back through a portal.

When our queen was crowned, a seer spoke of this day. She said when the first group of our people vanishes, prepare to move to a new world. Then the trunk of our home tree split and a seed fell out. Our queen has guarded this seed for a hundred and fifty years now, waiting for this day. When she comes to this world, the seed will gently compel her to move to a location. And when her king quickens her, the seed will sprout, and she will be able to plant it. As long as the tree grows, we will prosper and remain healthy, tied closely to the tree.

Yrswen stood speaking reverently. "She is the bearer of the seed of Yaggdrissl. Once again, the world will see the magic and open the way to Asgard."

"Oh, wonderful." Said Merlin. "Things are about to get very complicated."

"In what way?" Asked Sir William.

"Well, for one thing, that will open the way for the return of the old gods and strong magic. We will start to see dungeons spawn."

"What do you mean, Merlin? Every castle has a dungeon."

Merlin gave a dry chuckle. "Not those kinds of dungeons but caves and towers where monsters spawn. Tarija, how many types of dungeons were in your world?"

Tarija hummed, then placed her finger over her lips, finally speaking. "Eight main dungeons that I can think of offhand. Naturally, there are many variations on each type, even combinations."

Merlin said. "So an eight base would give you two hundred fifty-six kinds of dungeons before you hit a repeat."

Tarija's eyes widened. "How do you know this wizard? That is a closely guarded guild secret."

Sorry, I am from a far future where that is simple binary math. It is based on one and zero or, if you prefer, on or off. For example, if we increase the number of base dungeons to sixteen, you will get one thousand twenty-four possible combinations.

Tarija squeaked. "You know all the secrets of dungeon building? We know we can push a dungeon to be a specific type if we feed it the right things, and we also know this must happen when the dungeon is still level one."

"Oh, actually, no," Merlin said. "It is a good thing the Duke hired you, as they will need a battle dungeon to train their men in."

I gasped. "Wait now. You can train a dungeon, or...no, you can teach a dungeon to make war?"

Tarija said. "Well, yes and no."

We can guide it so it will form small armies. They could be as small as fifty men and up to five hundred or more. I say that because I have never seen one of more than five hundred men, and I think that was the King of Keramanda's military dungeon, at level twenty. I went there for my guild to learn small-unit tactics for dungeon raids. So I only reached the fourth floor where we did training for up to one hundred men.

"That will be one more worry for us. We do not have enough troops now." Said, Sir William.

"Sir William, you misheard me," said Merlin. "Troops are no good for clearing dungeons. That would be Tarija and the adventurer's guild she is setting up. Duke Grandson pay Tarija another nine hundred gold. She is not only setting up the guild but is now Sir-William's military advisor on dungeons."

Tarija gasped, her mouth opening and closing, but no words came out.

Finally, Master Sergeant Thomas grabbed the back of her neck and pulled her in for a deep kiss.

We all cheered at the action.

I laughed, "Digby, you heard Merlin. When Milady Tarija recovers enough to stumble down to the treasury, you may pay her that extra nine hundred gold."

"Stormavgaard," I said. "It looks like we will be bringing that guild over as soon as possible."

"Most assuredly, Duke Guy. Sergeant Thomas and Tarija can help me tomorrow, and I shall bring the guild advance party over in two days. It will only take that long because I need a dragon from that side to link to."

"Very well, we can table that discussion for later. Is everyone done breakfast?" I asked. I heard no complaints and said. "Then let us go meet our new queen."

We all began to file from the hall.

Stepping from the keep, we saw a gleaming carriage. Looking around, I saw Captain Geoffrey and Sergeant Mackey had the men of the escort formed up. I also saw Sir Penrose standing to one side.

I said. "Sir Penrose, do not wait for more dispatches. I want you in front of the king in two days. If I have more urgent messages from today, I will ask to have the valkyries deliver them to you."

"Yes, Milord, we will leave right now."

"Good, man, move out."

I saw Stormavgaard hand Merriam and then Lady Sophia up into the carriage when I turned back to the carriage. Alvos then climbed in and sat opposite my wife. Merriam turned to Stormavgaard. "Lord Dragon, join us in the carriage for the ride out."

Stormavgaard replied. "I think I will."

I pointed to a stable boy. "Return Milord's horse to the stables, as he will not need it for this trip."

The boy grabbed the reins and led the horse off.

Looking around, I mounted my horse and saw everyone else was ready.

"Captain, move us out." Captain Geoffrey led the cavalcade at a leisurely pace.

Yrswen lept to the footmen's platform at the back of the carriage. Six valkyries surrounded the carriage, and the other eight took to the air.

Merriam giggled. "Milord Stormavgaard, your valkyries have garnered some attention from the townspeople. They are in awe of the beauty that flies above them."

Stormavgarrd laughed. "Very beautiful but quite deadly."

Sophia smiled. "Women have been deadly, with or without combat skills throughout the ages."

Stormavgaard laughed. "Very accurate, Milady."

The group in the carriage chattered quite happily as we moved through the forest. Merriam became quiet as we grew closer to our destination and looked around pensively. Suddenly she said. "Something is watching us with ill intent."

"Good. Another skill is beginning to manifest." Said Sophia.

"Interesting." Said Stormavgaard. "You are manifesting danger sense. It is a valuable trait for a leader to have."

"Edwin, be a dear and stop the carriage now." Blurted Merriam.

Edwin pulled back on the reins stopping.

Merriam flipped her hood on, pulling her bow from the case.

By this time, Sir William and I had ridden back to the carriage to ask why they had stopped.

"Something is watching us." Said Merriam.

"Where at?" I asked.

Merriam pointed to the left.

"I should send some men."

"No, it is only the one, and I shall take care of it." She paused, drew her bow, and fired a flaming arrow into the woods. Merriam then pulled a second time and held her fire. The first arrow slammed into a log, passing through and piercing an orc through the chest. A warg then lept, and Merriam fired again, and her flaming arrow hit the warg's head. It exploded, leaving nothing but a body.

Looking around, she said. "It was just the one."

"Maybe I should send some men just to investigate."

"Nevermind." I watched as three Valkyries landed where the orc was.

Stormavgaard said."I think we need not worry about this any further. Orc scouts tend to range far and wide and do not report back quickly. This one could have been from that Warband you destroyed."

"Very well," I said. "We shall resume our journey as we are only about a half-hour from our destination."

As I predicted, we arrived a short time later.

Stormavgaard said. "You should all remain here with the carriage. Where is it safe." The valkyries all took off and landed around the edge of the clearing stepping into the woods a bit. Stormavgaard moved out into the center of the clearing. Transforming into his dragon, he carefully burned a circular area in the center of the clearing.

He returned to his human form and pulled a wand from his storage, and Stormavgaard marked symbols in the burned area. He stepped outside the burned area and raised his hands, chanting a formula.

The circle began to glow purple through red into yellow, green through blue like a rainbow, and the ring started to tip like the lid in a barrel as it reached indigo. Everyone began to murmur as the arch formed began to turn. It spun part way around and then headed back the other direction stopping on a northwest facing. The indigo glowed brighter, receding to the edge of the half-circle. The rest began to shimmer with a silver color. Stromavgaard drew a small cylinder from his storage bag, which started to glow green as he tossed it through the archway. The group gasped as the object hit the arch and vanished.

Merriam said. "How strange. I expected it to land on the ground on the other side, not disappear."

"I think it did." Said Merlin. "Not in this world. I believe it will have formed a guideline on the ground on the other side for the elves to follow.

A few minutes later, elves began stepping through the archway. The first group armed with bows spread out, forming a perimeter, and moved to the edge of the clearing. The next elf stepped through the archway in a white gossamer-thin robe, clearly female. The woman seemed to glow with an inner golden light.

"God, she is gorgeous." Whispered Merriam.

Those four words seemed to cut the string, and the twenty-five escort knights slammed to the ground. In unison, the men stepped forward, dropping to one knee and slamming a fist to their breastplate in worshipful salute.

The queen stepped forward, kneeling before Stormavgaard, and spoke in a musical language.

Stormavgaard said. "Queen Evadhi, you need not kneel to me. I am not the one you seek, but he will be on his way soon." Taking her hand to ease her back to her feet. "Please, Your Majesty, speak common, which is the language of this land and is colorful and expressive."

The Queen tilted her head. "It shall be as you ask Stormavgaard. We are very grateful to you, Dragonlord. We have waited long to meet our king, and we are happy to abide a bit longer as this land smells rich with growing things." As she spoke, many more elves came through the archway, walking around to examine the plants and trees in the clearing.

"Your Majesty, allow me to introduce you to your hosts and future subjects."

"Very well, we shall meet these gracious people."

Queen Evadhi seemed to float across the ground toward us as if she did not wish to disturb the grass beneath her feet.

As they approached, Merriam whispered to Robyn. "Almost makes me want to give up men."

And he whispered back. "But you are stuck with us now, my love."

Merriam giggled, covering her mouth as the queen approached.

Everyone bowed low or curtsied as Stormavgaard introduced us.

"Your Majesty," I said. "I would offer my humble castle as your abode until we can build something more appropriate."

"We thank you, Your Grace. We are sure your castle will be adequate, as we are used to a simple cabin in the forest."

"Surely it cannot be?" Exclaimed Merriam. "You must have lived in a magnificent castle in your other world."

Evadhi smiled gently. "No, Milady. Until we mate our king, we live a simple life. Our people govern themselves quite well. I am merely there as a counselor and arbiter of disputes, and the king will rule my people while we guide and nurture."

"That is how every marriage should work." Said Merriam with a giggle.

"Yes, you understand, so your marriage will bear much fruit.

Merriam laughed. "With these four. I will bear more than fruit."

The Queen's eyes lit up when she broke out in a musical laugh. "We think we shall become good friends, Merriam."

Sophia said. "Good, the prophecy moves on as foretold."

Stormavgaard said. "I saw so few problems it should not need much tweaking."

Sophia said. "But one must always be aware where it can diverge."

"Truth." Said Stormavgaard. "We need to close this one with the orb destroyed."

Sir William stood frowning at the elves pouring through the portal.

"There is something wrong with our people, Milord?" Asked the queen.

"Sort of, Your Majesty. I am not sure where we will put all your people."

"There is no need to worry about our people Sir William. They will camp near your castle while looking for suitable locations for a town."

"Perchance, you can show us some dense thickets we can build in?"

Stormavgaard then spoke up. "You may not understand, but elves mostly live in trees on platforms, so a large thicket of oak would be most suitable."

Will Scarlet said. "I know just the place. You remember Robyn about halfway between Nottingham and the Dwarven village. Great oaks around open fields, then the hill with the rings of oaks around the crown?"

"Oh, yes." Said Robyn. "I was thinking of building a house there myself for Merriam before all this happened."

"Would you be willing to show some of my people this place?" Asked the queen.

"Yes, Your Majesty, most assuredly." Said Will.

"Whoa, stop there, Sophia; I feel the prophecy is playing games with us."

"Your Majesty, are you feeling a pull from the seed?"

Queen Evadhi pulled the chain out of her robe. Holding it out, so the cage around the seed swung free, she whispered an Elvish word. The seed gave off a greenish glow and began to pulse. It then swung up and pointed westward.

Robyn grunted. "That is the direction of the hill,"

Stormavgaard laughed. "As I thought. Any divergence is locked when an event concludes, and a new event unfolds."

Merlin grumbled. "I was afraid of that. Sophia, check the wording of the original prophecy, as I think it has changed."

"Alvos send five of our builders with this man. Colvs, send an escort as well."

"Go ahead, Will, and stop by the town to grab lunch and supplies on the way," I said. "We will see you tomorrow or whenever you get back."

Stormavgaard said. "I will send the twins with Will so that I can see the location through their eyes. I will then be able to fly the queen out there to see the place firsthand."

Yrswen pointed at the twins and flipped her wrist at Will. "It is done, my Lord Dragon."

"Please, Your Majesty, join us in the carriage for the ride to Nottingham." Said Stormavgaard.

"We are excited to spend some time talking with these ladies."

Captain Geoffrey as Her Majesty's guard, is more than suitable as an escort. You will remain here with your men to escort the people to Nottingham. The northwest side of the town should be ideal for the elves for a few days."

"Yes, Milord, it will be done as you say."

"I will have the service group bring tents and food to help tide them over."

"Right, Milord, we will be along as soon as possible."

The queen spoke. "Worry not for my people as we have many supplies in our wagons. Remember that we have been preparing for this for over a hundred years."

Merlin suddenly cried out. "You have silkworms? Your Majesty, your people, cultivate silkworms?"

The queen smiled brightly. "Yes, Milord, silk is one of our best exports, and our tailors and seamstresses make wonderous garments from the worm's silk."

"By all the God's granddaughter, you will wear one of the most glorious materials ever to touch human skin."

Merriam giggled. "Really, grandfather, you are most dramatic."

"Ha." Merlin laughed. "Tell her, Your Majesty, of the wonders of silk undergarments."

The queen laughed musically, reaching into a pocket in her dress. She pulled out a long strip of cloth. Handing it to Merriam, she said. "This is an old scarf I made several years ago."

Merriam moaned, rubbing the material against her cheek. "It is so soft and smooth, and the color is so vibrant the stitching is not even worn."

Merriam looked up. "By several years, you mean you made it and put it in your drawer and never touched it until yesterday?"

The queen laughed. "No, I made that one about fifty years ago and wore it quite a bit. It gets washed once a month only because I have several scarves."

Merriam said. "My God. How much would this be at guild price?"

"A scarf like that, brand new, five silvers, maybe six depending on the pattern and stitching in the design."

"What about a gown like mine in silk?"

The queen grinned. "That dress with that level of detail in the stitching... And please do not get me wrong... For that lower quality work, fifty silvers."

Merriam and Sophia's eyes almost bulged from their heads.

Like they were connected by strings, Merriam and Sophia pulled purses from their dresses, giving them to the queen. "For clothes, many clothes of all kinds. Please."

I groaned. And the queen's laughter rang through the forest.

CHAPTER

24

Arriving back in Nottingham without incident, I left the group long enough to give Captain Paulson orders about the elves coming.

I then rejoined the escort leading the carriage through town. People bowed in reverence to the queen's beauty as she smiled, waving at the children running alongside the carriage. Entering the castle grounds, Edwin stopped the carriage in front of the doors to the keep Jamie, then hopped down and opened the door letting the stairs down.

Stormavgaard handed the Ladies down as Denby opened the doors to the keep.

"Your Majesty." Said Stormavgaard. "This way, if you please."

Denby pounded his staff three times as the queen made the last three steps over the portcullis. He then called out in a strong, clear voice.

"Her Majesty Queen Evadhi of the Elves."

At the last word, a fanfare blew, and a large flag was raised to the castle's highest point. It was dark green with a silver tree in the center.

"Thank you for your warm welcome, chamberlain." The queen said.

"Your Majesty," Denby said, bowing low. "Refreshments have been laid out in the formal reception hall."

Stormavgaard escorted the queen into the formal reception hall and to the throne. The mayor and several other town leaders were present for the reception.

"Please rise." Said the queen. "We are not your queen yet, so there is no need for such formality."

The queen sat on the throne, and servants stepped forward, offering trays of drinks and sweet pastries.

Taking a goblet of wine and sipping, she nodded her head. The servants moved away, offering wine and pastries to the others.

The queen's guards quietly filed in, standing directly behind the throne and along the walls.

"Your Majesty," I said. "My people have cleared the second-floor south wing for you and your guards. The remainder of your close staff are on the floor above you, and Denby has also assigned two maids for you. They are preparing a bath so you may refresh yourself before tonight's formal reception."

"There is no need for all this, Milord Duke. As mentioned before, we lead a simple life although the bath sounds glorious."

Stormavgaard said. "As soon as the king hears of your arrival, he will be here as quickly as possible."

"We are sure the king will be expeditious coming here once he has learned of our presence."

"Yes, I may not be here when the king arrives. Sir William will be filling my role as Senechal."

Sophia stepped forward, addressing me. "No, Milord, some things have changed. You will be delayed for a time as the queen brings information about the prophecy's fulfillment."

"Yes, Your Grace." Said the queen. "The orb will change your world in many ways, as it has brought monsters to terrorize and magic to enhance your world. Unfortunately, this also comes at a price we will have to discuss once my king arrives."

Sir William gave a half bow. "It shall be as you say, Your Majesty."

"In that case," I said. "Allow me to introduce some elders."

"It would be our pleasure."

The queen spent some time speaking with the town elders.

Denby then ushered forward a pair of maids.

"Your Majesty, these are Veronica and Madeline. Your maids for the duration of your visit. They will show you to your quarters."

"We thank you, Denby. Please lead the way, ladies."

"That went well, I think." As the queen left the hall and the others began to disperse.

"Yes, it did." Said, Sir William. "Let us retire to the study. I have a message to write post haste."

"What an interesting one it will be." Giggled Merriam. "How do you tell a king his unknown bride has arrived on our doorstep?"

"Yes, you see the crux of the problem." Sir William laughed.

"How quickly can we get this message to the king?" Asked Sophia.

"I could send a team of valkyries to deliver it." Said Stormavgaard. "They could have the message there before nightfall."

"Bloody hell Lord Dragon." Merlin laughed. "I can see some pompous official trying to stop them from walking in and the resulting slaughter."

Robyn chuckled. "Well, the king did say he wished to remove some of the deadwood in the court.

Merriam began laughing.

"And what has you so amused, my love?" I asked.

Still giggling, she pointed at the valkyries.

They stood caressing their spears and nodding eagerly.

"The king will only have arrived in Cambridge last night or early this morning," I said. "A four-day march for a whole company. Sir Penrose is traveling light, which should take only a day and a half. He would likely arrive there late tomorrow morning."

"So valkyries could catch Sir Penrose when he makes camp tonight. They can then give the message to him to deliver to the king."

"That might be less nerve-wracking than having five valkyries descend on Cambridge castle."

"Yes, I think that takes care of that. The valkyries will bring the message to Sir Penrose, and they can join in as part of his escort." Said, Sir William.

"Yes, Milord." Said Stormavgaard. "That should reduce the number of bodies that need disposal in Cambridge."

Pulling his desk over, Sir William took out pen and paper and began composing a letter.

Writing half a page, Sir William reread what was written. Grunting, he crumpled the page and tossed it in the fire.

Sophia giggled. "Perhaps I should write the letter, Milord. You are too much of a military man to compose this missive."

"Yes, Milady, perhaps you are correct." Sir William said, giving up his seat for Sophia.

Sophia quickly composed a letter explaining the queen's arrival, the valkyries, and Lord Stormavgaard. She also wrote of changes to the prophecy that may have dire consequences. Sophia concluded by requesting the king's presence to help resolve these issues. Signing it, she held it up for Sir William to read.

William quickly read the letter. "This should get his attention without making him panic."

Sophia took the letter back, folding and sealing it using her signet.

Sophia handed it to Stormavgaard, saying. "It is now in your hands to get to Sir Penrose."

Taking the letter, Stormavgaard handed it to Yrswen. "Can you show her approximately where Sir Penrose will be?"

Yrswen gave the letter to Malhe and said, "Your flight gets this task."

They stepped over to the map table with me. I said. "This is the roman road leading to Cambridge. It is usual for fast messengers to stop at this river crossing and a way station is there where riders may change horses. That was where Sir Penrose planned on stopping."

Stormavgaard said to Malhe. "Hand this letter to Sir Penrose, and you may join his company."

"At once, My Lord Dragon." She said, taking the letter and walking from the room, calling her flight.

They will be there in about two hours. Then I would think half a day to read the messages and recover from the shock. About four days and the king could be coming through the gate.

I chuckled. "I believe the first part of your estimate is spot-on, but I disagree with the rest. I think the king will be in the saddle by high tea, spend the night at the ford, putting him here in three days."

Merriam giggled. "I wager ten crowns the king stumbles through the gate on a half-dead horse in two days."

Both men said. "You are on."

Robyn laughed and shook his head. "You just cannot resist a wager, can you, my love?"

Merriam laughed. "I love taking other people's money. It is fun."

"We shall have to wait and see." Said, Sir William.

"Now on to other business. Alvos, you say your people can make these storage bags?"

"Yes, Milord, I make several types. Women like the bracelet, whereas men seem to prefer a ring. I have made a few as earrings and even a necklace."

"Mine is this ring on my right hand."

I asked. "How do the bags work if people can wear them in many diverse places?"

"It is in the magic of them. That is why the ring is the most popular and versatile method. The owner needs to push the item against the ring and think store. If the thing is too large to hold, place the ring against it and say store. A bracelet on the wrist would be just as versatile and easy to use."

I asked. "So how do you get it back out again? For that matter, how do you know which item you are getting?"

Alvos laughed. "It is simple. I reach toward my ring and think of the object I want, and I can then reach in and pull out this book. When I read what I wanted, I push it back against my right-hand think store, and it is gone."

"How could one possibly keep track of everything in their bag?" Asked Merriam.

"That is simple as well." Said Alvos. "One needs to say storage inventory, and then a list will appear before your eyes showing what is in each slot and how many."

"What supplies do you need to make the storage bags?" I asked.

"Some silver and Mythril wire to make the jewelry. Then it is just a matter of enchanting the peace to create the storage space."

"How much will they hold?" asked Robyn.

Alvos replied. They will hold ten items in a hundred slots. Now, this is where it gets complicated. One space could include ten bags of a hundred gold pieces or even a thousand gold pieces. Or it might be ten plates of hot food which will remain as fresh as the day a cook prepared them. However, a large item like this desk may take up to four slots. So you can see this number will vary depending on what you are taking."

"I see." Said Robyn. "So I could take ten arrows or ten quivers of fifty arrows."

Alvos said. "Our archers carry their arrows in quivers that way."

"That could be very handy, my love." Said Robyn. "We would not have to make arrows as often on our journey."

"Or not at all." Said Merriam. "We would need two slots for camping gear, and the valkyries would have to leave those two places open when they come as replacements, and they could then carry a resupply in those two slots."

"A most excellent idea, my love," I said. "They could also use those slots to bring other things we may need."

We should only need two or at most three tents." Said Robyn.

I said. "I would think, one for us and the other four."

"We will have to wait until we get our bags to see how much space a tent takes up." Said Merlin.

"Yes, I agree. We will table this discussion until we have the storage bags." I said. "We need to send a fast courier to Dworkin to get the Mythril wire. I have more than enough silver in my treasury for the jewelry. Alvos, how much Mythril do we buy?"

"Storage wire comes in a standard roll of a hundred arm spans and costs one platinum bar. The wire is difficult to make, so storage bags cost ten gold each for a bracelet or ring."

"Too bad we do not have the bag built into our armor. We will be wearing that most of the time." Said Merriam.

"It will not work." Said Alvos. "Due to the protections woven into the armor, the spells would counteract each other."

"In that case, no, my love, we will not be compromising your armor," I said.

Stormavgaard looked outside. It was still a couple of hours until dark. "I have business with Dworkin, so I will fly up there and bring the wire back."

"Come with me down to the treasury, and I will get that platinum."

"Okay." Said Stormavgaard, and we walked out of the study.

"Well," I said. "I should start planning for the king's arrival."

"I will look after that. You just look after the military side of things, Sir William."

"Very well, Milady."

"This will be fun." Said Merriam as Sophia and their maids followed her out the door. We could hear their giggles fading down the hall.

Shaking my head and rubbing my eyes, I muttered. "I think that was a mistake."

Merlin chuckled. "You did say the woman could plan a party."

Robyn laughed. "I also heard royal wedding bells."

Alvos said. "I am not sure of your customs for weddings, but a royal wedding for elves is very different.

When the queen chooses her king, they will spend some time together in public. A dinner usually works best for this. The queen and her chosen sit and talk, getting to know each other. The conversation will last until dark when the queen will walk out into the garden and meditate until dawn. She will then come to the king's bedchamber bringing him a cup of water and bread, kneeling on the bed, and feeding him. The queen wears nothing but the necklace holding the seed during this time.

"Whoa, that may be a problem."

"Yes. People of our time are not used to nudity, as we are very repressed due to our religious beliefs."

"Perhaps there is a way around that." Said Alvos. "This event should be held at our encampment, and you could invite just a select few of your more liberal-minded people."

How many would you require to attend this ceremony?" I asked.

"One witness for the king is needed, but many more couples would be better due to the nature of the ceremony. Remember, this is a grand celebration for us, and every elf in the village will be there."

Merlin said. "That would be the job of Merriam and her mates, Stormavgaard and his valkyries. Possibly Sergeant Thomas and Tarija."

"That is a good idea," I said as I entered the door.

"I thought we would need to wait to hold the ceremony. Should it not be held at your new home?"

Alvos said. "Milord, you are right. I got so excited about having my queen find her mate. We must hold the ceremony where the queen will plant the tree. Great magic will be released when the tree is planted, turning a large area into spring. It will be this place that would be called Elvenhome."

"I think perhaps we should take the rest of the afternoon to rest up and prepare for this evening." Said Merlin.

"I agree." Said, Sir William. "We need to be ready for tonight, and we can have the servants summon us an hour before the festivities begin."

Everyone left the study and headed for their quarters to prepare as needed. Robyn and I collected Merriam from Sophia's room on the way.

We headed for our rooms to find Alicia fussing with a dress.

Merriam giggled. "Whatever are you doing, my dear?"

Alica gasped and curtsied, saying. "I am having trouble with the trim on this dress, Milady. It pinches here and causes wrinkles."

Merriam walked over, looking closely at the place where the wrinkle was. Merriam said. "Here is the problem." She reached into the back for something twisting her hand. She pulled her hand out, and the crease went away, holding up a bent pin. "The seamstress left this. It would appear."

"How did you see that, Milady?"

"I noticed a tiny hint of silver." She replied. "You could not see it because you were standing in the light."

Alicia curtsied. "Good, you will be able to wear this dress tonight, as the green will set off your eyes and hair nicely."

Camila said. "Oh, yes, Milady, green is your best color."

Starting to remove our armor, both girls blushed and squeaked. "We will go... yes, go do something". They bolted from the room.

CHAPTER

25

"You two are naughty men." Said Merriam giggling.

"No, Milady," I said. "If we were naughty men, we would have had our way with them even if we had not survived the experience."

"Oh, you would have survived." Said Merriam. "I may have even joined. Now help me with these buttons."

We glanced at each other, seeing the same look of lust in each other's eyes. We slowly moved towards Merriam, and her pink tongue flicked out to lick her suddenly dry lips. As Robyn reached her, he began kissing her soft lips. I pushed her hair over one shoulder from behind. As Robyn kissed her deeply, I began undoing her buttons, kissing and licking the back of her neck. When Merriam's shoulders became exposed, I started nibbling and kissing my way down her back. Robyn took over, tugging her dress off her shoulders, and began to nibble at her neck.

Merriam reached for Robyn's cock, standing stiff in front of her, but he pushed her hands away.

Robyn murmured in her ear. "No, my love, hands at your sides."

Merriam whined. "But I want to touch someone."

"My love, this is all for you. You are not allowed to touch until we have you undressed completely."

By this time, I had reached the last button undoing it. Kissing and licking at the base of her spine, I kissed my way back up to her shoulders.

Robyn then pulled her dress off her arms and let it fall to the floor. I grasped her hips and nibbled over to the tie on one shoulder. Robyn cupped her breasts and nibbled his way to the other bow. We then undid the bows with our teeth, allowing her chametz to fall away and drop to the floor.

I worked down her back while Robyn began kissing and licking Merriam's breasts. Undoing the last two ties with my teeth, I let her final undergarment fall to the floor. While nipping at her neither cheeks, I slid my hands down each leg, removing her stockings and slippers. I then licked from her crease to her neck, sliding my hands up her sides. Cupping her breasts, I pulled her back against my chest.

Robyn gently moved down her stomach, kissing, licking, and nibbling. He worked his way over each hip bone and back to the center above her pubic hair. Sliding his hand down to her right knee, Robyn lifted her leg, pulling the material away from around her foot. He then kissed and licked his way from her knee back to her groin. He then repeated the same process with her left leg except, this time, I grabbed the back of her knee and held it up, spreading her open. Using his thumbs, Robyn spread the lips of her vagina. Smelling Merriam's arousal like a fine wine, he licked from her taint to her clit, swirling his tongue around that hard bud.

Merriam shuddered and gasped, moaning loudly. Her squirming pushed her ass back against me rubbing my cock between her bottom cheeks. This caused me to moan and thrust against her, and I pinched one of her nipples. Robyn pushed two fingers into her pussy, and Merriam shook in orgasm, crying in pleasure.

Chuckling, I said. "I think she is ready now."

"Yes." Said Robyn. Pulling back and standing, he lifted her other leg as we carried her to the bed. Robyn laid back on the bed, legs wide, his erection pointing stiffly, nearly touching his belly button.

Merriam crawled between his legs, took his erection in her shaking hands, and stroked it.

I fixed my eyes on Merriam's glorious ass. "This is a beautiful sight."

"I am sure it is." Robyn groaned as Merriam licked the head of his cock. "You better hurry up. I will not last much longer."

I climbed onto the bed behind Merriam. I rubbed the head of my cock over her pussy, gathering moisture. I slowly pushed into her. The slow penetration caused her to moan around Robyn's cock.

I then pulled back and slid into her faster, bottoming out. I began speeding up to keep time with the bobbing of Merriam's head on Robyn's cock.

Merriam's vagina clamped and fluttered as she screamed in orgasm around Robyn's cock in her mouth. With a roar of release, we pumped her full of our seed.

Merriam sighed as Robyn pulled her up against his body and kissed her.

I lay down beside them, running my hand over Merriam's back.

Merriam then leaned over and gave me a deep kiss as well.

Robyn said. "Well, we should see if the water is still hot enough for a bath."

Merriam giggled. "I do not want to move. You make a nice bed."

"As much as we like this position," I said. "Your ladies in waiting could walk through that door and get another severe shock."

Robyn laughed. "This is true. One of them may even faint this time."

"No." Merriam laughed. "They are made of sterner stuff than that."

"Then stay like this," I said. "Alicia and Camila will get a good view of my seed leaking from you."

"Oh, fine." Said Merriam giggling. "We best go wash up then."

"You will be wearing your formal doublets and breeches for dinner tonight."

Standing, she headed to the bathroom with us following behind her.

Robyn chuckled. "You are right, Guy. It is the best view."

Merriam giggled and put a little extra sway in her hips.

We smiled and slapped an ass cheek, then laughed at her squeak.

We found the tubs still warm enough to bathe. We quickly wet Merriam and washed her with a soft cloth and sweet-smelling soap. We then helped her into a tub to rinse off.

We quickly washed and climbed into tubs to rinse off ourselves.

We then got out and helped Merriam from her tub. Using soft towels, we dried her off. We quickly dried ourselves and followed her from the bathroom.

We stepped over to the wardrobe to get dressed. The door opened, and in traipsed Alicia and Camila, followed by Mary, who turned and closed the door.

"Milady Sophia sent Mary to help with your hair." Said Camila. That was when they noticed Robyn and me standing there naked.

"Oh, my exclaimed Mary, you are right. They do have huge..." Alicia clapped her hand over Mary's mouth, cutting her off.

Camila giggled, blushing brightly.

Merriam gave out a belly laugh. "Let us get my shift on, and you can do my hair."

Alicia said, "come help me." As she yanked Mary's arm, pulling her attention from ogling us as we dressed.

We chuckled as we finished dressing. Stepping over, we kissed Merriam on the cheeks. I said. "We will see you in the study."

We stepped through the study door to see Sir William looking out the window. Milady Sophia was in her customary place by the desk.

Merlin sat by the fire, looking through a large book. Friar Tuck, who must have just returned, sat beside him.

"Here it is." Said Merlin. "A whole section on healing magic."

"This would be most helpful." The Friar replied. "I must copy this down and send it to the brothers. The order will need to learn this, as healing will become our most significant task."

"It could not hurt." Said Merlin. "Healers are honored and respected in every realm, more so in a world of magic. We will have to ask Alvos about this."

Tarija came through the door with Sergeant Thomas. "I can help with some of that, Milord Merlin."

Healers of any type, particularly clerics, are sought by adventuring groups for dives and quests. We are fierce in protecting our healers, as they are the most vulnerable in any party. The problem is that some monsters know this and will target them first, leading us to target ranged attackers first. My teams always had one defender with the healers as their only task.

In most cases, a healer will form a close relationship with one, what we call a meat shield, and they will remain together for life. As they become adept, the healer will learn buffs for strength, speed, and power they can apply to party members, especially their shield. Alvos will help you understand the magic for buffs, but the elven healers will teach you better healing magic.

"Yes," I said. "Alvos is a good person. Knowledgeable in most forms of magic. Friar Tuck, how were your travels over the last few days?"

"Very tiring, Milord Annabelle carried me to every village in the area so I could heal their people."

Robyn laughed. "I swear that mule has more knowledge of your job than you."

Sophia giggled. "Like any good companion, she knows what you must do. Knowing that you will soon leave the area, she ensured your people were well cared for."

"Yes, I managed to cure over a hundred people of various ailments in the last three days. The bonus was I also performed three weddings and two baptisms."

"So, performing good work for God," I said.

"What good works would those be?" Came a voice from the doorway.

Turning, we all curtsied or bowed. "Your Majesty." Said, Sir William. "You surprised us. We discuss our Friar Tuck's work over the last few days."

"Your Majesty." Said Friar Tuck, dropping to his knees in supplication. "Are you an angel sent by God?"

Evadhi laughed musically. "Good Friar, I am the queen of the elves, and I have come to plant the tree of life, making our people one."

"Please, Your Majesty, sit by the fire," Sophia said. "The stone of these old castles are very cold."

Smiling, Evadhi replied. "As long as I carry the seed, I am wrapped in the warmth and sunlight of spring."

"The heat from your radiance bathes the world in love and healing." Said Friar Tuck.

"I do so love when the good Friar gets all squishy and poetic." Laughed Merriam coming through the door.

"Please, Your Majesty, sit with me on the settee so we can chat until dinner." Said Merriam, curtsying to Evadhi

Sir William said. "Milord Stormavgaard approaches. Edwin Jaime, take the carriage out to meet them."

"Milord." The boys jumped up and ran out of the door.

Sir William smiled, shaking his head. "To have such enthusiasm and vigor again."

"They are like a pair of good gloves, as they fit perfectly and respond well to your touch Milord." I laughed.

Sophia smiled. "They will have bright futures one day, Milord Duke."

"You have seen something for them, Milady?" Sir William asked.

"Nothing for you to worry about, for now, Milord." She said with a mysterious smile.

"How much longer do you have Sophia?" Asked Evadhi.

Sophia said. "Not much longer now. When this prophecy fulfills itself one way or another, my time will end. Then my task will be to raise the new oracle."

"That will be a long time without guidance." Said, Sir William.

"The gods will send visions as needed to guide the people. It has always been since the dawn of time. When one falls by the wayside, another takes up the mantle."

"So very true, Your Majesty." Said Robyn.

The queen said. "This room is comfortable and seems to serve many purposes. What do you use it for exactly?"

I chuckled. "This is my office, Your Majesty. I would typically conduct my day-to-day business here, and Sir William has taken it over as a war room and a place to discuss strategy in comfort."

"Ah." Said the queen. "The room is conducive to relaxation and deep thought, and my council should adopt a similar space for day-to-day business."

"Yes, Your Majesty, we use the formal reception hall to make announcements or receive dignitaries. Then there is the great hall for formal dinners and balls and a dining hall for my people. As leaders, we dine at that table and discuss business while eating." I pointed at the map-covered table.

"So this room serves many purposes, and I like this much better than having a separate room for each function."

"Yes, Your Majesty," I said. "We find the study most useful for planning."

There was a knock at the door, and Stormavgaard entered. "Your Majesty, Milords, and Ladies. I have returned from a successful mission." He said, holding out a roll of wire to Alvos.

"This is perfect, Milord Dragon." Said Alvos. "I will begin crafting the rings and bracelets of holding in the morning."

"Milord Stormavgaard, what was the other purpose of your mission?" Asked the queen.

"Oh, yes, Your Majesty, I had to discuss some of the requirements for my eyrie with Dworkin. I have also arranged for upgrades to my valkyries armor and weapons. While their spears and shields are legendary God-forged, their equipment is only excellent for the most part. I have arranged for the dwarfs to create the highest standard 'S' class armor and weapons. The eight with me have been fitted, and we will pick theirs up tomorrow. The rest will go get theirs when they return."

"What is the difference between what you are getting and what my men are equipped with?" I asked.

"The armor your companions received is of high 'A' class, excellent as it is known. What my valkyries will receive is called epic. The only higher rank of armor and weapons is Godly, and that would be where your bow stands, Milady." He said, turning to Merriam.

"Oh, I like that." Gushed Merriam. "And having excellent armor is not bad either, I think?"

We all chuckled at that.

Stormavgaard got a distant look on his face and then spoke. "Your Majesty, the scouts have arrived at Will's location. According to the twins, I believe it is a perfect place full of magic and earth power."

Merlin said. "It must be where the ley lines meet. There are numerous places around England, such as Stonehenge, and the orb moves between these locations, searching for the right one."

"What do you mean?" I asked.

"Merlin says that the orb is looking for a specific location." Said the queen. "Most of these hubs produce earth power but a few vent evil away from the earth."

"Yes." Said Merlin. "What the orb is looking for precisely. One such place is near Kesh in ancient Sumer, where I trapped the orb for the first time."

"It matters not." Said Merriam. "We will capture the orb, and Stormavgaard will destroy it."

We laughed when Merriam's stomach growled at the end of her declaration.

The queen smiled. "We fear the need for food has taken the edge from your fierce declaration, Milady."

There was a knock at the door then Denby stuck his head in. "Your Majesty, Lords, and Ladies, dinner is ready for you now."

"Excellent." Said Stormavgaard holding out his arm for the queen. "Allow me to escort you, Your Majesty."

"Thank you, Lord Dragon." She said, rising.

The rest of us followed in order of prominence behind the queen and Stormavgaard.

Merriam giggled. "We are like a small army marching to battle."

Robyn laughed and replied. "Most receptions are a battle of one sort or another."

I chuckled. "A battle of words and wits. There are always those wishing some advantage over those in power."

"I believe this will be a much more sedate affair." Said Robyn. "Those here will adopt a wait-and-see attitude as they are not strong enough to seek advantage. They may try to gain favor or two, but that will be mainly from the Duke."

"Such is the way of power and those seeking it." I said as we paused at the door to the grand hall.

Denby pounded his staff and began announcing everyone in rank from low to high. We all marched in and stood behind our seats at the head table. As Denby pounded the staff announcing the queen and Stormavgaard, everyone stood in their places.

All bowed or curtsied as she passed, taking her place before the throne. The moment she sat down, everyone rose from their bows and sat.

The servants began streaming from the side doors of the hall, bringing steaming platters of food and jugs with wine and ale, placing them before the diners. Stormavgaard took it upon himself to serve the queen. Two elves stepped forward, passing their hands over the dishes.

Merriam quirked her eyebrow. "Whatever are they doing, Your Majesty?"

Evadhi said. "It is their function to check for and remove poisons from my food, and it is a magical technique that they possess."

"I see." Said Merriam. "I suppose there are all kinds of dangers in the world, not only for royalty such as yourself."

"Well, it certainly seems to be a safer system for the testers." Robyn laughed. "Our royal tasters have to eat the food."

The queen said. "That must be stressful for those people."

"Yes, it is." Said, Sir William. "They are well compensated, and families of any that die get land and a stipend to take care of them."

"Oddly enough." Said Robyn. "There is great competition for the position among fourth sons and daughters."

Sir William said. "There is not much likelihood of them ever receiving an inheritance, which gives them a chance to gain some prestige."

"I believe using magicians is a far better option." Said Merriam. "Your magicians will be in great demand in court."

Evadhi smiled. "My people would be most pleased to have the work."

After that, conversation petered out as we concentrated on eating. As dessert appeared on the table, guests moved around.

Conversations sparked up in many locations around the hall.

A group of minstrels struck up a lively tune as a group of young ladies began dancing.

"Oh, good." Said Merriam. "Denby has arranged for some entertainment for us."

Evadhi beckoned Alvos over. "Have we also provided for this entertainment?"

"Yes, Your Majesty, some of our musicians and dancers will be performing next."

"Good." Said the queen.

Next, some young men join the girls to perform more traditional dances. And as they finished up and bowed low to the queen, she laughed and clapped with delight. "This was wonderful." She cried out. "We are most pleased with your display."

The young people left the floor smiling happily.

A flute began a low warbling tone, followed by a harp. An elven woman flowed out onto the floor with intricate steps. A soft drum thumped as she moved about the floor, and an elf man began high-stepping onto the floor. As the music changed, they began to flow together, whirling and touching, ending with the man dipping the woman.

As the music ended, Merriam clapped enthusiastically. "That was so wonderful."

The queen said. "That was the dance of two lovers meeting."

Sophia said. "I like that one. It was intimate."

A new tune began, and the queen said. "This one is a harvest dance." Six more pairs joined the dance. They started a twirling of movement that was almost hard to follow. As the music began to slow, the audience began to pick out some motions used for harvesting. They were reaping, digging, picking, and other typical movements. As the music stopped, each dancer froze like statues in their poses.

The hall erupted in cheering and clapping for the performance.

The elves performed a few more dances to everyone's delight.

The queen finally said. "We shall retire now. If we are to accompany the Lord Dragon on the morrow, we need to be well-rested."

We rose and bowed as the queen stood, taking Stormavgaard's arm. They left the hall, followed by the queen's guard and the valkyries.

"That was a most successful party Milady." Said, Sir William.

"I am pleased you enjoyed yourself." Said Merriam. "However, I cannot take all the credit because Sophia helped, and Denby executed the plan perfectly."

"No, it was your plan." Said, Sir William. "To you as hostess go the honors."

"Well, my loves, it is time to post ourselves by the door and thank our guests for attending." Said Merriam.

Glancing around the hall, Robyn chuckled. "I would say more than a few of our guests will still be here for breakfast, as it would seem some have drunk themselves into a stupor."

"Yes, those can sleep it off where they are." Merriam chuckled. "Those that can still stand can be sent home."

The group moved over to the door, saying goodnight and thanking those that could leave.

"Denby, have the people designated for cleanup throw blankets on the remaining guests, and they may then do the best clean-up they can and retire."

"As you wish, Milady." Said Denby.

"The night staff will take care of it, and your breakfast will be in the study in the morning."

"Thank you, Denby," I said.

CHAPTER

26

Walking down the hall, we heard music coming through the door. Quirking our eyebrows at each other, Merriam put a finger to her lips. Slowly opening the door, we slipped inside to a most delightful sight.

Camila and Alicia were dancing while Camila played a pan flute. Both girls were stark naked, trying to copy the elves' moves during their first dance. Camila lifted her leg while Alicia slipped under it, raising one of her own behind her and locking their ankles together. Camila then used the leverage to lean back, so the tops of their heads were touching. They collapsed to the side on the divan in a tangle of legs and arms.

They both scrambled to cover themselves as we laughed and clapped.

Both girls were crying as Alicia, terror in her eyes, peeked over the divan and blubbered. "Milady, please do not dismiss us. We did not know it was so late. We were excited about this dance, but our clothes got in the way."

"Girls, we will not dismiss you." Said Merriam. "As we have repeatedly said, you need to overcome this shyness. Come now, help me get undressed, and we will talk."

"Yes, Milady." Said both girls as they looked around for their clothes.

"Do not worry about your dresses. You will not need them for a while." Merriam then moved to her dressing table while the girls removed her clothing. Once they had removed the pins to let her hair down, Merriam beckoned them to follow her. Merriam entered the bathing room with the girls trailing behind her.

We gathered goblets and a jug of wine sitting by the fire to wait for them.

I finally broke the silence with a question. "I wonder what Milady has planned for these girls?"

"I suspect we will be doing a little womanly training."

"I suppose you are right. Sweet things like them should not be left to wither on the vine."

Robyn laughed. "I must admit they rouse some rather unwholesome thoughts in my head."

Hearing some giggling coming from the other room, Robyn asked. "Should we go peek, Guy?"

"Not really, Robyn. Sometimes anticipation can be much more fun than watching."

"Yes, but the show can be much more arousing. We may be invited to join in if we are caught looking."

Setting my goblet down, I said. "You are right. You have me there."

Standing, we both padded quietly to the doorway. Merriam had left the door partway open as if anticipating we would peek. What we beheld had us both rock hard in an instant.

Merriam was gently guiding the girls, pressed together, kissing. Merriam whispered something, and the girl's tongues started to dance around each other's mouths. With their arms around each other, she guided their caresses lower, soon fondling and gripping each other's bottoms. It, of course, pulled their lower bellies together, causing their clits to rub. The girls began moaning and grinding hard against each other.

Merriam then guided one hand from each girl up to fondle the other's breast and then whispered to them again, and they began plucking at the nipple of the other girl. That got a collective gasp and whimpers from both girls.

Merriam then directed them to bring the hand on their ass around between their legs. She said. "Slide your middle finger down, gather some moisture from the opening, and bring it back up around the clit. Now go back down and collect some more juices around the clit. Keep going until you have it good and wet."

Soon the girls were humping and grinding against each other's hands with abandon. "Now," Merriam said, "slide your middle finger inside her pussy and rub your thumb against her clit."

Both girls screamed as they climaxed.

She then kissed both girls as she held them against her. "That was very good she said. Now, lick your fingers clean and taste each other."

The girls complied, moaning a bit at the flavor.

"Now, I shall teach your pretty little mouths more than just kissing."

"Milady?" They both stuttered.

"First, Camila, sit on the table edge and bring your heels up to the loops. Come, Alicia, see how her flower opens up. Now observe," and Merriam began to demonstrate. Licking up from Camila's taint, she swirled her tongue around the girl's clit.

With her bent over like that, Merriam's ass presented a stunning picture for the men, and they knew she had seen them and was doing it deliberately. We could see how slick her pussy was with the juices running down her legs, wetting her inner thighs. Alica was bent over, presenting her pretty little bottom, her thighs also slick from her juices.

Merriam brought her hands up, spreading Camila's vagina lips open. She began probing the entrance to her vagina, and Camila was squirming and moaning for her part.

"Watch closely," Merriam said as she pushed her middle finger into Camila's opening. She then gently began to pump the finger in and out while flicking her tongue around the girl's clit. "When you do this, try not to puncture the hymen. If you curl your finger slightly, you will feel a rough patch at the top of the vagina, and it is not hard to find. Make a come hither motion with your finger," using her other hand to show Alicia the motion. "This will bring extreme pleasure, and she will climax very quickly." Pulling away, Camila moaned from the lack of stimulation.

"Camila, you are very delicious and wet. Alicia, it is your turn."

Alicia eagerly bent forward, licking from taint to clit, twirling her tongue around the clit several times, and spreading Camila's pussy lips. Coming back down to the entrance of her tunnel, Alicia speared her tongue into the hole, moaning slightly.

Camila cried. "Yes, more." Grinding her crotch against Alicia's face.

Merriam was gently fondling Alicia's pussy, making her squirm slightly. As Alicia began fingering Camila, Merriam did the same to Alicia. As Camila started to climax, Merriam praised Alicia.

"Next time we do this, we will teach you about anal." Merriam slipped her finger into Alicia's butthole.

Alicia screamed as she shuddered from her climax.

"You like that, do you?" Asked Merriam.

"Milady." Alicia moaned. "It felt strange but good."

"That is encouraging." Said Merriam. "But it will be a lesson for another night." And she then had the girls switch places. Then proceeded to teach Camila the same lesson she had, Alicia. Of course, this ended with Alicia screaming in climax and Camila getting the finger in the butt hole. The only difference was that Camila ejaculated a small stream of fluid from her pussy.

Both men groaned at that sight.

Both girls let out squeaks as they tried to cover themselves.

"Now, girls, what did I tell you about covering yourself. After that performance, look at the lust in their eyes. You have nothing to be ashamed of."

"Milady is right," Robyn said. "You were a delight to behold."

"Yes, your performance was spectacular," I said. "You should be proud for learning your skills so well."

Merriam giggled. "Yes, they have more lessons to learn yet. Come kneel beside me, girls, and learn to use your talented tongues on men."

We grinned, stepping forward in front of the girls."

"When we do this, girls, keeping your teeth covered by your lips is essential. Their skin is very soft, like velvet. Go ahead and stroke them, giving your wrist a slight twist as you go. Now using plenty of saliva, licking from the base to the tip. Keep running your hand over the shaft spreading your saliva around to lubricate their cocks."

"Excellent, now lick around the head. That is it. Take it into your mouth as far as you can go."

Both girls got about halfway down the shaft before they began to gag. "You will get better and be able to take it deeper with practice. Keep pushing your limits when you get to the same point; this will help you take more. Make eye contact. His face will tell you how well you are doing. Keep your hand working in front of your lips to help spread saliva making it more manageable."

We held our hands behind our backs, trying desperately not to force the girls before they were ready.

Both girls began moving faster as they got the hang of the rhythm.

"Good." Said Merriam. "Spread your knees a little wider to give yourself more balance. Now gently cup and fondle their balls with your other hand."

Both girls moaned, causing delightful vibrations for us. We each began thrusting as we could not help ourselves.

Merriam slid her hands down the girl's backs, running her fingers down the cracks of their asses into their pussies. That caused them to moan, sending shivers up and down our spines even more. Merriam grinned up at us, and she could see we were very close to cumming, and the girls were peaking. She pulled her fingers from the girl's pussies in a rush, shoving them up their asses. It caused both girls to lunge forward and scream as they climaxed.

Which caused us to ejaculate into the back of the girl's throats, and swallowing and choking, the girls pulled back in surprise. Our next shot of cum sprayed their faces and all over their breasts.

Both girls squirmed and gasped as Merriam pulled her fingers from their asses.

We both chuckled, grabbed a wet washcloth, and wiped the girl's faces. They tried to protest this act, but we hushed them.

Relax, girls." Said Robyn. "We do this for our ladies after sex."

"It is called aftercare," I said.

"Oh yes, girls." Said Merriam. "The feeling of being cleaned up after sex is relaxing."

We carefully laid the girls back onto the floor, spreading their legs and lifting them. We quickly tasted their sweet pussies. Then we gently cleaned them up and walked the girls back into the sitting area. We brought them onto our laps on the settee and poured them a goblet of wine.

The two nearly exhausted girls downed their wine in a couple of gulps.

Robyn chuckled. "That will go right to your heads." He then poured them some water.

"We should have probably given them water in the first place."

Merriam giggled. "You are probably right. It would not do to send my ladies-in-waiting ravished and drunk off to bed."

"It matters not." Said Robyn. "I will throw on breeches and a shirt, then escort the young ladies to their room."

"Oh, Milord, that is not necessary." Said Alicia. "We can find our room with no problem."

"No." Said Robyn. "I insist. A gentleman must escort young ladies to their room late at night."

"Very well, Milord, we should get going. It is very late." Camila said as she stood, heading for the door.

Merriam smiled. "Camila, you should perhaps put on your dress."

Alicia giggled as Camila spun around, blushing.

I laughed. "Perhaps we have the girls too relaxed about nudity now."

"Yes, we may have gone too far in the other direction." Merriam laughed.

Both girls giggled a bit as they slipped on their dresses and shoes.

Robyn laughed, pulling his boots on. "While I do not mind the view, people may get a little upset if our maids run around naked."

Both girls giggled as they headed for the door.

"Have a good night." Said Merriam. "I do not expect you to early tomorrow morning."

"Yes, Milady." Said Alicia. "Although it may not matter."

"No." Said Camila. "One of the night servants comes around and wakes everyone before dawn."

They both curtsied as they went out the door.

"Well, that was a thoroughly enjoyable evening, my love."

Merriam laughed. "Yes, I had fun. While I did not orgasm, I gave the girl's a few."

"Yes, I am sure it will be an experience they will never forget."

"That was my plan." Said Merriam. "Next time, I will better taste those sweet little pussies. You will get to ride their asses. We will preserve their maidenheads for their wedding night, but everything else is fair game."

"I like the sound of that, and will Will and Jon get to play this little game?"

"Oh, yes, my love, they will be joining. Meanwhile, as soon as Robyn returns, you will take me to that bed and use me how you will."

As we reached the top of the stairs, the girls turned to go down.

I asked. "Where are you quartered?"

"In the servant's quarters where the rest of the maids live." Said Alicia.

"Well, this will not do, and I will speak with Milady Merriam about this. You are ladies-in-waiting, not servants. While you are looking after Milady, you should have your maids. You should always be on the second floor near our quarters, close to your lady."

"Oh, Milord, I do not think that would be proper." Said Camila.

It is proper." I said. "Your jobs are to train the maids that will replace you. As a new Lady, I realize that Merriam does not know of this, but Denby should."

Well, Milord, we share a room, so would it be possible to share one when we move upstairs?"

"I do not see why not if that would make you comfortable."

"Thank you, Milord. We are here now." Said Camila as she opened the door.

"We will bid you good night." Said Alicia.

"I would look at this room you have been stuck in," I said. I looked around at a dresser, two wardrobes on the wall, and another dresser under the window. On the other wall were two beds that amounted to no more than a couple of cots pushed together.

"How long have you been sleeping in here?" I asked.

Alicia replied. "Since we were ten when we moved here from the nursery. We then started doing menial cleaning tasks."

As we grew, we got more physical jobs that needed someone taller. When we turned fourteen, we began doing maid work. At first, it was just for other servants or senior staff. At sixteen, we started working upstairs, but that was mainly dusting as we had very few guests over the years we worked there.

"Yes." Said Alicia. "Milady came along, and everything changed. I am thrilled to be serving Lady Merriam; she is kind and easy to please. We are not beaten."

"Well, you can put your mind at rest. Your Lord and Lady would never beat you or mistreat you. It is your last night in these beds, and mark my words tomorrow. There will be changes."

"Yes, Milord, thank you, Milord." The girls said in unison.

Walking out, I closed the door and headed back upstairs down the hall.

I closed the door firmly as I stepped into our quarters.

"Merriam, you will need to inspect the servants' quarters in the morning. Your ladies-in-waiting share a room no larger than our bed."

"Oh, really," Merriam replied. "Have some wine, and we will leave those things for the morning. I will go on a rampage then."

The following day dawned with a distinct chill in the air. The door opened and in swept Alicia and Camila. "Good morning, Milords Milady. I hope you all slept well."

Camila opened the curtains and said. "There was a light frost overnight. I believe it will turn into a nice warm day."

Merriam stepped from the bed and walked over to Alicia. Pulling her into a hug, she said. "I am sorry for your living conditions, my dear." She then took Camila into her arms, hugging her. "I will make this right today."

"Not to look like you have been complaining, I plan a surprise inspection of the servant's quarters. We will get all the ladies-in-waiting into better quarters. As for the rest of the servants, it will only be a temporary measure." Merriam said and then kissed Alicia and Camila.

I chuckled. "You have struck a nerve with Milady. She will put things right now."

"Yes," Robyn said. "It appeared to be a domestic problem under household affairs."

"That is right, gentleman, and you best go save me some breakfast."

"Yes, my love." We both laughed, quickly dressing and heading down the hall to the study.

We entered to find one of the servants replacing candles while another built up the fire. "Milord." The one replacing candles said. "We are sorry this was not done earlier. Friar Tuck was sleeping in the chair over there, and we did not wish to disturb him."

"I see." Said Robyn. Walking over, he gave the Friar a shake. "Whatever are you doing sleeping here, Tuck? You have a perfect bed just down the hall."

Friar Tuck snorted and shook himself awake. "What is this, Robyn?" He looked around blearily. "That is right, I came up here to finish writing notes on healing magic, and I also finished my report to Father Superior. After breakfast, I will send this post-haste to the monastery."

"It is just north of London, is it not?" Robyn asked.

"Yes, a small town is growing there, and we have not decided on a name for it yet."

I said. "I will send a squad of my men to deliver your message, as I am not comfortable sending out single messengers."

"That is most gracious of you, Milord. I thank you."

Merriam and Sophia walked in, giggling with their heads close together.

Sir William followed behind, shaking his head in amusement.

I said. "I hope you both slept well."

Sir William replied. "Very well."

Everyone turned to the door as Yrswen and a queen's guard stepped into the study, followed by Evadhi and Stormavgaard.

Everyone bowed, greeting the queen as she swept through the door.

Evadhi said. "Please, everyone, relax. There is no need for such formality amongst this small group."

"Thank you, Your Majesty," I said. "I am sure breakfast will be served shortly."

As everyone settled around the table, servants began bringing in food.

Stormavgaard sighed. "I am famished."

Laughing, Merriam said. "You have a busy morning of flying ahead of you."

"Oh, that is light work and will hardly stretch my wings. But it was another vigorous night as my valkyries are pretty feisty."

Yrswen blushed. "We were only following your instructions, Milord."

Robyn laughed. "Sounds like someone else had a fun night."

Merriam giggled.

The conversation died down as everyone began eating.

CHAPTER

27

It was near dusk when I spotted Sir Penrose and his men. They were still about a mile from the ford. I could see the break in the terrain caused by the river in the fading light.

As we overflew their formation, I heard distant sounds of fighting. I quickly signaled my sisters, sending Malhe and Rangilde ahead to investigate. The rest of us promptly landed in front of Sir Penrose.

The column stopped as we landed a short distance in front of them. Nodding my head to Sir Penrose, I said. "Hail and well-met, Sir Penrose. I bring other dispatches for the king." I then reached into my bag and handed them to him. "I also sent two sisters to investigate the sounds of fighting ahead."

"Thank you, Eyldana." Sir Penrose replied and then called back to the column. "Rest check weapons and armor. We may fight shortly."

Then my sisters came in and landed behind us.

Malhe said. "About two hundred orcs are attacking the motte-and-bailey by the ford, and it seems to be just a single Warband."

Rangilde said. "They are the usual disorganized mob not that dangerous for fortifications."

Sir Penrose said. "That may be ladies, but the men manning these places are more guards than soldiers. We need to strike them from behind and break their formation.

"That will be easy." Said Eyldana. "Your knights drive a wedge into their backs, and your other men can start pushing outward. My sisters and I will fly in and hit the flank, tearing them to pieces."

"Sounds like a solid plan." Said Sir Penrose. "We will leave the wagon at the edge of the woods, and the archers can shoot from there, protecting the wagon and covering our flanks."

"Excellent," I said. "Once you have got the orc's attention, we will hit the greatest flank from the rear.

Sir Penrose mounted his horse. We took to the air again as they moved at a trot. As we reached the wood's edge, I saw it was only about four hundred yards from the tree line to the motte-and-bailey. Many orcs were dead, focusing on the gate, and there seemed to be more on the riverside.

Sir Penrose and his men broke from the tree line. The knights quickly formed a wedge speeding up to a canter, and pikemen slipped to either side of the wedge, moving in a solid formation.

The archers spread out under the edge of the trees, calling out targets as they got set.

The knights were sixty paces from the back of the orcs when seen. Sir Penrose and his men couched their lances and charged. As the lances fouled or snapped, they dropped them pulled their swords, and began hacking around them. They began to slow as the number of orcs facing them increased. By this time, the pikemen had hit the opening made by the knights. The archers started raining arrows on the orcs. They targeted leaders and any orcs trying to rally. The men on the walls cheered and renewed their efforts.

The larger group near the river turned their attention to Sir Penrose, so my sisters and I flew over the river. Giving some quick hand signals, we spread out. We drew our sabers and began a delightful slaughter while hitting the ground running.

My sisters and I soon fell into a battle trance. The orcs fell like wheat before a scythe. Backing away in fear, some tried to run, but we cut them down with extreme prejudice. When they realized they could not run, there were not enough to mount an effective defense. I soon found myself standing in front of a surprised Sir Penrose.

Shaking myself from my trance, I asked. "Where are the rest of the orcs?"

Sir Penrose chuckled. "There is no rest. We have slaughtered them all. Mostly you and your valkyries, but we helped."

I grinned, looking around. "Well, that just calls for feasting and drinking." I sheathed my weapons, clapping Sir Penrose on the shoulder. "Come battle, brother, let us go meet the defenders."

Chuckling, Sir Penrose grinned. "Yes, you were something of a surprise for those men. They look at you nervously, and we should calm them down a bit."

We walked toward the motte as the gates began to open, and a large armored man stepped out with an escort.

Sir Penrose said. "Milord, I am Sir Penrose from the Duke of Nottingham's command bearing dispatches most urgent for the king. This is Eyldana Home-Wand, and her Valkyrie sisters sent with further updates."

The armored man said. "I am Sir Rodrick, Captain of the Baroness of Bedford's men. Can you explain to me what these creatures were and who they are? Until recently, I have seen nothing like this, as there have been other monsters like werewolves and other creatures."

"I can help you with some of this information," I said. "My sisters and I are Valkyries sent by the Goddess Freya to protect my Dragonlord Stormavgaard. We are blood bonded to him as mates and guardians, fighting for this land as my Dragonlord directs. We are not here to harm the people, so you may relax."

Sir Roderick grunted. "That is easy for you to say, but I saw you fight, and it was terrifying."

Sir Penrose laughed. "Invite us to board and see another side of them. There are more men here than I would have expected, Sir Roderick."

"Yes, we were escorting Milady the Baroness to Cambridge. She had only recently come to power when her mother died. Her father died years ago during the crusade, so she must be confirmed in her position."

Sir Penrose said. "I understand, captain. We lost many good men on the crusade; alas, most of the scum seem to have survived. Unfortunately, you missed the king and one of our companies passing through."

"The commander of the bailey told us of that. They had left for Cambridge, and we only arrived at noon."

"Please, Sir Penrose, come and meet the Baroness. She will be delighted to have news of what is happening."

As we headed for the bailey, I contacted Stormavgaard reporting the battle. He said he watched most of it through our eyes, congratulating us on a well-done job.

As I led my horse through the gate into the motte, I saw several grooms coming forward. Handing my reins over, I patted the man on the shoulder and said. "Give him extra oats and a good brushing. He fought well today."

"Yes, Milord." The young man said.

We then proceeded towards the bailey, where the doors were opening. A petite young woman exited from the door smiling brightly.

My heart seized at this vision before me. Stepping forward, I bowed low as Sir Roderick made introductions.

Baroness Sylvia spoke in a most musical voice. "I am happy to meet you, Sir Penrose and Eyldana. We were fortunate you showed up when you did to help us."

Eyldana giggled, nudging me from my stupor.

"We are most happy to have been of help, Milady. I must say, though, Eyldana and her sister Valkyries made the job much easier."

Eyldana laughed. "You would have taken a bit longer and had more kills, but it would have made no difference. Those orcs were dead the moment you hit the back of their formation. There may have been no problem, but they still worked up an appetite. Milady, do you have meat and ale for us?"

The baroness giggled. "Yes, come inside. Servants are preparing food now, and we can eat and discuss your prowess in battle. I watched the fight from the tower and was most impressed with your skill."

I felt my face flush at her praise. "It was nothing, Milady, just discipline and good training. Milord Duke and our men have been together for a very long time."

We reached a long room set up as a dining hall by this time. The Baroness led us to the table where pitchers of ale and tankards sat. I

241

turned to my sergeants. "Let the men eat their fill but only two mugs per man."

"Yes, Milord." The sergeant's replied.

Eyldana remained with me as the other valkyrie spread out amongst the men.

The baroness sat at the head of the table, and we sat on one side while Sir Rodrick and Sir Porter sat on the other.

The baroness smiled as I quickly poured a goblet of wine for her.

Eyldana giggled as she poured ale for herself and me.

The baroness sipped her wine. "Now, please tell me the news. We have been relatively isolated in Bedford, and I have only just learned of the return of the crusade."

"Yes, Milady," I said. "When we returned, Sir William the High Commander released most of the army. We had orders to bring the treasures from the crusade to Nottingham for the regent. Then..." and over the next hour, I brought Milady up to date. She was an attentive listener gasping and giggling as my tale unfolded.

It was getting late when she finally asked me. "Will you be accompanying us to Cambridge, Sir Penrose?"

I thought to myself as I rubbed my scalp.

"Milady, there would be no point in you going to Cambridge. The dispatches I carry have such significance that the king will likely leave for Nottingham immediately, and I suggest you leave here and make your way to Nottingham at your best speed. I know this would be about four days for you, but I think we will catch back up with you tomorrow night with the king. The king will be moving very fast once he reads these dispatches."

"How disappointing, but I suppose you are right. I will miss your delightful company and hope we meet again soon."

"Milady, you are a delightful woman, and I would love to know you better."

Baroness Sylvia giggled. "I would get to know you better, Milord."

Standing, I bowed, taking her hand and kissing her knuckles. "Until we meet again, Milady, my heart will only know desolation."

And we walked from the hall seeking our bedrolls.

Eyldana laughed as we crossed the motte. You totally smite her, Sir Penrose. Did you see her squirm as you told your tale?"

"I noticed no such thing," I said, blushing.

Again Eyldana laughed. "You could have had her on the table, and she would have loved every moment."

"Really, Eyldana, is that all you valkyries think about?"

"Pretty much, except for battle, because they are fun." She laughed.

Entering the barracks, I removed my outer armor and rolled into my bunk. Eyldana quickly pulled off her leathers, climbing into the other bunk.

Dawn began to break the following day as we rode from the motte. We quickly loaded the wagon and half the men onto the ferry. Working the ropes, we pulled the empty ferry back, drawing our loaded one across. Loading up while the other group unloaded and pulled us across the river.

We then set a challenging pace for Cambridge. We did not worry about ambushes with valkyries flying overwatch and made good time.

We arrived in Cambridge late morning, and the valkyrie's landed, joining our formation as we slowed to enter the town. We rode straight to the palace, where Captain Jeffrey met us.

Dismounting, I saluted Captain Jeffrey.

The captain returned my salute and asked. "Why are you here so soon after we left Nottingham?"

I laughed at his concerned look. "Let me see where to start. I have urgent dispatches that must be in the king's hands. It is a tale of dwarves shifters. valkyrie's a dragon, and elves with a queen." The captain's eyes kept getting wider, jaw-dropping open as I spoke.

"Dragons, you say, and an elf queen? It is madness, but seeing the king's reaction should be fun. Very well then, most of your men can go to the barracks there and rest. You can come with me to the king."

This is Eyldana, Captain Jeffery. The leader of this…? What do you call your teams?"

"Flights and three flights make a squadron." Eyldana smiled.

"Yes, of course, you said that the other night at the party."

"You did get drunk, and I am surprised you remember anything before I poured you in bed." Eyldana laughed.

Turning on his heel, the captain chuckled as he led the way, and we marched behind.

Eyldana was grinning like a cat who got the cream. I looked at her and said. "You know this is serious business?"

"Oh, yeah." She said. "But it will be fun."

I snorted. "You have no idea."

Eyldana kept giggling as we entered the palace.

Inside, some officials tried to stop us, but Captain Jeffrey just pushed them out of the way. And we marched through the doors to the throne room.

The king heard a petition from some lord.

Jeffrey interrupted him. "Your Majesty, Sir Penrose bears urgent dispatches from Sir William in Nottingham, and this is Eyldana of the valkyries with him."

Eyldana opened her wings, dropping to one knee, saluting a fist to her breastplate.

"Your Majesty, I bear greetings from my Dragonlord Stormavgaard."

His eyes widened, and a slow grin spread over his face. "Rise, lady Eyldana, Sir Penrose. Come, we will go to my private office."

The Lord, petitioning, and a court official protested. "The business of the court is essential, Your Majesty."

The king glared at the official. "This is far more important than the petty squabbling of many thieving Lourdes."

The king led us through a side door and down a narrow hall. We entered an unremarkable door into a large ornate office. The king tossed his robe of office onto a nearby chair, taking a seat behind his massive desk.

"The dispatches Sir Penrose." The King held out his hand. I opened the pouch at my waist, handing the King the packets, updates, and letter.

"Goodness, Sir William, must-have striped a full goose to write these dispatches. Okay, Sir Penrose, what order should I read them in?"

Eyldana giggled. "Save the one from Milady Sophia until last."

I chuckled. "Your Majesty, start with the big one. It deals with the dwarves and a rearmament program for the army and training schedules. Then the second would be this one here, Your Majesty, as it contains a proposition for restructuring the army I wrote. Most important is the one from Milady Sophia."

"Very well." The king said, taking a dagger and slitting the packet open. He reached in and pulled out the message. "What material are the letters written on?"

"Oh, yes, Your Majesty, that is something else I have to show you. If the Captain shows me the way, I can go get it now."

"Yes, go ahead. I will read these while you are gone. Milady may relax." The king said, ringing a bell by his desk. "I will order freshments for us while you are gone."

"Your Majesty," I said. The captain and I left the room.

"What are we getting for the king?" Asked Captain Jeffrey.

"It is a large box of gifts for his majesty. Not heavy, just a bit bulky, and takes two men to carry. Little-Jon carries one by himself, but you know how big he is."

"Yes." The captain laughed. "He is rather large for a man named little."

"Captain, even he jokes about that, saying it was his mother's fault." We laughed as we walked into the courtyard to the wagon, and I hopped in back, pulling the chest to the tailgate.

"You are right. It is a large box. But it does not seem very heavy." Captian Jeffery said as we lifted it off the back.

"Yes, you see this armor I am wearing? It is a thousand times stronger but weighs one-tenth of yours, and it also has magic enchantments built right into the armor. We'll be able to display some of it when we get back to the king."

It was not long before we were back in the king's office, and I saw his scribe also there. "Your Majesty, this chest contains some gifts from the Duke of Nottingham and Dworkin."

"Now, this first thing will explain the paper you are reading from."

I pulled the pole frame from the box and set it beside the king's desk. I then got the desktop to place on the stand. I then went back and got the smaller mobile desk for the scribe. Helping him put it on was no problem. I then opened the top of the desk, taking out two pens and some paper. I laid the paper on the desk and one of the pens in the groove. I then showed the scribe his paper and pens in a drawer on his desk. I then showed them how to fill and use the pens.

"By God. This desk is a princely gift."

I chuckled. "Yes, Your Majesty, and a steal at only five gold."

"You jest, Sir Knight." Scoffed the king shaking his head. "This is worth thousands."

"No, Your Majesty, that is the guild price for these desk sets. A new pen will cost you one gold, and a refill of paper and ink which come as a set is also one gold."

"Some of that would be described in the documents sent to you by Dworkin. All of the prices are fixed so that each person makes something.

You will make some mistakes learning to use the pens, but the price is so low that it will not be a problem. There are also two extra refills in the chest for you."

Eyldana was smiling over on the settee, sipping tea and nibbling on pastries.

"We will leave you to your reading, Your Majesty, and just sit quietly over here."

The king spent three hours reading through the dispatches and grilling me with questions. Eyldana helped with some of them, mainly about Stormavgaard and the valkyries. Captain Jeffrey sat more or less in stunned silence.

Finally, the king asked one of the funniest questions. I stood before his desk. "The scriptorium banner was added when they decided I would carry messages. Initially, it would have just been three." I called out, "dark," and the tabard disappeared, showing plain silver.

The King asked. "How is this possible?"

"The armor is Mythril, Your Majesty, imbued with magic. All the tabards are just a magic script enchanted to the Mythril. The Dwarves told us it takes magic to work Mythril."

I called out "for the King," and the rampant lion tabard appeared. Smiling at the king's surprise, I called "for Milady," and the emblem of Sophia's own appeared.

"Well." Said the king. "It is undoubtedly pretty. How does it stand up in battle?" I smiled as Eyldana giggled. "You are going to love this part."

CHAPTER

28

"Captain, please get one of the guards to run and get me a spare breastplate."

Captain Jeffrey walked to the door, stuck his head out, and spoke to a guard. The guard returned with a stand and armored breastplate a few minutes later.

I told the guard. "Strike that breastplate with your sword as hard as possible."

The guard did so, leaving a dent and a small gash in the plate.

"Just as I would have expected." Said the king. "Our guards' equipment is the best armor money can buy."

Eyldana stood from the settee. "May I borrow your sword?" She asked the guard.

"Yes, Milady." Said the guard handing her his sword hilt first. I was standing, hands at my side, facing the king.

Eyldana swung around and slammed the sword into my chest. I grunted a bit at the impact but hardly moved. The king, mouth wide open, leaned over the desk, and Captain Jeffrey had moved to draw his sword to stop her. The guard just stared.

Eyldana giggled. "Oops, it broke." She said and looked at the shattered blade and hilt in her hand.

"But." Said the king. "There is no mark on you, Sir Penrose."

Captain Jeffrey stepped around, running his fingers over the breastplate. "I can not even feel a scratch. How is this possible?"

"That is just how strong this armor is. The footmen's armor is just as strong and looks like their leathers. I can take a longbow arrow to the chest at twenty-five paces without a mark."

"Now, for the next part of the demonstration," I said. "Your Majesty, use my sword and strike that armor." I unclipped my bastard sword from my belt, handing it to the king, hilt-first sheath and all. "Whatever you do, Your Majesty, only grab the hilt, and the sheath, do not touch the blade."

The king grunted and almost fell back when he took the sword. "My God, it is light. I could wield this for hours." He then drew the sword looking at the etchings on the blade. "This is a work of art and not meant for battle."

"You might not believe this, Your Majesty, but an apprentice made that blade in two hours. They produce these by the dozens every day. Go ahead and strike that armor as hard as you want."

The king swung at the armor and spun around, almost overbalancing. The two pieces of breastplate and broken stand fell to the floor with a clatter.

Captain Jeffrey breathed reverently. "I want one, no, I want ten."

"By God, yes." Said the king. "One for each day of the week."

By this time, Eyldana was laughing hysterically. I chuckled along as I took my sword back, clipping it on my belt.

"When you get to the dwarf village, Your Majesty, you will be fitted for your armor. It takes a half-day to fit, but it is worth the time. I have been wearing this armor for four days now and feel as fresh and comfortable as the moment I put it on."

"What? No pinching or binding anywhere?" Said Captain Jeffrey.

"Nowhere, Sir Jeffrey, it is more comfortable than my best nightshirt."

The king shook his head, walking back around the desk.

"Guard, get some help and remove this clutter."

The guard shook himself. "Yes, Your Majesty." He dashed out and was back in a few seconds with another guard, and they carried the broken stand breastplate and bits of sword out.

Taking the letter from Lady Sophia, the king began reading. His eyebrows slowly rose as he read the message. Muttering for a moment, he reread it.

He looked at me and asked. "Is this truth Sir Penrose? You have seen this elven queen?"

"I have, Your Majesty. She is much too beautiful to describe. Not because I cannot but because I do not have the words."

"Very well." Said the king, "Meet me in the courtyard in twenty minutes. We ride for Nottingham."

"Yes, Your Majesty, we will be passing the baroness from Bedford. Baroness Sylvia was coming to Cambridge to have her patent confirmed. Her mother recently passed, so she is the last of her line."

The King tilted his head as he looked at me. "You have an interest in this young woman, Sir Penrose?"

Eyldana laughed. "He is besotted, Your Majesty." Captain Jeffrey and the king chuckled.

The king said. "Things could get fun when we get to Nottingham."

Eyldana laughed harder. "You have no idea, Your Majesty."

The king grunted. "Are all you women so mysterious?"

"It is the gift all women receive from the Goddess Gia."

"Right then, I need to get my armor on. Then collect my squire and bannerman, and we will meet you at the stables." The king just shook his head.

"Yes, Your Majesty." We bowed and left the office.

"Captain Jeffrey, we will leave our wagon here, as I expect the king will want to move fast. We can stop at Durobrivae tonight for a hot meal. But we will require some trail rations for the march."

Captain Jeffrey replied. "That will be no problem. We can set you up with small packs and water skins."

"How is your night vision Eyldana?"

"We have magic to enhance our vision in the dark."

"Good," I said, reaching into the wagon's back. "I only brought three extra hoods."

"Hoods?" Asked Captain Jeffrey.

"Yes," I said. "The hoods replace our armored helmet and offer as much protection as the rest of our armor. Here try it on so you may see. Make sure that ridge is to the back."

Captain Jeffery pulled the hood on and gasped. "It is incredible. I can see so clearly and breathe so well." Turning, he looked into the stable. "I can even see the stable's back like it was brightly lit." He then removed the hood handing it back. "This armor must be costly."

I laughed. "You are going to be sadly disappointed. My entire suit of armor and for my horse, including weapons, cost twenty gold."

"My God, my armor cost me a hundred gold, and that was just for me, no weapons and nothing for my horse."

"Yes, and now you see the benefits the dwarf guild brings us."

As my men formed up and stable hands brought the horses out, other men brought us small packs and water skins.

The king, his bannerman, and squire walked up at that time.

"Are we ready to move out?" The king asked.

"Yes, Your Majesty," I said. I handed him and his companions the hoods. "You will need these when it gets dark, Your Majesty. When you put it on, make sure the ridge runs down the back of your head."

The king said. "Incredible, I can see so clearly. These hoods are part of the armor?"

"Yes, Your Majesty, those are generic hoods the Dwarves use for mining. They offer the same protections as our armor, but they are not fit for one person."

"Yes," the king said. "I thought it seemed loose. We will not have to stop for the night."

"No, Your Majesty," I said. "The plan is to stop at Durobrivae for a hot meal and change horses for the men. Our chargers should be able to maintain a trot and canter with just an occasional stop for water."

"Yes, I would like to be in Nottingham tomorrow afternoon. It is only eighty miles."

"I thought as much, Your Majesty. You should meet Baroness Sylvia at Durobrivae, as I believe that will be as far as they get today."

The king chuckled. "You seem to be taken with the Baroness, Sir Penrose."

I had the grace to blush. "Yes, Your Majesty, she may look like a delicate flower, but there is steel in her spine."

The king laughed as he mounted his horse.

"Captain Jeffrey." The king said.

"Yes, Your Majesty?"

"You will bring your company and follow at your best speed. We will be in Nottingham for a while, so I want your men armored like Sir Penrose."

"Yes, Your Majesty, we will be there in three days."

"Excellent, captain, carry on." And we began riding out of the palace grounds.

As we trotted through town, the king asked me. "Sir Penrose, what was your reasoning behind the proposed restructure?"

Your Majesty, I won my spurs at Medina. But when we reached the Holy Land, I saw that the mixed patrols we sent out either saw nothing or got massacred. I talked to some survivors, and they told me there was a lack of coordination. That made me think, what if we trained our men in smaller units?

This group of men would be called a platoon and be the smallest unit. Then four platoons make a company with a headquarters platoon to make two hundred twenty-five men, three fighting companies, and a service company would make a battalion.

"Interesting," said the king. "We will discuss this further when we slow again." He picked up the pace to a canter, and the valkyries took to the skies.

The king laughed and yelled at me. "That is a sight to behold."

Stromavgaard chuckled as we were finishing our breakfast.

"What has you so amused?" Asked the queen.

I just got an update from the valkyries we sent with Lady Sophia's letter. The motte-and-bailey at the ford was having trouble with a couple of hundred orcs attacking. Sir Penrose formed his men and hit them in the rear. When they were distracted, my valkyries hit them from the flank. Eyldana said the slaughter was magnificent, but there were not enough orcs to have fun.

I chuckled. "That does not surprise me after the other night's demonstration."

"No." Laughed Stormavgaard. "But the best is yet to come. Apparently, a young and beautiful baroness of Bedford was there, and Eyldana told me they were both quite smitten with each other. Sir Penrose suggested the baroness come to Nottingham to meet the king, as she still has to be confirmed in her position."

"Oh, my." Merriam laughed. "We are going to have fun."

Sophia's eyes became unfocused.

We all paused as she shuddered back to herself then she spoke. "Yes, I see you, Merriam, and the king taking both of them under your wing, and they will be a force in the future."

"Ding ding." Robyn laughed. "I hear more wedding bells."

We all laughed at that.

The queen smiled. "A grand opportunity. We elves have our ceremony now; I can see how your weddings work. It may not be necessary, but I will need to marry your king in your ways to satisfy your people."

Sir William said. "I suspect you are right, Your Majesty. Once you return to Cambridge, there will be a huge wedding."

Stormavgaard grinned. "Your people are giving me many opportunities to add to the dragon archives. Already many dragons have contacted me for information."

"Speaking of contacts," Stormavgaard said. "Tarija, I have made arrangements to bring some of your guild members here tomorrow."

"Fantastic, Lord Dragon. It will be good to see my friends again." Tarija replied.

"Have you managed to make any progress on the guildhall?" I asked.

"Not enough to make a report yet, Milord. But I did go see the huntsman barracks and looked at the land, and there should be enough room there depending on what my guild builders say."

"You have dwarfs in your guild?" Sir William asked.

"Yes, Milord, adventurers come from every walk of life, every race. The urge to see another place or go on an adventure can take anyone."

I laughed. "This is very true, Lady Tarija. That thirst for adventure is what grabbed many soldiers."

The queen smiled. "Many of those third and fourth sons and daughters you spoke of last night will want to join."

Sir William laughed. "They do not know how hard adventuring can be."

"Those who have the wrong skills or are less adventurous will not last long, and those who do last will get the best training and support we can provide."

"Speaking of support, Your Majesty, mind if I poach a few of your elves to assist in the building effort?"

The queen laughed. "You may have a few, Lady Tarija. But I also have a town to build first."

"I understand, Your Majesty. I just need a couple to help with planning for today."

"I have no issues," said the queen. "Right now, I get to fly on a dragon's back for the first time. I must say I am pretty excited."

Merriam laughed. "It is quite exciting, Your Majesty. I am sure you will love it."

Merriam stood curtsying. "I will take my leave as I have some domestic affairs."

"Be gentle with them, my love. They have had quite the upheaval here in the last week." I said.

"I will." She said, kissing my cheek and walking out.

The queen then rose, and we all did as well, bowing. Stormavgaard offered his arm, walking her to the door.

Jamie and Edwin bolted from the room ahead of them to get the carriage.

"I am not sure how many guards she will be able to take, but with Stormavgaard and his valkyries along, she should be safe enough."

Sophia smiled and said. "They will have no problems today."

Escorting the queen down the stairs, I said. "I can carry ten passengers, Your Majesty, if you wish to choose your party based on that number. With my valkyries as your escort, we will have no trouble.

The queen said. "I will take Sorac and Colvs and seven guards, which should be sufficient for my party."

"Yes, Your Majesty," I said, handing her into the carriage. I entered and sat beside her Sorac got in and faced the queen. Colvs paused a moment flicking his wrist and pointing, then got in the carriage. One elf mounted the footmen platform, and six others surrounded the carriage."

When we got to the field behind the castle, we dismounted the carriage, and the boys headed back.

I took a few minutes to explain the procedure for mounting and riding as I had a harness now made by the dwarves. Transformed and loaded my passengers.

"Hang on tight," I said. "Taking off from the ground is rough." I then gathered my haunches and launched into the air with a powerful beat of my wings. The valkyries took off behind me and formed up on my flanks.

The queen laughed gailey as I rose high in the air.

The queen shouted. "This is a wondrous mode of transportation, Lord Dragon. We are delighted with the spectacular view."

"All of my passengers say much the same thing, Your Majesty. Believe me when I say nothing gives me greater pleasure than flying." I rumbled a chuckle.

Yrswen laughed and called down from above us. "Milord Dragon is right; there is no greater freedom than being able to fly."

I quickly pointed my nose and headed for the twin's location. As we approached, we could make out the circle of great trees around an open field. Then a large hill with trees and an opening at the crown. I changed my course slightly and began circling so the queen would have a good view. I slowly tightened the circle and lowered my altitude to land at the crest of the hill.

There was a pool of water bubbling up from one side of the crest, and it ran down the hill in a series of small waterfalls and pools into the forest surrounding the hill. We could see the stream running off toward the south.

I lowered my passengers to the ground and transformed myself.

I could feel the tremendous power radiating from the hill. Will Scarlet and the twins led the scouting party toward us from the trees.

The queen walked over to the spring dipping her hand into the water. tasting some, she said. "This is the purest spring water I have ever tasted. My body vibrates with the power of this hill." Pulling the necklace from her dress, she walked towards the center of the hill. The seed began glowing brighter and brighter. She stopped as the light began to pulse.

Pulling her necklace's chain out, she let the cage dangle freely, moving it around slowly. The greenish light pulsed faster as she moved it and then suddenly stopped. A beam of green light shot into the ground with a blinding flash. The light went out, but we all still saw after images.

Tucking the seed back into her robes, the queen took a staff from her bag and set it in the hole formed there.

She then turned and declared in a resounding voice. "This is where the home tree shall grow." Evadhi smiled as tears ran down her face. She walked over to Stormavgaard. "Let the archives show I have completed my first Royal Quest." There was a resounding "CHIME."

Turning to two of the builders, the queen said. "Make a road from the outer ring to Nottingham." Turning to two other builders, she said. "You will make a road from the outer ring to Dworkin's village." To the first two, she added. "Lead our people back here as quickly as you can." She said to the rest of the elves. "You may begin construction of Elvenhome."

CHAPTER

29

Turning to me, the queen said. "My Lord Dragon, if it would not be a burden, may we now visit the dwarf village. I need to make a pact with Dworkin for trade."

I said. "That is not a problem. My valkyries have armor there to collect."

I moved away from the others to transform and loaded them up. I then looked at Will Scarlet. "Will you and Little-Jon be okay making your way back to Nottingham?"

"Yes, Milord Dragon, we can scout the area as we go. I would also like to see these elf builders make a road."

I chuckled. "You will be amazed and entertained." I then turned and launched into the air with my valkyries. It was only a short fifteen-minute flight to the dwarven village, where we landed again.

Dworkin came marching out of the gate with several men while I unloaded my passengers and transformed.

When they reached us, the men all knelt, bowing low, and Dworkin said. Your Majesty, thank you for blessing our village with the glory of your light."

The queen stepped forward. "All rise. Dworkin, may the greatness of your works stand for eternity."

"Hoorah," the dwarves shouted. "Thank you, Your Majesty we have things for you and much to discuss."

"Yes, Dworkin, we must set up trade between our peoples. It may be some time before exotic woods are available, but we can still set up agreements."

"Well, Your Majesty, most of those agreements are already in place, as we still have the contracts we made in our other world."

Sorac spoke. "Yes, Your Majesty, we hold the same contracts. It will only be dusting them off and changing some place names."

"Thank you, Sorac I did not know this."

"It is quite all right, Your Majesty. You have enough other things to worry you. You may let us look after these small details."

Dworkin huffed, smiling. "Come, let us have lunch as we have a few things for you."

"Whatever would you have for us?"

Dworkin laughed. "Eat and drink first, presents later."

I chuckled. "Anticipation does heighten the surprise."

The Valkyries giggled as the queen laughed musically.

Dworkin chuckled. "Yes, you ladies get presents as well. But I see there are two more, so Bordoff show these lovely ladies to the armorer for measurement, and they can join us after for food."

"Aye, Dworkin, this way, ladies, please."

The Dwarf led the twins off to get fitted.

By this time, we had reached the long hall. Guiding the queen, I sat her at the head of the table. Dworkin sat on one side, and I sat on the other.

As the others sat, dwarfs began bringing platters of steaming food and chilled ale. "Ah," I sighed, taking a drink. "We must hurry and teach our hosts the spell for chilling food and drink."

We struck up a general conversation as we began eating and drinking. A short time later, the twins joined us and started eating. Yrswen laughed at the confused looks on their faces.

"You look like we did yesterday."

"Yes," said the twins in unison. "We have never been so thoroughly posed and measured."

The queen laughed. "Are they as bad as my tailors and dressmakers?"

Yrswen giggled. "Much worse, Your Majesty. They even measured how much our nipples bounced swinging a sword."

Runeror said with flushed cheeks. "They even measured the gap between my legs in various positions."

The queen flushed red. "My, that does sound very intimate."

Dworkin rumbled a laugh. "It is easier for you ladies. You have no dangly bits to take into account."

We all laughed at that as the ladies blushed even brighter.

Dworkin beckoned a Dwarf over and whispered in his ear.

The Dwarf left the hall as the random chatter continued.

Then Dworkin stood bowing to the queen he began to speak formally.

"Your Majesty Queen Evandhi, the day you were crowned Queen of the Elves and received the seed of the home tree, we were given a commission. The first part of that commission was the necklace and cage where the seed resides. I had despaired we would never fulfill the second part of the commission, and it appears the prophecy knew better than simple dwarves."

The dwarf Dworkin sent out returned at that moment, holding an exquisite wooden chest.

Taking the chest, Dworkin placed it in front of the queen.

"I now present my masterwork and the fulfillment of our commitment to your people."

The queen gasped, reaching out to run her fingers over the Mythril inlays on the surface of the chest.

Raising the lid, she sat open-mouthed, gasping at the chest's contents. Inside was a matching necklace, earrings, and tiara containing robin egg-sized emeralds surrounded by diamonds. A filigree web of Mythril strands held the jewels.

Tears streaming down her cheeks, her fingers ran over the emeralds, and they all began to glow with power. "We had thought these gems lost ages ago during the race wars."

Doing some quick research, I chuckled. "Interesting, Your Majesty, while the settings were damaged beyond repair when the first queen died, the emeralds were recovered. The prophecy has been working toward this moment longer than I had thought."

"What have you discovered?" asked the queen, drying her eyes.

A quest for heroes commissioned in the third century of the new age recovered them. They fought many battles and lost quite a few members but found the jewels in several dungeons. They brought the jewels to the dragon, who offered the quest. A series of seemingly random events occurred when you were crowned and received the seed.

An elder elf approached Dworkin and commissioned the royal jewels, and he died of old age before the Council of Elves was informed. Then the ancestor of the dragon who had recovered the emeralds received a vision, and he delivered them to Dworkin for the commission.

Dworkin said. "Yes, I recall him now though he never told me his name." The dragon handed me a box with those emeralds wrapped in velvet inside. He said for the queen's commission. Of course, I researched those emeralds, fearing a curse. All I found was that my first great ancestor completed a commission for the first Elven Queen. I found one rough drawing and a list of enchantments."

I have made these as close as possible to the originals, and the enchantments I have used are much more powerful. While you wear these jewels, my queen, none but your king may touch you, and not god wrought weapons nor magic will pierce the shield.

I grunted. "Your Majesty, those are some potent magics. But I am sure there is a caveat, as there always is."

Dworkin chuckled. "Yes, Your Majesty, the magics will not activate until you have been quickened and planted the seed. I also had a vision while making this commission. The vision spoke an enchantment through me, tying the power to the tree of life. This jewelry will not only protect you but the tree itself. Alas, the memory of that enchantment ended with the vision. I have not been able to recall even one moment of that vision; I just know I had it.

I said. "That is very interesting. I can feel the shield power and vitality boost, but I cannot judge a source, and it is pulling ambient mana to itself right now."

The queen said. "This is an incredible gift, Dworkin. I will be eternally grateful to you and your people for this, knowing it is your one masterwork."

Another dwarf entered the hall and murmured in Dworkin's ear.

"Lord Dragon, the armor for all your ladies is ready, including the twins."

"Your people must have worked hard to complete the twin's armor so fast."

"It is no problem, my Lord, as it is the most valuable commission we have had in many years. My people are grateful for your patronage."

I chuckled. "Come, girls. I see you dancing in your seats with excitement. Let us get your new equipment and armor." Giggling, they all dashed for the door causing a jam-up as they tried to get out.

Shaking my head as I followed, the queen walked beside me, giggling. "The right present will make any girl giddy with excitement."

"Yes, Your Majesty, it is easy to please these girls." I laughed.

As we approached the women's armory, we heard delighted squeals as the girls put their new armor on.

When they stepped from the door, I could hardly contain the evidence of my arousal. The girls wore low-cut bustiers with a center strap up to a collar. Around their hips were a wide thick belt and short skirt of the same material. They had heavy boots laced to the knees and a simple skull cap that held their hair behind their ears, all made of Mythril. Everyone could see the top did not cover my dragon mark on their breasts.

"Well, I see that this armor exposes more leg and skin than their old armor."

Yrswen stepped forward, drew on her Shield, and pulled out her short spear. She cried, "to battle." Suddenly armor slithered and covered all the exposed skin. The skullcap extended a shield down the back of their neck and another over their faces.

"Oh, my." The queen gasped. "Those are gorgeous."

"Yes," I said. "The armor certainly cost me enough."

The queen laughed. "This armor will shock your hosts when it retracts."

I laughed. "That was the idea. These people need to loosen up a bit."

Yrswen giggled. "The men will have far more difficulty than the women. Their pants will be so tight from arousal they will not be able to bend over to bow."

The entire group laughed hard at that.

Then the valkyries said. "For my Dragonlord." And the armor retracted back to a halter and skirt.

Yrswen said. "They have a slotted flap on the back to allow our wings to extend. There is even a razor-sharp ridge on the leading edge of our wings. Protecting them from damage and making them weapons as well."

I said to the girls. "Let us go shock our hosts."

"Yes, please." They said in unison.

Laughing, I led the group out of the Dwarven village, thanking Dworkin again on the way."

Once I had transformed and loaded my passengers, we returned to Nottingham.

We made it to the ford in excellent time. We still needed both

ferries to cross as we now had horses in place of the wagon.

The king again began to question me on the formations I had proposed. "So what is this company command platoon made up of?"

"Your Majesty, three cooks, a blacksmith, farrier, tailor armorer, two engineers, and two healer apprentices. The apprentices would drive the supply wagons. Then twenty pikemen, ten knights, their squires, ten archers, and the captain. For a total of fifty-three men."

"So, a company would have fifty archers, one hundred infantry, fifty knights, and twenty support people for two hundred eleven men."

"Yes, Your Majesty, plus the commanders for fifty-five knights and ten squires to give us two hundred twenty-five men. Although these numbers are tentative, we could play with them for balance."

"I agree." Said the king, mounting his horse. "We will continue later, and let us ride."

We quickly moved from a trot to a canter to resume our journey.

As I was coming in for a landing, I could see the boys had the carriage there. I unloaded my passengers and transformed into my human form. We headed for the carriage as the valkyries landed. The boys stood stock-still staring at the valkyries.

Yrswen giggled, walking up and gently closing the boy's mouths. "You will catch flies like that."

I opened the door and handed the queen into the carriage, taking my place next to her. Once the boys resumed their seats, we started trotting towards the castle.

I thought quietly to myself, smirking. My valkyries anatomy is doing interesting and distracting things under those short skirts.

The queen giggled at my smirk. "Milord Dragon, you are smugly transparent."

"Yes, Your Majesty, but you must admit they are a thing of beauty."

She laughed. "They are fifteen things of beauty, and all those things have thorns."

"Yes, Your Majesty, I would have never done this if I was not confident they could defend themselves."

"Yes." The queen laughed. "Shock and awe. In the case of the town, folk here staring and drooling."

I laughed uproariously. "Yes, Your Majesty, men have little thought for tactics when the blood of their brains is occupying their groins."

Reaching the doors to the keep, I opened the carriage door and lowered the steps. I stepped down and handed the queen down.

Edwin had finally joined Jamie on the ground. Turning to the boys, I said. "Let this be a lesson to both of you on focus. Times are changing, young men, and you will meet many more female warriors. You may even fight them. You must learn to focus on the eyes. Now return the carriage to the stables and meet us in the study. There may be errands for you soon."

"Yes, Lord Dragon," the boys shouted out. They then scrambled up to the carriage seat and drove away.

The queen giggled behind her hand. "Do you think they learned their lesson today?"

I laughed. "No, Your Majesty, my valkyries will need to spend some time beating them black and blue on the training field for the lesson to sink in."

The guard room door slammed open, and Sergeant Mackey marched out screaming. "What the bloody hell are you gawking at? A blind man with two left feet could take this castle. Eyes front, or I will blind you myself."

"There, Sergeant Mackey has the right of it, and I am just not soldier enough to train young boys."

Yrswen giggled. "No, but Milord certainly knows how to take a young woman to task." The rest of the valkyries laughed as well.

I just chuckled and rolled my eyes.

The doors opened as soon as we got to them. The duke's eyes widened as he saw the valkyries and addressed the queen. "Your Majesty, did you find the site to your satisfaction?"

The queen smiled. "Yes, your Grace, the location suggested by Will and Robyn was perfect. Our people will move as soon as the road is completed and will be gone by dawn. Myself, my guards, and a few advisors will remain here until the king arrives."

"I see, Your Majesty, we have all scattered to do various mundane things this afternoon. If you wish to retire and rest, your maids are drawing you a bath."

"Yes, thank you, your Grace. We believe that is sound advice."

And the queen left for her room, surrounded by her guards.

"Whatever were you thinking of Stormavgaard? If anything, that armor looks less protective than they had before."

I chuckled. "That is the beauty of it, Lord Duke. Show him how it works, Yrswen."

Yrswen stepped forward, calling, "to battle." As her armor covered her, she also called out her wings."

The duke's eyes widened. "What interesting armor. Are those blades on your wings?"

"Yes, they are narrow wedges of my armor extending to cover my wings' leading edge."

"God's they will be deadly in combat."

Yrswen's lips spread in a feral grin. "When I dual-wield, it will be like I have four swords."

"By all the gods, I want to see that battle. But do not show Merriam your armor yet, please. I do not know if I could handle her wearing a set like that."

Yrswen laughed. "Too late."

Merriam's voice came from the stairs. "Show me what?"

The duke turned to see Merriam coming down the stairs staring wide-eyed at the valkyries.

Yrswen said, "guard." And her armor retracted.

Merriam gasped. "That is the most gorgeous thing I have ever seen."

"My love."

"No."

"But."

"No."

"Please?"

"God, Merriam, you are distracting enough in your armor. We would be standing around like drooling idiots if you wore something like that."

"Can you not control them, Stormavgaard?"

I was grinning wide as my valkyries fell over, laughing hysterically at the byplay.

"Oh, no, this is much too entertaining. Please continue your battle with Milady. Although I think you may wish to concede defeat."

"Fine," the duke's shoulders slumped. "How much did it cost?"

"A thousand gold each set."

"And they can add the enchantment I already have? I wonder?" Merriam asked. "But could they also add a flaming wing enchantment?"

"I do not know if that would be possible, Milady, but the rest of your enchantments would be no problem."

"I need to talk to grandfather. Maybe I can make flaming magic wings."

"My love, if you try, please take it outside. We do not need you burning down the castle with guests inside."

"Yes, my love, I will be careful." She gave him a peck on the cheek and ran upstairs.

"I know this is going to end badly."

"I am sure she will learn safely between her grandfather and a few elven magic teachers."

"We can only hope so."

CHAPTER

30

As we headed toward the stairs, Stormavgaard said. "I think the queen has the right idea. Yrswen, find Denby and have a couple of casks of ale sent up to our quarters. We will relax for the rest of the afternoon."

"Yes. my Lord Dragon." She grinned vivaciously.

I said. "I will see you later, Stormavgaard." And I headed for the study.

I walked in to see only Merlin and Alvos standing by the table.

"Is no one else here? And did Merriam not find you?"

"No," Merlin said. "Milady Sophia and Friar Tuck are at an empty barracks with some elves planning an infirmary."

"Sir William went to lay down, and Robyn went with Sergeant Thomas and Tarija to the guild site. Why is there some problem?"

I chuckled. "Not yet. But Merriam has seen the valkyrie's new armor, and it is revealing would be an understatement."

"That sounds interesting," said Alvos.

"Interesting is one way to put it, but now Merriam wants to try adding flaming wings to her armor."

"Oh. Yes, I see where that could be disconcerting." Said Merlin.

"Terrifying is the term I would use."

Alvos laughed. "Well, for the enemy at least. I wonder if she is strong enough yet? But she does have a tremendous amount of control with her bow."

Then Merlin said. "I think she may have enough power."

"I could scan her." Said Alvos. "We know she has the phoenix trait, and with how she uses the power?"

The door banged open. "There you are, grandfather." As Merriam came, marching in.

"Hello, granddaughter, what has you in such a tizzy?"

"I was looking at the valkyrie's new armor, and when I get mine, I want to manifest flaming wings. But can you both teach me how to do that?"

Alvos said. "There are three mages who will be able to help. I will need to scan you to see your levels, Milady. You may not be strong enough even if we could teach you."

"Yes, I can see that, and that might be a problem, so go ahead and scan me."

Reaching into a pocket in his robes, Alvos drew out a stone. "This is the same type of stone the guilds use to determine a candidate's ability for an apprenticeship, and guilds also use them to rank adventures."

"When I place it in the palm of your hand, think status."

Merlin grunted. "This will also test whether or not we get a leveling system."

Alvos said. "Yes, I never thought of that. I could have used this to see what type of system you will have. We will find out now." He placed the stone in Merriam's palm.

She thought status, and a screen appeared above the stone. Merriam said. "That is a strange way to list things."

I do not see a thing.

Alvos said. "Milady, turn away and say share status."

Merriam turned, so we were behind her to one side, then said. "Share status."

Merriam Sherwood Bonded Harem	
Guy Sherwood/Paladin Robyn Loxley/Ranger Will Scarlet/Rouge Little-Jon/Barbarian Alicia/Maid/ Battle Dancer Camila/Maid/Siren/Battle Dancer	
Alignment	
Phoenix Kin / Druid / Fire Mage	
Abilities	Level
Archer	40
Sword Master	20
Fire Mage	16
Druid	12
Health 400/400 Rec 1 per min x5 fire boost	Mana220/220 Rec .5 per-min x4 Kin boost
Stamina 30	Int 30
Dex 35	Str 25
Con 25	Luck 15
Available Skill Points 60	
Skills acquired	Description
Hearth Mistress	Those in your home are made welcome and comfortable. You have undeniable skills in homemaking and managing staff.
Fire Shot / Flaming Arrow DP 100 per point of mana	Able to use fire magic to produce flaming arrows scalable. One mana to max avalable mana.
Fireball DP 10 per 5 Mana	It can produce a small ball of flame to cast and be held to make a light to see. Cost five mana per min. Scalable. You can also absorb fire to replenish mana or heal. Advances to Flame Blast at level 20.

Druid Herb Lore	The herbalist has a broad knowledge of herbs used in healing birth control and poisons. Advances to basic Alchemy at level 15

Merriam asked. "So what is with the skill points, and how do they work?"

I laughed. "The fascinating item I see is Alicia and Camila as battle dancers and part of our harem.

Alvos chuckled. "You must have had intimate relations with them like sex."

Merriam blushed, and I said. "You could say that."

"Back to your question, Milady. You simply scroll down the list to what you wish to change and think select. If you did it right, the item you selected would flash. When you have made your choice think, add points and the number."

Alvos said. "Just for practice, you can never go wrong on this think intelligence; when it flashes, think, add five points."

Merriam followed the instructions and added five points toward intelligence, making it thirty-five.

Merriam giggled. "That felt funny, like someone tickling my brain. Although I feel I understand this chart better."

"You understand how this works now." Said Alvos.

"Now, the next question is determining what path you wish to take."

"Path?" Asked Merriam.

"Yes," said Alvos. "On which tree do you wish to concentrate? Your archer level is potent, and that bow does not need much added. However, your spell-casting is very weak, and if you wish to use flaming wings, that needs to become stronger."

"Okay, so what would you suggest?"

Alvos thought for a moment rubbing the tip of one ear. "Well, your wings are available, but they cost forty skill points. Because you are phoenix kin, there may be perks."

"What do you mean perks?"

"I am not sure, but it may reduce mana cost to use the wings. It could also be other things like your health and mana recovery increase."

"So instead of twenty mana to use my wings, it may only cost ten."

Alvos chuckled. "No, it would be more like twenty mana per minute reduced to ten mana per minute."

"Oh, darn." Said Merriam. "So sixteen minutes of flight as opposed to eight."

"No, more like eleven as opposed to five. It would be best to land before your mana runs out, minus your reserve. If you are a hundred feet in the air, your wings disappear when you run out of mana, and you become a rock. Also, as a mage in battles, you must conserve your mana. You never want to let your levels drop below thirty percent on average."

"Ouch, that would be very unpleasant."

"But I want to develop those wings and have some ideas for battle surrounding them."

"Usually, you would get one skill point per level with five on the fives and tens."

"So, technically, I should have nearly two hundred points. Why do I only have sixty available?"

"I suspect points were automatically applied as you learned a new skill. At what age did you receive your bow?"

"Eleven, I think I went to bed one night and dreamed about a lovely lady, and she gave me the bow. I woke up the following day, and it was beside me on the bed."

"Okay, when did you first draw the bow?"

"I could sort of draw from day one but only a few inches. It was funny because I got so frustrated the arrow would only fly a few feet and plunk into the ground."

We all chuckled at that.

But I pulled that bow every day for four years. I pulled until my fingers bled. I had my mother bandage them so I could continue. My father finally took me to the tanner and got my first gloves. But it was my fifteenth birthday. I remember it clearly. I was in the woods at the back of the house, and an eight-point buck stood there two hundred paces away. I took out my best arrow, knocking it I drew, taking the buck in the heart. Of course, I was too small to move the buck, so I had to run to get my father to bring in my kill.

"There," said Alvos. "Now, you see what I mean by progress and gaining skills. You have had this bow for how long now?"

Merriam giggled. "Well, a woman does not like to reveal her age but let us just say over 300 years."

Alvos' eyes widened, and he said. "Interesting, you passively gained forty levels in archery without a leveling system. I guess you broke level forty when you were able first to use flaming arrows, which would have also leveled you up in your fire mage skills."

"Fascinating," Merlin said. "I think you should focus on fire and druid skills for now. If you look down here, flaming wings are available for forty points. But greyed out next to it is phoenix flight, and I bet it becomes available when you reach level ten or twenty flaming wings."

Alvos said. "I agree that flaming wings will turn into phoenix flight."

"Yes, of course," Merlin said. "It would be a progression upward rather than a new skill. But the critical point is that it will advance your fire skills simultaneously."

"I have a question," I said. "Can the skills list be focussed? To show fire-related magic, and then to only magic available?"

Merriam said. "It is confusing with all the unrelated choices mixed in."

"Of course, said Alvos. "I was overwhelmed in my excitement, as I have not had this many choices in hundreds of years."

Merlin chuckled. "Yes, I feel like a kid in a candy store with a gold piece to spend."

We all laughed at that image.

"However," Alvos said. "Milady. Focus on fire magic and think only related."

Merriam did, and suddenly the list was much shorter.

"Good," said Merlin. "Now, we can see where flaming wings fall. Some of these skills and spells are very cheap. But you can see now that flaming wings cost so much because it is an ability that will change your class."

"Oh," said Merriam. "I do like the idea of becoming a phoenix."

Merlin began laughing. "Do not select it yet, granddaughter, as we must prepare. First of all, you will need to have the proper attire."

Alvos chuckled. "Yes, that may be a good idea. Let us go to the elf encampment."

I innocently asked. "Why would Merriam need special attire?"

Merlin and Alvos both laughed as Merlin gasped out. "Because there could be an uncontrolled burst of flame that would turn her clothing to ash, leaving Merriam standing naked. Well covered in soot but still entirely naked."

Merriam's eyes widened as I grinned. "Yes, that may be somewhat embarrassing in mixed company."

I laughed. "Okay, fine, let us go get the carriage."

Merriam giggled. "Do you have a large pouch of gold, my love?"

"Umm, yes, why?"

"Because I will need a whole new wardrobe that is fireproof."

I groaned. "Very well, grab your maids, and I will take you shopping."

Merriam giggled and dashed from the room.

Merlin laughed. "Oh, yes, the devious mind of a woman who wants a new dress."

"Or an entire wardrobe."

We laughed as we headed down the hall to the stairs, meeting the three giggling breathless women.

Alvos said. "Milady, perhaps I should carry the stone to prevent accidents in close quarters."

"Oh, yes," Merriam said. "Here you go," and she handed it over.

"So, out of curiosity, try bringing up your status now."

Merriam focussed for a moment with an adorable scrunch of her nose. "Oh my God, there it is. I can see it now."

"I can not see a thing."

Alvos said. "That is because she did not say share status. We must think of the word status to bring up the screen for ourselves. But you must say share status out loud to share it with another person."

"Oh," I said. "That makes sense, as you would not wish everyone to see you checking your status."

"No," said Alvos. "That information is personal to you and should not be shared lightly."

"Yes, that brings up an important point." Said Merlin as we climbed into the carriage. "Merriam could not see her status until she held the stone, but now she can. May I have the stone for a moment, Alvos?"

"Certainly, Merlin," Alvos said, handing it over.

Merlin held the stone for a moment. Then handed it back and got a focused look. "It is as I suspected. We are going to need a lot of these stones. Grandson, you try it, take the stone and just think status if the screen appears, hand the stone back and think close screen. Then think status to bring it up again."

I took the stone and thought of the word status. To my surprise, the screen appeared before me, and everyone could tell it worked because of my reaction. I thought close, the screen vanished, and I handed the stone back. Sitting beside Merriam, I said. "Share status." And my screen appeared before us.

Merriam giggled. "It is fantastic. I can see your status. You are soul-bound to me, Robyn, Will, and Jon."

I thought close, and the screen vanished. "Yes, but it is very distracting. I will need to sit with a trainer and review my options, as I also have many skill points to spend and many decisions about my path."

"Yes," said Merlin. "Sophia and I can help with some of it, but you need a skilled Battle Master to choose those related skills."

"I can see where guidance becomes very important when choosing a path."

Then I groaned as a thought struck me.

"What is it, my love?" Merriam asked.

"I just realized I will have to write a whole new training schedule for my entire army."

Merlin laughed. "Oh, yes, that will be fun. The king will need trainers everywhere to open all his people's skills."

Merriam giggled. "I hope the queen does not mind that your people will be very busy for a few years, Alvos."

Alvos chuckled. "I think Stormavgaard will be put on the spot for this one. He will need to bring trainers from Magic Academies if they are willing to open branches in a new world."

Merriam laughed. "The kingdom will be a mess for a while, as it will take some time for this to sort itself out."

Merlin laughed. "Talk about living in exciting times. I wish I could be everywhere to see the results, good and bad."

"Yes, but we must secure our kingdom first, as the chaos will make our quest much harder."

"This is true," said Merlin. "But we are here to let our little bit of chaos ensue."

I laughed. As we dismounted, to hand the ladies down. The maids sat quietly wide-eyed, holding hands in one corner.

Alicia begged Merriam. "Do we have skills, Milady?"

Alvos chuckled gently. "Yes, my child, everyone has a skill tree. For some, it may be mundane, and for others, it could lead to greatness. Would you like to see yours?"

"Oh, yes, Milord." The girls said eagerly.

Merriam stood behind the girls as Alvos handed Alicia the stone.

Merriam said in her ear, say "share status," and Alicia did.

A screen popped up in front of her, and she almost dropped the stone in surprise.

Merriam giggled. "Careful now. Let us see you are Alicia Benson, Lady-in-Waiting."

"That is your title now, and it may change as you age." Said Alvos.

"This is interesting under skills. You are a level one harem battle dancer bonded to Merriam Sherwood." Merriam said. "What would that mean, Alvos?"

Alvos flushed slightly and chuckled. "Well, Milady, it means they have some dancing skills which can be helpful in battle, and she just needs weapons training to go with it. Harem means, as you recall from your status, you have had sex with her, and she is becoming part of your harem."

"Oh." Alicia squeaked, blushing furiously.

Merriam chuckled in her sultry way. "That is very interesting. Let us see what Camila says."

Alicia handed the stone over, and Camila said. "Share status."

Her name popped up, Camila Sanchez, Lady-in-Waiting. Below that was a level two harem battle dancer/siren.

"Oh," said Camila. "Mine is a bit different. What does siren mean?"

"You play the pan flute so beautifully. Perhaps that is part of it?"

Alvos laughed. "It is the perfect combination, Milady. You have a pair of battle dancers, one of whom can sway people's minds by playing her music while they both dance. Miss Alicia has a sweet clear voice, and teaching her to sing will also give her the siren status. Once trained, they will make devastating personal bodyguards. I know the perfect trainers for them."

"Come, this way." Said Alvos. He led us to a large tent. Ducking his head inside, he spoke for a moment to someone, and a lovely elf woman came out.

Alvos said. "This is Milady Merriam and her harem, maids Alicia and Camila. Milady requires a fireproof training suit suitable for archery and melee, and the girls need beginner harem training clothes."

"Milady girls, this is Windgust Artisan, the queen's seamstress.

Windgust smiled brightly. "Oh, a new canvas to paint. A beautiful set of curvy sculptures to adorn. Come this way, my lovelies. You gentlemen may go take tea while you wait."

"Oh, yes, Lady Windgust, we want no part of what goes on in there." Alvos chuckled.

"My love, just remember you have others to meet, and dinner will be in a few hours."

The girls giggled as they followed the elf into the tent.

CHAPTER

"Come," said Alvos. "We will go over here and have a drink. He led us to a table in front of another tent. An elf came out and asked what we would like. Alvos ordered for us, and she went inside, returning quickly with a tray. A flask of wine, delicate glasses, and two plates with pastries were on the tray. The one was steaming and, Alvos said. "These are warm because they contain meat and vegetables. The other ones contain fruit and nuts."

Alvos spoke briefly with the elf in his musical language, and she nodded and darted off.

Alvos poured some wine for us. "I have sent her to seek the trainers for Miladies, and they should be here shortly."

I looked around, and we chatted amicably about what I was seeing.

I saw a picture of happy people going about their day. There seemed to be a little extra energy in their steps, and Alvos said. "That is due to the anticipation of moving to Elvenhome."

Soon three elves approached, along with two creatures I had never seen before. They looked identical, with a greenish cast to their skin and hair like leaf-covered vines. They looked fourteen but moved with the fluid grace of dancers and spoke together in musical voices.

We all stood as the five got near.

"Good," Alvos said. "You are here. I present my Lord Duke Sherwood of Nottingham. He will be holding your commissions." The elves all bowed, and the other two giggled.

Alvos pointed to the female Elf, "Milord, this is Alpenbender Sunsinger," pointing to the first man, "Loyal Archmage. And finally, we have Groveshard Battlemage."

"And last but not least, to train your harem maids, we have the dryad sisters Sprucebramble Dancer and Locustlimb Chorus. They are battle dancers, and Locustlimb uses her voice to stun enemies. They may be small, but look at their weapon type."

The Dryads pulled fans from their waistbands, flicking them open with practiced ease. They held them out so I could examine them closely. I saw the four fans decorated similarly, with spines ending in sharp points almost invisible to the eye. The Dryads snapped them closed, and I saw they formed a dagger point. "What a fascinating weapon," I said.

"Yes," they said. "But the fans are also an essential part of the dance, as it is a fundamental battle technique."

"My sister can also sing them into a stupor. We would not demonstrate that here as it would cause too much disruption."

"I see," I said. "Our maids are only level 1 and 2 and relatively young. We saw the other night that they show some promise and flexibility."

"Good," said Locustlimb. "Flexible is very important for a battle dancer. My sister and I will demonstrate in front of them so they may see and we may judge."

"So, how much for the girls' training?"

"Level one and two?" Asked Sprucebramble. "Do we have control of their skill selections?"

"Perhaps with Milady's approval?"

Sprucebramble said. "I only ask this because we made mistakes in our skill selections, and some of them cost us many points to fix and much time training. She should have final approval if they are to be Milady's bodyguards."

"I agree, so how much for the commission?"

"A hundred gold and a garden inside your castle walls."

"I am sure Nottingham does not have a garden; however, the new castle and the one at Derby will have gardens. My people will be moving there when it is complete until we build the new castle here."

"We understand." Said Locustlimb. "The garden can wait. Their training will not be complete for several years. But we will also train any other maids in the castle, which will make a good defense against spies and assassins."

"We have a deal of one hundred gold per month and control of all the gardens in the new castle."

"No, you misunderstood my Lord, one hundred gold per year, and we only ask for one garden."

"One hundred gold per year is fine, but I thought you may want to take care of all Milady's gardens because you are dryads and work with plants and flowers."

They both dropped to their knees, clasping hands with tears running down their faces. "Thank you, my liege. We are bound to you, body, and soul forevermore."

Eyebrows raised, I turned to the laughing elves. "What exactly did I just do?"

"Take their clasped hands in yours, Milord. Pull them to their feet and say I accept your bond forevermore."

Reaching down, I took their four tiny hands in mine, pulled them to their feet, and said. "I accept your bond forevermore."

Alvos said. "Now about what you have done. Do not worry, for it is a glorious thing."

Dryads can wander through the forest for centuries without ever finding a mate. You see, they cannot bind themselves to a place of their own to have children. A master must bind them. And trust me on this, they are cautious about whom they choose. There have been many evil men who have attempted to bind dryads. Because of the benefits, they bring to a place. You need to send word to the dwarves about your bond. The gardens of your new castle will be spectacular creations. Their crafters will have to discuss with the dryads the shapes of the gardens. This benefit will spill over into your lands as your two dryads look for a particular flower bush or tree. Your farmlands will become healthier and more productive.

"Excellent," I said. Looking down, I saw the dryads were still crying and hugging. Taking a knee so my head would be on a level with them, I wrapped an arm around each of them. "Please stop crying. Enjoy this moment that came about by accident. My people will love you and take good care of you."

They both smiled as I spoke. "You misunderstand us again because you do not know dryads. We are bound to you now as part of Milady's harem."

"Really, my love, have you been adding to our harem behind my back?"

I heard Merriam's voice behind me. Smiling at the dryads, I said. "Oops, it just happened, my love. By definition, I accidentally bonded these two dryads to our castle and you."

Merriam looked past my shoulder. "Oh, they are pretty little things." Her eyes lost focus. "There they are, Sprucebramble and Locustlimb harem battle dancers."

She hugged and kissed both of them.

It was then that I noticed the open back of her leather armor. "That is an attractive look that accommodates your wings, my love."

Merriam giggled. "You think mine is interesting? Look at those two."

I turned to see Alicia and Camila blushing and fidgeting with their not clothes. I looked them over as they turned even redder. "Attractive almost clothing you have there, ladies." They wore small cups over their breasts and a tiny string bottom covering their pubs. Their collars on their neck, wrists, and ankles supported gossamer-thin opaque material. Pale green for Camila enhanced her golden skin and a rose color for Alicia, highlighting her skin's paleness.

"Well," I said. "Those will certainly distract any assassins attacking us. Or any invaders at all. I need to find you all jobs in the convent. My love, you are really doing your best to get me killed by distraction."

The dryads giggled behind me, and Sprucebramble said. "This outfit is meant for a dance to entice and arouse Milord and Lady. It is a basic dance taught first, the dance of seven veils. A headpiece goes with it and has the seven veils held by keys. The first five keys unlock the cuffs and collar, and the last two unlock the top and bottom. It is a bedtime dance that will take a few days, but we will teach them."

"Speaking of distractions, Alicia, Camila, these are your trainer's Sprucebramble Dancer and Locustlimb Chorus. We will find you a place to train that is secluded."

"Milord," said Alicia. "There is a large room in the lower keep once used for training in inclement weather. On the opposite side of the treasury hall, it is not used now since the new training area was built."

"Excellent, it will be posted immediately exclusively for your training. I will allow the valkyries to train there if it is large enough. The dryads have offered to train all maids in battled dancing, as this will serve to protect them and boost the castle defense."

"Very well, young ladies, that is not suitable attire for walking. Get changed now into something more appropriate."

"Yes, Milord." They giggled. "We just wanted to show these off."

I grinned. "The outfits certainly do show you off."

The four girls ran off to the tailor's tent, giggling.

"Well," said Merlin. "They certainly hit it off well."

"Yes, but I am not surprised," I said. "Those girls are prime examples of innocence in youth."

Merlin laughed. "By its look, my granddaughter is working to change that."

"Oh, hush, grandfather, introduce me to these lovely people."

Alvos chuckled. "First, there is Alpenbender Sunslinger." She stepped forward and bowed. "Then Loyal Archmage and Groveshard Battlemage." They both stepped forward and bowed.

"A pleasure to meet you all." Said Merriam. "I assume you are to be my trainers?"

"Milady," said Alpenbender. "We three are well-versed in fire magic." Alpenbender made a gesture, and flaming wings appeared from her back.

Merriam gasped. "They are beautiful."

"Thank you, Milady." Said Alpenbender as she dismissed them.

Loyal Archmage spoke. "I train fire mages in spells and incantations. I also advise on skill trees."

Groveshard Battlemage said. "I train young mages in battle magic: attack and shield magic. Fire magic is good for heating your tea or bath water. But on the battlefield, while you try to cook your enemy, every other mage and the ranged attackers will be trying to kill you. The first rule of battle is to kill the mages, then progress down a list. It starts with mages, ranged attackers, rogues, stealth fighters, brawlers, and defenders. That is why a defender covers every battle mage, and for the same reason, every healer has a bonded defender. Because when I say kill the mages first, I mean the healers."

I grunted. "Well, I guess that is my job. I must defend our cleric, Friar Tuck."

Loyal Archmage's eyes widened. "You have a cleric? Blessed by your gods?"

"Yes," I replied. "Why?"

"You must bring him to me at once or bring me to him. I must get to your cleric as he is much more powerful than any healer. These two can train Milady in what she can learn now."

I raised my eyebrow. "Well, I can arrange that if you insist."

Looking around, I saw the dryads and maids coming from the tent. "Come, Loyal, I have a young man you need to meet." Gesturing, I waved the girls over to the carriage as well.

"Get in, girls. You are heading back to the castle to claim your training room."

"Jamie, this is Loyal Archmage. When you return to the castle, you will find Friar Tuck and introduce him to this elf."

"Yes, Milord." Said Jamie.

"Edwin, when you return to the castle, find Denby and tell him. These girls have exclusive use of the training room in the lower keep, and no others may enter it except for the other maids. Alicia can explain that part herself. Alicia, Camila, you girls must find suitable quarters for your trainers. We should be back by dinner time. Edwin Jamie, you can come back and collect us an hour before dinner."

"Yes, Milord," said Alicia and the boys.

As I turned away, they drove off, and I rejoined the others.

"Can we go see what Milady can do?"

Alpenbender laughed. "We shall go out here into the open field, as there will be less chance of mishap there."

Groveshard Battlemage chuckled. "Yes, I remember when Alpenbender achieved her wings. It took the water mages two hours to beat down the forest fires. And the local dryads a week to heal the trees."

Alpenbender giggled. "It is not my fault he made me mad."

Alvos laughed. "Yes, but you both made up quickly."

Alpenbender laughed musically. "Hey, the makeup celebration sex was fun while covered in the soot and ashes of our clothes."

Merriam laughed hysterically while the rest of us chuckled.

"Okay, so I can see why you wanted me to get unique clothes for this. Now how will it work?"

"Oh, that is simple." Said the battlemage. "We will stand here, and you will go over there. Wave when you open your status screen, and I will put a shield over you. Then like Alvos told you, select flame wings and think, add points."

"And poof, I will have wings?"

Alpenbender giggled. "More like whoosh standing in a ball of fire. The grass around you will be incinerated, but you have fireproof clothes, so you will not be naked. That will last a few seconds, then you will have two wings, and you will suck in the fireball, so we can drop the shield."

"Okay, then let us do this." Merriam said and marched about twenty paces away.

I grunted and said. "This will not harm Merriam, will it?"

"No," said Alpenbender. "She is immune to fire. Closest I can describe the feeling is being immersed in a warm bath, and fire becomes a very comfortable thing, so you do not even think about picking up white-hot steel. Now, watch it is about to happen."

Merriam nodded and waved, and Groveshard cast a shield.

After a moment, Merriam held her arms as if to say. What now?

Then with a mighty whoosh, she burst into a giant fireball. After a few seconds, it vanished as she sucked it back into herself, and she stood there, eyes wide, and a gorgeous pair of flaming wings appeared from her back.

Groveshard grunted. "That went well. Even the fires in the grass were sucked back into her."

Alpenbender said. "Yes, I did not get that part quite right. But as I said, I was angry at the time."

We chuckled as we walked over to Merriam.

"My love, those are genuinely spectacular."

She turned, looking over each shoulder. "They are beautiful. I love them. Now I have to see the dwarves again for some new armor."

"Yes, my love, I concede your point. You will need armor like the Valkyries."

Alpenbender said. "Now recall your wings. You have had them out for almost five minutes."

Merriam said, "recall," and her wings vanished.

"Now call up your status so we can see it. We need to figure out how much mana the spell takes and calculate how long you can keep the mode."

Merriam Sherwood Bonded Harem	
Guy Sherwood/Paladin Robyn Loxley/Ranger Will Scarlet/Rouge Little-Jon/Barbarian Alicia/Maid/ Battle Dancer Camila/Maid/Siren/Battle Dancer	
Alignment	
Phoenix Kin / Druid / Fire Mage	
Abilities	Level
Archer	40
Sword Master	20
Fire Mage	17
Druid	12
Health 400/400 Rec 1 per min x5 fire boost	Mana200/220 Rec .5 per-min x4 Kin boost
Stamina 30	Int 35
Dex 35	Str 25
Con 25	Luck 15

Available Skill Points 15	
Skills acquired	Description
Hearth Mistress	Those in your home are made welcome and comfortable. You have undeniable skills in homemaking and Managing staff.
Fire Shot / Flaming Arrow DP 100 per point of mana.	Able to use fire magic to produce flaming arrows scalable. I mana to max avalable mana.
Fire Spark can light fires and candles.	Can hold a small flame to light the way. Cost 1 mana-min. Advances to fireball at level 10
Fireball DP 10 per 5 Mana	It can produce a small ball of flame to cast and be held to make a light to see. Cost 5 Mana per-min held. Scalable. You can also absorb fire to replenish mana or heal. Advances to flame blast at level 20.
Flame Wings Manifest wings of fire for a limited time 1/20 Level 20 is required for Pheonix Shift.	Flaming wings cost 20 mana per/min 20/max mana. Caution, you will fall if your mana runs out in flight. Advances to Pheonix flight at level 20. Pheonix Kin boost X.25 mana.
Druid Herb Lore	The herbalist has a broad knowledge of herbs used in healing birth control and poisons. Advances to basic Alchemy at level 15

Merriam called up her status, looking at mana which said two hundred over two-twenty.

"Scroll down to your flame wings," said Groveshard. "Something is wrong with this, as a first-time use should have consumed far more mana than that."

"Yes, I recall that it was using eighty mana per minute in the beginning.

"By my calculation, this will give her eight minutes of flight time," I said. "That will leave the one-third cushion you all speak of."

"Look, she is back to two-ten mana."

"Milady, you have tremendous mana recovery. Quickly Alvos a sand glass timer." When her mana ticked to two-twelve, Alvos held up the glass, and we waited to flip the glass the third time Merriam's mana ticked to two-fourteen.

"Two mana per minute," Alvos said. "Could that be her druid half pulling mana from the earth so fast?"

Merriam said. "I know my cabin is on a ley line because I always feel more energetic there."

"Okay," said Groveshard. "That will be an experiment for another day."

"Now, let us see what flame wing says."

"Yes." Said Merriam, and she scrolled down to it.

Alpenbender gasped. "This is incredible."

"Due to the Pheonix kin perk, flaming wing costs one-quarter of the standard eighty mana. If this follows the usual pattern, it will cost her ten mana per minute in one hundred XP when Merriam levels up the skill."

"Wait," I said. "Do you mean that when Merriam reaches level twenty, it will only cost one mana per minute?"

"This will be a potent skill." Said Alpenbinder.

"I have ten times your mana, and I am a level sixty fire mage, but it still costs me ten mana per minute of flight."

"What does this line at the bottom mean?" Asked Merriam. Level twenty is required for Phoenix shift."

"By all the gods." Said Alpenbender. "When you raise this skill, you will become a goddess."

"What?" Merriam squeaked.

"Excuse me?" I exclaimed.

"Yes," said Alvos. "Something legendary and only seen twice in all the realms."

CHAPTER

32

Merriam said. "I think we can discuss that tomorrow or the next day. I want to try flying for a bit."

Merlin chuckled. "Your limit is eighteen minutes of flight time because you recover two mana each minute. You only use eight."

"Not too high or too far, my love. Remember, you have a time limit."

Merriam kissed me gently on the lips. "Not long, I see the carriage is headed this way again."

"Okay, my love, have fun."

Merriam stepped away and called her wings out.

"I will join you, Milady." Said Alpenbender. "Flying is tricky at first."

"You must crouch, jump, and think flap to your wings."

Merriam said. "Right, crouch, jump, flap, crouch, jump, flap, crouch, jump, flap."

Merriam crouched, jumped, and flapped, slamming face-first into the ground.

The four of us stood there laughing.

Alpenbender giggled. "It is not that funny, gentleman. This skill is very tricky to learn."

Merriam picked herself up off the ground with a look of raw determination on her face.

"I flapped too late?"

"You have to flap at the same time as you jump."

"Okay, got it now."

She got two flaps and six feet off the ground before turning and spiraling in for another crash landing.

I ran over to help her up. "That was close, but I saw your fight feathers dip on the left wing and raise on the right. Is that significant?"

"Yes," said Alpenbender. "You must pay attention to your flight feathers. Keep them curled slightly down to take off. That is what gives you an extra lift. Once you are flying, you can straighten them out for a faster flight. Then for turning, if you lower the flight feathers of your left wing, you will turn to the right. You turn to the left if you lower your flight feathers in your right wing."

"You are lucky I am here to help you. I spent many weeks watching birds learn this."

"Yes, I will get this right if it kills me."

"It better not, my love. If you kill yourself, I will not speak to you again."

They all looked at me like an idiot and then laughed when they got the joke.

When we had settled down, I said. "My love, you have got this fly for me."

Merriam thought for a second and took two running steps flapping her wings. She quickly rose to thirty feet and then gently turned towards us.

"Yes." She screamed. "I Can Fly!"

I laughed as she followed Alpenbender through several maneuvers.

Then, ten valkyries flew around Merriam, swooping, diving, and laughing gaily.

"Milady." Yrswen cried. "Your wings are glorious."

And I could see from the ground that they indeed were. The wings flowed from yellow on the leading edge to red on the trailing edge, with tiny flickers of flame moving over them.

Alvos called out. "Time, Milady, you have used too much mana.

Merriam came in for a landing but forgot to back her wings and fell forward, sliding along on her face. Fortunately, the ground was soft, so she did not damage anything except pride and a bloody nose.

"I think, my love, you should practice takeoffs and landings when you have recovered your mana tomorrow."

Spitting dirt from her mouth, she said. "Yes, that is likely a good idea as she recalled her wings."

The other flyers swooped down, landing gently, laughing and giggling, gathering around Merriam, congratulating her.

"Well," I said to Merlin. "I think that was a reasonably successful afternoon."

Merlin chuckled. "Yes, and pretty entertaining as well."

"And you grandfather, what did you discover when you looked at your status? I saw your eyes go very wide in shock."

"Well, I have discovered I am a level ninety storm mage."

Alvos and Groveshard gasped in shock.

I said. "That must mean you have many points to spend on upgrades."

Merlin chuckled. "Yes, many points."

"You are going to keep the secret, grandfather?"

"I wish to read more of Alvos' books on lightning magic before deciding for a little while."

"Yes, I do not know anyone who has lived long enough to get to level ninety. Most of us magic teachers reach the level sixty range. You are of an age that you wish to retire from adventuring and settle down by then."

"Well, I have been looking after this world for nearly ten thousand years. My task is close to being done, but I do not feel the least bit tired."

"Whatever happens now, the carriage is here, and I believe it is dinner time."

"Quickly bring up your status again. Let us check your mana," said Alvos.

Merriam said, "share status," and her screen came up. "Oh, look, I have leveled up my fire magic and am now level seventeen."

Merriam Sherwood Bonded Harem	
Guy Sherwood/Paladin Robyn Loxley/Ranger Will Scarlet/Rouge Little-Jon/Barbarian Alicia/Maid/ Battle Dancer Camila/Maid/Siren/Battle Dancer	
Alignment	
Phoenix Kin / Druid / Fire Mage	
Abilities	Level
Archer	40
Sword Master	20
Fire Mage	17
Druid	12
Health 387/410 Rec 1 per min x5 fire boost	Mana78/240 Rec .5 per-min x4 Kin boost
Stamina 31	Int 35
Dex 35	Str 26
Con 26	Luck 20
Available Skill Points 17	
Skills acquired	Description
Hearth Mistress	Those in your home are made welcome and comfortable. You have undeniable skills in homemaking and managing staff.
Fire Shot / Flaming Arrow DP 100 per point of mana	Able to use Fire Magic to produce flaming arrows scalable. One mana to max avalable mana.
Fire Spark can light fires and candles.	Can hold a small flame to light the way. Cost 1 Mana-min. Advances to Fire Ball at level 10

Fire Ball DP 10 per 5 mana	You can produce a small ball of flame to cast, and it can be held to make a light to see. Cost 5 mana per-min held. Scalable. You can also absorb fire to replenish mana or heal. Advances to flame blast at level 20.
Flame Wings Manifest wings of fire for a limited time 3/20 Level 20 is required for Pheonix Shift.	Flaming wings cost 5 Mana per/min 5/max Mana. Caution, you will fall if your Mana runs out in flight. Advances to Pheonix flight at level 20. Pheonix Kin boost X.25 Mana.
Druid Herb Lore	The herbalist has a broad knowledge of herbs used in healing birth control and poisons. Advances to basic Alchemy at level 15

She scrolled down to manna seventy-eight of two-forty.

"That can not be right?" She said.

"Yes, the twenty mana from your level up needs to be recovered just as if you used it."

"Okay, I see here I got one Con. one Str. and one Stamina, and five Luck?"

"Those stats are tied to physical skills and should go up. Except for luck, that may have been because you did not kill yourself crashing."

Scrolling further, she brought flame wings into view. "Level three already." She shouted.

Alpenbender said. "That is to be expected with the amount of mana you have and how small the cost is. You have more flight time than I ever did when I started, and you may break that level twenty before the week is out."

"Well, my love, if my math is right next time, you will have thirty-two minutes of flight."

Merlin grumbled. "At this rate, granddaughter, either the cost at that level will be zero, or you will get five minutes flight for each mana point spent."

Merriam giggled. "Yes, apparently, I can become a Phoenix and goddess."

The valkyries all fell to their knees, genuflecting. "All-Father, the legend of the Phoenix is reborn."

Merriam stamped her foot. "Will you people stop bowing to me? I am not that special, and I will not change. I am going to remain the same person I have always been."

Yrswen stood, tears in her eyes. "You do not understand, Milady. The legends say, in short, the Phoenix Reborn will prevent Ragnarok, and that is the final battle that will destroy the world."

"Oh, well, we can deal with that later. Once Stormavgaard has destroyed the orb, we can worry about the world's end. Right now, I am hungry; let us go eat."

We climbed into the carriage. As the valkyries flew back to the castle, we invited Apenbender and Groveshard to join us, and they accepted.

The sun had set an hour before when the gates of Durobrivae came into view.

As we approached, I heard a buzzing and flicked my shield out in front of the king, and an arrow bounced off. I bellowed out. "Who shot an arrow at the king?"

"Sorry, Your Majesty, he is a new guard just hired because we have lost many men."

"Well, do not let it happen again. Now open the gate."

"Well done, Sir Penrose." The king said to me. "Most would have ordered the man's head on a pike."

"Yes, Your Majesty, but most would not have heard that arrow, and it was a feeble shot. I am guessing the young man had sweaty hands, and the arrow slipped from a half draw."

"That was sharp of you to figure that out just from the sound."

"When you have been hit by a few of my Lord Duke's practice blunts at night, you quickly learn to pick out the sound of an arrow."

The king chuckled. "He did that?"

"Yes, Your Majesty. Ask Sir William. He got hit twice before he learned noise discipline."

The king laughed as we rode up the street towards the keep.

As we rode up to the doors, they opened. A man stepped out with a slip of a girl I was hoping to see.

"Your Majesty, I am Baron Loric. We were not expecting you until tomorrow."

"My mission is urgent, baron. We are only stopping for a hot meal if that is available."

"Certainly, Your Majesty, I can feed you and your men while my grooms look after your horses."

"Thank you, Baron Loric." The king said, dismounting.

I dismounted with him walking up the stairs, and I bowed. "Baroness Sylvia, I am pleased to see you made it here safely."

"Yes, Sir Penrose, the roads were clear, and we made good time."

"Excellent," I said. "May I present His Majesty, King Lionel Claymore. Your Majesty, this is Baroness Sylvia of Bedford. The baroness curtsied as the king stepped forward.

"Sir Penrose has spoken highly of you, Baroness Sylvia. We will speak more once we have eaten a bit and washed the dust from our throat." He took her hand and brushed his lips over her knuckles.

"Thank you, Your Majesty. I shall place myself in your service.

The king whispered to us. "Clever girl."

The king turned to catch the baron's dark look. "Come, Baron, lead me to your table and a tankard of ale." The baron led us through the doors and into his dining hall. Trying to strike up a conversation with the king twice, the king waved him off.

The table had already been cleared, but servants quickly brought food and ale. The king said. "Sir Penrose, you will escort the Baroness for me."

"Yes, Your Majesty, I would be delighted." I sat the baroness opposite the baron next to the king, then sat beside her.

I caught the quick flash of anger across from me and smirked.

I leaned to the side and murmured in Eyldana's ear. "Be ready. The baron has designs on Sylvia, and I do not think they are good. The king is playing a game, and we must protect them both."

She raised her mug to her lips, covering her mouth. "We will be watchful."

Leaning over, smiling, I murmured to Sylvia. "Keep your eyes open. The game is afoot."

Sylvia smiled. "I certainly am grateful to you and your men, Sir Penrose, for rescuing us at the ford."

"It was our pleasure, baroness. The fight was only some light training for my men, as the valkyries killed so many we hardly broke a sweat."

Baroness Sylvia laughed musically at that.

"You are such a charmer, Milord."

"Would you like some of this Milady? It is a wonderful ham."

"No, thank you, Sir Penrose. I had my fill at dinner. I want for nothing now. Well, except perhaps to finish my journey to Nottingham."

"I spoke with Captain Jeffrey before we left. His company will catch up with you tomorrow, and he plans to finish escorting you to Nottingham."

"I would be delighted to meet with some of your other friends. All your men seem so polite and disciplined."

"Hogwash." Said the baron. "Pretty soldiers in pretty uniforms and not a fighter among them."

The king chuckled as he ate and drank his ale.

Baroness Silvia replied. "You do not understand Baron Loric. These thirty men and five valkyries faced two hundred orcs and slaughtered them in about thirty minutes."

The king grunted, grinning but continued eating.

The baron said. "I am sure it may have looked that way to your inexperienced eye. There were no more than thirty or forty poorly equipped, ill-trained monsters. My men have fought many of them and taken heavy losses."

"You call Milady and me liars?"

The baron said. "Just young and inexperienced. When did you win your spurs within the last year, I wager? And the Baroness and I will be wed soon, and you will be gone from this place. Is that not right, Your Majesty?"

The king chuckled and finished his tankard of ale. Slamming the mug on the table, he rose and said. "It is time for an audience."

Standing, I assisted the baroness, and she took my arm. The baron had attempted to come around the table, but the king intercepted him and let him out of the dining hall. I whispered to Eyldana. "Position three to protect the King and two to cover the baroness as we followed along."

Eyldana nodded and flicked her wrists. The valkyries mounted their shields and spears. Eyldana and two others moved up behind the king and the baron. The other two moved in behind us. I smiled at the baroness. "Just in case. Where are your captain and guard?"

The baroness frowned. "Being confined to barracks, I only had my maid with me."

I said. "That will change very shortly, Milady. I have an idea of the plan, and our king will sort the baron out."

She smiled and said. "Thank you. You have rescued me again."

"That is my job, baroness, and my pleasure." I glanced back, getting confirming nods. The rest of the men were ready.

The king walked through the doors to the baron's throne room. The baron turned, eyes widening slightly at the valkyries behind him.

"You and your men may stay out here Sir Penrose."

And the king said. "No Baron Sir Penrose and his men are required for this audience, and it concerns Sir Penrose intimately."

The baron frowned. It looked as if he would protest but remained silent.

The king strode down the length of the audience chamber, stepping up to the throne and turning. Eyldana moved behind the throne with two of her valkyries flanking her. The baron stood one step down and to the side of the throne. I stopped the baroness at the end of the aisle, and my men spread out around the hall at parade rest.

The baron sneered at me, turning to the king.

The king said. "This audience is now in session." And he sat on the throne.

"The first order of business, Sir Penrose, step forward and kneel."

My eyebrows shot up, but I did as the king commanded, kneeling on the bottom step.

The king stood drawing his sword, bringing the tip down to tap my right shoulder. "For outstanding service to the Kingdom, We pronounce you Baron of the Realm at large." He brought the sword over and tapped my left shoulder with his last words. "So shall it be proclaimed rise Baron Penrose."

I stood gasping. "Thank you, Your Majesty. I will not let you down." I then stepped back beside the baroness.

Baron Loric was glaring at the king and me but made no sound.

The king commanded. "Baroness Bedford, step forward and kneel." Sylvia stepped forward and knelt in the same position I had. He placed the sword tip on her right shoulder. "Before God and these witnesses. We confirm your patent of nobility. We Proclaim you, Baroness Sylvia of Bedford." He had tapped her other shoulder during the second part of the proclamation.

The baron finally blurted out. "Good, my liege, and you may now proclaim my betrothal to the baroness."

The king smiled, looking at the baron. "We are the King and decide what proclamations to make."

The baron blushed red as he backed down, bowing to the king. "Yes, my Liege."

The baroness spoke. "My Liege, I accept your proclamation."

"Baron Penrose, take your place beside the Baroness. Before these witnesses and God, I Proclaim the betrothal of Baron Penrose to Baroness Sylvia Bedford. Henceforth Sir Penrose will be named Baron Bedford. May they serve the crown well and bear many heirs."

The king sat back down on the throne.

As the king was about to speak, the baron growled and threw down his gauntlet before me.

"I Baron Loric challenge Baron Penrose for the hand of Baroness Silvia."

The king grinned widely. "Excellent, Baron Penrose, you have my blessing to accept this challenge."

I smiled back. "Thank you, my Liege." I bent down and took up the baron's gauntlet. Tossing it to Lorick, I said. "I find your manners boorish and unseemly, as you obviously have no regard for the feelings of others. You may choose your weapons as you please. I have my sword, and that is enough."

The baron turned to one of his men. "Get my shield armor and battle-ax." The man ran out a side door.

The king beckoned a servant and said. "A comfortable seat for Milady and a tankard of ale for myself. Would you like some wine, Milady, while we watch the show?"

Sylvia replied. "Why I thank you, Your Majesty, I could use a small goblet to sip on."

"And a goblet for Milady, hurry along now."

I escorted Sylvia to the king and kissed her, then moved to the open area in front of the throne. Looking back to the king, I saw Eyldana had placed herself behind and between the seats, and the other four valkyries were in the front and back on either side. Around the rest of the hall, my men had spread out among the barons.

My pikemen grinned tightly. None of us had shields, and the baron's men did. I smiled as the baron stomped over to the other side of the open space. He wore his battle armor and helmet with a full face shield. He had a kite shield strapped to his left arm and carried a large battle ax in his right. I quickly saw his movements would be slow and clumsy. Sylvia sat glancing between us with a concerned look on her face. I grinned impishly at her and pulled my hood over my head. I then drew my beautifully engraved sword and stepped to the on guard.

The baron snorted. "A pretty knife welp will look good above my mantle."

I just rolled my shoulders and beckoned him forward with my left hand.

With a roar, the baron lurched forward, attempting a shield bash. Light on my feet, I slipped left around his shield. I cut the strap holding the left pauldron with a flick of my wrist. The baron spun around clumsily. "Standstill, coward." I stepped back from the wild swing of his ax, danced around his right side, and cut the strap for his right pauldron.

The baron growled. "Stand and fight." I chuckled. "Very well, you asked for it." The baron swung at me again, only this time I stood my ground, deflecting his ax with the flat of my blade. Switching to a downward strike, I sliced his shield in half lengthwise.

"What?" Loric squawked. Stepping back, he tossed the shield aside. Then did he notice a deep cut on his forearm. "That is not possible." He growled.

The king chuckled. "It is impolite to play with your prey, Sir Penrose."

"Yes, Your Majesty, I apologize."

The baron raised his ax for a mighty overhand swing as I stepped forward, slashing across his abdomen. With a soft 'urk,' Loric fell to his knees. As his hands came forward to support himself, the pauldrons dropped from his shoulders, baring his neck, still in the same motion spinning around to my right beside him, I brought my sword down, lopping his head off.

Looking to the chamberlain, I said. "Would you mind getting someone to clean up this mess? I do apologize, but these things happen."

The Chamberlain stuttered. "At once, Milord." Running from the room.

CHAPTER

33

The king laughed. "Baron Penrose, send one of your squads to find Milady's guards."

"Yes, Your Majesty," I replied. "Sergeant Clark, take some men and find Captain Roderick."

The sergeant snapped a salute. "At once, Milord."

"You there who is in charge of the late baron's men?" Asked the king.

The man replied. "I am Captain Carson, Your Majesty, in charge of the barony guard."

"Tell us of your situation." Said the King.

"Majesty." Said the captain.

Baron Loric was left in charge when his father went to the crusades. His father died early in the campaign, and the regent confirmed Baron Loric. The title went straight to his head, becoming overbearing and demanding. He was not the worst man to serve, but he did have designs on the Barony of Bedford. I have been captain since the previous one died in a fall two years ago. My Liege, I have not got enough training to command, and we have lost too many men from monsters due to my lack of training skills.

The king said. "It takes a solid brave man to admit lack of ability. I applaud your fortitude, and we will fix that problem."

The doors opened with a bang, and Captain Roderick marched straight to the baroness, falling to his knees and laying his sword hilt first toward her. "Milady Baroness, I offer my life for leading you into this trap. I have no excuse except that I had hoped to protect you."

The king held out his hand, smiling. "Please allow me to handle this punishment, Milady." The baroness inclined her head in agreement.

The king then stood, taking up the captain's sword and speaking. "You show great honor in admitting you made a mistake, and I am also impressed you offered your life to the baroness before asking your king's permission. For this display of contrition, I name you Baron Rodrick of Durobrivae. Rise Baron Roderick, and hopefully, when you draw this sword next, it will be in defense of our kingdom."

The new baron stood stunned, taking back his sword and sheathing it. "Your Majesty, I know not what to say. I never expected this."

The king laughed. "What do you say, Milady? Should I change my name to King Lionel The Unexpected?"

Sylvia laughed brightly. "I think it does not have the same ring, Your Majesty."

The king sighed dramatically. "Right, Milady, perhaps as a footnote. I will have to think about that."

"Now I need to mess up everyone's schedules even more. Sir William, Milord High Commander, will be very vexed with me."

"I am sure he will get over it, Your Majesty. Sir William and the Duke of Nottingham are very flexible thinkers."

"You have the right of it, Baron Bedford."

"It is why I cultivated Sir William in the first place. As he was so wise in choosing his replacement, the duke is just as adept at choosing his captains and officers."

"But enough preening. We have business to attend to before we get on the road."

"Milady Sylvia, can you ride?"

"Yes, Your Majesty, I can handle a charger without trouble. I am also pretty good with swords."

"Oh, baron, yours should be an exciting marriage." The king laughed.

Baron Rodrick said. "I taught Milady how to fight with falchions myself. While not a master yet, I can confirm that she is very adept."

"Yes," said the King. "I can see that falchions would fit her best by Milady's size. Good Milady, go find some leathers and weapons you will be riding with us."

"Baron Rodrick, keep your escort here as part of your baronial guard. I will be arranging for a new battalion to form at Bedford under Baron Penrose's command."

"Nottingham is the center of training for my new army. But units will be spread out as they become available. I may have to build an enormous castle in Nottingham."

I smiled at that but said nothing. The king would find out very soon.

The king then said. "Second company will be here sometime tomorrow. The Baroness will be coming with us, and they will no longer need to escort you. You can tell Captain Jeffrey what has transpired and the change of plan. Tell the captain to make their best speed to Nottingham."

"Yes, Your Majesty, I can do that, and we will top up their supplies if they need anything and send Milady Sylvia's luggage with them."

"I have spoken with Captain Carson, and I do not think he was part of the problem, as his only issue is a lack of experience, and he admits that. I think you will bring him up to speed and give him the training he requires."

"Yes, Your Majesty." Said Baron Rodrick, "I will take him under my wing and show him the way."

The light of my life, Sylvia entered with her maid dressed similarly. She had the hilts of falchions over her shoulders, and her maid had a saber at her hip.

Walking up, she bowed. "Your Majesty, we are ready to go."

I said. "Your maid is trained as well?"

Rodrick said. "The maid was more comfortable with a single sword, so I trained her with a saber, and she pairs that well with a buckler."

"Good, Milady, will have a companion she knows when she gets to Nottingham."

The king said. "All right, I will leave you to put your house in order, Rodrick. Come, let us get back on the road." We all walked out so the baron could see us off.

As we mounted, Rodrick walked up to us. "Milady." He said, taking Sylvia's hand. "I believe you have made a good choice in Baron Penrose. Fare you well, and I hope to see you again." Clasping forearms with me, he said. "I have raised the baroness like my daughter for the last six years. I now pass that task to you, so do not mess up, or I will come looking for you."

I chuckled. "You need not fear Baron. We will be around to visit from time to time."

"Good," said Roderick turning to the king. "Farewell, Your Majesty, and I will see you on your return trip. Perhaps you will be able to stay a day or two on your way back to Cambridge."

"I will be happy to stop over, Baron. You have an excellent ale here." We all chuckled, and the king said. "Let us move on." We headed for the gate.

Closer to the wall, I called out. "Open the gates, as the king has places to be and new people to see."

Sylvia giggled at that, and the king chuckled. "Really, Baron?"

"Oh, yes, Your Majesty, you have no idea what is in store for you." Kicking my horse to a canter as we rode on through the night. The valkyries sent up two scouts, and the rest flew above us in overwatch guarding the column.

Morning came, and we all met in the study. Merriam's maids and the dryads had taken to escorting her everywhere. I smiled at that, knowing she did not always need their protection.

Robyn Will and Little-Jon just chuckled at the additions to the harem.

Robyn whispered to me. "It seems our wife is collecting her own army."

I laughed. "We must start using the dining hall or eating in shifts." The others laughed, and Will quipped. "Well, if our wife would stop expanding the family until we have the new castle built, we should be fine."

"Oh, shush, Will, it was an accident." Merriam giggled.

Jon rumbled a laugh. "An accident perhaps but a happy one nonetheless."

"You men have filthy minds." Merriam laughed.

The dryads giggled. "Yes, please."

We all broke up laughing as we entered the study.

Sophia sat in her usual place smiling brightly. "There is a happy group Sir William."

Merriam shot back. "Not yet, but we are getting there."

Sir William chucked. "So, what are everyone's plans for the day?"

"Training for me." Said Merriam.

"Dancing and singing lessons for them." Giggled Sprucebramble.

Stormavgaard entered, escorting the queen with their close guard detail. On their heels followed Merlin, Friar Tuck, and the four Elves.

We all greeted the queen and each other.

Sir William looked around for a moment shaking his head. Waving his hands, Sir William called out. "Please excuse this old military man, but I live for organization. Now, what are everyone's plans so I may arrange escorts if need be."

Everyone laughed at that, and the queen spoke up. "I have no plans except to prepare an audience as my king approaches quickly."

Merriam asked. "Do you have an idea of when Your Majesty?"

The queen said. "By Stormavgaards estimation, they should arrive by noon."

"Perfect." Said Merriam. "Denby, she called."

And Denby popped through the door like he was expecting the summons.

"Yes, Milady?" He inquired politely.

"Have the audience chamber prepared for the king's arrival. Then have the dining hall ready for a celebratory feast."

"Yes, Milady preparations are in hand." And he left.

Merriam giggled. "How does he do that? It is so exasperating I can never catch him off guard."

We all laughed, and I said. "Magic, my love."

Merriam looked thoughtful, scrunching her nose. "Alvos, you should use the stone on Denby to see what it says."

"I can ask him if he would show you, but I would not wish to violate his privacy."

"You are quite right," Merriam said. "You can ask him, but I will not order it."

Stormavgaard chuckled. "I have an appointment with Sergeant Thomas and Lady Tarija this morning. I will be opening a portal for the advanced guild party, as they will only send those required for planning and construction. About twenty, if I am not mistaken."

"That is right." Said Tarija. "It will be twenty in the first group with ten wagons of supplies and equipment."

"Will I need to provide an escort?" Asked Sir William.

"No, Milord." Said Stormavgaard. "We can handle that. Once we get them to the road, they move pretty fast. We will be back before noon." Stormavgaard got a look of concentration for a moment. "I have let Eyldana know we need the king to arrive no earlier than one hour past noon."

"Good," said Merriam. "He will be hungry and unreasonable."

We all laughed at that statement.

"You are mean, my love."

"Ugh," said Merriam. "Did you see those pictures from Kristoff? This castle is a moldering pile of rubble compared to that. I wanted the king to see my new castle when he next visited."

Merlin laughed. "Yes, the grass is always greener. I will be over there by the fire reading."

Friar Tuck said. "I will be with Loyal Archmage and some Elvin healers in the infirmary. Bring your injured there so I can practice."

Merriam giggled. "I will be out behind the castle burning a few things and flying around to practice my takeoffs and landings."

"You should have Friar Tuck practice out there just in case."

Merriam squeaked and slapped me on the shoulder as we all laughed.

"Well, I did hear it was more take-off and crash landing." Will laughed as Merriam threw a biscuit at him.

Robyn chuckled. "The three of us will be staying near Merriam as we want to learn about our levels from Alvos.

Sir William said. "I think I will join you, gentlemen, for a while. I would like to learn a bit about this myself. Then we will be back here to meet with the captains and sergeants about preparations for the king's arrival.

Merriam giggled. "The king may wave at your men as he gallops past. Although you should make sure the streets are clear, leading to the castle gate."

Sir William chuckled. "I suppose you are right, Milady, but proper military decorum must be followed. I dislike slapdash formations when I have foreknowledge of impending arrival."

"Very well, let us go down and pile into the carriage. We have a very, very busy day. Just keep your afternoon open for the king. Your Majesty, enjoy the quiet for the morning, for I am sure it will be chaos after lunch." Sir William smiled, bowing to the queen. The rest of us bowed as well and exited.

"Come, let us go to our rooms and prepare for the audience." The queen said, leaving with her guards.

Sophia said. "Well, girls, what shall we do to occupy ourselves for the morning?"

Mary giggled. "We could go watch Alicia and Camila training?" Rose nodded eagerly.

Sophia laughed. "I thought it was off-limits?"

"Oh, no, Milady." Said Rose, "That is only for men. The maids are encouraged to participate. Something about learning to battle dance, whatever that means?"

"Oh, yes," said Sophia. "It is a deadly fighting technique for women, used mainly by spies and assassins. But I can see where it would enhance the defenses of Duke Sherwood's castle. Yes, we will go as I may wish to learn this myself, as I will no longer have a purpose once I mate."

"Milady," said Mary. "I believe Sir William cares for you greatly, and we will look after you as long as you need."

Sophia giggled. "We shall see what comes about."

They headed downstairs, quickly finding the training room. Knocking on the door, The girls heard a voice call out one moment. After a few seconds, they heard locks snapping and chains rattling. Then the door opened to show one of the Dryads peeking around it. "Oh, hello, ladies." She said. "Come in, come in." They turned to see locks snapping, chains rattling through loops, and a large, heavy bolt being shot home when they entered.

"Oh, my." Sophia laughed. "You like your privacy, do you?"

"Yes, Milady, very hush-hush must not reveal our secrets. Only women may know this information."

I looked around, and the floor was smoothly polished wood. And the other three were standing there naked. The dryads looked at ease, but Alicia and Camila were breathing hard and had a light sheen of sweat.

"Oh." Said Mary grinning. "I thought you were dancing?"

"No, must warm up the muscles first and learn proper breathing. Take your clothes off and join us."

"You can hang your dresses there." Said Alicia, pointing.

Where she pointed, I saw a bar with hangers on it.

"We will try this out," Sophia said, starting to undress. The other two quickly joined in, helping each other with buttons and ties in out-of-the-way places.

Once they were naked, they joined the other two in a line. Sprucebramble snapped her fingers, and her clothing vanished.

"How did you do that?" Asked Sophia.

Locustlimb said. "It is simple. We have bags of holding. So I think to store and snap my fingers, and clothes go to storage. If I wish to wear something for a particular dance, I think of the outfit and snap my fingers again." Suddenly, she was wearing a different outfit. "That is how we can make quick changes during a performance." She snapped her fingers again and was once more naked.

I am, Sprucebramble Dancer, but you may call me Spruce. It will take time, but you will be able to tell us apart soon. We will not mind you getting our names wrong. If you look at me and say Locustlimbs name, she will answer your question."

Sophia said. "That is no problem for me. I can tell you apart now, but the girls may take some time."

"Yes, seer, we know of your abilities from past encounters with your kind."

"You have met seers on the other worlds?"

Locustlimb giggled. "You misunderstand Sophia. We have always been here. As we are hundreds of years old, I have checked in with your ancestors to know when the time of prophecy would happen. It is the same with other fey creatures like fairies and imps, which remain hidden in the deep forests and glades."

"It is only now that we may show ourselves in at least reasonable safety." Said, Spruce.

Sophia said. "Excellent. How do we begin these exercises to warm up?"

CHAPTER

34

The group arrived near where I had been practicing the day before. Dismounting, we saw the elven encampment was gone, and in its place was a clearly defined road through the trees.

I said. "That did not seem to take long."

Alvos replied. "No builders, magic is potent. They essentially ask the trees to move aside, clearing a path."

Will said. "Yes, it was fascinating watching them make the road. The trees just slid aside to make the path."

"Oh, I wonder if my druid magic could do the same?"

"It is possible, Milady." Said Alvos.

"I will leave that for later and practice flying."

"Come, Alpenbender, and we will go over here away from the men."

"Yes, Milady Merriam, may I suggest a strategy?"

"Of course, Alpenbender, you are the one with the experience, and I need to learn from you."

"Very well, then from your stats, we calculate you have thirty-two minutes of flight time. I suggest only practicing flying for twenty minutes, which will allow you sixty mana to practice other fire magic."

"I see, so I should balance my training in all types of fire magic?"

"Yes, you do not want to focus on one skill to exclude the others."

"You suggest that I practice my druid magic on another day?"

"Well, Milady, you recover magic so fast you could perhaps do two training sessions a day."

I laughed. "Well, on days the schedule is not quite full, maybe."

Alpenbender also laughed. "Yes, sometimes it is hard to strike a balance."

"Well, let us see how long it takes me to learn takeoffs and landings smoothly."

"Yes, Milady, just remember when coming in for a landing, tilt your wings up slightly and cup them to catch the wind. It will slow you down enough to make a smooth one or two-step landing."

I thought about that advice for a moment or two while calling my wings out, muttering. "Okay, girl, you can do this," I took two steps forward and launched myself.

I quickly rose to about thirty feet and began to circle. "Okay, that seemed much less awkward than yesterday. Now let us try a landing without using my face."

Swinging toward Alpenbender, I lost altitude. And just before hitting the ground, I cupped my wings, stopping myself in mid-air. Before getting my legs under me, I slammed into the ground from about six feet.

Everyone chuckled as my wings vanished from lack of concentration. I spent a minute laying there gasping to regain my breath, then climbed onto my feet.

Alpenbender said. "Very close, Milady. I forgot to mention that as you cup your wings lower your feet and do not flap. Once they are cupped, just hold them steady unless you are going very fast and must stop in a hurry. Think about how a hawk circles up high, looking for prey. They pull their wings in when they spot a rabbit or mouse and stoop. They flair the wings, lower their claws and strike at the last moment. Using their knees and hips to cushion the shock of landing."

"Okay, I think I have this now," I said. Once again, calling my wings out, I took off. Each take-off seemed to be getting more comfortable, and I ought to get the landing.

Circling again, I once more came in from thirty feet up. At about six feet, I lowered my legs and cupped my wings. I landed hard, stumbling a few steps and falling to my knees.

"Okay, that was better."

Alpenbender said. "Your reaction time is beginning to speed up to match your flight movement. Have you noticed how much easier your takeoffs are getting?"

"Yes," I said. "It did seem easier than the last time."

"That is because you are beginning to do it rather than thinking it through."

"Oh. my God, you are right. It is like breathing; you do not think about taking a breath. Just do it."

"Yes, precisely that is how it works."

I turned away, took two steps, and relaunched myself. I circled up to thirty feet and came back in for another landing. This time I stayed on my feet, only stumbling a few steps.

The men cheered and clapped, and I smiled and took off again. Circling, I came in for another landing and gently set down, with only two steps. I did not think about launching myself into the air again just did it. After circling, I realized I had taken off from a standing start. I came in for another landing and settled feather-light on my feet.

"Yes, said Alpenbender. "You have mastered taking off and landing. Try a couple more times to set it in your mind."

I did as she said without even thinking about the take-off or landing, and it was easy and gentle both times.

"Perfect," said Alpenbender. "Now check your stats and see how much mana you have available above your minimum safe levels.

Calling up my stats in my head, I scrolled down, realizing there were changes.

Merriam Sherwood Bonded Harem	
Guy Sherwood/Paladin Robyn Loxley/Ranger Will Scarlet/Rouge Little-Jon/Barbarian Alicia/Maid/ Battle Dancer Camila/Maid/Siren/Battle Dancer	
Alignment	
Phoenix Kin / Druid / Fire Mage	
Abilities	Level
Archer	40
Sword Master	20
Fire Mage	19
Druid	12
Health 430/430 Rec 1 per min x5 fire boost	Mana160/280 Rec .5 per-min x4 Kin boost
Stamina 35	Int 37
Dex 35	Str 30
Con 26	Luck 20
Available Skill Points 31	
Skills acquired	Description
Hearth Mistress	Those in your home are made welcome and comfortable. You have undeniable skills in homemaking and managing staff.
Fire Shot / Flaming Arrow DP 100 per point of mana.	Able to use fire magic to produce flaming arrows scalable. One mana to max avalable mana.
Fire Spark can light fires and candles.	Can hold a small flame to light the way. Cost one mana-min. Advances to Fire Ball at level 10

Fire Ball DP 10 per 5 Mana	It can produce a small ball of flame to cast and be held to make a light to see. Cost 5 mana per-min held. Scalable. You can also absorb fire to replenish mana or heal. Advances to Flame Blast at level 20.
Flame Wings Manifest wings of fire for a limited time 7/20 Level 20 is required for Pheonix Shift.	Flaming wings cost five mana per/min five/max mana. Caution, you will fall if your mana runs out in flight. Advances to Pheonix flight at level 20. Pheonix Kin boost X.25 mana.
Druid Herb Lore	The herbalist has a broad knowledge of herbs used in healing birth control and poisons. Advances to basic Alchemy at level 15

I gained two intelligence points: stamina, strength, and dexterity. Then I noticed my Fire magic had reached level nineteen. Health was four-thirty max mana two-eighty, and my remaining mana was one-sixty, which I thought odd until I realized I had recovered twenty mana while practicing.

I scrolled quickly to flame wings and gasped. "Very strange, Alpenbender. I have gained three levels in fire magic and four in my Flame Wings."

"So I am now seven of twenty to reach phoenix shift, and my mana cost is down to five per cast."

"Oh, said Alpenbender. "You are advancing so rapidly."

"I hope not too rapidly. I would not want to hurt myself or someone else."

"If you use care and instincts through each change you make, you will be fine. Also, you now have ten more skill points, and I recommend waiting until you get phoenix flight before using them."

"Yes, I suppose it may cost me skill points for the phoenix shift.

"Yes, that is a possibility that may cost even more points than you have. Then you will have a decision to make."

"But I do not think I will have a choice; I will have to save. I feel I will need that power before this is over."

"Come now, Milady, we can play catch with some fireballs. We fire mages play this game to improve control and accuracy."

I asked, intrigued. "How does it work?"

We stand back to back, march ten paces, turn and throw a fireball. We will set ourselves up so there is nothing flammable in range behind us. The idea is to catch a fireball, absorb it, and throw another back with the same hand. You may aim for any part of the body, from the knees to the elbows. The idea is to get faster until one of us misses.

"This sounds like fun. Let us do it."

We found an excellent safe line around us and placed ourselves back to back.

Counting to three and we began pacing ten paces. We would be two-thirds of the max range for a fireball at twenty paces. Reaching the launch point, we both turned and threw a small fireball. Alpenbender's fireball came at my chest while mine went a bit wide. I caught hers, and with a slight reach, she caught mine. Absorbing our fireballs, we both shot one back. This time, I was a little more accurate as that would have hit her body if she had not caught it. I caught hers before it hit my knee, absorbing it and throwing one back. It continued for about fifteen minutes, getting faster and faster. We both grinned until an errant throw from me landed short and between her feet. I could not help myself as I had started laughing, and her fireball hit me in the stomach. I slapped my hand over it, absorbing the fire, and just fell laughing. Alpenbender laughed as she drank the fire from the grass around her feet.

Standing finally, we walked over and hugged each other, I said. "That was fun."

"Yes," Alpenbender said. "It is even more fun when there are four or five mages in a circle tossing fireballs at each other. When we build the academy, a room twenty-five paces in diameter will be installed and made fireproof. Students just learning can miss without fear of burning anything up. We make a room so each elemental magic student can practice."

"Oh, I get it," I said. "Each element can absorb its own like lightning, water, fire, and air."

"Yes, once battle mages are advanced enough to learn shields, they start to practice against each other. We only use the lowest level of our magic for that training, and the idea is to hit the other person's magic to deflect it or cancel it.

I scrunched my face, thinking. "But how do you see air?"

Alpenbender giggled. "Air magic leaves a slight shimmer like heat waves on a hot day. It is hard to detect, but you can see it if you know it is coming."

"Okay," I said. "I can see where that is possible, but I do not think I am ready for that level yet."

"You are not that far away, Milady. Like you, age and maturity are far easier to train than adolescent children."

"Children? How old are people when magic manifests?"

"Between ten and fifteen years, it depends on the circumstance. And younger ones who are angered or hurt cause them to manifest. In my case, a boy threw a rock at me, and I threw a fire spark back."

"Oh, God, we need to get the word out to the soldiers and Sherriffs men. These people know nothing of magic and could accidentally burn the town down before realizing it."

Rushing back over to the men, I called out. "My love, Sir William, we have a problem. Well, at least a potentially dangerous situation. Alpenbender informs me that people first manifest magic by accident in a fit of lust, anger, or other strong emotions. She also tells me it happens anytime after age ten."

"Will Jon get to the barracks and inform the Huntsman and Sheriff's men of the situation. Sir William Guy, you will need to educate your soldiers. A child in a fit of anger or pain could spark a fire, like a sudden bar fight, robbery, or rape. The thing to remember is to calm them down and make sure they are safe. Then gently bring them to the guildhall we will be building. There are people there that know what to do. Alvos, do you think the elves can train these people at least enough to make them less dangerous?"

"Yes, Milady." Said Alvos. "For now, the best place would be the guild hall. We will send elves to establish a magic school as soon as we can build one."

Robyn said. "Okay, Will, find your patrols and tell them. Jon and I will go to the barracks and tell the rest of the team, then Jon can go out and tell his people in the woods."

"Duke Sherwood, you head for the fourth company and tell them I will do the same for the fifth company." Said, Sir William. "We can meet back at the castle and tell the first company, and then I will send a message to the third company in Derby."

My husbands gave me a quick kiss, jumped onto their horses, and rode off quickly, Sir William among them.

I said. "We had better head back to the castle if needed to fight fires."

Alvos said. "It is a good thing we have a variety of mages in the queen's guard. I think she numbers ten, which can use water or fire magic."

"That would be most helpful," I said.

"Yes, please." Said Alpenbender. "We can only absorb so much fire before we need a place to vent it. Ice mages would be helpful because they can make ice for us to melt, venting magic. Remember, we cannot be hurt by fire, so we can run into burning buildings to save people."

After about two hours of running around, we gathered back at the castle. By that time, the potential disaster had been averted. I had stopped at the queen's quarters and asked if we could borrow her fire and water mages if needed. The queen also suggested using the ice mages and giving the fire mages someplace to use up the flame they would absorb.

Sir William said. "The letter is written now. How fast can we get it to Derby?"

Stormavgaard said, walking through the door. "One of my valkyries could get there in about fifteen minutes. What are we in a hurry to deliver?"

I giggled. "A dire warning and solution to a problem we just discovered."

"A problem, Milady?"

"Yes," I said. "The sudden and possibly accidental manifestation of magic in children from ten years. It will be a frightening experience as our people know nothing of magic."

"Oh," Stormavgaard said. "I never thought that could be a terrible thing."

"Yes," said Sir William. "Everyone ten and up in the world is a potential disaster waiting to happen."

Stromavgaard took the letter handing it to Yrswen. "Send two girls to Derby with this letter and ask Kristoff if he can spare any builders for the guildhall."

"Yes, Dragonlord at once." With a wrist flick, she indicated Sofreir and Agione. "Take this letter. Talk to Kristoff and get three stone brothers here fast."

The two valkyries quickly left.

"Right," said Sir William. "With that taken care of, how long until the king arrives?"

Stormavgaard got that distant look in his eyes again. "About one hour, give or take."

I called out, "Denby."

Denby stuck his head in the door. "Everything is ready, Milady." And he ducked back out.

"Just once," I growled.

We all laughed, breaking the tension.

Sophia, the maids, and dryads all entered. Sophia plunked into her chair and grabbed the goblet of wine Sir William offered her. She said. "Whew, that was hard."

Sir William raised an eyebrow. "What was, Milady?"

"Oh, I was just learning to dance with the maids."

The Dryads giggled. "Milady learned about exercise and getting sweaty."

"Yes, said Alicia. "But the hot bath afterward was divine."

Locustlimb laughed. "Yes, getting all soapy and slippery together was fun."

The maids and Sophia blushed as the rest of us laughed.

Sir William said. "Well, I think that is enough. And we must go get ready for the king's arrival now."

We all agreed and began leaving to change.

"I will need a bath after my training," I said.

"Yes, Milady." Said Camila. "We have your bath ready and had baths prepared for your husbands in the communal bathing rooms."

"Good," said Sir William. "We will meet back here as quick as we can get ready. Then we may escort the queen to the audience hall."

I giggled. "Then the fun begins."

Sophia's laughter followed us into the hall as we went to clean up.

We were back in the study half-hour later in our best doublets and hose. Merriam wore a gown in shimmering green silk. Jewelry set off her hair and eyes with lovely red stones and diamonds.

Of course, I could see how this gown molded itself to her figure.

Stepping forward, I put my hands around her waist. "Stunning my love as always." And I kissed her cheek.

Merriam giggled as Will, Jon, and Robyn closed around her.

The queen laughed musically at our group as she walked through the door.

We all stepped away to bow, and the ladies curtsied.

"Hum." Said Merriam. "Speaking of stunning, Your Majesty will knock the king off his feet."

Sir William grumbled. "And the rest of the men as well."

We all chuckled as I said. "The people will get used to it, Sir William. Soon all the castle maids will be dressed like Alicia and Camila. The girls in question stood together, wearing a white blouse and short black bibbed skirt with black slippers and white stockings. While showing a large expanse of the leg, their outfits still covered their modesty, if just barely.

Merlin laughed. "In the time I came from, they would have been called eye candy."

"Harumph." Sir William grunted. "Yes, they seem to catch the eye."

Sophia giggled. "I cannot wait to see Mary and Rose in the same thing."

While blushing furiously, the girls stared at Alicia and Camila.

The queen laughed brightly and said. "Seeing battle dancer maids does take some getting used to, but you will love it when they learn to dance."

Sophia laughed. "Their teachers are outstanding, so it will not take long."

The dryads giggled and replied in unison. "Thank you, Milady Sophia."

It was almost startling to hear them as they were so small and lost in the crowd. Being under five feet made it very hard to keep track of them.

Stormavgaard said. "Your Majesty, I think we should proceed to the audience chamber."

The queen replied, taking his arm. "Yes, Milord Dragon, it is time I met my future king."

We all gathered and moved down to the audience hall, entering and taking our places.

The crowd gasped, and many blushed when they saw the queen. She was dressed neck-to-toe in a white gossamer gown that hid nothing but covered everything. Merriam quickly distracted most women with her gorgeous shimmering gown in green silk.

I spoke to the queen while we waited. "Your Majesty Windgust Artisan and several seamstresses need to move here for a time, as their skills will be in great demand among the ladies."

The queen replied. "It is our sincere belief that our seamstress guild will be able to teach your seamstresses our skills. Yes, the school will take time, but it will happen."

"Thank you, Your Majesty. I am grateful you show such willingness to help my people."

The queen laughed lightly. "I do not wish to sound contrary, Your Grace, but we are your people now."

"That is true, Your Majesty, at least our king's people."

Suddenly there was a clatter of hooves in the courtyard.

CHAPTER

35

It had been a long night of hard riding for us, and we had had no encounters, which was perhaps a good thing. The only delay had been that blasted deadfall. It only took an hour, but I did not regret making sure the road was clear.

I had been thoroughly impressed by the young Baroness Sylvia. Despite the hard night riding, the girl showed some backbone. I could see the weariness on her face, but she still sat tall in her saddle. I chuckled to myself as I glanced at young Penrose. He was equally impressed with her stamina but still hovered in a worshipful way. He moved closer as we trotted along, saying. "It is not far, my love; we will see the town just around this bend."

She smiled at Penrose. "That is a good thing. As much as I love riding, I am saddle sore."

Her maid giggled from behind her. "Milady, I am sure the duchess has some cream the baron may rub on your bottom to make it feel better."

I laughed as the baroness gasped. "Angela, you are naughty. I may have to spank you."

"Yes, please, mistress." She giggled.

I laughed hard as Penrose's face turned bright red. "Yes, dear baron, yours will be a fun marriage."

"Aye, Your Majesty, I suspect it will."

I leaned forward slightly as Nottingham came into sight and slapped my horse on his shoulder. "Come, old friend, you have done well. One last push, and you can have all the oats and carrots you want." I kicked my horse up to a canter, and we thundered up the road.

I do not know what it was, but I felt something pulling at the back of my mind. The feeling had been getting stronger the closer we got to Nottingham to the point it was almost a compulsion.

The next thing we saw was the fifth company in parade formation beside the road leading into town.

I waved at Captain Robert and Bell, calling them to join us as we rode past. I was not stopping for anything now. We rode into town at an easy canter stopping in the courtyard before the steps of the keep. Tossing my reins to a groom standing there, I said. "Take good care of these horses. They have ridden hard all night with little rest. Let them drink a bit, then cool down before feeding them."

The young man replied. "Yes, Your Majesty, we will take good care of your horses, and they will be ready again by morning."

I turned to Penrose. "Let us go."

Young Penrose and his knights formed up behind me with the baroness on his arm. I saw the unusual flag flying from the battlements and the Duke's banners. Just as my foot struck sparks from the top step, the doors to the keep opened.

The duke's chamberlain Denby stepped out, banging his staff and announcing.

"His Royal Majesty Lionel Claymore King of all England." At his last word, there was a fanfare, and my royal banner broke out beside the other flag.

"Denby, it is good to see you," I said.

"Thank you, Your Majesty. We are always happy when you visit."

"Haha." I laughed. "Now, what have my Duke and High Commander been doing?"

His lip almost twitched into a smile. "It has been somewhat disturbing Your Majesty in a good way. I will announce you if you follow me to the audience chamber."

I sighed mightily. "Very well, I guess the bath will have to wait."

"Not for long, Your Majesty baths are being made ready for you and your companions now."

"Oh, yes, that reminds me, Sir Penrose is now Baron Penrose of Bedford. With him is Milady Sylvia, Baroness of Bedford, his betrothed."

Denby's eyes widened slightly. "Thank you, Your Majesty. I will be sure to announce them correctly. This way, if you please."

Walking to the doors of the audience hall, I said. "Baron Keith and Baroness Sylvia, move forward. You will lead, and I will enter with your men as an escort after suitably shocked gasps as you take your places."

"Yes, Your Majesty." Said Keith, stepping forward with Sylvia on his arm.

Sylvia giggled. "I wish I had had time to get dressed better. Fighting leathers are not exactly court attire."

I chuckled. "You would look lovely in anything, my dear, and strange times call for unusual attire."

I stood slightly to the side as Denby pounded his staff and announced the baron and baroness.

They marched up the aisle to the front at a dignified pace. I smiled as Sylvia tugged on Keith's arm to slow him down. They were in place, and it was my turn. The compulsion to enter that chamber was becoming almost painfully physical. What the devil was happening to me? What had William and Guy cooked up and gotten me into now?

The Chamberlain's staff banged three times. And I started moving as Denby called out. "His Royal Majesty King Lionel Claymoore Ruler of all England and Duke of Normandy." As he finished, I cleared the doorway and looked down the aisle. My world came to a stop for a moment. The vision before me was like taking a solid punch to the gut as I gasped for breath. Rising from the throne, glowing softly from within, was an Angel of God. Even from this distance, the smell of spring struck me, causing me to take a deep breath. I began moving, almost running. I marched up the aisle, dropping my helmet and gauntlets. As I reached the steps before the throne, I unclipped my sword holding it before me. As I fell to my knees, I laid it at her feet.

"As God is my witness, I have seen your glory and lay my sword and kingdom at your feet. Command me as you please, my queen."

Her musical laughter was a balm to my soul, soothing me like nothing else. Then she spoke, and I was complete.

"Rise my knight in shining armor, take up your sword, for it is I who should kneel before you. You are my Lord, King, and mate ordained by prophecy. My people are your people, and we will be bound as one."

"May I hear the glory of your name, my queen?"

"My name is, Evadhi, The Guardian. She said as she touched the strange device hanging between her breasts. I sucked in a sharp breath as my eyes were drawn to those glorious orbs of woman flesh. My face grew warm as I snapped my eyes back to hers. She giggled briefly, eyes shining.

"Evadhi," I breathed, taking her hand and gently kissing its back. "A name as beautiful as the goddess who wears it."

Smiling, she said. "You have sweet and charming whispers to make me swoon. It would be best if you announced our betrothal before your people. Then we may feast and celebrate."

Then she smiled. I did not want to do anything but bask in her glory. But I finally forced myself to move. I did still apparently have a kingdom to rule. Turning to the people gathered for this audience, I declared. "Before God and this gathering, I proclaim my betrothal to Queen Evadhi of the Elven people." It was then that I noticed the tears in the eyes of most of the people, and a soft chime rang out.

There was a moment of silence as I finished. Then the audience roared approval, cheering as bells rang from the towers. The companions stepped forward to congratulate us both and Baron Keith and Baroness Sylvia.

After a moment, I said. "Come, Your Majesty, Baron, there are servants outside the hall who will lead you to a room where you may bathe. They have clean, comfortable clothes to wear while you celebrate. Baroness Sylvia, you are a bit of a surprise but allow my Ladies in Waiting to lead you and your maid to my quarters. There they can assist you in getting cleaned up and find something suitable for you to wear."

"I thank you, duchess," Sylvia said, curtsying.

I laughed, taking her arm. "We are going to be friends, and it is just Merriam. Alicia and Camila look after the baroness and her maid."

Both girls curtsied. "Yes, Milady, we have suitable clothing for them."

"Excellent," I said. "Now run along, girls."

"Your Majesty," I said. "Shall we retire to the study to await your betrothed?"

"Yes, Your Grace." Smiled the queen as we linked arms heading for the door.

Duke Sherwood held up his arms and called for attention. "Good people, please step over to the dining hall and relax. We will rejoin you as soon as the king's party has refreshed themselves, and then we will have a double nuptial celebration."

As we left, the hall headed upstairs, and the crowd followed, moving into the dining room.

I giggled and said to the queen and Sophia on her other side. "Did you see the look on the king's face when he first saw you, Your Majesty?"

Sophia laughed. "It looked like he had been struck between the eyes with a quarter-staff."

Evadhi laughed musically. "Yes, he did appear quite stunned, but it was at that moment I knew he was the one. He saw nothing but my eyes as he marched up that aisle."

Sir William chuckled behind them. "I thought his heart would stop, Your Majesty, when he looked down as you touched the seed."

The queen laughed as we entered the study. "But he looked up quickly enough to stop drooling all over me. When he took my hand, I must admit I almost jumped on him."

We all laughed at that image, sitting down to chat while waiting for the others.

Thank goodness for my iron self-control so I would not embarrass myself while bathing. We entered the room to see steaming tubs and servants preparing more. We all started to strip as other servants gathered our discarded bits of armor and clothing.

A servant said. "Your Majesty Baron gentleman, we will have these things cleaned and placed in your quarters."

I replied. "Thank you. Do I still have the same corner room?"

"Yes, Your Majesty." The server replied. "We have also added an extra cot for your bannerman. Baron Penrose, the room next to the kings, is available for you. Quarters are tight with all our guests, and the Baroness and her maid will be put in Milady's maid quarters."

Baron Penrose said. "We do not wish to impose or put the duchess's ladies out."

"Oh, no, Milord, the maids have become close to their dryad trainers and bunk with them."

I sighed and grunted as I settled into the hot water grabbing the tankard of ale I drank deeply. Setting it down, I said to the servant. "All this must have been quite the upheaval for you?"

"In some ways, Your Majesty. Much has changed, but the duke and duchess have brought new life into these old halls. Most of us find it quite refreshing, although I am sure that will wear off."

I laughed. "Yes, newness is always exciting for a short time. By the time it wears thin, chances are we will be gone again, and things will settle down."

"As you say, Your Majesty, but I somehow doubt it with the duchess." He chuckled.

"Would you gentlemen like a haircut and shave?" Said another servant.

"Yes," I said. "Just because we smell nice. There is no need to look like a bunch of ruffians."

Baron Penrose chuckled. "I think my love likes this look on me, but she has not seen me in any other state."

I laughed. "Good, this is a chance to impress her."

Penrose chuckled. "Yes, Your Majesty impressing the ladies is essential."

"Do not worry, baron. Our ladies will have us domesticated soon enough." Everyone chuckled at that statement. I laughed as I got out of the tub to dry myself.

Looking at Jeffrey and my Bannerman, Clarence, I said. "You young men may join Edwin and Jamie for the celebration, as there is no need for you to hover over me like a pair of hens."

"Your Majesty." They chuckled.

All cleaned up, and we headed for the study at a fast pace. I had been too long away from my queen.

I strode in, waving everyone down before they could start bowing. Walking straight over, I took my queen's hand, bent over it, kissed her knuckles, and then sat beside her. I realized just how much I had been missing before meeting her.

"My queen, as much as I would like to sink into your gaze and forget the world, I must tear myself away. Events have transpired in the last week, leaving me feeling like I am staring at an oncoming avalanche. Being in your presence makes me feel calm and ready for anything."

"My king, there is much to learn and discuss, and we will have time to learn about each other soon. My advisors inform me that Elvenhome will be ready for our mating ceremony in three days. Because the ceremony takes two nights and the day between to complete, we will travel there the day after tomorrow."

I said. "This is good. What is with the see-through clothing you wear?"

Evadhi giggled. "This is all part of our ceremony. I wear this due to your people's sensibilities. Normally, I would strip except for my necklace and seed in the Elven royal mating ceremony. I would remain this way until we mate in the final part of the ceremony. A ritual baring of the soul before my king. It will all be explained to you by Alvos, my advisor."

An elf stepped forward, and Evadhi pointed to him.

Looking, I saw an elf of great age and wisdom. "We are pleased to meet you, Alvos, and I hope you can explain this more fully."

Smiling, he said. "I will explain it all to you, Your Majesty. Have no fear. Your part of the ceremony is relatively simple."

Merriam giggled. "It is all performance-based."

The companions behind her laughed.

"I am glad this amuses you. I have work to do?"

"Yes, Your Majesty." Said, Sir William. "First, as you have met your betrothed, other introductions are in order."

"Yes, they most certainly are," I said. "I see two I know but dressed most unusually."

Alicia and Camila blushed, curtsying. The dryads behind them giggled.

Merriam said. "You know my Ladies-in-Waiting, Your Majesty. These are dryads, Sprucebramble Dancer, and Locustlimb Chorus. They are training my maids to be harem battle dancers."

My eyebrows shot up. "Harem? Battle dancers? What do you mean?"

Merriam giggled. "My maids and I had an adventure with Guy and Robyn the night the queen arrived. They have been added to my harem, but we have also learned that they are level one and two battle dancers and sirens. Alvos will show you the stone in a moment to activate your status. But first, I will show you something I have learned.

Merriam stood and moved over in front of the fireplace. Once she had the room, she called forth flaming wings.

I gasped in shock, sliding back hard in my seat. "Are you part demon, Milady?" I could feel the heat radiating from her wings.

Merriam giggled. "No, Your Majesty, it is but part of my fire magic. Although my next level says phoenix shift."

"This cannot be possible. The phoenix is a mythical bird, not real."

Alvos chuckled as Merriam recalled her wings and sat back down. "Now, Your Majesty, please hold out your hand." Alvos placed an oddly carved stone in the palm of my hand. "Now, Your Majesty, my queen can help you speak share status."

"Okay," I said, "share status." And I was startled beyond belief for the second time in a few seconds. A screen had popped up before me, showing much information.

Lionel Claymoore Betrothed to Evadhi The Guardian	
Alignment	
Paladin Monarch Lion/Superior	
Ablities	Level
Paladin	40
Monarch	35
Archer	20
Sword Master	45

Commanding Presence	30
Rally	25
Status	
Health 420/450 REC 5 per min	Mana 600/600 Rec 2 per min
Stamina 40	Int38
Dex 25	Str 35
Con 30	Luck 21
Avalable Skill Points 238	
Skills Aquired	Decription / Cost
Commanding Aura At level 40 becomes Voice of Command 30/40	Use your Aura to reinforce orders causing your men to obey quicker. Costs 3 Mana per level (scalable)
Sword Master Becomes Legendary Swordsman at level 50 varies with the weapon 45/50	You are close to becoming a legend, but your Dex and Con hold you back. Dex Con min 40
Rally Becomes Inspire at level 40 25/40	Rally wavering troops within 100 feet. Costs 10 Mana per 100 men (scalable) 10-minute cooldown
Skills Available	

Evadhi said. "This, my king, is your status screen. It is very personal to you and should never be shared with anyone you do not trust implicitly. At the top, it shows your name and that you are betrothed to me. Below that is your alignment Paladin Monarch and... Oh, my. Lion/Superior? Is that what I think, Alvos?"

"May I look, Your Majesty?" He asked.

"Yes, please, do as my queen trusts you, and so shall I."

"Thank you." He said, coming around behind us. "Please, scroll down to available skills near the bottom. Now, focus and say shifters. Ah, yes. As I expected, Your Majesty, you have not met all the requirements for the skill, as you need to have INT CON and DEX at forty to unlock it."

"So, how do I do that? Better yet, what will happen?"

Evadhi panted excitedly. "Something extraordinary that has not been seen in centuries."

Alvos cocked his head to the side, looking at both of us. "Umm, we better wait before doing this, as it could get embarrassing for everyone."

"What do you mean?" I asked.

"Well, you will be overwhelmed by your senses, vision, hearing, taste, and smell. You will have a strong urge to dominate, and your mate's arousal will be the trigger."

Evadhi squeaked, drawing my attention. She was blushing down to her... and I covered my face, groaning. "Yes, let us not do that yet."

The rest of the group laughed.

"Next, we have a list of abilities and your levels, health, and mana. And your status in critical areas. Then you have a lot of available skill points, and we will speak much more on this in private."

"Good because I do not understand this next section."

"It is self-explanatory. On the left are skills you have acquired. On the right is a description of each skill and what they involve. As we work on your stats, I will help you understand these categories."

"Below this section is a list of skills and abilities you may purchase for skill points."

"That, my love, is the quick overview to understand more of the conversation."

"Yes, thank you, my queen and Alvos," I said. I was raising her hand to kiss it again.

"We can review this more thoroughly during our private time later in the ceremony."

Alvos said. "Think close, Your Majesty, and the screen will disappear."

I did, and the screen blinked away.

"Anytime you want to look at your stats, just think status, and the private screen will pop up again. Remember that no one may see your stats unless you share them aloud."

"There is also no greater dishonor than demanding to see a subordinate or captive status."

Merlin stood by the windows looking out when he turned, saying. "Oh, hell. It would seem it never rains, but it pours. Grandson, you need to see this. Jamie, go find Friar Tuck and tell him to get the infirmary ready, and he may, in fact, already be there."

The Duke walked over to look out the window, and I followed out of curiosity.

I asked. "Is that...?" Trailing off in dismay.

"Yes," said the Duke frowning. "It would appear Captain Doerner has found something terrible. Please, everyone, remain here while I go deal with this."

I followed the duke as we hurried down to the courtyard. The duke called for Denby as well. Stepping out of the keep, we were in time to see Captain Doerner lead his column through the gate.

Glancing into the first wagon passing, I could see several female figures wrapped in blankets.

The duke said. "Denby bring female servants to help washerwomen, and older women would be best."

"Yes, Milord, right away," Denby said.

I called the wagon drivers. "Over there is the Infirmary." And I pointed to the converted barracks.

"Yes, Your Majesty." The drivers called back.

"Captain Doerner." The Duke said. "Please come with us to make your report."

I saw Friar Tuck and some elves rushing out of the Infirmary to help. Then I saw several women hurrying from the servant's door towards wagons. Nodding at that, I followed the captain and duke.

We returned to the study, where everyone was waiting anxiously.

I said. "Ladies, it would perhaps be best if you retired to the duke's quarters while the captain makes this report."

"I will remain." Said Merriam. "I have seen this many times before, and I will help once I know more."

My queen said. "I would remain because my people will be involved in healing."

The other women left, heading to the duke's quarters.

CHAPTER

36

"Very well, captain, now report your findings."

"Yes, Your Majesty."

We moved quickly to the coast, finding nothing on the way. Before reaching Manchester, we turned south along the coastline to the first village. It was, as described, burned out with nothing remaining. The weather had removed any marks from the strand, so we had no clues there. However, my scouts found scattered bits of clothing on the road leading south. We followed the trail for a half-day until we saw smoke further away from the coast.

Raiders were attacking a village. We immediately proceeded to engage these raiders and try and save the town. Unfortunately, we were too late for the village but did save fifteen women and girls from a much worse fate. All the men were dead, and the women left alive were stripped naked and bound at the edge of the village. We quickly dispatched the thirty raiders we found. There were three boys whom I suspect would have been trained to bolster their ranks. I kept one raider alive to question him. He said there were many more further south on the coast.

We loaded the women into the raiders' wagon, giving them blankets to cover themselves, and moved on. We arrived at the next village near dusk. We could hear the screams of women and the laughter of men.

My scouts reported men loading loot onto longboats. It confirmed they were Norsemen raiding the coast for slaves and plunder. They had already killed the men in this village but used it for a base. Waiting for dark, we attacked and killed the raiders, numbering about seventy.

Once again, I question one of the men discovering the existence of two more raiding parties to the south. We found another group of twenty women naked in a pig pen in various states of having been assaulted. I could not find any clothing, and one of the more coherent women told us the raiders had burned everything they owned. She said by its sound, the raiding parties would be back that night as they were leaving before dawn. We moved the women into one of the larger huts giving them blankets and food and lighting a fire to keep them warm. We then set up ambushes.

It was not long before the first group of raiders showed up. They had a loot wagon, ten naked women, and five young boys tied in a slave line following the wagon. My archers took out the raiders before they knew what hit them.

We brought the wagon into the village and put the new women in the same hut as the others.

Resetting the ambush, it was not long before the final group appeared. They had eighteen women but only two boys and two wagons of loot. Dispatching the men of this raiding party, we returned to the village.

Speaking with the more coherent women, we gathered that the raiders were looking for breeding stock. The main reason, I believe, was to start a new clan.

We remained there for another day, caring for the women to help them recover some strength. Two women died from the abuse during that time, and we lost another on the return trip.

Searching the longboats and wagons, we found very little of value. The stores on board the boats were mostly meat and sacks of grain. Some gold copper and silver coin and a bit of jewelry belonged to a couple of more well-off women. We put it together in a pouch to be used for the women's care and split it between them.

We loaded them onto wagons and returned here as quickly as possible. The boys seem to be in better condition, along with most women. A few younger girls are terrified of men, and a few women are skittish. We had the stronger women to take care of them and brought them all with us.

"Good," said Merriam. "We will employ all of these women and the boys. Her eyes gleamed for a moment as she called. "Denby."

Denby stuck his head in the door. "Friar Tuck and the elves are healing the worst injured. They will, of course, heal them all, but they are concentrating on the worst cases for the moment. Our women not needed are helping the rest with baths and feeding them, and my mother is interviewing them for positions in the castle staff." He then ducked back out again.

Merriam's shoulders slumped. "Okay, I admit defeat. He is just that good."

We all chuckled.

Duke Sherwood said. "Thank you for your concise report, captain. You did excellent work saving those women and boys and preventing further raids. You may rest and refit for the balance of the day. Then join Captain Anders at the dwarf village for your rearmament tomorrow."

"Rearmament Milord?" Asked Captain Doerner.

"Yes, Captain Doerner, Captain Anders has all the details and the funds for your equipment. We are equipping every man in the army the same way. Trust me, and you are going to like what you are getting. The equipment is ten times lighter and a thousand times stronger."

"Yes, Milord, Your Majesty, I will take my leave." Saluting, he marched out.

Sophia walked in giggling. "Milady Merriam, your harem battle dancers, are gaining new members."

Turning to Evadhi, I asked. "Can you explain to me what this woman is talking about?"

My queen giggled most delightfully. "Let Milady Sophia explain, and it will become clear."

Sophia laughed. "Your Majesty, the dryads and Milady's maids Alicia and Camila have been recruiting aggressively. At least twenty younger women have agreed to join the harem training the dryads conduct."

"Okay," I said. "I get that part. Now, what exactly is a harem battle dancer?"

Evadhi smiled. It is an art form and skill for women. It teaches them dances that are at once erotic and deadly. The added siren ability can lure unsuspecting men into dropping their guard, making them very easy to kill. Their skills also make them excellent as counterspies and counter assassins. They add a great deal to any castle's defenses and security.

Merriam giggled. "It would appear I have started a new business that will be much more fun than a bordello."

Robyn groaned. "With all these women running around half-naked, I will spend the rest of my life in perpetual arousal."

I laughed uproariously at that. "Could that be such a terrible thing, Baron Robyn?"

"Harumph." Said Robyn. "Probably not, but you will find out soon enough on your own, Your Majesty."

We laughed at the surprised look on his face.

"Here is Baroness Sylvia. You look exquisite, my dear."

Baroness Sylvia dropped the perfect curtsy and replied. "Thank you, your majesty. I feel much better now." She then went and wrapped herself around Keith's arm. He leaned down, kissing her on the cheek.

A huge man entered the study, trailed by five scantily clad women. He was with Sergeant Thomas and another sizeable muscular woman clinging to the sergeant's arm.

Sir William began laughing.

I glared at him. "What is so bloody funny?"

He chuckled a bit more and replied. "The look on your face, Your Majesty. May I introduce the Dragonlord Stormavgaard accompanied by five of his valkyries."

"Master Sergeant Thomas, you know, and the lovely woman attached to his arm is his mate Tarija of the Snow Elk Clan, and she is the head of our adventurer's guild."

"The Dragon Council sent Stormavgaard to assist and advise us from his world. He has already been more than helpful in many ways and has unparalleled knowledge of races and governments."

Stormavgaard stepped forward. "Well, met Your Majesty." He clasped forearms with me. "I place myself at your service to assist as I may. I will tell you now that I am an ambassador and advisor, as dragons only fight when they are directly threatened. My valkyries are my guard and my harem. You have already met Eyldana and her team, so you are familiar with valkyries."

"Eyldana and her team were most capable during my time with them. I must say, though, that these valkyries are dressed differently."

"Yes, I have upgraded their armor and their more mundane weapons. Yrswen, please show the King your improved armor." Stormavgaard grumbled a chuckle as the rest of us laughed.

She stepped forward saying, "to battle," and her armor transformed, covering her from head to toe.

I gasped, sitting heavily, staring. "The wonders never cease, and this armor is as good as the dukes?"

Yrswen chuckled. "Guard." And her armor transformed back. "No, Your Majesty, my Dragonlord paid more for our armor, which is much better. Eyldana and her team will be heading to the dwarf village tomorrow to get their new armor."

I said. "It would appear I need to go meet these dwarves soon."

Evadhi clasped my hand. "You may go tomorrow, my king. I insist you be as well protected as our guard." I heard chuckles from behind me.

I turned to see ten elves, half male and half female.

"These are your guards, my queen?"

Elvadhi smiled, laughing. "Our guards, fifty in total, half male, half female. They are all warriors and battle mages."

I raised my brow, attractive. "Now, where were we?"

"Dwarves and armor." Yrswen giggled.

I chuckled. "Thank you, my dear. In that case, I guess I will ride up there tomorrow."

Stormavgaard laughed. "We will fly up there tomorrow morning, so no wasted time."

Merriam giggled. "Yes, I have to go and get some new armor."

"New armor, Milady?" I asked innocently.

Merriam laughed. "Yes, the armor I got before does not allow for my wings. So I will get something similar to what the valkyries have."

My eyes widened, knowing they did because I could see everyone else grinning. But I managed to bite down on my tongue before saying anything foolish.

"Yes, Milady Tarija, you will be heading the adventurer's guild?"

Tarija said. "Yes, Your Majesty, I will head this world's branch of the adventurer's guild. The guild master of my branch is old and does not wish to relocate, so he will continue to run the reduced guild there. Most adventurers from my chapter in the other world have expressed the desire to come here. Many of them are like me, cat shifters, some other shifter races, but most are non-shifter races."

My brain, of course, was still stuck on a cat shifter.

Sergeant Thomas rumbled a laugh. "You have lost him, my love. Perhaps you should show him."

Tarija laughed as well. "Yes, you are right. He is stuck on cat shifter."

The rest of us laughed as well.

Tarija glanced around, stepped to the side of Sergeant Thomas, and then she shimmered like a heatwave. And suddenly, a giant white cat with jagged black stripes stood before me.

"Oh my God, she is gorgeous."

And then Sylvia stepped forward hesitantly and whispered. "You are so beautiful and big." The giant cat purred, grinned, and then licked her face as only cats can do. She giggled, stepping back. "eew." Baron Penrose laughed, handing her a handkerchief to wipe her face. Tarija rumbled deep in her chest and then shifted back.

"Sorry, Milady." She laughed. "Sometimes, I cannot resist wide-eyed innocence."

Baroness Sylvia laughed. "Your cat form was just so beautiful I could not resist either."

"Do not try that with a bear shifter or wolf. We cats tend to be more playful than those others."

Sergeant Thomas barked a laugh. "That is because you tend to play with your food, my love."

Tarija laughed. "But you like it when I play Ulysses."

Everyone laughed as he blushed.

"Oh, that reminds me, Master Sergeant Thomas," I said. "Do you recall Tonya and Tanya?"

Sergeant Thomas's eyes went wide. "Yes, two former students, Your Majesty."

I chuckled. "I made some inquiries, and apparently, you made quite the impression on those young ladies. They refused all efforts to be married off separately, and their father despaired of ever getting them out of his house. He was delighted when I asked him to send them my way. I am sort of disappointed to find you now married."

"Mates, Your Majesty." Said Tarija. "We are soul bonded lovers much more permanent and intimate." She said with a wicked grin. "Once I hear this story, I may be interested in meeting these young ladies."

We all laughed as Sergeant Thomas covered his face, groaning.

"All right," I said, ticking off my fingers. "We have dwarfs, elves, and an elf queen I am to marry with pleasure. Then we have a dragon valkyries shifters, of which I have seen a cat. Oh, and dryad battle dancers and a most glorious queen I am to marry."

Merriam giggled. "And I have flaming wings and may be able to turn into a phoenix soon."

"Yes, that too, and I will get married."

Evadhi giggled beside me, gripping my hand.

I groaned. "I need to drink a lot."

In the background, the dryads cheered. "It is party time."

We headed out the door, so Evadhi and I were the last.

A giggling group of maids and dryads led the way to the dining hall. Then Master Sergeant Thomas and Tarija. As announced, we all moved into the hall, taking our places at the tables. Stormavgaard was announced just before us and entered with his five valkyries taking his place next to them. Everyone in the hall rose to face the door as we were announced. I walked down the aisle with Evadhi gliding along beside me. We both smiled at the people bowing as we passed. Finally, taking our places at the head table, I said.

"Rise, my friends, let us eat and drink in celebration, for it is not only my betrothal to Queen Evadhi. It is also the betrothal of Baron Penrose and Baroness Sylvia." We sat, and all the rest followed suit.

As soon as we were seated, servants brought food from the kitchens. I recognized many of the dishes right away but not all. "My dear duchess, what are these new dishes I see?"

Merriam giggled. "It is something the elves have cooked up."

Alvos laughed. "Your Majesty Denby approached me asking if any traditional dishes were served at these ceremonies. The one before you is a traditional dish served at royal ceremonies."

"Well," I said. "We must try a little bit of all of the offerings." I then served up samplings from several dishes and set the plate before my queen. I then helped myself to the same dishes. I poured Evadhi a goblet of wine and myself a tankard of ale. I was about to dig in when Evadhi held up her hand.

"Wait, my king, they must be checked. Two elves stepped forward and passed their hands over each dish and our cups and plates. Both nodded to each other and bowed to the queen before stepping back.

"They have determined that the food is safe we may eat now. These elves will stay nearby and check a new dish each time you serve yourself."

"What were they checking for?"

"My love, they check for poison and can detect binary toxins."

"Binary toxins? What are they?"

"My queen giggled in that most delightful way again. "They are poisons that come in two parts, and separately they are benign but are highly toxic when mixed. So one may have been cooked into the meat, and the other sprinkled on the vegetables."

"Oh, I said. "That seems rather complex and time-consuming. If I do not like someone, I will stick my sword in them and invite anyone who does not like me to try."

That elicited another of those delightful giggles. "Some are more cowardly than warriors, so I also have guards."

"Yes," I said. "Annoying creatures, guards, always watching your every move. Sometimes I think they would follow me into the privy if they could fit."

Evadhi burst out in musical laughter. The sound was a balm to my soul.

Dinner continued with idle chatter all around the tables.

CHAPTER

37

The entertainment performed during the dessert course was a resounding success. There was magic and juggling, dancing and singing. Even the dryads performed a demonstration battle dance. I could see the king was impressed and whooped at its end. I had also noticed our maids had brought a large group of the victims to see that dance. Even from the head table, I could see their eyes shining with determination.

The final cap to the entertainment was when the king led the queen onto the dance floor. He then turned, beckoning Keith Penrose and Sylvia Bedford. Once they got on the floor, the musicians started a slow, intimate tune. I discovered that King Lionel and Keith Penrose were both accomplished dancers. Guiding their ladies around the floor like it was the most natural thing they had ever done.

I leaned over to Guy and asked. "How do they get time to learn to dance like that?"

Guy and Robyn sitting next to him, both chuckled. "A master swordsman must be balanced, graceful, and aware of his surroundings." Said Guy. "Mind you. I can guarantee Keith never had as pretty a partner as he does now."

Robyn laughed. "No, it would have been another smelly squire."

I giggled. "So, as squires, you are forced to dance together?" And I lost it laughing hysterically.

Guy and Robyn laughed with me. "Like to take a turn around the floor with me, my love?" Guy said.

"Yes, please," I said. Guy led me around the dance floor like it was his most natural element. Then suddenly, in the smoothest move I have ever seen, I was being led by Robyn. And I saw Guy with Alicia. Then I was back in Guy's arms, seeing Robyn with Camila. Next, I danced with Jon, giggling because he was not as smooth as Robyn or Guy. But he made up for his lack of finesse in brute force and strength. And Guy and Robyn kept dancing with Alicia and Camila. Next, I found myself in Will's arms. He was also an accomplished dancer. And Jon was dancing with Alicia and Camila while Robyn and Guy led the dryads. Finally, we all came back and sat down, breathing heavily.

I looked over and laughed, pointing, and my men chuckled.

Keith was sitting at the table with Sylvia in his lap, and she had her head on his chest, half asleep.

I walked over to him and said. "Keith, I think it is time we put your lady love to bed."

"Yes," he agreed. "Two days and a night without sleep, my love is exhausted." He kissed the top of her head.

I beckoned Alicia and Camila over, saying. "Girls, please show the Baron where his lady love will be sleeping. I am reasonably confident he can easily carry her to bed."

Blushing, the girls said. "Yes, Milady. We will tuck her in and then go get your chambers ready."

Thank you, girls. "We will see you in the morning, Keith."

"Yes, Milady, goodnight." He stood holding Sylvia like she weighed nothing. "Lead the way, Alicia." He said. Giggling, Alicia and Camila headed for the door leading Keith.

I came back over and sat down, and the king laughed.

"You should have left them, Milady. Young Penrose looked quite comfortable holding her in his arms."

I laughed. "I am sure Keith was, but he would need the privy at some point."

The king laughed until tears ran down his cheeks. "Oh, Gods." He finally gasped. "That was an inspiring vision of hopeful love at its most desperate."

Evadhi laughed. "It is a simple solution. Just toss her over your shoulder, and you are good to go."

"My queen." The king gasped. "Such crass disregard for your partner's dignity." And then we all burst out laughing.

And the king finally clapped his hands. "Even I find myself becoming sleepy, and I am tired enough that I may miss dawn for once."

Guy chuckled beside me. "I doubt that Your Majesty, you never missed the dawn after several straight nights of battles."

The king chuckled, rising to his feet. "My queen, allow me to escort you to your door. I pray the time flies when I can carry you through that door for a night of bliss."

Evadhi stood, clasping the king's arm. "I agree, my king, but the wait will build our anticipation. The first time we mate will be a significant event."

We walked from the dining hall and up the stairs.

Turning to me, she gave me a brief kiss on the lips. "Soon, my king, sleep well."

"You too, my queen." I waited as she entered her chambers. Two female elves outside her door giggled and smiled gently.

I smiled and chuckled back. "Ensure the queen's rest is undisturbed." I turned and walked away to my bed.

I smiled, watching the king and queen leave. "Come, gentlemen, it is time to bid our guests a good night."

Robyn chuckled. "You have done it once again, my love. It would appear at least half the guests will be here for breakfast."

I said. "It would seem you are right, love. We still have to see off those that can leave."

Will chuckled. "I have men outside to escort them home."

"Oh, Will, that was so thoughtful." I turned and kissed him.

Jon laughed, clapping him on the back, nearly knocking us over. He rumbled. "See, I told you it would be a good idea, Will."

I giggled. "Because of my reaction?"

Jon gave me a peck on the forehead. "Yes, my love. Will was unsure if it would be the right thing to do."

"Oh, well, protecting our people is always paramount, and that is your job, and I am glad you think of these things."

The dryads sauntered over, giggling tipsily. "A fun party, Milady. I hope we can have more." Said Sprucebramble.

Locustlimb added. "Milord's dance very well, and I look forward to more opportunities."

The men chuckled, and Guy said. "The dancing was fun and educational. As small as you girls are, you are powerful."

They both giggled, and I said. "And how did your charges take to your little demonstration?"

"Oh, yes," Sprucebramble laughed. "All twenty-two girls are excited to become battle dancers, and six of them wish to become part of your harem."

Locustlimb laughed. "Yes, they were the least abused and prettiest of the victims, as they were merely stripped and groped to ensure their virginity."

Sprucebramble took up the story. "The raiders told them they would be breeders for their king. And now, because their families were murdered, they have no place to go."

"When you finish your trip to the dwarf village." Locustlimb continued. "Come down to our training room, and they will pledge themselves to you."

"Oh," I said with a tear in my eye. "Well, I would be happy to take these girls on, and they do not need to pledge to me but the duke."

Sprucebramble laughed. "You misunderstand, Milady. It is a ceremony making them part of your guard, and you have already done this with Alicia and Camila by accident."

Locustlimb giggled. "Your little adventure with Alicia and Camila is why they show on your stats as harem battle dancers. Your ceremony was not entirely correct, but the system accepted it. We will assist you in completing the ritual correctly."

Sprucebramble continued. "When we are done the ceremony, they will be bound to you, body, mind, and soul, as are your mates."

"Oh, dear," I said. "How will I keep eight ladies-in-waiting busy? I have enough problems keeping an eye on Alicia and Camila."

Locustlimb laughed. "We ten will also be body servants for your mates, and we will care for you as one protecting you with our lives."

We all gasped at that statement, the men's arousal becoming evident.

Sprucebramble giggled. "Although we may need something to stand on to wash the big one."

We all laughed uproariously at that image. The dryads barely came to Jon's belly button, as he was so tall.

This entire conversation had been interspersed with thanking drunken guests as we saw them out the door. Finally, the line of those who could stagger out ended.

Denby ushered us out, saying. "Good night, Milords and Ladies. We will take care of this mess. The venue for breakfast has been changed, as the study is no longer large enough for you. We have taken the liberty of rearranging the library, as this will give you room for all your extra guests, including guards and maids."

"Thank you, Denby," I said. "We will see you in the morning then."

We left the hall and headed upstairs with the dryads giggling and clinging to Jon. I hung on to Will's arm as Robyn and Guy followed along.

I giggled as we climbed the stairs. "We are becoming quite the spectacle as we head for bed."

Robyn laughed. "Imagine it with eight more pretty girls dressed in maid uniforms."

"Now, that would be a spectacle. We will impress those at court when we finally show up." Guy laughed.

I laughed brightly as Will threw open the doors to our chambers. We all stumbled to a stop while the dryads giggled.

There before us were Camila and Alicia, kneeling naked on the floor.

"What the...?" said Guy.

"Devil?" said Robyn.

"Is going on?" I completed.

The Dryads rushed forward, giggling.

Sprucebramble adjusted the girls' positions, opening their knees to shoulder-width and placing their hands palm-up on their thighs.

"Now say the words as we taught you," said Locustlimb.

Both girls blushing, said. "We are yours to command, Milady."

I blushed at the sight before me. "Well, that was unexpected. I know not what to say."

Sprucebramble giggled. "Step forward, Milady. Now, place your hands on their heads and, in this case, say. You may serve me by getting me ready for bed, pets."

I stepped forward, placing my hands gently on their heads and saying. "You may serve me by getting me ready for bed, my pets."

The girls rose, leading me to the dressing table, where they sat me down. Alicia let down my hair to brush while Camila began undressing me.

I heard the groans from behind me and glanced over my shoulder. My mates stood there with raging hard-ons tenting their hose. At least one of them had the presence of mind to close the doors behind us.

Alicia and Camila blushed and giggled as they saw where I was looking.

The Dryads giggled. "You get Milady ready for bed, girls. We will assist our masters for now." Said Sprucebramble.

Locustlimb giggled. "This will become easier when there are more of us to help. It will take time, but we will acquire a large enough harem to work in shifts."

Guy said. "Ten will be far more than we can keep up with, and hope to satisfy our wife."

Sprucebramble laughed. "With thirty points in your stamina and constitution, you will be more than capable, masters."

Robyn said. "Status." Looking at his screen. "Let me see, I have many points to spend but only need to add four to my stamina and five to my constitution." He mused. Getting a brief look of focussed concentration, he nodded. "There, done." Shivering slightly. "What?" He said. "That was a bit of a rush."

Locustlimb laughed. "Have you all got your status unlocked?"

Jon rumbled. "Yes, Alvos unlocked ours this morning, but I do not need to add to my stamina or constitution. They are both over thirty."

Will laughed, looking Jon up and down. "That does not surprise me in the least." He then checked his stats and nodded himself after a moment of concentration. He then shuddered. "Whoa, Robyn, you are right. That was a rush."

After a moment, Guy said. "Yes, a rush is a good description, and it is like having a big bucket of ice-cold water dumped over me."

Robyn chuckled. "Yes, that was the feeling."

I glanced at my stats and quickly added seven points to my constitution.

I looked at the dryads. "Have you been working with Alicia and Camila on their stats?"

"No, Milady." Said Sprucebramble.

"We promised Milord Duke we would consult you before making changes." Said Locustlimb.

Sprucebramble continued. "As they become stronger and level up, we will guide them in their choices. Those choices will always be their's, and we can only be a guide."

Alicia said. "We belong to you, Mistress, and will do as you say."

I smiled, hugging the girls. "That is lovely, but as the dryads say, we may only guide you as the ultimate choice is yours." I slid my hands down their backs, squeezing their bottoms. They squeaked as I said. "Get me undressed so we may have some fun."

The dryads giggled as they pushed Jon down onto the settee so they could climb up and reach to pull off his shirt and tunic. They then jumped down to remove his boots and socks, finally pulling him back to his feet so they could grab his hose to pull them down. "Oh, my, he will be much too big for virgins."

Locustlimb said. "We might be able to take him, but the rest of the harem will not yet."

Spucebramble said. "The other masters will have to stretch them out first."

Alicia and Camila were blushing furiously, undressing me to the dryads, commentary, and peaking when they could.

"Do not worry, girls' my husbands will be very gentle." The girls shuddered and gasped as I reached between their legs to see how wet they were. They were both dripping wet. Bringing my hands up, I allowed them to clean their juices from my fingers. I asked. "Have you girls been practicing?" Both nodded their heads as they sucked on my fingers. "Good," I said. "Come wash the sweat from my dancing off." They followed me into the bathing room.

Stepping to the center tub, the girls began to pour ladles of water over me as I stood on the grate. The men walked in and stood watching, except for Jon.

The dryads dragged him over to the left-hand tub, which was the largest. They grabbed a bench to stand on and began scooping water over him. We all laughed at the tiny dryads wetting the giant Jon down, then grabbing sponges from a soapy bucket; they began to wash him.

I watched them while the girls rinsed me off and settled into my tub to soak. I laughed as I saw the dryads were as covered in suds as Jon was, as he had been running his hands over them, getting the suds in every crack and crevice.

The dryads then rinsed him but not themselves, pointing to his tub to soak. They skipped over to the other men to help Alicia and Camila. It involved a lot of giggling and groping as well. Soon they were all washed, and my men climbed into their tubs. Getting four tankards of ale from the cask by the wall, they brought them to each of the men to enjoy. Alicia then went and got me a goblet of wine.

As they sipped and felt how cold the ale was, I said. "Whoa, did someone finally get the chill spell?"

Sprucebramble said. "We have that spell, Milady, as it is part of our harem training. All the girls will learn this spell and one for heating mulled wine as they become available to harem maids early.

Jon rumbled. "I think I will miss this the most on our trip."

Robyn laughed. "You will not find ale in most places we are going, as wine is the drink in most lands. When we get to the Holy Land, we will not even find wine as the Arabs think it is evil.

Jon laughed. "Then we best make that part of the trip short."

I laughed. "We can always ensure room so the valkyries can bring a cask in their bags of holding."

"Oh, they can. Thank the gods for that idea." And we laughed.

I then stood to get out of the tub and froze. Everyone stared at the water cascading off my body.

Alicia and Camila came forward with soft towels to dry me. We had been watching them dry themselves and each other.

Jon also stepped out of his tub, and the dryads giggled as they climbed back on their benches with towels to dry him.

As the girls finished with me, Guy stepped out of his tub, and they quickly grabbed fresh towels and started drying him. The Dryads were done with Jon, and they dried Robyn as he stepped out. Then we laughed as all four of them dried Will with considerable groping on his part.

CHAPTER

I took Wills' hand, leading him to the bed.

We sat side-by-side on the edge of the bed as the others came from the bathing room.

Wilfred slid his hand between my legs and asked. What happened to your hair, my love?"

"Alpenbender explained that the fireball burned all the hair off my body from my eyebrows down when I transformed."

"But not the hair on your head or your eyebrows?"

"No," I said. "Alpenbender told me it is a function of the magic within us. She told me that elves get pubic hair when they reach the age of twenty and that puberty lasts thirty years."

"Wow," said Will. "I do not know if I could have survived thirty years. I was a raging lunatic for the five I needed to mature."

I giggled. "I can imagine. But do you like how smooth I am?"

"Yes," he said. "It makes you very soft."

"Well," I said. "Get used to it because it is permanent. Alpenbender tells me the elves have a cream to remove hair from the body."

"Oh, really?" Asked Guy. "I find hair down there very uncomfortable, and when I lick a woman there, it gets in my mouth."

I laughed. "I will get some but only for the pubes and between your legs. I like the feeling on my nipples from your chest hair, and Jon is like a big furry rug."

The Dryads giggled as they made Jon lay back on the lounge and rubbed themselves on his chest like two kittens. With Jon caressing and fondling their bottoms, spreading their juices around.

I laughed at the sight. "Well, that takes care of those three, it would seem."

"Yes," chuckled Will. "Although I would like to have them all over me."

"You will get your chance." I laughed. "But first, you are going to service me. Now sit up against the headboard in the center."

"Yes, my beautiful general." He laughed. He crawled over and arranged some pillows for comfort. I reached into the drawer and grabbed the bottle of lube.

I climbed over and straddled Will's erection facing the foot of the bed. I pointed to Guy, who was holding Camila. "Lay with your head here and your feet to the bottom of the bed. Robyn, you will do the same on this side," I pointed to a spot on my left. They both did as I asked.

"Camila, straddle Guy's face and suck his cock. Alicia, do the same thing for Robyn. Now I can watch you both and help get you ready for them" Quickly arranging themselves to my satisfaction and moaning, I slid myself down over Will's shaft.

I began sliding up and down Will's cock, watching as the girls stroked the men's cocks. The men, in turn, licked their pussies, causing each of them to moan.

Glancing over, I saw the dryads, each straddling one of Jon's legs and humping their wet little pussies as they took turns to lick, suck and fondle Jon's cock and balls.

I reached back and poured some lube down the crack between my cheeks.

"Use your hands Will and get my ass ready too."

I leaned forward as he began to finger me, sliding back and forth on his cock. I then leaned over, flicking my tongue over each girl's puckers. That got a muffled squeak from both of them, translating into groans from the men. I then poured lube onto their asses. My men got the hint pushing a finger into their bottoms, causing them to wiggle and moan louder. The men inserted a second finger and began twisting their hands, opening the fingers to stretch the girl's asses wider. I quickly poured more lube into their holes so they could force a third finger in, and the girls shuddered and screamed around the men's cocks as they began to climax. That set the men off, and they shot ropes of cum down their throats and on their faces when they pulled back too soon. I giggled and moaned, moving faster as my climax overcame me. The clamping of my vagina set Will off, and he bucked beneath me, filling me with his cream.

I looked over at a roar from Jon just as his cock began to fountain cum into the dryad's faces and mouths. They giggled and slurped as their four little hands milked Jon's cock dry.

Lifting myself off Will, I gasped as his cream ran down my thighs and dripped onto his balls. "Now, my ass," I said. And he lined his cock up as I slid back onto it.

I had been used enough there now that it felt perfect, and I shuddered.

"Alicia, Camila, turn around and slide those cocks into your asses. Take your time. It will be uncomfortable initially, but you will soon love the feeling."

Both girls turned around as the men held their cocks steady the girls spread their ass cheeks and slowly lowered themselves onto their bulbous tips. As they got lined up, I said. "Remember to push back with your ring like you are going to the bathroom and relax." Both girls grunted as the tips popped in them.

They bottomed out, sitting on the men's laps moaning. The men clasped their hips in their hands. They both groaned, holding the girls still. "Wait," I told them. "Do not move yet. Allow your passage to adjust to the penetration. As it feels good, start to move."

I looked to see one of the dryads on Jon's shoulders as he cupped her ass and licked her pussy. Her musical moans identified her as Locustlimb. Sprucebramble grunted and squealed in delight as she squatted down, pushing Jon's massive cock into her tiny opening.

I began riding Will's cock in my ass as he reached around to play with my nipples. "God, yes," I moaned as he pinched them harder.

Alicia and Camila begin bouncing on the rods in their asses, moaning as their pert tits bounced up and down. Their eyes were glazed with lust as they looked at me, and they began pinching and tugging at their nipples. Both men held their waist with one hand to help steady them and slid the other hand between their legs to rub their pussies. It got squeaks from both girls, and they began to move faster, and I sped up as well, matching them and playing with my pussy. We all screamed in orgasm together, and as our rings clamped around the men, they grunted and began filling us with their hot seed.

Locustlimb squealed, grabbing Jon's hair as she began to squirt juices over his face and down his chest. He grunted and thrust upward with his hips, almost throwing Sprucebramble off his cock. She grabbed him by his chest hair and pushed back a mix of his cum, her juices flooding out around the cock buried in her.

I grinned lustily and said. "Alicia Camila, switch and allow Robyn and Guy to take your final virginity." The girls gasped as they slid off the cocks, hot cum trickling down their legs. They changed places, whimpering slightly at the sight of those cum slicked cocks. Robyn and Guy grinning, flipped the girls onto their backs, heads to the foot of the bed.

"I like that," I said. "Is that not a lovely view Will."

He leaned over with his cock still deep in my ass. "Yes, impressive."

We watched between their legs as both men slowly slipped their cocks into the virgin pussies beneath them.

"Oh my gosh." The men bent forward, kissing their foreheads and whispering words of encouragement. Clenching around Will's cock as small blood bursts trickled from their openings. Both girls cried out in pain at that final push.

They both stayed still, letting the girls adjust to their size as the pain faded.

Robyn and Guy started to pump into them with increasing pleasure when the girls began squirming. I went a couple of rounds with Jon while the dryads had fun with Will. When I returned to the bed, I saw Alicia and Camila cuddled in a cum covered, exhausted sleep Robyn and Guy were spooning them from behind. Jon had fallen asleep on the divan, so I crawled into bed, and Will and I cuddled the dryads between us, passing out.

I think this is the first time I awoke without morning wood since puberty. Even the delightful warmth of Alicia's ass did nothing to make me stir. I grunted, sitting up to see the first steely light of dawn glow in the windows. The dryads sighed and stretched in the pile of bodies near the head of the bed. They giggled as Will stirred and Merriam mumbled. "Just five more minutes."

Robyn sat up, yawning and stretching. "That was a good night's sleep."

I chuckled. "Because we fucked ourselves into exhaustion."

Will laughed. "This is true. I have never cum that many times in one night."

Jon grunted. "I suspect we may have to get used to it."

The dryads laughed, and Sprucebramble said. "Yes, there will be much fun to come breaking in your harem."

Merriam moaned. "Yes, I am looking forward to that, just not the morning after."

Camila gasped as they both came awake. Blushing red, Alicia said. "Oh dear, I fell asleep."

Camila said. "We must hurry. We are late."

Robyn and I laughed, and Merriam smiled and said. "You are where you are supposed to be looking after us, so you can not possibly be late."

"Yes, no, Milady." Alicia squeaked. "When the night servant wakes us, we must get ready and go down to get our orders for the day."

The Dryads laughed, and Locustlimb said. "No, you are a harem maid for your mistress and your masters."

Locustlimb then said. "We only report to our Mistress for our orders and obey our Masters only with Milady's approval. I spoke with the chamberlain so that he will know this."

"Oh, my," said Merriam. "Will that not create a conflicting dynamic within the staff?"

Sprucebramble said. "No, Milady."

It is an essential hierarchy within the harem. Right now, we are the only two fully trained harem battle dancers, and it is our job to teach the others. When eight are prepared enough, we will take on an apprentice from the castle staff. We explained this to the chamberlain to know who to hire and when. We told Denby that being chosen by us would promote them.

Locustlimb said. We will first interview them and check their stats to see their suitability. If they refuse, they are disqualified and will not be interviewed again. We handle this in the same way guilds interview potential apprentices. Of the twenty-two girls we interviewed for our training, only six had the harem and battle dancer abilities in their stats.

Sprucebramble said. That is why usually there would be three people at an interview. One is the person hiring, one would be the person training, and lastly, a guild clerk to record any transaction.

Locustlimb continued. We dryads are the trainers, and Denby hires all staff for you, Mistress, so he is present. Now that an adventurer guild is being established, we may employ their clerk for a small fee to record transactions.

Sprucebramble then said. We have arranged for the guild clerk to come here to interview the girls with Denby this morning properly. We will also have a scribe write down the procedure for the king so he may proclaim it law.

Locustlimb giggled. It is a good thing we must use the stones to unlock status. As the guilds spread over the land, they could post the rules to see how they worked.

I said. "I can only see one problem with this. The guilds will also have to employ criers to read the rules as most people in this land can not read."

"Oh, yes, I forgot this." Said Sprucebramble. "We will tell the guild clerk, so he knows to include this in his instructions."

"Good," I said. "We should head down for breakfast now."

We cleaned ourselves up and got dressed for the day during this time.

Robyn and I took Merriam between us, and the giggling dryads latched onto Jon. Will wrapped his arms around the blushing Alicia and Camila as we headed downstairs.

Entering the library turned dining room where the shelves had been turned, making a large open area in the center. Tables had been arranged in a hollow square allowing us to sit on the outside. At the same time, servants could move around the middle laying out dishes.

We said our greetings as we moved over to sit and eat. Merriam went and sat with Sophia while I sat between two valkyries. The rest of us sat wherever.

The king laughed. "I love these informal meals you have, Duke Sherwood."

"I find they promote a good working relationship between everyone."

The king chuckled. "That is an important factor, and I may start implementing these things in Cambridge. But what I find most interesting is that our guards and staff can eat in shifts, allowing us to speak together of pressing matters."

I laughed as a report was handed to me by one of the men.

Looking at the report, I said. "Oh, that is good news."

"What news is that?" Asked the king.

"Two hundred knights, five hundred armsmen, and three hundred archers have been reported a half-day march from here. It seems several tradesmen also accompany them."

The king raised his brow. "Baron Penrose, would that be enough men?"

Keith frowned, thinking for a moment, grabbing a piece of paper to check the numbers. "Yes, my liege, we could form two battalions with a few knights and archers leftover."

"Good," the king said. "Duke Sherwood and Sir William can put their heads together this morning and decide which companies we want to use for this."

"Now, besides those who can fly on their own, how many are we taking to the dwarf village?"

Stormavgaard chuckled. "I can carry ten, Your Majesty, so that is your limit."

The king laughed. "So, me, my bannerman Clarence, and Jeffrey. Baroness Sylvia and her maid need appropriate armor. I assume you would like to come along, Baron Penrose?"

"Yes, my liege, I will pay for Milady's armor myself. I would also like master Alvos to unlock their stats so we know what should be appropriate."

"An excellent idea Baron. We should also look into unlocking the men's stats as we equipment them."

"That would be an excellent idea, Your Majesty," I said. "Unfortunately, we did not know about unlocking stats before, but Dworkin's people should know how to do this."

Alvos said. "Yes, Milord, all guilds have a clerk. They will also have people to teach your men how to make good choices when choosing their skill tree."

I said. "It will take time, but we can develop methods for teaching all our people by training the men. Then as the guilds spread out, they can carry people with them to teach others. Eventually, those teachers can be brought together to form schools."

The king said. "Duke Sherwood, you have spoken the words on my mind. Now is there any other business that needs attending this morning?"

The dryads giggled. "Not for you, Your Majesty but your queen."

The queen smiled. "And what would you need of me, Sprucebramble?"

"Just your permission, Your Majesty. We would like to hire Windgust Artisan to make the right clothing for our battle dancers for a few days. We would also need one of your crafters to make bags of holding for them."

I groaned, shaking my head. "How much Sprucebramble?"

She giggled. "Eighty for the bags and one hundred or less for clothing; then we will need weapons. I will lend milady one of my fans, so she may have the dwarves make enough for everyone and some extras as we will need forty of them eventually. They only cost one gold each which is not too bad."

I thought for a moment. "What about armor?"

Locustlimb said. "We will use adjustable leather harnesses for now. The girls will not need dwarf-made armor until they are fully grown."

I grunted. "Digby, give the dryads a five hundred gold account they may draw on. And replenish it as they show receipts for reasonable expenses. You can also give Milady Merriam two thousand gold for her armor and harem weapons."

"As you command, Milord." Said Digby.

"See me before you leave, my love, as I have some ideas."

"Oh, I like the sound of that," Merriam said. We all chuckled.

The king clapped his hands. "Is that it for the morning business?"

"I believe so, Your Majesty," I said as the others around the table nodded.

Standing, he bowed and kissed queen Evadhi and said. "Later today, my love."

Merriam ran over and gave me a quick kiss, then she and the dryads followed Digby to the treasury.

Stormavgaard said. "Those going with me can meet me in the courtyard in twenty minutes."

Will said. "Jon and I will take some huntsman to Elvenhome to escort Windgust back here."

"Good idea," I said. "We will see you when you return."

CHAPTER

39

As we stepped out of the dining room, the baroness said. "Give us a few moments, Your Majesty, as we ladies need to change into something more appropriate for riding or flying."

I chuckled. "Indeed, Miladies, we will await you in the courtyard."

Giggling, they ran off upstairs to get changed.

I chuckled at the expression on Young Penrose's face. "You will get used to that baron. Ladies seem to require a wardrobe change for every occasion."

Evadhi laughed musically, sending a spike of pleasure down my spine. "We are creatures of habit, my king, and must always look our best on any occasion." She then kissed me on the cheek and headed for the stairs.

I stared mouth open, at seeing my queen walking up the stairs. She knew I was watching and put a bit of extra sway in her hips.

Stormavgaard chuckled, patting me on the shoulder to break my trance. "Watching our women walk away is something we will never get used to."

I grunted and shook myself. "That is something that will never wear thin."

Stormavgaard laughed. "Not in a thousand years at least."

We stepped out into the courtyard, and I saw grooms with several horses, including mine and Baron Penrose's chargers.

"What goes on here, young man?" I asked as I took my reins.

He said, bowing. "Milord has instituted an exercise program for the horses not being used. We grooms take turns exercising the more restive horses and take them out for a half-hour of cantering in the fields behind the castle."

"That is an excellent idea," I said. "I know this fellow gets grumpy when he has not been ridden for a while."

The young man laughed. "Yes, Your Majesty, they all do. Although I will admit, the chargers are more to handle because of their training."

"Well, carry on, young man, and we will be back shortly."

There was a commotion at the gate as the duchess and other ladies stepped out of doors.

A high-pitched squeaky voice came from near the gate. "Unhand me, you ruffians. I have an appointment with Sprucebramble Dancer."

One of the guards, laughing, called out, "Sergeant of the guard to the gate."

"Oh, dear," laughed Merriam. "A moment, Your Majesty, I will take care of this."

I chuckled and followed along to see what was going on.

The two dryads and the lady's maids scampered out the doors to follow us, giggling.

One of them said. "Sorry, Mistress, we forgot to tell the guards."

Merriam laughed. "Dears, you must remember the men are on edge due to the monster attacks when we first arrived here."

"Sorry, Milady, we will remember for next time and make a list of anyone we expect."

"That is a perfect idea." She said as we arrived at the gate.

"Milady, Your Majesty," said the sergeant, bowing. "This creature demanded entrance, saying he has an appointment."

"Creature?" The tiny man exclaimed. "I will have you know I am a gnome of the highest standing. As I told these ruffians, my name is Jose Rosario Enrique Vasquez, gnome and clerk of the Sherwood Adventurers Guild."

Merriam stepped forward. "We are pleased to meet you, Sir Vasquez. I am Duchess Sherwood of Nottingham, and these are the dryads Sprucebramble Dancer and Locustlimb Chorus. You will be meeting with them and my chamberlain this morning."

"A pleasure to meet you, most gracious duchess." The gnome said, stepping forward and bowing. "Please call me Jose as a clerk. I may be necessary to the guild, but I am a humble man."

Merriam smiled. "It will be a pleasure doing business with you, Jose. You may accompany the girls to Denby's office, and they will provide refreshments for your meeting." Merriam said. "Sergeant Mackey, I thank your men for their diligence. Please place Sir Vasquez on our list of business associates."

"Yes, Milady," Sergeant Mackey snapped a salute.

I chuckled as I watched the dryads and maids surround the gnome and escort him into the keep. He was only three ft tall with a pointy hat on his head and shoes curled up at the toes.

We all returned to the carriage, where I handed the ladies up. "Make yourselves comfortable."

"Thank you, Your Majesty. "They all giggled.

Stormavgaard climbed in with the ladies. And Edwin closed the door, climbing up into the driver's seat. I mounted with the other men and followed the carriage out the gate. The valkyries spread out around us as guards.

I rubbed my brow as I saw the exciting things trotting did to the Valkyrie's anatomy. Baron Penrose groaned, and I said. "Yes, this will take some getting used to."

Glancing back at my bannerman and squire, I chuckled at them, staring at the valkyries. I said. "Decorum, gentleman, those ladies would break you into tiny pieces without putting a hair out of place."

The closest valkyries laughed and grinned at the boys. "It might be fun, though." One of them said.

I laughed at both boys blushing furiously.

Stopping in an open field behind the castle, we dismounted, handing our reins to the grooms. At the same time, Stormavgaard dismounted and handed the Ladies down from the carriage.

"Do you have enough mana for a thirty-minute flight, Milady?" Asked Stormavgaard.

She smiled. "Yes, Milord Dragon, I have an almost unlimited range with my recovery rate. I use two mana per minute to fly, and I recover that every minute with bonuses."

Stormavgaard said. "You are incredibly powerful, Milady. I can not wait to see you break level twenty. A phoenix transformation has never been recorded in the dragon archives. I am constantly bombarded with questions asking you if you are ready."

Merriam blushed. "I am delighted and embarrassed to be the object of the attention."

"I am glad to see the attention turning to you milady and away from me."

Stormavgaard laughed. "Oh, no, Your Majesty, all dragons have our eyes on both of you. You are both about to participate in something unprecedented in all our archives."

"Yes, well, perhaps we should proceed," I said.

Stormavgaard laughed, walking away. I made to follow, but Merriam held me back.

"Wait here, Your Majesty. Stormavgaard requires ample space to transform."

"Oh yes," I said. "I suppose that is true." My eyes widened as I watched him shimmer and transform into a giant dragon.

"God's," I said. "What idiot storyteller said a knight could kill a dragon by charging him with a lance?"

Sylvia giggled. "I think I read that story, and the author is long dead."

"Damn," I grumbled. "I would have found that miscreant and killed him myself or fed him to Milord Dragon."

Stormavgaard rumbled a chuckle. "Deer and sheep are much tastier than you humans."

I laughed. "I can get on board with that pork is pretty good too."

Baron Penrose chuckled. "A large steak is tasty as well."

I said. "We just had breakfast, and I am getting hungry again. Let us get going."

Stormavgaard turned his claw up, and Merriam explained how to mount.

Seeing the excitement in Sylvia's face, we allowed her to sit at the front with the baron behind her, then her maid, then myself and the boys behind me.

Stormavgaard rumbled. "Hold on tight. The launch is always a bit of a jolt for passengers."

I let out an excited whoop as Stormavgaard launched himself into the air. The ladies shrieked and laughed as everyone else yelled at the sensation.

A few moments later, I saw the valkyries form around Stormavgaard. To my right, I heard Merriam's laughter. She laughed when she saw me looking, "There is nothing quite like flying. My first time on Stormavgaard was fun. But this having my wings is the best."

"Yes," I said. "I think I would love to be able to fly. That may not be as my status showed last night, as I did not see anything indicating flying, and I did not make any changes as I will wait for Evadhi to advise me."

Stormavgaard rumbled. "That is a wise idea, Your Majesty. We have lived with stats all our lives, and we are taught from a young age how to use them. And your people will be seeing them as adults with established patterns already in place."

I said. "Yes, I found the information overwhelming and the number of selectable choices quite large and confusing. I am content to wait until my queen can advise me."

Merriam giggled. "I have three advisors who have helped me quite a bit, Your Majesty. Alvos has been helpful and does not mind having his brain picked for information."

Stormavgaard chuckled. "I think he immensely enjoys the attention, making him feel young and valuable again."

Merriam laughed. "Not only helpful, but I saw him flirting with one of our older maids last night at the party."

I laughed at that. "Well, good for Alvos."

Merriam pointed. "There; Your Majesty is the dwarven village. Hang on, and we will be landing in a few moments."

Merriam flew ahead as I saw the gate opening and, with a whoop of joy, flipped over and dove for the ground. She flared her wings and came to a smooth one-step landing in front of the gate at the last moment. The valkyries all laughed and began peeling off to do the same thing. Fortunately for us passengers, Stormavgaard came in for a more sedate and smooth landing.

Raising his claw for us to dismount, he transformed back as we moved towards the gate.

Stormavgaard chuckled as we approached the group. "Milady, you are becoming quite adept at controlling your flight."

Merriam blushed. "I thank you, Lord Dragon praise coming from you is most encouraging."

"Your Majesty, this is Dworkin Clan, leader of the dwarves. Dworkin, this is His Majesty King Lionel Claymoore."

"Your Majesty," Dworkin and his companions bowed. "We are most grateful you have come to see us so soon."

"Please rise, friends. As soon as I learned about you and saw your craftsmen's skill, Dworkin, I would have done a great disservice not meeting you immediately."

Dworkin laughed. "At least as soon as you could tear yourself away from your new queen."

I laughed, clasping his arm. "You at least understand my position. The war between desire and duty often requires compromise."

"Aye, Your Majesty, we Dwarves understand these things. As much as we love to craft, a pretty girl will still turn our heads."

We all laughed at that

"Come, Your Majesty, we have much to discuss over ale, and my people have some fittings to do." Dworkin flipped his wrist, and one of his men hurried off.

"Dragonlord, you have brought the last of your valkyries to be fitted."

"Yes," Stormavgaard replied. "Some other women need to be fitted."

Dworkin laughed. "This is good. More people to show off our wares."

I laughed. "There is no need for you to pander for customers, as you will be swamped with much business for a long time."

Dworkin chuckled. "We need to train more of your craftsmen first. We are unlocking stats for the company craftsmen and teaching them."

"That was one of the things we were going to ask you about, Dworkin," I said.

"We wanted to know if you could unlock the men's stats as you outfit them. If you had someone to spare or if we should get some elves to come here and do it."

"We could start doing this, Your Majesty, as soon as our raw material inventories are adequate. We have not started on the armor for these men yet as we have been building them a barracks and training ground."

"We will outfit twenty-five men daily to unlock their stats and teach them once they are measured while the armor is being made would be easy."

"That would be most excellent," I said. "I cannot see a more efficient way of doing it." Then I frowned as I got a thought in my head.

"Dworkin, what are your twenty-five men per day based on?"

"Your Majesty, that is based on your heavy knights. It is not so much their armor but also that of the horses that take the time."

"Ugh, I should have brought my charger with me."

"Oh no, Your Majesty." Said Dworkin. "All these chargers are nearly the same size within one or two hands. You may just point out one the same size as yours, and we can make that armor no problem."

Baron Penrose said. "Your Majesty Sir Gilmore's charger is the same size as yours. He is a rather large fellow, and we needed the biggest charger we could find for him."

Dworkin said. "Excellent, we have the measurements for that horse. I remember him because he tried to bite through my wife's pauldron."

"Oh dear," I said. "Was she injured?"

Dworkin laughed. "No, but the horse was slightly stunned when she punched him between the eyes."

We all laughed at that.

"So, Dworkin, the point I was getting to is your people did the armor for Baron Penrose's men in one day, correct?"

"Yes, Majesty, I see. Is that how you would like us to equip the army?"

I said. "Yes, that is the smallest unit in the new army as we are restructuring it."

Dworkin grabbed an abacus from another dwarf, and his fingers flew as he flicked the beads. Looking up, he said. "We can do this if I shift some work to others."

"Excellent, Baron Penrose will give you the new battalion structure to work from."

The baron pulled some papers from his pouch and handed them to Dworkin. The dwarf scratched his chin as he read through the pages and said. "This will take twenty-five days for each battalion."

I chuckled. "Perfect, that will not change the schedule at all."

The dwarf that ran off came back with three tankards, one for me, Baron Penrose, and Dworkin.

I raised my tankard and said. "Too many years of friendship and good business."

Dworkin replied. "And much profit for us and taxes for you."

We laughed and then drank deeply.

"There you go, Your Majesty, step inside, and my people will get the measurements for you and your companions."

I went inside with Jeffrey and Clarence.

"Now, Milady Duchess, what business do you have for me?"

"Well, you have noticed I am not wearing your excellent armor made for me the last time I was here. I have since acquired wings and require an upgrade. I pulled a large pouch from my bag of holding. Here is the gold for armor similar to the valkyries. I may soon have the phoenix shift ability, so it must be fireproof."

Dworkin's eyes widened. "You will become a goddess?"

"So my elven trainer tells me, and Milord Stormavgaard seems to agree."

Stormavgaard said. "Eyldana, lead your team inside the dwarves; know what to do."

"One moment, ladies," Dworkin said and ran inside, hollering. "Elsa come here, wife, gaze at your masterwork."

Dworkin returned, leading his wife. "Milady, this is Elsa, my wife. She is the master smith that worked on your previous set of armor. Now tell her your problem and let her decide."

"All this attention is embarrassing. Okay, Elsa, I need armor to release my wings in. I had an upgrade a few days ago that allowed me flaming wings. But I am one level away from the phoenix flight. So I have been saving all my status points until I find out the cost."

Elsa gasped, eyes widening, and fell to her knees genuflecting. Her shoulders shook as she sobbed out. "Milady goddess, I had despaired ever finding a reason for my masterwork."

"Please rise, Elsa. I am not a goddess yet and am uncomfortable with the bows I get as a duchess."

Elsa stood, tears still streaming down her face.

I cringed. "So, how much for a masterwork?"

Dworkin chuckled. "Masterworks are priceless, as they are the one thing we live to create. They are typically given freely to someone extraordinary, and none is more special than you, Milady."

Elsa said. "We may have to wait until you shift the first time."

"Does the first time make a difference?"

"Yes, Milady, if you change in form, we may need the armor to reshape itself or automatically store in your bag of holding."

"Like Stormavgaard and the way his clothes store when he shifts?"

"Yes, Milady, or you may be able to do a partial shift where armor will work. Like wolves can take the werewolf form, cats can assume the werecat form."

"Oh, Gods, stop making the king's armor. Just take his measurements."

Dworkin's eyes widened. "Milady, is there something wrong?"

"Not yet," Merriam said. "But he has an available ability called lion superior."

Dworkin grunted and raced into the men's hut.

Stormavgaard chuckled. "Perhaps we will see a second masterwork."

Elsa giggled. "It would be the third, including my husband's one for the queen."

"Oh, yes, Stormavgaard said. "Three masterworks in so short a time from one clan is unprecedented. Most clans go hundreds of years between masterworks."

Elsa chuckled. "Most masterworks end up waiting for the right person in a vault. It is sad for those dwarves who make something that great never to see the person it was meant for."

"Yes," said Stormavgaard. "It is a sad thing. I know the completion of a masterwork is a time of grand celebration for dwarves.

I had been standing quietly, concentrating on my stats. "Oh, I will be right back." I stepped away and launched into the air.

I groaned. "Bloody excitable women. Yrswen escorts for Milady."

Yrswen giggled, took two quick steps, and launched herself into the air along with four other valkyries.

Dworkin came back out and said. "It is done, and there was a crash as a dwarf came rolling through the door."

Dworkin chuckled. "Well, almost done. A couple of my master craftsmen are still discussing who will get to use their masterwork for the king.

Stormavgaard chuckled. "Your discussions tend to be a little feisty."

Dworkin laughed. "We are a passionate people."

But wait dear reader, the tale continues in…
The Paladin's Phoenix

As Merriam grows into her new powers, the world mobilizes for and against her. The prophecy adjusts to the circumstances opening new realms of possibility.

ABOUT THE AUTHOR

David Hunt fell in love with books at the tender age of eleven. Initially, he did not always understand what he was reading, but a dictionary was never far away. Being an introvert, he was surprised to fall in love and get married at twenty-one. Throughout his marriage, he never stopped reading. Retiring brought new challenges with boredom because David still liked to work with his hands. Fortunately, the rapid growth of technology lent a helping hand. Dictation software has become the window to his fertile mind. There are many stories in there, of which this is just one.

Printed in the United States
by Baker & Taylor Publisher Services